Marjorie and Claudette

Marjorie and Claudette

Published by The Conrad Press Ltd. in the United Kingdom 2021

Tel: +44(0)1227 472 874
www.theconradpress.com
info@theconradpress.com

ISBN 978-1-914913-44-0

Printed and bound in Great Britain by Clays Ltd, Elcograf S.p.A

Typesetting by The Book Typesetters
www.thebooktypesetters.com

Cover design by James Price
www.theartofjamesprice.com

The Conrad Press logo was designed by Maria Priestley.

Marjorie and Claudette

Elaine Somers

1

Boarding-school

The run-up to Easter was always the most tiring part of the school year. Marjorie had five girls hoping to study English and Modern Languages at Oxford University. This had demanded a huge part of Marjorie's free time, preparing them for A-level exams and ensuring they got the necessary grades. She had arranged to go on holiday with Claude, her friend from Rouen in France. Like Marjorie, she was a language teacher teaching English in a school close to her local town.

By contrast Marjorie taught in a rather exclusive girl's school in Hampshire where she was head of languages. The thought of spending her Easter break with her parents was something she wasn't looking forward to.

Marjorie had not always lived at home. She was born in India, in the hills high above Madras. Her father was a lieutenant colonel in the Indian Army, a highly qualified eye surgeon who found working with the pioneering removal of cataracts not only interesting but satisfying. Most of his working life was spent in Madras, among the Indian people.

Marjorie and her sister Daphne were brought up by their Amah, a loveable woman who could neither read nor write but who knew how to love children. Her only contact with her mother was when they were brought each day for tea in the garden when they were supposed to be well behaved, seen but not heard.

Her father had engaged tutors to educate his daughters. Marjorie absorbed knowledge so fast that the day came when there weren't any tutors available who could educate her at a higher level. Daphne, on the other hand, had been bought a pony for her sixth birthday and spent every moment she could, riding, cleaning and grooming her pony. Recognising his elder daughter's remarkable intelligence, he found a boarding-school in England which could also accommodate Daphne's pony.

Saying goodbye to her mother was not at all emotionally difficult for Marjorie but saying goodbye to her Amah broke her heart. She knew she would not be able to write to her as there would be nobody to read it to her, so goodbye really was goodbye.

In the dorm at night, she would cry herself to sleep feeling utterly alone. Many of the other girls would be feeling the same but Marjorie had never had a friend before and didn't know how to communicate with other girls.

She would dream of the sunsets in Madras where her Amah would be beside her at that magical time before nightfall. Her Amah never slept more than ten feet away from her, there to comfort her when the demons of the night came to torment her. There was no one now to chase them away. Sometimes she would imagine herself back in the garden with her mother.

She loved watching the ritual of boiling water in the silver kettle and pouring it over the leaves in the silver teapot before pouring it into delicate china teacups. She would remember sipping it and breathing in the scent of bergamot. She would wake up to the reality of washing her face and hands in cold water, drinking milky tea and eating lumpy porridge and hard toast.

Her saving grace was her ability to learn. Languages came easily to her ear and English literature fed her soul. Daphne, meanwhile, won so many rosettes there was no more space above her bed. She was also brighter than average and got through exams with ease, in order to get back to her pony. Marjorie did have a friend by now, a girl called Louisa, who asked Marjorie to come and stay with her for half term while Daphne stayed behind with some other girls who also had ponies.

It was the first time she had experienced what family life was really like. Louisa's father was also a surgeon but in a local hospital. She felt very proud when he told her how much he admired her father. Her mother was the kind of mother Marjorie had read about in books.

Louisa's mother sat at the table at every meal, asking the children about their day and taking them to the cinema, something Marjorie had never experienced before. She tucked them into bed at night and planned picnic lunches during the day. Marjorie longed to be a real part of their family.

Christmas was spent with Aunt Margaret, her mother's unmarried sister. The house was warm and welcoming with a Christmas tree in the drawing-room and fires in all the downstairs rooms. On Christmas morning there were books for Marjorie, cosy jumpers and fur-lined boots. For Daphne there was new riding gear and a blanket for her pony.

They ate their turkey dinner in the dining-room in front of a glorious fire. In the afternoon they watched television together, a totally new experience for them and one which Aunt Margaret had provided just for them.

Marjorie formed a relationship with her aunt which made going back to school a great deal easier. Her aunt sent her hampers from Fortnum and Mason and shampoo which made her rather wild hair just a bit easier to manage. Louisa included her in everything she did and told her that her mother had invited her to stay again at half term.

Life was getting easier and the demons had stopped arriving uninvited as they had before. She constantly achieved the best grades it was possible to get and her exams in June held no fear for her. She wasn't exactly popular but she was accepted and she asked for no more. Louisa was talking about studying Physics, Chemistry and Biology for A-levels as she planned to study Medicine at Oxford University just as her father had done.

Marjorie's father had studied Medicine at Trinity College in Dublin, but Marjorie was being encouraged to study English and Modern Languages at Oxford. With Louisa talking about them being together, she decided that was the route she wanted to take. Two years later, with the best grades she could have wished for, her father and Aunt Margaret accompanied her to Oxford along with her luggage and a trunk almost full of books.

Marjorie settled into her room at St Hilda's while Louisa had her room in St Anne's. They continued to see each other but both of them threw themselves into their studies, Louisa so she could follow her father and Marjorie simply because she soaked up knowledge like a sponge. She didn't find it easy to befriend other students but there was a group she felt comfortable with. They realised how privileged they were as women, being able to study on an almost equal footing with their male counterparts.

One particularly studious young man asked her out for lunch and to the student bar. Whilst he seemed to enjoy her company, it was her intellect that attracted him and that was all that Marjorie looked for in him but was sadly disappointed.

She did learn to smoke cigarettes and drink endless cups of coffee. She joined the debating society where she was respected by many of the other students, but not befriended. She was neither happy nor unhappy. She had had a letter from her father telling her that he and her mother were coming home. He had accepted a position in a major hospital lecturing to young doctors wishing to specialise in eye surgery.

Aunt Margaret arrived to collect her at the end of Trinity term and drove her home to stay with her. Her mother and father were due to arrive in July and had agreed to rent a property near Reading in Berkshire until they found a house they could agree to buy. Her father had seen the end of the British Raj in India coming and wanted to be back in England. Marjorie was neither pleased nor sorry about their return. Meanwhile she would enjoy her time with her aunt, the only member of her family she really related to. She was grateful for the comfort being with her aunt gave her.

The summer passed lazily, days of lying in the garden, listening to the steady buzz of the bees, drinking homemade lemonade, listening to music, learning about her aunt's childhood and about the brothers she lost in the Great War. It was probably the nicest summer she could remember since she left her Amah behind.

2

Oxford

By the end of August her parents had set up home in Sonning, a village near Reading in Berkshire. It seemed like an awfully big house for two people, but Marjorie's father insisted that she was to choose whichever bedroom she would like for her own. She walked round them, trying to look enthusiastic, eventually deciding on one at the back of the house looking over the garden and beyond to a copse of trees in a very large field.

It appealed to her imagination and was inside a turret which made it even more interesting. It had an anteroom where she could keep her books and turn into a study if she wanted. Her father would be lecturing in the main hospital in Reading and it would be good to be closer to the country. He was obviously trying hard to make her feel at home, but her mother seemed at a total loss to find something she could do.

Marjorie realised that her mother had probably never looked after a house before, having had an army of servants in India. Her father realised he needed to employ a housekeeper, one who could also cook as her mother had no previous knowledge. Mrs Harrison was chosen, a kindly woman past middle age but who had previously been a cook in one of the large, neighbouring houses. She insisted she would not be doing any scrubbing, so Dorothy was employed to not only clean the house but also attend to the laundry. Marjorie's mother had never ironed a shirt in her life.

Marjorie and Mrs Harrison began a friendship of a kind, not one her mother would have approved of but one which was born out of mutual respect. Marjorie liked being in the kitchen while the housekeeper prepared dinner or had a pie in the oven. There was a four-oven range with a rocking chair to the right of it. Mrs Harrison had placed two large cushions on it and there she sat with the teapot beside her on the range.

'I don't care whether it's summer or not, it's good for me back sitting by the heat when I'm not having to be on me feet,' she would tell Marjorie. 'You young ones have no idea what it's like to have a bad back like I have. When I was younger and up at the big house, I were on my feet for more than twelve hours at a time. Them big dinner parties they had were nothing normal. We had the old king you know once upon a time. Real gentleman, he was, thanked us all before he left. Now tell me again what it is you're studying?'

There was always a cup of tea ready for Marjorie every time she came down to the kitchen. If there weren't any scones there was fruit loaf spread with butter. 'Just you eat up now. You'll not get good food when you go back to that college of yours.'

Marjorie didn't tell her that she got one good meal a day and the rest of the time it was just tea and biscuits made in her room. Mrs Harrison always went upstairs to ask Marjorie's mother what she would like her to cook for the colonel when he got home. Her mother never once came downstairs.

Mrs Harrison shed a tear when Marjorie went back to Oxford. 'I've enjoyed our little chats, miss, and I'll look forward to seeing you when you get back at Christmas,' she said, handing over a large tin containing a fruit cake she had baked especially for her.

Her mother merely wished her well and told her to work hard, something she had never had to do. Her father drove her back, this time with two large suitcases. Thankfully the porter took them up to her room while Marjorie gave her father a quick look around St Hilda's. Her room, although small and simply furnished, was described as a palace compared to her father's room at Trinity.

'Everything is different these days, my dear,' he said, 'but I'm sure Oxford is different from most universities. Delighted you're enjoying it, my dear. Let me know when you're ready to come home and I'll come and collect you.'

There was no display of emotion when her father said goodbye, and Marjorie was grateful for that as she didn't feel she really knew her father very well.

Michaelmas Term was barely eight weeks from start to finish. Marjorie applied herself to her studies and debated regularly within the debating society. She became quite well known for her views and beliefs, but it was the only time she mixed with any of the other students other than during lectures. She was known as a blue stocking, something which really didn't bother her at all. It did, however, bother some of the male students who liked to feel their intellect was higher than hers.

She did accept one invitation to have a glass of wine in one of the bars, but soon realised that the Hon. Herbert Bagshot was merely trying to find flaws in her knowledge. She hadn't time to be bothered by him and others like him.

She did confide about it to Louisa during one of their rare dinners together. She was delighted to be told that this particular person wasn't terribly popular among his peer group for being too boastful of his own achievements and would have liked nothing more than being able to go back and brag to everyone how he tripped you up and how you'd fallen for him. 'The fact that you only had one date with him proves to everyone that you had not.'

However, it did make her even more cautious of relationships with any of the opposite sex. She stuck to the group of girl friends she felt comfortable with and ignored any man who showed an interest in her.

When it was time to go home in December, she phoned her father to inform him she would be ready the following afternoon. He told her he was terribly disappointed that he couldn't pick her up as he was performing surgery but would send someone to collect her. The 'someone' turned out to be her aunt Margaret and she couldn't have been more pleased.

After the porter placed her luggage in the boot of her aunt's car, Margaret suggested they go for a slap-up afternoon tea. 'But Aunt, I'm not exactly dressed for anywhere nice,' Marjorie protested. 'I thought I would just be coming home with some driver my father sent.'

'Hmm,' her aunt said, looking sideways at her niece. 'What you need is a hat, a really nice hat. Let's go to Henley-on-Thames. I know a very nice little hat shop just across the way. Then we will have our tea.'

Marjorie was wearing a charcoal grey coat with heavy black stockings and black shoes with a strap which were quite fashionable for her. Her aunt chose for her a pale blue cloche hat which suited Marjorie surprisingly well. She picked a blue cashmere scarf to go with it, fastened by a large silver brooch. Black leather gloves and a boxy handbag were the final touches.

The restaurant Aunt Margaret chose looked out over the Thames and was incredibly busy, but as one of the waiters recognised Margaret, they were ushered to a table for two in the corner. Marjorie felt really embarrassed when a waitress came to take their coats.

'Give us a moment, dear,' Margaret told the girl. After she had gone, Margaret instructed Marjorie to take the coat off and then wrap the cashmere scarf over her shoulders. 'And don't remove the hat,' she warned.

Marjorie was wearing a cream blouse under a grey cardigan. The scarf over the cardigan was going to be a great improvement. The skirt was very simple and needed no adornment.

'I'm going to have to have a shopping spree with you over the holidays,' Margaret said. 'After all, your father isn't exactly penniless. I'll have a word over Christmas.'

Marjorie relaxed and her only worry was how many pastries she could manage. Aunt Margaret also introduced her to Earl Grey tea. 'No milk, just a slice of lemon.'

Marjorie was delighted that her aunt agreed to stay for dinner. Mrs Harrison, knowing Marjorie would be home, had made her favourite stuffed pork fillet. The stuffing, she had told Marjorie, was her own recipe which she had shared with no one. 'Unless of course, you decide to learn to cook yourself. Then I might be persuaded.'

Her father was late home, explaining that he had had to demonstrate this particular operation to a group of doctors studying under him. 'It was a worthwhile procedure, I have to say, but I'm sorry I couldn't collect you, my dear. I'm sure, however, that Margaret was a lot more fun.'

'She certainly was, we had tea at Havershams, absolutely scrumptious,' Marjorie announced. 'And Aunt Margaret took me to her milliners and bought me a hat, scarf, gloves and handbag. I'm ready to go anywhere now,' she beamed.

'Henry, this girl really does need a new wardrobe. After all, she's going to be looking for a teaching position next year. It's important she looks smart,' Margaret told him.

'Oh dear, I have no idea about those things. I leave it up to her mother. Why don't you go into town and buy whatever she needs?' he told his wife.

'Darling, I'm much too busy in January, I'm sure Margaret will be delighted to go with her,' she suggested.

'I'd love to,' Margaret replied sweetly. 'I know you're going to be busy playing bridge and lunching out. Marjorie and I will have a wonderful time. Won't we, darling?' she asked, winking at Marjorie.

'Oh, we will. Father, may I?'

'Of course you may, my dear. Remind me to give you a cheque, Margaret, please.'

With a sigh of relief Marjorie turned her attention to the pork which was, as usual, absolutely delicious. Margaret complimented her sister for finding such a treasure to cook for them.

'Well, if she's good enough for the King of England, she's good enough for me,' her mother replied. Suddenly, both Marjorie and her aunt coughed into their napkins.

'Oh, you are so right,' her aunt managed to answer after composing herself, while Marjorie took a long drink of water. Maybe being home isn't going to be so bad, Marjorie thought to herself as she hugged her hands round a cup of hot chocolate Mrs Harrison had just made for her.

3

St Catherine's

With double first degrees behind her, Marjorie needed to find a job. She had looked everywhere she knew to look but found very little to encourage her. Just as she had decided to accept a post not ten miles from where she lived, Louisa's mother rang her. Firstly, they talked about how Louisa was doing with another year at Oxford ahead of her, then the subject switched to her own position.

'Darling, I'm sure you already have a wonderful position to go to, but my sister rang me today and told me that the school her daughter attends is looking for a language teacher. Apparently their present one has had to take early retirement owing to family problems - her elderly parents to look after, poor thing - and so they are actively looking right now.'

'Oh really?' Marjorie replied, 'Where is the school exactly?'

'Well, that's just it, you see; it's in the Channel Islands, in Jersey, between France and England and would suit you beautifully, don't you see? English, French and Spanish. Right up your street. Would you be at all interested? It's a rather special girls' school.'

'Well I would actually.' Marjorie replied, 'I have been offered a post near to home, but I'd much rather be away, so that suits me perfectly.'

'Marvellous, darling, I'll get straight back to my cousin and see what we can arrange. Thanks awfully, Marjorie dear, I just know you'll be perfect for the job. My cousin's daughter just adores the school and it has its own beach which I know you'll love. Bye for now, darling.'

Felicity, Louisa's mother, was true to her word and in July Marjorie boarded an aeroplane bound for St Peter in Jersey. The headmistress herself collected her and drove her to the school to see what the school had to offer her.

On the way Miss Toogood pointed out various places of interest and shops she might find useful. She manoeuvred her Morris Minor between two enormous granite pillars with wooden plaques announcing St Catherine's. The drive to the school seemed endless but Marjorie was assured it was exactly half a mile to the front door.

Parking the car, Miss Toogood beckoned Marjorie to follow her to the majestic porch, complete with pillars, which shadowed the magnificent front doors. Waiting for the door to be unlocked, Marjorie turned around and saw the sea glimmering no more than a quarter of a mile away.

'Splendid, isn't it?' Miss Toogood announced before opening another inner door leading to the hall. Inside Marjorie stood and gazed upwards to where the staircase rose, the steps in marble, the handrails in dark mahogany, to the atrium at the very top of the stairs.

'Built for a very wealthy French aristocrat in the last century. Italian of course, as you note from the architecture. A chateau wasn't good enough for him, I'm afraid. Then the silly man got shot and the family had to sell. Now, come along and I'll show you round.'

The classrooms were small, made from bedrooms, but were

wonderfully comfortable and well furnished. The boarding apartment was at the back, hidden from the great house itself, but with the views down towards the sea.

Marjorie was captivated, more so when she was shown her own apartment, complete with sitting-room, bedroom, bathroom and a very small kitchen. Her main meals would be taken with the boarders. The original ballroom with its beautiful parquet floor was now used for assembly. The conservatory was now the art room and the drawing-room a wonderful music room, complete with a black ebony grand piano.

Marjorie found the whole house quite enchanting and couldn't wait to get to know it all. Seeing her credentials, knowing that Marjorie had herself gone to boarding-school away from her parents was a huge advantage; the fact that she was free to start right away was another.

A drive around the island followed a very enjoyable lunch. The island itself was beautiful and the beach Miss Toogood showed her was just perfect for bathing and within walking distance from the school.

Miss Toogood herself was a headmistress who Marjorie instinctively felt was someone she would enjoy working with. She guessed that she was in her fifties, with strong features and eyes that demanded you look her straight in the face. She was, Marjorie imagined, strict but fair. Talking about her students she obviously cared greatly about their welfare and wanted them to have some of the happiest days of their lives in the school, but they had to show willing to learn and have respect for others.

She wouldn't take any nonsense either and had little time

for the girls from very rich parents who wanted everyone to do things for them. They had to make their beds in the morning, ensure the dorms were tidy and treat the cleaning ladies with respect. Matron, she informed her, had a big heart until she was crossed, and girls rarely misbehaved twice.

On the way back to the airport, she was formally offered the position and she had no hesitation in agreeing. She would return to the island on the twenty-first of August, eight days before the boarders would return and ten days before the day-girls began the new term. That way she would have time to be acquainted with other members of staff and come under the scrutiny of Mrs Farmer, the matron.

'Don't worry, she won't bite you,' Miss Toogood smiled, 'she will be your strongest ally if you have a problem. Quite a few of the staff live in town with about five teachers living in. The food, I can promise you, is excellent. Parents paying that kind of money want their girls to be properly fed. We have our own vegetable garden and in September as many apples as you can eat. The locals speak English or French or both, so it's an advantage to know the language, so they can't pull the wool over your eyes.'

At the airport they shook hands. 'I'm delighted you're joining us,' Miss Toogood said, 'I think you're going to fit in very well.'

Somehow or other Marjorie felt very assured and excited at the prospect of a new chapter in her life.

Marjorie assumed her mother would be delighted not having Marjorie around the house, but that was not apparent by her attitude. 'Don't you like English schools? I'm sure I have no idea why not,' was her first comment when Marjorie told her.

'Mother, I understand that you and your sisters never worked, but times have changed and I'm really looking forward to teaching at St Catherine's. You would love it if you actually saw it, but I don't suppose you'd like to come and visit.'

'Actually, dear, I'd like to see it after hearing your description,' was her father's reaction. 'I thought your mother and I might take a little trip over at Easter. What do you say, dear?' he asked his wife. 'I'd rather like to take a flight and I believe there are some superb hotels on the island. Why don't we, dear?'

Her mother's ears had pricked up after hearing the words 'superb hotels', and she was obviously giving it some thought. Two minutes later she uttered the words, 'Well, if you insist.'

Marjorie and her father shared a secret smile.

And so, complete with suitcases of books and the trunk she used at Oxford, Marjorie sailed from Portsmouth to Jersey to begin a new chapter in her life.

Aunt Margaret had insisted on a shopping trip to provide a new wardrobe suitable for her position and a couple of off duty outfits which she felt might be useful. Her father had accompanied her to the bookshop she loved in Reading to stock up for reading in her leisure time. He had also deposited some money in a bank account with which to begin her working life.

Mrs Harrison had baked her a large fruitcake, just as she had when sending her back to Oxford. 'Look after yourself, dearie,' she told Marjorie with tears in her eyes. 'You go and enjoy yourself and I'll keep an eye on you old Mum and Dad, it's your time now.'

It was just that, Marjorie thought as her father and Aunt Margaret drove her to Portsmouth. This is the time I shall spread my wings, and then, as though she was being rather fanciful, she decided that no one was going to clip them. Her father and her aunt waved goodbye at the pier as the ferry made its way towards the channel.

She had a shiver of excitement at the thought of living in that beautiful building. She also gave a thought for the new girls preparing to leave home for the first time to go to boarding-school. She would make sure none of them would ever feel as lonely as she did when she left India.

Walking out on deck, she watched as the English shore disappeared, then turned her eye towards the land which was her destination. Shivering as the wind took up, she pulled her coat tightly around her and allowed the wind to ruffle her hair.

4

Miss Toogood was waiting at the front door when Marjorie's taxi pulled up at St Catherine's. She called to someone behind the door to come and help and to Marjorie's relief a well-built young man in dungarees appeared, pushing a trolley. 'Nicolas, this is Miss Fitzpatrick. Please take her luggage to her apartment.'

Although her trunk was not overly large, it contained a lot of books and her suitcases were also full. She was so relieved when Nicolas reappeared with a large trolley and had no apparent problem lifting the luggage firmly on top of it. 'I'm so sorry, there does appear to be quite a weight in them,' she stammered as she tried to help.

He merely smiled in response, showing a mouthful of very white teeth, emphasised by his sun-bronzed skin.

'Nicolas is our handyman,' Miss Toogood said. 'He can fix almost everything, the only problem being the older girls seem to find him rather attractive, so I keep my eye on him. Now, come into my sitting-room and I'll order us some tea or coffee, whatever you prefer.'

Tiredness had suddenly overwhelmed Marjorie as the last few days had been so busy, packing her clothes, trying to make lists so she didn't forget anything and last-minute shopping for toiletries which would have to last until

Christmas. Miss Toogood indicated for her to sit down on the sofa opposite her chair. As if by magic, the door opened and a girl about her own age dressed in a pale blue dress and white apron appeared.

'Excuse me, miss, but Mrs Bradley would like to know, do you prefer tea or coffee?'

'Thank you, Celeste, what would you prefer, Marjorie?'

'Coffee would be lovely, thank you.'

'Two coffees please,' Miss Toogood replied.

For just a moment Marjorie felt as though she was in a top hotel, not a school. The curtains and furnishings were made of chintz, showing peacocks and roses in pinks and blues. The bay window overlooked the gardens and beyond to the sea. The fireplace bore signs around the marble surround that the fire was often lit.

Miss Toogood looked directly at her. 'So, Marjorie, I hope you found the information I sent you helpful. I thought it best to acquaint you with the other members of staff on paper, then it will be easier to put a name to the face as you go along. You should find it easy to settle in, the staff are all very pleasant and we pride ourselves on working well together. You won't meet them all together, but as they arrive, I will introduce you.'

Before Marjorie could reply, the door opened and Celeste returned carrying a tray containing white china cups and saucers, plates, scones and slices of fruitcake. She smiled warmly at Marjorie as she handed her a cup of coffee.

'That will be all, thank you, Celeste, we'll manage ourselves,' Miss Toogood told her.

Celeste nodded, smiled again and left.

'Celeste is Nicolas's sister, she has been with us since she left school. Now, where were we? Ah yes, the staff. Take your time getting to know them. You're the only new member we have this year, so it won't be difficult. Breakfast is at eight, lunch at twelve, tea at five and supper at seven. Now, have a scone, all freshly baked today.'

Later in the afternoon as she started to unpack, Marjorie had the feeling that she was really going to enjoy teaching here. The surroundings were magnificent, the school itself more than adequate and her apartment, although small, just about perfect.

She was so grateful Aunt Margaret had insisted on buying her new clothes. Wearing them, her aunt assured her, would give her the confidence to face the unknown. Hanging her three suits up, she brushed the creases down with her hand and hung them carefully in the wardrobe. Although the colours were suitably quiet, grey, beige and navy, the shirts she would wear with them could be varied each day. She had also bought some corduroy trousers to wear with her boots when exploring the island.

After unpacking and hanging up all her clothes, she decided to leave her trunk until later. She turned the armchair by the window around, so she could look out at her new home. The window was small and overlooked the vegetable garden, but there was a glimpse of the sea further down the fields belonging to the school. She could see a small ship which must have just left the harbour, reminding her that Jersey was also a holiday destination. She hoped she would manage to go down and explore the local town before school began in earnest.

She suddenly felt tiredness come over her again and, removing her shoes, she lay down on the bed.

She gasped when she eventually woke up as her watch told her it was now six o'clock and she had to meet Miss Toogood in her sitting-room at 6.30. She realised she wouldn't have time to bathe, but she could change her blouse, fix her hair and be downstairs in plenty of time. She opened the window to let in fresh air to wake her up properly and as she breathed in the kind of salty air you could only experience close to the sea, she thought once again how fortunate she was.

Knocking on the door and being told to enter, Marjorie was surprised to see another person sitting on the sofa where she had sat earlier. 'Ah Marjorie, this is Mrs Farmer, our matron and head of boarding. She has come back a day early. Mrs Farmer, meet Miss Fitzpatrick.'

Marjorie found herself looking into one of the friendliest faces she had ever seen. Her eyes were literally twinkling and her pink cheeks and smiling mouth with laughter lines made Marjorie feel welcomed without her even speaking. 'Delighted to meet you, my dear, I hope you'll be very happy here, but then again I know you will,' she said, shaking Marjorie's hand vigorously. 'We'll soon have a bit of colour in those cheeks,' she added.

Marjorie found herself smiling back and, releasing her hand, she sat down on the other side of the sofa. 'I've arranged for us to have dinner in here, much nicer than sitting in the big dining-room. Celeste will bring it in at seven,' Miss Toogood explained. 'Can I offer you both a glass of sherry before it arrives?'

'Oh, I'll not say no,' Mrs Farmer replied. 'What about you,

Miss Fitzpatrick? It's just what you need.'

Marjorie nodded as Mrs Farmer thrust a glass in her hand.

Miss Toogood lifted her glass towards Marjorie. 'Here's to a great year ahead of you.'

'I'll second that, you'll not be long fitting in,' Mrs Farmer added, raising her glass.

'I'm sure I will, how could I not be in such a lovely place?' Marjorie replied. 'And I'm really excited to meet the girls when they arrive.'

'Ah now, I'll be introducing you to the boarders,' Mrs Farmer told her. 'I'll tell you the ones you need to look out for, the ones that need a little bit of attention and the ones that can occasionally step out of order. But we have ways of dealing with that, so don't you worry. You can come to me whenever you're worried about anything.'

Marjorie remembered what Miss Toogood had told her and smiled. She was so different from the matron at Marjorie's old school, she wondered if the girls knew just how lucky they were.

After they had finished their sherry, which Marjorie was sure had gone to her head, Miss Toogood showed them through an internal door to a small dining-room with a circular table and four velvet upholstered chairs. 'Let's all sit where we can admire the view,' she suggested. 'By this time next week, you won't have time to.'

Enjoying a wonderful dinner with crab for the starter, Dover sole for the main course and late strawberries from the garden served with shortbread and fresh cream, Marjorie realised that Miss Toogood had been right about the standard of food. Celeste brought some local cheeses served with sliced fruit before serving coffee back in the sitting-room.

'Tomorrow is a day you might explore the town,' Miss Toogood suggested. 'Nicolas will drive you in and show you where the bus stop is to bring you back. Is there anything you need to ask?'

'Not that I can think of right now,' Marjorie replied. 'I'm sure I'll find my way around and then on Tuesday I can familiarise myself with the classrooms and of course the Boarding department.

'Yes, m'dear, I'll look forward to showing you around,' Mrs Farmer beamed, 'and my own apartment is next to yours, number three, so just knock on the door whenever you need me.'

With that reassuring thought Marjorie bid them both goodnight and made her way back to her apartment.

Just two minutes after Marjorie had returned, she heard a knock at the door and found Mrs Farmer standing on the landing.

'I was just thinking, with it being your first night here, why don't you have breakfast with me in the kitchen in the morning. I'll introduce you to Cook and bring you up to date with the other teachers. Now, sleep well, my dear, for I'm ready for an early night myself.'

'Did you have far to travel?' Marjorie asked.

'Bless you, no, dear,' Mrs Farmer laughed, 'I live on the island. I have my own little house there although I sleep here during term time and only go home once a week.'

'So, Mr Farmer takes care of it when you're away?'

Mrs Farmer gave a hearty laugh. 'No, my dear, there is no Mr Farmer, he ran off a long time ago, but I'm very happy on my own thank you. Now, off to bed with you, goodnight.'

Marjorie could imagine just how Mrs Farmer must treat the boarders. She was the kind of mother figure everybody wanted to have. It was a nice feeling knowing she was just next door.

Leaving the rest of her unpacking until the morning, Marjorie undressed and collapsed into bed, the window open and the distant sound of the sea lulling her to sleep. She thought: When I make some money and find some time, I'm going to buy a house, right by the sea so I can always go to sleep like this.

Trying to imagine just where that house might be, she fell into a deep, restful sleep.

5

Breakfast with Mrs Farmer was a pleasant start to the morning. They made it themselves as Cook was not due in until the afternoon but had left cereal and a freshly baked loaf for them. Mrs Farmer chatted away while she showed Marjorie around the kitchen. When it was made, they ate at a table where Mrs Bradley and Celeste ate along with the other kitchen staff who would be back on duty by the weekend.

Marjorie felt so comfortable around Mrs Farmer, she was so grateful to have this time together getting to know each other before the girls came back and term began. When they had finished eating, Mrs Farmer suggested Marjorie go upstairs and get herself ready to go into town and she would inform Nicolas to bring the car round. It was a beautiful day but, unsure of the weather, she pulled a light raincoat over her dress and grabbed her handbag.

Nicolas was waiting for her by the steps of the staff door and opened the passenger door as soon as he saw her. Marjorie, never particularly comfortable with members of the opposite sex, especially young men, wasn't at all sure whether to speak or not. Nicolas, however, had no such sensitivities at all. Once they were through the gates, he turned his head to look straight at her, regardless of the fact that the road was more of a lane. He smiled broadly at her which made her even more uncomfortable.

'First time on the island for you, no?' he asked her, his French accent obvious.

'Well, the second actually, if you count my interview,' she replied, praying he would take his eyes off her and turn them back to the road.

'But is the first time you go to into St Aubin?' he continued. 'I have been living here for all of my life, so if you like to go to St Helier to drink wine or dance maybe, I can tell you where to go.'

'That's awfully kind of you, but I actually don't dance.'

'That is no problem, I can teach you if you like,' he offered, once again looking at her.

Why on earth can't I think of something suitable to say? she thought to herself. I feel like I'm an awkward schoolgirl again instead of a mistress at the school.

'That's awfully kind of you, but I really won't have much time to do things, it's my first teaching post and I need to do lots of preparation,' she managed to say.

'Ah, I see, I understand, you are worried, no? But you must not worry, Miss Toogood is a very good lady. She has been very kind to myself and my sister. My mother, she used to work at the school, but she died when we were still very young, so Miss Toogood give us both jobs when we leave school. You have met Celeste I think.'

'Oh yes, I have met her. She seems like a very nice girl, very kind, very polite.'

'Not at all like me then?' He laughed, loudly. 'Yes, Celeste is very like our mother. I am maybe like my father, but I hope not,' he added, the laughter leaving his face. 'He left us and went back to France as soon as I began working, but that's ok, we are all right, we manage better without him.'

Marjorie stared at him, this time his eyes were straight on the road ahead. 'I hope I didn't say anything to offend you,' she stammered.

Once more his eyes turned towards her. 'Oh but no, it is I who offend you. It was foolish of me to, how do you say, talk about myself. You must forgive me. Please, let me make it up to you. Let me come back for you, for I finish today early. I will pick you up just here,' and he pulled the car to a halt by the side of the road.

'No, really, there is no need. Just show me where the bus stop is, I shall be absolutely fine I assure you.'

'Please, just this once I will come for you. I did not do my job properly, so when I pick you up, I will show you I know how to behave, please.'

There was something about his face, his expression that changed her mind. 'Well, if you promise to just this once, then that is very kind,' she heard herself saying.

'Excellent, I thank you, I will be back in two hours if that is good,' he called to her through his window.

'Yes, that will be fine,' she replied and immediately crossed the road.

St Aubin was beautiful, she could see that immediately, but first she needed to find where the shops were. Two minutes later, she was standing in front of a shop selling newspapers, postcards and books. She purchased some postcards to send home and let everyone know she had arrived safely. She would write letters when term began.

She was pleased to see quite a good selection of books and paused to examine the titles. She found a chemist's shop just next door, which was useful to know, and some delightful small shops selling paintings and drawings of local landscapes.

Continuing to walk down the hilly streets, she at last saw the harbour appear below her. She could see where the artists drew their inspiration. The collection of small pleasure boats in every colour imaginable stood apart from the more serious fishing boats. She walked alongside them, watching some of the fishermen tending to their nets, others just sitting out on deck staring at the sky. She imagined they were looking for signs of any change in the weather, while some smoked pipes and others watched the tourists walk by.

Although it was late August, she could feel the warmth of the sun on her face and she found a space on the wall where she could sit down. This was so different from home, so different from Oxford and for the next few months it would be her home. She had noticed a restaurant, very French, where people were sitting outside drinking coffee and reading newspapers. There was a perfect table in full view of the harbour, and she pulled up a chair and sat down. She ordered a café au lait and pulled out her postcards and began to write.

The first one she addressed to her parents.

Dear Father and Mother,

The island is even prettier than I imagined. I am writing this from a café by the harbour in St Aubin. There seems to be no shortage of good hotels and I'm

sure you would both love it. I will write to you when
I'm settled in and term has begun. I trust you are both
well.

Love,
Marjorie

She wrote another one to Aunt Margaret and one to Louisa's mother to let her know how happy she was to be at St Catherine's. After finishing her coffee and paying the waiter, she walked along the promenade, admiring the historic buildings before she began to walk uphill again, exploring the cobbled streets and the wonderful variety of houses. She felt as though she might be a million miles away from home, the air was so bracing and the architecture entirely different.

She had always been attracted to the sea, even in India when they had summer holidays to the State of Kerala on the Malabar coast. Back then she loved to sit quietly, just looking out to sea and imagining. Her biggest dream was of having a house of her own by the sea, somewhere she could lie in bed at night listening to the lapping of the waves.

Looking at her watch she quickened her step knowing that Nicolas would be waiting for her very soon. She wished he wasn't, not because she didn't want him to drive her home but she would have liked to explore a little longer. Then she reminded herself she had the rest of the year to explore the island. She was to have a day off each week although often it would mean two half days depending on her classes. She would read up a little more about Jersey and at half term she would hopefully travel around the island.

Nicolas was waiting for her at the exact spot he left her. He had his window open and his elbow out. As he saw her approach, he quickly wound up the window and opened his door before stepping round to open her door from the other side.

'Honestly, there was no need for you to come back, I feel awfully guilty,' she began, but ignoring her he checked she was safely inside before closing her door. He drove forward for two hundred yards and then pointed to a small lay-by where several buses stood.

'That is where you catch the bus back, miss; Number Eighteen drives right to the door of St Catherine's.'

Marjorie made a mental note and then thanked him. They drove in silence for the next five minutes before he spoke.

'I hope you can forgive me for speaking to you this morning. To be honest, I forgot you were a mistress in the school because you are so young and the others are... older. I hope you would not tell Miss Toogood I was disrespectful. It will not happen again.'

Marjorie really didn't know what to say. She had felt uncomfortable about him offering to teach her how to dance but in every other way he had been kind and thoughtful.

'There really isn't any need, I won't be saying anything to anyone I can assure you,' she replied. 'It's our secret.'

'And I can assure you, miss, that if you ever find yourself in trouble, you must come to me and I will fix it for you.'

He said it so seriously, Marjorie had to smile. 'I hope it won't be necessary but I will keep it in mind and you will be the first person I will come to if I should.'

She was relieved when he smiled back at her. In an odd way they had become friends and she was pleased about that. They drove through the gates and right to the door of the staff quarters where once again he leapt out to open the door for her.

'Thank you so much, Nicolas, I'm very grateful,' she called to him as she made her way through the door. He nodded and she was happy to see him smiling again.

'You're back early,' Mrs Farmer announced, looking at her watch. 'I thought it would be at least three o'clock before we saw you. Just as well I kept you a sandwich. I'll make you a cup of tea and if you don't mind, I'll have one with you. Did you find your way around?'

Shaking off her coat, Marjorie hung it on the hook behind the door and sat down where Mrs Farmer indicated at the table. 'I found the shops and I made my way down to the harbour and back by the esplanade.'

'Good, someday we'll go together. Now eat this up, it's ham and mustard and tea will be ready in a minute,' Mrs Farmer said, placing a plate with four cut sandwiches in front of Marjorie. 'Then I'll take you upstairs and show you where the new girls will sleep. But first I'm going to enjoy this tea,' she added, pouring the amber liquid into the white china cups.

'Did Nicolas show you the bus stop, was he helpful?' she asked.

'Oh yes, very,' she replied taking a bite of the sandwich, 'this is delicious, did you make it?' she asked.

'I made the sandwich, Mrs Bradley boiled the ham,' Mrs

Farmer replied, 'which makes me believe there will be roast ham for dinner. So young Nicolas behaved himself?'

'Absolutely,' Marjorie replied, her mouth full, 'he could not have been kinder.'

'I'm so glad to hear that. Nicolas can be a bit of a boy at times, but the head has told him he has to behave himself or he's out. I blame the girls myself; they throw themselves at him. He's a handsome lad, it must be said. Shouldn't really be working in a girl's school but there's not a lot of work to be had on the island especially with all this talk of war. His mother used to be the housekeeper here, but she died, poor woman. The father's a bad one to put it mildly. Thank God he left the island, he was a terrible burden on those kids with his drinking and gambling. Here, let's have a slice of Mrs Bradley's fruit cake while no one's looking.'

They washed up and tidied the kitchen, 'so Cook can't complain,' and then headed up the stairs together. Mrs Farmer waited while Marjorie left her coat back in her room and then she led the way up to the dorms.

The dormitory Mrs Farmer showed Marjorie around was much better than the one that Marjorie lived in for nearly five years of her young life. The beds were comfortable with coloured sheets and cosy blankets. Each girl had a generous-sized bedside cabinet with its own key. There were plenty of radiators and the bathroom had ample basins and four baths.

She was taken back to her thirteen-year-old self, looking at the beds lined up on two sides of the room. She had never slept with her Amah more than a few feet away; there she had to share a room with nineteen other girls. She remembered crying into her pillow with no one to offer words of sympathy. She hoped there would be no girls at this school treated the same way. And if there were, she would make it her business to find out and deal with it.

Tomorrow the new girls would arrive. It would be a whole new world for them and in many ways for herself. She felt very much the new girl here, but she had Mrs Farmer to look after her. Well, she would stand side by side with Matron to ensure these girls enjoyed a better experience than she herself had.

With that, she closed the door behind her and followed Mrs Farmer to where the older girls slept. They were all so blessed to have such a wonderful matron and she was blessed to have her as a friend.

6

Friday morning saw the atmosphere in the house change. There was so much to do, new staff arriving, new boarders arriving from ten in the morning. Marjorie had breakfast with Mrs Farmer, which was a much less leisurely time, before heading up to the dormitories to check everything was as it ought to be.

Fortunately, the sun was shining which made everything look brighter. Marjorie thought it all looked perfect but Mrs Farmer's attention to detail meant altering a pillow here and a blanket there. By the time she was satisfied it was past nine o'clock and the first girls would arrive in less than an hour.

Nicolas drove the school bus down to the port along with two of the housekeeping staff to make sure the girls knew where to go. There were only six girls on the first bus, all travelling alone, and after unloading the luggage and ensuring the girls were safe with Mrs Farmer and Marjorie, he headed off to the airport to collect the next five girls. The remainder would arrive with the lunchtime ferry.

After a name call, Mrs Farmer introduced herself as Matron and Marjorie as mistress in charge of year one. The girls, all in casual clothes, followed them up the back staircase until they arrived at the dormitory where they were allocated their beds.

'Because you've arrived first, you lucky girls have the beds nearest the back windows, but don't tell the others,' Mrs Farmer told them, putting her fingers to her lips.

The girls replied with nervous smiles as they opened their bedside lockers and tested the mattresses. Marjorie really felt for the youngest two, first time away from home and having to share with other girls who as yet were strangers.

When Mrs Farmer finished giving them all their instructions about bathrooms, lights out, et cetera, Marjorie stayed behind to sort out any problems the girls might have.

One girl stood out for her. She was small and thin with long, skinny plaits and glasses. She seemed to be just one step ahead of tears and her eyes remained glassy as she looked up at Marjorie. Checking her list Marjorie realised that she was only just eleven years old. Her name was Hermione Montgomery Needham. Such a big name for such a tiny girl, Marjorie thought to herself.

She sat down on the bed beside the girl and when Marjorie asked her, 'Is this your first time away from home?' her reply was a whispered 'yes'.

From the information she had, she realised that the child's home was in Kenya. 'You've come a long way,' Marjorie remarked, 'Did you travel alone?'

'Daddy came with me,' Hermione replied, 'but he had to fly back after he left me on the ferry.'

'When I was just a little bit older than you, my sister and I had to fly from India on our own,' Marjorie told her quietly. 'We went straight to boarding-school and at first I was a little bit scared, but in a few days, I felt so much better.'

'Did you like it?' the girl asked, in a very small voice.

'Not on the first day,' Marjorie replied, 'but then when I got used to it, I really liked it much better. The food is much nicer here though, we got horrible food and we had to wash in cold water, can you imagine?'

The little girl's eyes opened wide on hearing this. She stared into Marjorie's face and asked, 'Will I have to wash in cold water, even in wintertime?'

'Goodness no,' Marjorie laughed, 'we have lovely warm water here and in wintertime we have lots of radiators, you won't be cold, I promise you.'

Hermione managed a very small smile, but her eyes were much less haunted.

'Now, be a good girl and have a look at what you need for your locker. The luggage will be up soon and you can get yourself sorted. Lunch will be at twelve. I'll take you down with me. Would that be better?'

'Yes, thank you,' and this time the smile was much broader.

The other five girls all looked much older, all but one. They were chatting amongst themselves, the girl with ginger hair tied back but rebelling against the band that held it in place, stood just a little further back. Marjorie had a quiet word with her and suggested she might like to go to lunch with Hermione, but she was anxious not to isolate her from the others.

Feeling that she would have been better served with a degree in Psychology, Marjorie was relieved to see the next group arrive with Mrs Farmer. This group had travelled with their parents who would all have lunch with Miss Toogood while their offspring settled in. 'This is the worst weekend, I promise you. After this it gets a lot easier,' Mrs Farmer told her.

And it did.

Marjorie had met with all fifteen girls by supper time. They were allowed to read books or play board games until eight o'clock, after which they went back to their dorm and had to be in bed by 8.30pm and lights went off at 9pm. Marjorie noticed that Hermione put herself to bed and immediately began to read. The ginger-headed girl, who turned out to be the Hon. Victoria Longley, did the same.

Marjorie was delighted to see their beds were beside each other. Although Victoria was a little older and a little taller, she thought they might well have a lot in common. She wished them all goodnight, had a little chat at every bedside before switching the lights off. Being August there was still a lot of light behind the windows and she imagined both Hermione and Victoria might read for a little longer. As it was just what she would have done, she simply closed the door behind her.

Monday morning saw all day girls return. There were only three of them in first form, which meant she had a class of eighteen who today would have their first introduction to French language. The three local girls, all there on scholarships, were bright girls who were equally as much on edge as the boarders, so Marjorie made the first lesson as enjoyable as possible and they were all quite annoyed when the bell rang indicating it was time for them to move on.

Tea break in the staff room was all a little hectic, but Marjorie was treated like one of them from the moment she walked in. They were all aware she was younger and in her first teaching position. Each one offered her their support although she imagined some were more sincere than others.

The Latin mistress, Marjorie thought, looked like a little

bird with a hooked nose and beady eyes. She was quite unlike her initial appearance, with the warmest handshake and an assurance she was there for Marjorie whenever she was needed. 'I've been teaching for forty years now, the last twenty-five on the island, not much I haven't come up against, so you just tap me on the shoulder when you need something.'

Her name, Marjorie discovered, was Laura Finch. Miss Finch, it appeared, was respected by everyone, especially the headmistress for her superior knowledge.

By the end of the week Marjorie felt physically and mentally exhausted. She was delighted not to be teaching on Saturday and although she couldn't leave the premises, her time was her own.

The first-formers were having their first hockey lessons that morning, something she herself had never excelled at but she enjoyed taking part. When she realised Hermione was terrified, having never seen a hockey stick before, Marjorie assured her that she would be keeping an eye on her and so Hermione reluctantly made her way out to the hockey pitch.

Hermione looked so out of place in her hockey skirt so big it threatened to fall off her. However, to everyone's surprise she was remarkably quick. She learnt quite quickly and dribbled the ball as fast as the older, much taller girls. Victoria was the first over to congratulate her on doing so well and Marjorie was delighted to give her an encouraging thumbs up.

As the girls had time off for leisure after lunch, Marjorie retreated to her room to read and prepare lessons for the following week. She was sitting with her back to the window when she heard a tap on the door. Thinking it might be Mrs Farmer, she shouted, 'Come in!' But instead of Mrs Farmer, there was the tiny form of Hermione standing in the doorway.

Marjorie got up to go over to her and had to stoop over to hear the tiny whisper. 'What is it, Hermione?' she asked in her kindest voice.

'I was just missing my mummy and my sister so much and I wondered if you could tell me what to do. What did you do when it happened to you? I don't want anybody to see me crying,' she explained, her eyes welling up with tears.

'You'd better come in,' Marjorie told her, 'although it's strictly against the rules. Anyway, just this once, sit down and I'll tell you what I used to do.' Marjorie sat down facing her and told Hermione about her first days at school.

'You see I didn't know my mother very well when I lived in India. I had my Amah, you would call her your nanny, do you understand?'

'Yes, I do. I had a nanny in Kenya but I didn't like her very much, she looks after my little sister, but Mummy was much nicer.'

'Well, my Amah was the nicest person in the whole world.' Marjorie spoke quietly. 'At night-time she would sleep on the floor outside my room in case a snake came in under the door. So, when I went to school, there was no one looking after me, although of course there were no snakes,' she smiled. 'So, at night-time, when the lights went out, I used to cry and put the covers over my head so no one could hear me.

'Then I remembered what my Amah said before I left her. She said, "When you feel sad at night-time, look up into the

45

sky and find the moon. Always remember, I am looking at the same moon and thinking about you." So, I used to gaze at the moon and think of her and then I would fall fast asleep. When you write to your mother, tell her you are looking at the moon and she can do the same.'

Hermione looked straight at Marjorie with eyes opened wide. 'Yes, I will do that, I will write to her today,' she replied solemnly.

'And you know, it's all right to cry sometimes. I'm sure everyone in the dorm feels sad at night and that's ok.'

'I think I heard Victoria crying last night,' Hermione confided, 'but I didn't know what to do.'

'Well, if I was you, if you hear her tonight, just whisper to her that it's ok to cry, and you feel sad too.'

Hermione gave a very small smile and stood up.

'Thank you, Miss Fitzpatrick, I will go now.'

'I'm glad, Hermione, and remember, Matron knows just how you are feeling, it's how most girls are feeling now, but it gets better and better every day. Never be afraid to talk to her. Now, off you go, see you at supper time.'

Marjorie thought for a while before going back to her book. She was glad she could identify with children like Hermione and Victoria. She also remembered what a huge difference Louisa had made to her life, bringing her home to her family. She hoped one of these girls would be just like Louisa was and become a special friend to Hermione.

She thought of Matron as she called her now and realised how well she had helped to make her feel more at home. Friendship was what everybody needed, and she was happy to help any of the girls in need.

She went back to her reading chair, lifted the book to read and one page later fell fast asleep until she was rudely awoken by the supper bell.

7

Marjorie settled into her first month of teaching at St Catherine's. Just as she had hoped, the new girls had settled equally well. Hermione was a studious girl, did well in all her subjects and excelled in English and French. She was lively and happy with just a few hiccups which Marjorie considered quite natural. Family birthdays made her long for home but by the following day, she was back to her normal self.

Victoria was perhaps not quite as bright but still rose above average in most subjects. She missed her pony most of all. Marjorie explained to her that the pony would never forget her and would be delighted to see her when she returned home to France.

Marjorie was overjoyed when Victoria invited Hermione to her home for half term. They had forged a friendship that Marjorie thought was very like her own relationship with Louisa. The rest of the girls seemed to be a happy bunch and as their form mistress, she was presented with very few problems.

Nicolas was always extremely polite when she met him around the school. One Saturday, when the tap on her wash hand basin was leaking, she had to call upon him to fix it for her. He had fitted a new washer in no time at all and also hammered in a nail so she could hang a watercolour she had treated herself to, from one of the art studios in the town. He hung it for her and stood back to make sure it was hung correctly. Seeing that it was, he was in the process of packing away his tools when she asked him if he would like a cup of coffee. He hesitated before accepting as though it might not be the correct thing to do, but Marjorie insisted it was perfectly all right.

'Who taught you how to do these things, Nicolas?' she asked him. 'You seem to be able to do almost anything.'

'I suppose it must have been my father,' he replied, 'he could build anything with his hands, and I used to go with him when I was young. When he was in his workshop I used to sit and watch him for hours. Seems like a long time ago,' he added quietly.

'He certainly taught you well,' Marjorie told him, 'but I'm sure you must miss him. I hope you don't mind me asking, but what age were you when he left?'

Marjorie poured his coffee and pointed at the milk and sugar so he could help himself. She took the lid off the biscuit tin and offered him one.

'I suppose I must have been almost eighteen, so it's not that long ago. He was seeing someone just a little older than I was and it was difficult for Celeste and I to have her around. He went back to France with her and said we could live in the house for as long as we need to. We've managed ok thanks to Miss Toogood.'

'I think it works both ways, Miss Toogood must be very glad to have you as you seem to do a bit of everything. Do you hear from your father much?'

'About once a month but I'm taking Celeste to France for Christmas, so we'll see him then. We're staying with our grandmother in a village close to where he lives,' he explained. She was, how do you say, *la mère de ma mère.*'

'Your mother's mother,' Marjorie smiled, 'you're very lucky, I never knew either of my grandmothers. I was born in India and they were both gone before I came to England.'

'Celeste is very close to my grandmother,' Nicolas explained, 'some day we want to go and live with her, but first we must make some money to take with us. Then maybe I can make her house bigger and we can look after her.'

Marjorie smiled at him, 'you're very kind, Nicolas, you have a good heart.'

'When I behave myself, you mean,' and he laughed. 'Really, I am not interested in young girls in this school, they just get me into trouble. You know sometimes they hide on me in my workshop, then they jump out to surprise me,' he added, his tone more serious. 'I have to tell them, you will lose me my job.'

'That does seem rather unfair, I will keep my eye out and deal with them personally if I catch them. Goodness me, look at the time, I promised I'd watch the hockey match. Thank goodness it's not raining.'

'And I must go too. Thank you for the coffee and for your kindness. I don't talk to the other teachers like this,' he assured her, 'but you are different. So is Matron,' he added as an afterthought. 'You must call me whenever you need some help or need a lift into town. 'But not with the dancing of course,' he added with a very cheeky smile.

When he had gone and as she was washing the cups,

Marjorie thought how she could understand why the older girls felt attracted to him. He really was like some of the men she had seen in films, much more attractive than the men she met in Oxford. But then again, she thought, I was only interested in meeting men on an intellectual level. What a boring girl I must have been.

Gathering her coat around her tightly and wrapping a large woolly scarf around her neck, she stepped into her wellingtons and headed out to the hockey field. For October it was quite wintry but the air was fresh and the sound of laughter coming from the hockey pitch encouraged her to quicken her step.

There was only time for her to write two letters when she got back, one to Aunt Margaret and one to Louisa letting her know how well her appointment to the school was going. She found herself telling Louisa about Nicolas, even going into detail about his dark eyes and swarthy skin. She asked the question of Louisa: *Were we really such blue stockings that we wore blinkers? I certainly don't remember ever finding anyone attractive and yet, given the number of men at Oxford, there must have been some. Perhaps I'm only noticing Nicolas because he is the only man around for miles. He actually has a lovely soul and I have a feeling he will do something meaningful with his life.*

She thought about this after she had put her pen down and wondered what caused her to feel that way about Nicolas. She certainly had no desire for any kind of romance in her life, she was too intent in moving on with her own life, but there was something about the boy that struck a chord in her.

She dropped a quick note to her parents just to let them

know how well she was doing and also because she daren't let them find out she had written to Aunt Margaret without writing to them. She addressed the envelopes and put them in her bag so she could leave them into the post-box downstairs.

After supper with the girls, she bumped into Miss Toogood who asked her if she would pop into her sitting-room for a minute or two. Slightly concerned, Marjorie sat upright in the chair waiting for Miss Toogood to appear. She hoped she hadn't done anything she shouldn't have and was relieved to see the headmistress smile broadly as she walked into the room.

'There you are, Marjorie dear, I just wanted to read you something which I believe you will be pleased to hear. It's from Hermione's mother and she has asked me to convey her thanks to you. I'll read it to you, shall I?

'*My husband and I would particularly like to thank Miss Fitzpatrick for the extra care she has given to Hermione. It was one of the most difficult things I have had to do, letting our daughter go to live in a different land away from everyone and everything she has ever known. Whilst we were aware that she showed some academic excellence for her age, she is not particularly robust and I wasn't sure she could cope to the extent that I was prepared to go there and bring her home.*

'*As it was, Miss Fitzpatrick gathered her under her wing and taught her not to be afraid. Her letters are quite different now, full of talk about the school and her friend Victoria. I am sure this is all to do with Miss Fitzpatrick's encouragement as Hermione writes with such fondness of her. Please tell Miss Fitzpatrick I will never look at the moon in the same way again.'*

Folding the letter and replacing it in the envelope, Miss Toogood removed her reading glasses and looked directly at Marjorie.

'Well, I'm not going to ask about the moon, but I am going to ask how you managed to turn things round for Hermione and Victoria also, I believe. What is your secret of helping children overcome their fears? Matron tells me you've wiped away quite a few tears in the dorm at night.'

'Oh dear, I'm not quite sure it's a secret. When I arrived at boarding-school at thirteen, I was expected to be old enough to look after myself. In fact, I had never slept entirely on my own before as my Amah slept on the other side of my door. I cried into the pillow every night until I remembered what my Amah told me I was to do. I was to stare at the moon at night and remember that she was staring at the same moon thinking about me and making sure I was well.

'When I started doing that I felt better until eventually I fell asleep without looking for the moon. It's quite simple really, just an assurance that you're not alone. In Hermione's case it was very like my own, we both came from hot countries full of exotic colours and different sounds and then were plunged into schools in a country quite alien to us.'

'So, it's as simple as that, is it?' Miss Toogood smiled. 'I don't think it was. You have an empathy with these children many of us wouldn't understand. I'd like to thank you personally for the work you've done well above what you were expected to do. I really hope you're happy here as Matron and I are so happy to have you. Your teaching is also very satisfactory, so I hope you have a good rest at half term. Are you going home?'

'No actually, I'm staying here. I thought it would be a good time to see more of the island and Matron has also offered me a weekend with her which I've accepted.'

Miss Toogood rose from her chair signalling to Marjorie that she was free to go. 'Thank you so much, headmistress, I really appreciate what you've told me,' she said, 'and I'm very happy here.'

'Excellent, now go and do whatever you do in your spare time, I'm glad we've had this little talk.'

Mrs Farmer was standing on the landing, about to turn her key in the door. 'Everything all right?' She asked having seen Marjorie enter Mrs Toogood's rooms.

'Yes, couldn't be better actually. The Head just wanted to tell me she's pleased with my work.

'And so she should be,' Mrs Farmer replied, 'you've been a blessing to all of us with the first formers this year. I've no idea what I would have done without you. Fancy a little nightcap?' she asked, making sure no one heard her. 'I've a nice bottle of brandy and I think it's just what we both deserve.'

Marjorie returned to bed later that evening and fell asleep as soon as her head touched the pillow. It was almost halfway through term and she felt as though she fitted in pretty well. That positive thought and the rather large glass of brandy gave her a very warm feeling indeed.

8

The year continued and under her instruction, Marjorie's pupils flourished and Marjorie herself blossomed into an excellent and confident teacher. The new year saw her return to school to a classroom full of children delighted to be back. Much to her amazement Marjorie realised she was back to the place where she actually belonged.

That summer she travelled to France with Louisa who was preparing for her final year in Medicine. Felicity had insisted her daughter needed a break and Marjorie was the person she could most relate to. They travelled to Provence to stay with relatives of Louisa's father who owned a chateau within walking distance of the coast. They spent mornings swimming and lying on the beach, reading and discussing their futures. Evenings were spent sitting on the verandah overlooking the sea and trying to ignore all talk of war. The two of them sat alone, away from the family, talking about their hopes and fears.

One evening was different. Louisa explained that she had met another medical student two years ahead of her who was carrying out research for a paper he was writing. At first it was a meeting of minds but now she confessed to Marjorie that it had also become a meeting of bodies. She was concerned that it would disrupt her studying now that she was approaching her final year, so they had agreed to see each other just one night a week. She hadn't told her parents, she knew they wouldn't approve, but when she returned they were going to spend a week together. 'You do understand, don't you, Marjorie?'

Marjorie didn't. She tried to think about the men she had met at Oxford but not one caused her to feel as Louisa felt now. Over the last year the only man she had been involved with was Nicolas. While she had to admit she thought him terribly handsome and easy on the eye, her thoughts had not gone beyond that. Louisa, she realised, was much more attractive than she herself and could now be described as very pretty, where at school she was pleasant looking. It did make her wonder if love did that to people. If she did meet someone, she would perhaps be more open to the idea.

The rest of the summer was marred only by the constant talk of war. Marjorie's father insisted on listening to every news item on the radio and the newspaper headlines every day was talk of Hitler and his army marching ever closer in Europe. She spent time with Aunt Margaret which she always enjoyed, read for hours lying in the back garden, went to Brighton to the Grand Hotel with her parents and read some more. She tried to block out all the bad news and concentrate on the good.

She was actually delighted to return to Jersey, to her own rooms, with Mrs Farmer waiting with open arms to welcome her back. This year she was not in charge of the new girls, of whom there were very few, but she was still sent for to carry out her 'magic' and help the new boarders to settle in. Her own girls, now proud second formers, seemed rested and ready to start working, apart from a few first-night tears which she dealt with.

In her French class she noticed their accents had improved and now, with a new vocabulary, they were anxious to try it out. At weekends she would take several of them shopping using only their French to find what they needed. They were so much happier and so much more confident that Marjorie didn't notice that half term was just a week ahead of her. Once again Hermione went off to France with Victoria and as there were few boarders left, Marjorie decided to do as she did last year and stay on the island.

She thoroughly enjoyed herself and spent a full day with the boarders left behind by organising a picnic around a fire, a treasure hunt within the boarding department and had them act out a play which they loved. On another day she took a picnic with Nicolas and Celeste, including a flask of soup, sandwiches and a flask of coffee to go with the fruit cake from home, sent in a parcel by Aunt Margaret.

In it, there was a letter from her father full of news about the war. He had heard through friends in the army that the Germans were planning to occupy the Channel Isles which obviously included Jersey. She had decided not to think too much about it until she was on her own. Right now, she was going to enjoy her day out as Nicolas had been given the use of the school car. They drove round the island and the places he took them to were off the beaten track with wonderful views over the coast. They chose a space high up but sheltered where they could watch the tide roll in on the beach below them.

It was a wonderful autumn day with the colour of the leaves on the trees providing a wonderful backdrop to the hollow where they sat now. Nicolas had thrown a large tartan rug on the ground and Celeste pulled out a tablecloth and spread it over the rug. Nicolas was not his usual good-humoured self and while the girls laid the food out he stood, arms folded, staring out to sea.

Celeste whispered to Marjorie, 'He is worried about the Germans occupying France. Our father wrote us a letter about it saying that many young men were preparing to fight for their country and he thinks we should be there.'

Suddenly Nicolas turned round and threw himself on the rug, before accepting a bowl of soup from Marjorie. Celeste and Marjorie talked about some of the girls who appeared every time Nicolas started to wash the car or chop up logs. 'They are mad in the head,' Celeste said, pointing a finger in the side of her head. 'I mean what is interesting about my brother washing a car?' she added with disgust.

'I rather think they see your brother differently from you do,' Marjorie replied with a broad smile. 'After all, he is the only man in the school and he is rather handsome,' she added, lowering her tone. Nicolas appeared not to hear them as he devoured several cheese and ham sandwiches washed down with homemade elderflower juice.

'Are you going to share your thoughts with us, Nicolas? You are so quiet today,' Marjorie asked.

Nicolas pulled up his knees and took the last of his juice before replying. 'My thoughts are dangerous I think and not for young ladies like you,' he replied, managing the smallest of smiles. 'I don't like what is happening in Europe, in France, while I sit here doing the kind of work that will not make any difference.'

'You may think that but a lot of people would think

differently,' Marjorie told him quietly. 'I, for one, am very glad to have you around and I'm sure that goes for all the teachers. You really do fix everything for us and the school couldn't manage without you.'

Nicolas looked, listened, then spat out his next words.

'None of that is important. If the Germans come here, there will be no school, no little jaunts in the school bus, no more walks along the beaches. No one will be safe. I need to go to France and stop the bloody Germans. Oh, I'm sorry, please forgive my language.'

'That's ok, I rather agree with you, my father refers to them as bloody Germans too,' Marjorie told him. 'But look, Nicolas, you are going home to see your grandmother at Christmas. That's what you must do. If you go sooner, the Germans will question you. You must think about Celeste, she needs you here, we all do.'

The journey home was quiet as the three of them considered the conversation they had just had.

After that Marjorie found herself buying a copy of The Times every day. She also listened to the radio in the kitchen where they gathered at night. The news wasn't good for the children to hear and so they shielded them as much as they could. However, not all the boarders returned after half term and those who did were full of what they had heard from their parents or read for themselves. The mood in the school altered. Children became anxious and their parents were writing to Miss Toogood for the kind of advice she couldn't give.

Eventually an emergency staff meeting was called during lunch hour when prefects and kitchen staff were left in charge. Arrangements, she told them, were being made for the overseas boarders to return home as soon as possible. Teachers who felt the need to leave would be advised to go home as soon as their arrangements were made. She, Miss Toogood, would remain until the last child had left and if it was advisable to do so, she would keep the school open under a skeleton staff.

After a telephone call with her father, Marjorie was told to return to London as soon as she could. Her sister Daphne had now been moved to the War Office and would remain in her mews cottage nearby.

It was a very solemn afternoon when classes recommenced. Marjorie tried as hard as she could to keep it all as normal as possible but at the end of the afternoon she sought out Hermione and Victoria and the other first form boarders to tell them she would keep them up to date as soon as she could. She told them not to worry, that she would be looking after them until the moment they left. She took extra time at night with the girls before lights out to assure them they were perfectly safe.

Hermione's father had decided to fly to England and take Hermione home with him but had to wait until suitable flights from Kenya could be arranged. In the end it was decided that Hermione would return with Marjorie and stay with her at her parents' house until his arrival. Victoria returned to France by ferry. On the day that Victoria left, she and Hermione held on to each other and sobbed. Marjorie wiped their tears and told them it wasn't goodbye, it was *au revoir*. Miss Toogood arranged for several other children to travel with Marjorie on the ferry and stay with them until their parents collected them at the port.

When Marjorie told Celeste that she would be leaving on Friday morning, there were tears as she went off to find her brother. She came back ten minutes later with Nicolas behind her. Marjorie asked him to promise her he would stay until the last child had left before sailing to France. He hesitated at first but when Marjorie reminded him he had a duty to Miss Toogood and the school, he nodded in agreement. 'Here is my address at home,' she told them. Promise me if you need me you will contact me, and please, Celeste, let me know you are both safe. Just a postcard from time to time will suffice.'

'I understand,' Nicolas said quietly, 'but when I am in France I must do my duty. I will make sure my sister and my grandmother are safe, but I will be doing whatever I can to keep my country safe from the Germans. I know you would do the same thing if you were a man, which of course you're not,' he added with a small smile. 'I always thought, if things had been different, that I would have taught you to dance,' he said with a broader smile this time.

'And if things were different, I might have let you. But maybe someday we can do that, when the war's over,' Marjorie replied, returning his smile. 'Celeste, look after each other until we're back together again.'

Marjorie had so much to do, she barely noticed the time. Mrs Farmer insisted on helping her pack, folding her clothes carefully and wrapping them in tissue paper. As Marjorie brought the suits that Aunt Margaret had bought her to begin her teaching career, her eyes filled with tears thinking how different her circumstances were now. Mrs Farmer silently wrapped her arms around her and without words they comforted each other. Mrs Farmer would remain in her house on the island.

'I'll not let those buggers take my home. I love it and that's where I'm staying,' she managed to say between tears.

It was a very different goodbye Marjorie said when she left behind the place she now thought of as her island home. The children were sombre as they sat together on the school bus. Marjorie sat at the front close to Nicolas as he drove. They didn't speak, there wasn't much to say. As he found someone to take the luggage from them he bade the girls goodbye. He reached out to shake hands with Marjorie but she ignored it and hugged him instead. 'Stay safe,' she whispered softly. 'I really need you to teach me to dance.'

Standing back from him she gathered the girls around her. 'Wave goodbye to the island,' she told them. 'We will all be together again when the war is over,' and she managed a bright smile. With her directing them in front of her, they boarded the ferry together.

Standing on deck she could see Nicolas, still standing where she left him. She lifted her arm and waved. He waved back and then turned and walked towards the bus, his eyes straight ahead. Marjorie said a silent prayer, that she would meet him again, that he would be safe until the war was over. Then she turned round to face the girls, a bright smile on her face. 'Right girls, let's go and sit downstairs shall we, I have a wonderful packed lunch to share when we get out to sea.'

They followed her, no one looking back until they sat downstairs with Miss Fitzpatrick. They knew they were safe with her, she always made them feel better.

9

England, 1939

Aunt Margaret was waiting for her in Portsmouth. Marjorie asked her to keep an eye on Hermione until she saw the other girls were all safely with their parents or guardians. Thankfully they were all there. Once their luggage was packed in the car, they set off on the journey home.

Hermione was very quiet and fell asleep ten minutes after they left Portsmouth. Marjorie explained quietly that there had been tearful farewells when they left school and of course no one knew when and if they would ever be back.

During the half hour she spent with Aunt Margaret, Hermione had explained that she really did want to go home to her family but she knew she was going to miss her friend Victoria and other friends. Margaret suggested they write to each other every two weeks and they would have so much to tell about life at home. She liked that idea but was still anxious about getting home. Her father had agreed to telephone Marjorie that evening to discuss travel plans. Hopefully his flight would arrive within the next couple of days.

Arriving home, both her parents seemed delighted to see her safely returned. Her father paid particular attention to Hermione, telling her he was very pleased to see her and hoping she would like her room. Marjorie suggested they go upstairs and get her overnight bag unpacked and then they could come down for afternoon tea. Hermione seemed quite pleased by that idea and ran quickly upstairs in front of Marjorie.

Mrs Harrison had put a very pretty pink quilt over the bed in the smallest guest room and left a bar of chocolate beside the bed. Hermione opened her bag and carefully laid out her pyjamas and her wash bag. She then placed the book she had been reading at school on top of her bedside cabinet. Marjorie then took her into her own bedroom in the turret so she could cuddle up on the window seat and look out to the garden.

Seeing Hermione sit on her knees with her elbows on the windowsill and her head in her hands, reminded Marjorie so much of herself at that age. It's how she sat in her room at Aunt Margaret's during school holidays. She had been a little older then, but still loved to gaze out the window into the neighbour's garden, wondering what kind of people they were.

The phone call came just as they had finished their afternoon tea. Mrs Harrison announced that a Mr Alex Needham was asking for Miss Fitzpatrick. Hermione looked up immediately with an anxious expression. That was her father's name. Marjorie assured her she could speak to her father as soon as she had the information she needed.

Mr Needham thanked Marjorie for her kindness in looking after his daughter and said unfortunately he would not be arriving until the day after tomorrow and would she mind if Hermione stayed another night. Marjorie assured him it would be no bother at all and she would happily drive her to the airport to meet him. He replied that he didn't know how he and his wife would ever thank her. Marjorie assured him it was her pleasure and then called Hermione to come and speak to her father.

When Aunt Margaret heard that Hermione was to spend another day with them, she proposed that she take both of them for a drive and out to lunch somewhere nice. Hermione, who had come back into the room with them, seemed delighted with the idea. She was even more delighted when Marjorie discovered that *Snow White and the Seven Dwarfs* was showing in the cinema the following afternoon.

Mrs Harrison had made chicken pie for dinner, followed by chocolate cake for afters. At eight o'clock Marjorie suggested Hermione have a nice warm bath before bed. When she was ready, Marjorie tucked her in and told her it was all right to read for an hour or so. When she herself came to bed two hours later, Marjorie noticed the bedside table lamp was still on, the book was lying open and Hermione was fast asleep. She quietly closed the book and left it on the table before wrapping the blankets round her and quietly switching off the light.

When Marjorie switched off her own light, she lay in the dark, thinking about the conversation she had had with her parents. Since she left the house at the end of August, her parents had installed blackout curtains in every room. On the floor below the hatstand, three square boxes sat, each containing a gas mask. Talk of rationing had begun and shopping was already proving difficult. Being out in the country, although not far from Reading, Mrs Harrison had ensured they had plenty of eggs and vegetables.

Marjorie's mother thought it wiser for Marjorie to stay at home where she would be safe. Her father meanwhile was still going by train each day from Reading to Euston where he could then walk to the Hospital for Tropical Diseases where he was working.

There was no way Marjorie was going to stay at home. If she had to give up teaching, she could at least do something for the war effort. She would investigate all the possibilities after she returned Hermione to her father. Her sister was working in the War Office, perhaps she could suggest something.

She thought of all she had left behind, a job that gave her so much satisfaction in a school she adored. She thought of Nicolas and Celeste and prayed they would be safe. She thought of Miss Toogood and Mrs Farmer and prayed they, too, would be kept from harm. The world had changed and her life with it. She must do her best, no matter what the outcome.

In the morning, Hermione was full of excitement for the day ahead. Aunt Margaret arrived at eleven although Hermione had been ready since nine. Dressed in her best dress with navy knee length socks, she had brushed her hair and held it back with a navy Alice Band. It was cold outside, so Marjorie suggested she wear her heavy school coat she had travelled in.

Once they were ready Aunt Margaret drove them into Reading to do a little shopping. She parked the car and as the three of them walked towards the shops, she spotted something and beckoned for them to follow her into a small shop across the road. Once inside she spoke to the girl behind the counter and asked to see the red scarf in the window.

'Certainly madam, I have some more just here,' and the girl pulled open a drawer from behind her and placed it on top of the glass counter. 'Here we are, here's a red one,' she said, pulling a red knitted scarf from the bottom.

Aunt Margaret immediately took it from her and wrapped it around Hermione's neck. 'There now, that's much better,' she said, 'what do you think?'

Hermione looked at herself in the mirror and smiled.

'I like it very much,' she replied.

'And look down here, I have the gloves to match,' the assistant told them, pointing to a drawer visible under the glass counter.

'Here you are, these should fit you,' she said, offering Hermione a pair of knitted red gloves which totally matched the scarf. They fitted perfectly and Aunt Margaret told her not to bother wrapping them up, Hermione would wear them just as they were.

'Now, no one will think you're wearing a school coat, it looks much nicer with a splash of colour,' she told her.

Next stop was the book shop and Marjorie could hardly wait to examine the new titles. Aunt Margaret took Hermione over to the children's book section and encouraged her to browse. Marjorie chose *Rebecca* by Daphne du Maurier, not her usual kind of book, but she had heard about it and wanted to see for herself. She also chose *The Tree of Liberty* before going over to see what Hermione liked.

Hermione was sitting beside Aunt Margaret with several books on the table in front of her. Aunt Margaret had suggested *Little Women* and Hermione thought *Anne of*

Ingleside looked interesting.

'I shall buy you both,' Marjorie insisted and took them, with her own selection, to the desk to pay.

The rest of the morning was spent browsing round all kinds of shops, Aunt Margaret suggesting that she and Marjorie should purchase some silk stockings as they might soon be difficult to find. 'I imagine luxury things like this will be rationed, so I'm stocking up while I can.'

They then carried their parcels into the restaurant Aunt Margaret thought was the best in Reading and after enjoying a lovely lunch, they all agreed it was. Hermione really blossomed in their company and was wonderfully entertaining through lunch. She explained to Aunt Margaret what life was like on the plantation that her father owned and how her brother was due to go to boarding-school next year and her sister was still a baby although she was walking now and could talk quite well. She told them how she and her brother had their own ponies and how she was longing to ride again. She was enjoying herself so much she forgot to be anxious.

After lunch they headed for the cinema. Hermione had never been to one before and Aunt Margaret and Marjorie themselves were thrilled to see it through her eyes. They had excellent seats and as the lights went down and the music began, she was on the edge of her seat. Although Marjorie had seen the film before, she enjoyed it so much more with this child for company.

Aunt Margaret took Hermione's coat off and Hermione hardly noticed, so enthralled was she with the film as it started on the big screen. It weaved its magic for all three of them as Snow White appeared, larger than life and with the voice of an angel. All three were quiet when the film ended and the lights went up.

'I never wanted it to end,' Hermione whispered, 'I loved it so much. Thank you Miss Fitzpatrick and Auntie Margaret, I've had the best day ever.'

'I think, due to the special circumstances, that you should call me Marjorie. It's going to be quite a long time till we'll be back at school again.'

'I think I might find that a bit difficult for a while, but I will try,' Hermione answered solemnly.

'Whatever makes you feel comfortable,' Marjorie told her.

After dinner that night, Marjorie suggested to Hermione that she should pack a bag for the flight home. Her two new books and the notebook and pen that Marjorie bought her should go in it and maybe she could buy some sweets or chocolate as a snack when they got to the airport. Together they packed them into Hermione's overnight case and in the morning they would zip up her large suitcase and put it in the back of Aunt Margaret's car. Aunt Margaret had enjoyed Hermione's company so much she had offered to drive them both to the airport.

Seeing Hermione into bed with her book beside her, Marjorie went downstairs to join her parents. It was her mother who remarked how glad she was that Hermione was returning home to her parents. 'Because of the war, you mean?' Marjorie asked.

'Well yes,' her mother replied, 'but it's a shame a child so young should be away at boarding-school, she should be at home.'

'Mother, might I remind you I was at boarding-school when I was just months older than Hermione,' Marjorie remarked.

'Oh yes, dear, but that was very different,' her mother replied, 'We had no choice. There was nowhere in India where you could have received a good education.'

Whilst she knew it was probably true, Marjorie found it ironic that her mother could feel that way about another child. She couldn't remember her ever acting in such a maternal way with her.

The following morning after saying goodbye to everyone, Hermione climbed into the back of Aunt Margaret's shooting brake. She was very excited at the prospect of seeing her father again. She was quiet on the journey, silently looking out the window. Margaret parked the car and found a man who would take the luggage for them. She chose to sit in the car and wait for Marjorie. She hugged Hermione goodbye and Hermione hugged her warmly before following Marjorie. Now all they had to do was find Hermione's father.

Marjorie paid the man generously for carrying the luggage and then looked around her. There was a man by the entrance, his handsome face tanned although he was wrapped up in an overcoat. Seeing him, Hermione jumped into his arms, shouting 'Daddy, Daddy,' in her excitement. He held on to her with one arm, his other arm reaching forward to shake Marjorie's hand.

'Miss Fitzpatrick, I'm delighted to meet you. My wife and I have heard so much about you.'

'Very nice to meet you too, Mr Needham,' Marjorie assured him, 'Hermione has been a delight to have staying with us. I'm just sorry I'm meeting you under such difficult circumstances.'

'Difficult for us all, but especially people living here,' he replied. 'Please look after yourself, I simply don't know how to thank you. All I can say is that if you ever find time to come and visit us in Kenya, we would be so delighted to have you to stay.'

'Daddy, I've had the loveliest time you could imagine,' Hermione interrupted. 'Miss Fitzpatrick and Auntie Margaret took me for the most scrumptious lunch and then to see *Snow White and the Seven Dwarfs*. And they bought me these,' she added, pointing to the red scarf and gloves.

'What a lucky girl you are!' her father told her, looking at her smiling face. 'Well, I think we've taken up enough of your time,' he addressed Marjorie, 'please give my warmest regards to your parents. And Auntie Margaret of course.'

'She happens to be waiting for me in the car park, so I had best get back.' Marjorie leant over to hug Hermione and as she held her she felt tears well up in her eyes. Anxious that Hermione should not see them, she quickly turned round to leave. Hermione raced after calling, 'Marjorie, please write to me.'

'Of course I will, darling. Now, off you go. You've got a plane to catch.'

Mr Needham and his daughter stood side by side, waving after her until she left.

It was saying goodbye to Hermione that really brought home to Marjorie the significance of her leaving. This war was here and now. She had been cocooned from it in Jersey, the rest of the world had seemed a million miles away. St

Catherine's was an oasis of calm. She knew now it was the calm before the storm.

She saw Aunt Margaret wave to her from the car and was so grateful at this time to have her in her life. Tomorrow she would think about what she could do for her part in the war effort, but for now she was so glad to spend time with someone who really understood her. Aunt Margaret was that person.

10

The war effort

Marjorie woke next morning to the realisation that she was not home on holiday, she was home for the foreseeable future. Today she would have to find something to do, both for herself and to contribute her part in the war effort. She knew she couldn't become a nurse; she couldn't bear watching anyone suffer, she would be useless. She wondered if her languages would be of any use in the foreign office but thought perhaps whilst she could confer with the French or Spanish, she mightn't be good enough to translate technical papers.

Oh dear, what could she do? She sent up a prayer for guidance and then leapt out of her bed and prepared to start her day.

Her father promised he would ask around in the hospital to see if there was anything there but he suggested she ring Daphne in case she had any suggestions. She caught her sister just as she was on the point of leaving to walk to work. She agreed that Marjorie probably wouldn't be of any use as a Civil Servant, but she would consult with colleagues and ring her back later. Marjorie hoped she meant it.

Aunt Margaret had told her she wished she was young enough for service but had agreed to work as a volunteer in a hospital which had been designated as a convalescent home for injured servicemen. Marjorie was really pleased for her aunt but knew that it wouldn't suit herself at all.

She ate her tea and toast sitting in the kitchen with Mrs Harrison. 'Don't worry so much about it,' was her advice, 'you're only home a day or two and now you've ready to work again. Take your time, something will turn up, just you wait and see.'

Marjorie knew she was right but she needed to have a goal to take her mind off the war at least. The newspapers were full of what was happening in Germany and how Hitler wanted to destroy England and as soon as possible. She saw the photos of young men leaving their jobs, wives and families to go to war with very little training. Sometimes she wished she'd been born as a man. They seemed to have so much more freedom to do what they felt was right for them.

She had just finished having lunch with her mother when the telephone rang. It was Daphne. True to her word she had asked around but the only suggestion offered was that she become a land girl and work with the farmers. So many young men had gone off to war, there was a severe shortage of helpers to assist farmers with the land and with farm animals.

'The only other thing which might interest you is working in one of the munitions factories. It's highly necessary and not without danger, but as you're rather bright I imagine you could do jolly well. There's one just a couple of miles outside Reading might suit you. I'll find out and ring you tonight when I get home from work. You get paid for doing it, not a lot but it's something,' she added.

There was no point discussing it with her mother, Marjorie

knew, so she rang Aunt Margaret to see what she thought.

'Actually, darling, it's not a bad idea, I know it's a very important job, we can't win the war without weapons and in some ways, it might be rather fun. I'd go ahead if I was you.'

Marjorie decided to talk it over that night with her father. It would mean she could continue to live at home but with a sense of purpose in her life.

Her father agreed with Margaret that it probably was a sensible idea. 'You'll be with a lot of young women your age, much better for you than sitting at home with us.'

Her mother, of course, did not agree. 'Working in a factory, have you gone mad? All that education you wanted so badly so you can stand in a line with a screwdriver. Honestly, Henry, how can you support such a ridiculous notion?'

'It's not a notion, dear, there's a war on in case you haven't noticed. Half of our young doctors are joining up which is why I'm operating again. I think it's very commendable of Marjorie to want to do her bit.'

'Thank you, Father, I believe Daphne has arranged for me to go and see a munitions factory tomorrow. Then if they need me, I'll start as soon as I can. I'm sorry to disappoint you, Mother, but it's the best I can do right now.'

Her mother raised her eyes to heaven, rolled up her serviette and left the table without another word.

'Don't mind your mother, dear. You must remember, she lost both of her brothers in The Great War and it brings it all back when we discuss what's happening. I'm right behind you, so go ahead with my blessing.'

The following day Marjorie went with her father to

Reading Station. While her father got a train to Euston Station, she got a bus out to Theale where she was to have her interview. She really had no idea of what lay ahead, but she had brought a notepad and pen and hoped to follow instructions. Normally she would have had to go through the Labour Exchange but Daphne had spoken to someone who had bypassed that stage and so she went straight through to the factory.

Walking through a make-do building she was ushered inside and sent to the first table behind which stood a rather tough looking woman dressed in navy overalls. The first thing she asked was where Marjorie lived. When she explained she was living at home just outside of Reading, the woman laughed.

'Thank Gawd for that then, Ducks, you're not going to need digs 'cause there ain't any. Go over there and show Albert your papers and he'll tell you where to go.'

Albert was dressed in a well-worn suit, frayed shirt and tie. He seemed quite jovial.

'Show us your papers then, luv.'

Marjorie handed him a sheet of paper stating where she was born, where she had been educated, details of her degree from Oxford and her teaching experience. He examined it through glasses perched on the edge of his nose, looked at it, then Marjorie, then the paper again. He looked over his shoulder at the next table where an elderly man sat in a smarter suit and a freshly ironed shirt.

'Oi! Richard, we've got a smart one 'ere, right up your street.'

Marjorie moved to the next table, handed over her details

and waited for a response.

'I see, I see, I see. Right then, wait over there please, madam, while I consult with the manager.'

'Over there' was just a space against the wall. She stood there watching some other women being sent straight through the door. She wondered what was wrong with her. Why had she been told to wait? Five minutes later, the door opened and 'Richard' reappeared with another man at his side.

'Miss Kirkpatrick, will you step over here, please?'

Marjorie obediently stepped forward and waited to be told where she was to go. Were they not going to accept her?

'This is Harry, Miss Fitzpatrick; you will be working under him. We need someone like you on the assembly belt, but in charge of another fifty or sixty women. The guns we are making here can mean life or death for our airmen. There can be no mistakes. You have to see that none occur. Do I make myself clear?'

'Abundantly so,' Marjorie replied, 'but I have absolutely no idea how to make one myself, so how can I make sure others are doing it correctly?'

'Watch and learn, miss, watch and learn. You just watch me for a while, then you can supervise the others,' Harry told her. 'Now, let me find you a pair of overalls and we can get started. You'll have to ditch the shoes though. There's oil all over the floor. Wear a sensible pair tomorrow, there's no style in here I can tell you.'

He opened the door and Marjorie almost reeled back. There were hundreds of women, quite a few men, all under one roof with no windows. There were smells she could not identify but none of them were pleasant.

'Righty ho, this is where you'll be working, but first you and me is going to spend time together so you learn to know what you're doing. Step over to that table and I'll get what we need.'

Harry walked into a room that looked vaguely like an office and reappeared carrying a pair of khaki overalls covered in oil and paint stains, she imagined.

'It's all there is, I'm afraid, now slip into them and let's get started. You can use my office, just for today.'

As Marjorie had worn a suit under her coat, not imagining she could possibly be starting today, she folded her coat, jacket and skirt and placed them on an empty chair. The overalls looked ridiculous with her court shoes, but it was all she had.

As she walked out she felt all eyes upon her and felt incredibly self-conscious.

'Never mind them, just you mind me,' Harry told her. 'What you're going to be doing is to help assemble a gun which will be fired by the rear gunners in our planes. If it don't work, aircraft get shot down with the people in them. It's happened already, it ain't going to happen again under my watch. Now, what do I call you? Miss won't cut any butter round here.'

'No, of course not, please call me Marjorie,' she replied, 'I'm not a teacher any more.'

'Well, in a way, that's just what you'll be. I teach you, you teach them,' he nodded towards the sea of faces. 'Everybody has their bit to do. You start with this,' he said, holding a metal bar, 'you add this, this and this, and then you go on until you get this.'

He lifted up part of a long gun from under the table. 'Now, you have to remember, you got a brain, this lot out here mostly don't have. If they do they don't use it. So, you see, you are going to have to be a teacher all over again. The good news is you get a cup of tea in the morning and one in the afternoon. You have to make your own arrangements for lunch. There is a canteen but I don't recommend it.

'It's a bloody long day, pardon my French, but you'll get used to it and we work shifts, day and night. It'll be best if you stick to days when you've got these ones doing what you tell them, but you might have to do the same on nights.'

'Right then,' Marjorie replied, 'let's get started.'

'That's just what I like to hear. I'm a retired airman myself. You may not have noticed, but I only got one leg, so I'm not much use up there any more, but I'll make sure my mates are kept safe.'

Marjorie hadn't noticed his leg. Thinking back, he did seem to waddle a little but she thought it was just his gait.

'The Great War,' he explained, 'I was only eighteen, but that was a long time ago. Now, pull up that stool and let's get started. Today I'm your teacher!'

It was an incredibly long day. Harry shared his sandwiches with her and she was grateful for that. The toilets were the worst part of the day for her. She couldn't hear herself think and the women who eyed her up and down whispered 'Hoity Toity, Lah de dah,' loud enough for her to hear. She hadn't met any of them today; that was a treat for tomorrow, Harry told her.

Every bit of her ached when she got up to go home.

Stepping out of her overalls she hoped she'd be allowed to take them home to wash. She'd wear a pair of trousers tomorrow and some lace up shoes. She had to be back by eight in the morning. She just prayed she hadn't missed the last bus home. The bus from Theale was packed to the door. As it turned a corner she fell back on top of someone behind her and had to pull herself up again.

The person behind her, a woman with bleach blonde hair wrapped up in a turban, whispered to her, 'Don't worry luv, it gets worse, but I'll tell you who to avoid and who to be nice to. I watched you today working with Harry, I reckon you're bright, but you'll need to learn a lot of things before long. I'll teach you, if you're willing. My name's Irene, you just remember that.'

Marjorie had no idea if the woman was being kind or menacing, but as she got off the bus, she waited for Marjorie. 'Bring your own mug with you tomorrow and a bit of soap and mind you bring your lunch with you too. Bye luv, see you tomorrow.'

Marjorie decided then and there that Irene meant to be kind. Then she ran forward as she saw her bus home about to leave.

'You just made it, love,' the bus driver told her. 'If you're coming from the factory, you'll need to get the first bus if you can or you'll miss this one. Let me know how it goes and I can always hold on for a minute or two.' The bus driver was an older lady with a kind face. Marjorie hoped she was true to her word.

Walking the last mile home, she almost collapsed on the kitchen floor. Mrs Harrison had left her some casserole in a saucepan for her to heat up. There was a slice of apple pie for after a with a jug of custard. Her father was waiting for her and came into the kitchen where she was sitting at the table, too tired to get up.

'Well, my dear, I didn't think you were going to be so late. How did you get on?'

'Father, I'm too tired to tell you. Forgive me and on Sunday I will tell you all. Suffice it to say I'm to make machine guns for aeroplanes, eleven hours a day, six days a week. I need to sleep. Got to be up in the morning.'

'Then I shall take you to the station. It's the least I can do,' her father replied.

'Thank you, Father, I'll see you in the morning.'

Marjorie washed her face, cleaned her teeth and fell into bed exhausted. It had been the kind of day she couldn't have dreamed of. She asked God to give her the strength physically and mentally to succeed with it. At least she was doing something useful, those guns would save lives. It's what she wanted to do and had prayed for. *God must have a wonderful sense of humour*, was the last thought she had before falling asleep.

11

Marjorie woke to the shrill ring of her alarm clock. She just wanted to turn over and go back to sleep but she needed to choose comfortable clothes for work and make a packed lunch before she left home.

After her bath, she found an old pair of lace-up shoes with thick rubber soles which would be good for the horrible, wet concrete floors. She wore woollen socks underneath. She then found an ancient fair-isle sweater which went over a check flannelette shirt and under that a woollen vest. She pulled her thick hair into a plait before running downstairs to make her lunch.

She couldn't believe her eyes when she saw that Mrs Harrison had made it already, wrapped in greaseproof paper. Beside it sat an apple and a small tin containing biscuits.

'Well, your father told me about your work and how you wouldn't be home till eight o'clock at night, so it's the least I could do. I'll leave you something warm for you to come home to tonight. Slave labour it is, but knowing you, you'll take it all in your stride. Now hurry up and eat your porridge before it gets cold.'

True to his word, Marjorie's father was ready by the door to drive her to the bus depot. He was his usual smart self, in a dark grey suit, white shirt and striped tie.

'I'll start early and come home earlier,' he told her. 'It will be nice to have time to think before I start operating at nine. I'm glad there's some little thing I can do to help you, my dear, it's a very long day for you.'

'I'm so grateful to you, otherwise I would have had to be up at least half an hour earlier. I didn't realise just how exhausting it would all be, but I'm getting a half day on Saturday which makes it slightly better. Father, would you mind letting me off here? I don't want anyone to see me at the station getting out of a Jaguar. Right here will do, thank you so much,' and she got out at the side of the road and walked the short distance to the bus station.

There was a whole row of girls standing by the stop for Theale and Marjorie joined the queue hoping to goodness she wouldn't miss getting on the bus. She didn't recognise anyone from yesterday, so she kept her head down in case anyone spoke to her. They didn't and she felt herself pushed along as the bus pulled up. It was a stampede to climb on and the bus was already full when she got on with yet more people jumping on behind her. She stood, squashed on all sides by bodies gyrating with the movement of the bus. She held on to the seat closest to her, her other hand holding tight to her bag.

'Hello, ducks, you managed the bus then,' a voice from behind her spoke. Turning her head as far round as possible she saw that the voice belonged to Irene, the blonde girl who spoke to her last night. 'Don't make no difference whether you're at the front or the back of the bus, you'll still be squashed like sardines. Next bus isn't for seven minutes. It can leave you late, so take my advice and climb on, no matter what.'

Marjorie was grateful it was such a short journey and the bus pulled to a halt. She moved along with the crowd and was gasping for air when she eventually stepped off. Irene was waiting for her just a few feet away.

'Righty ho then, time for the holiday camp. You got your bus all right last night then?'

'Yes, thank you,' Marjorie replied, 'with a minute to spare. Did you get yours?' she asked politely

'What, me, on a bus? Nah, my digs is in Reading itself,' Irene told her. 'I was dead lucky to get a room to myself on top of one of the pubs. I get a bath an' all on a Friday night, so I ain't doing too bad. What about you, love, you far out of town?'

'Oh no, not far.' Marjorie wasn't sure what to answer. 'I'm only ten minutes away.'

'Good stuff. Now don't forget, just holler if you need something. I'll wave to you when we get in so you know where to look for me.'

'Thank you so much,' Marjorie replied, 'I really appreciate your offer.'

Both of them joined the queue to sign in for work. Marjorie fumbled in her bag for the card Harry had given her, then followed the others, handing her card to the lady she saw yesterday. She looked up seeing the name. 'Still with us, love? I thought you might have changed your mind. Nice to see you.'

Marjorie gave her a smile, lifted her card back and walked on.

Harry was in his office when she arrived at the table allocated to her. She walked to the door and knocked tentatively. Harry got to his feet and came towards her.

'Ah, so you made it on time. Good-oh, stick your coat on the back of the door but keep your bag with you.' She did as he said, then went back to the table where he was teaching her how to assemble the part of the gun allocated to Harry's department. He explained that he wanted her to start one part without his help, but he would be watching. She felt nervous at first, but she concentrated hard and remembered all he had taught her yesterday. When she had finished she handed it to him.

'Blimey,' he said, looking at it from every angle. 'Spot on, you have a hell of a memory. Let's try it three more times to make sure and then I'll have a check.'

She concentrated hard and completed five more before Harry came back to the table. Once again he examined it closely before taking the last one apart. 'Just wanted to see you didn't leave anything out and you didn't. To be honest I didn't think you'd manage it this quick, it's not even ten yet.'

Harry scratched his head a bit, then leaving the last bit down on the table, he walked past her. 'Right then, come with me and I'll show you what happens next.' Marjorie followed him across to a table ahead of them where six girls sat along each side facing each other.

'Ok you lot, this is Marjorie. From tomorrow you're going to be doing what she tells you to do. You will finish this lot today,' he explained, pointing to the table, 'and start on a new lot tomorrow. Marjorie will start you off first thing. Got that? No skiving, get on with your work and I want every piece of metal off this table by six. The bonus is, you get to go home early, but if one of you hasn't finished, the rest of you stay.

Got that, Gloria?' He was looking directly at a middle-aged lady wearing bright, floral overalls with her hair caught up in a turban, with a single brown curl escaping at the front.

'Yes, boss, got it,' Gloria replied. 'Don't you worry, Harry, we'll be done by six.'

Harry said to Marjorie, 'Gloria has her head screwed on, she has. She worked for one of those top dressmakers in London before the war, now she's working here and doing a good job. She's older so the other girls respect her. You need to keep on the right side of her. It's going to be your job to make sure every piece is done perfect like. Now, come over here and I'll explain how the assembly line works.'

Marjorie was so relieved when the tea trolley came around. She hadn't been able to find a mug in the house, but she found a large breakfast cup which she thought would do the same job. The man wheeling the tea trolley was very bald and very fat. The remaining hair was ginger and quite long. He reminded Marjorie of a monk except he was wearing a brown coat instead of a habit. Marjorie handed him the cup when he arrived beside her.

'What have we got here then? Never seen one of these before,' he said, looking over the top of his round, metal spectacles. Lifting it up and looking at the bottom of the cup, he read out, '*Wedgwood bone china*, very nice indeed. Look after it, love, or it'll get nicked, that's for sure. Now, milk and sugar?'

Marjorie was very aware of faces watching her. She saw them laughing amongst each other. She decided not to be bothered about it and just drank the tea. Ten minutes later Harry advised her to take her toilet break. Thinking about yesterday she wasn't looking forward to it but she kept her head down and slipped into the ladies' toilet praying nobody saw her.

Standing beside the cracked mirror she saw two women who turned round as soon as she walked in. Looking straight ahead, she saw one of the cubicle doors open and made a dash for it. When she closed the door behind her, she saw why it was vacant. It stank to high heaven and the contents had not been flushed away. She pulled the chain but nothing happened. She pulled it again and still nothing happened. She decided she couldn't stay another minute and opened the door to walk out.

The same two girls were still there sniggering. Other women started coming out from the cubicles but they stopped her going in. One of them walked down to the cubicle she had just vacated. Without going in, she shouted down the room, 'Who the hell was in there last? Whoever it was is a dirty bitch, ought to be ashamed of herself. Oh, hold on, it was you, wasn't it?' she said, coming up to Marjorie and standing beside her, hands on hips. 'Well, you might only drink from a china cup, but you don't even know how to pull the chain after you, do you?'

Marjorie felt all eyes on her as more people came in. She also felt rage coming up to her throat.

'It wasn't me and you damn well know it. You saw me going in, try to flush the toilet and come straight out again. For all I know, it could have been one of you. You were here before me. And come to think of it, aren't you on a five-minute break? Doesn't look to me you'll be home early. Now, if you don't mind, let me past. Please,' she added.

The two girls stepped aside with eyes wide and mouths closed, and she walked between them. As she reached the door she saw Irene, standing beside it. 'Well, good for you, girl, you told them. I followed you in to see if you needed help. Seems you didn't. You're tougher than you look, that's for sure.'

Marjorie smiled, but she was still shaking inside, proud of herself that she didn't show it. Realising both girls were from the table she would be working at the following day, she hoped they wouldn't try anything else to put her down. A couple of minutes later she saw Irene talking to Gloria. Gloria looked across at her and smiled. Marjorie managed a very small smile in return.

Harry had explained what would happen the next day. Every girl at the table would be given the parts. As Marjorie would demonstrate how to assemble the pieces and she would walk round the table making sure they did it properly. When they all got it right, they would work together as a team, producing as many as they could. Meanwhile Marjorie would keep on working, assembling as many as she could by herself.

They were given thirty minutes for lunch and they stayed at their desks unless they fancied the canteen. Marjorie stayed at her desk and laid out her lunch in front of her. Her cheese and pickle sandwiches were delicious and she ate them hungrily. When she finished she tidied her things into her bag before heading to the toilets. There were not many there this time as many of them went outside for a smoke. Gloria was there in front of her, her bright overalls making her stand out. Seeing Marjorie, she turned round and smiled.

'Seems you managed to look after yourself this morning, I hear. Well, don't you mind those two. You got to cut them some slack, they're both in rotten digs, get a slice of bread and jam for breakfast and a couple of sausages for dinner if they're lucky. It's no excuse for carrying on like that but I can see why they're jealous. They're good workers, mind you, so let's hope they prove that tonight. I could do with an early night.'

Marjorie had to laugh at Gloria's idea of an early night, but six was better than seven so she nodded her head in agreement. When they met again later at the wash hand basins, she told Gloria how cheerful her overalls were.

'Old pair of curtains I had and I hated the dirty old brown pair they gave me, so I ran them up for myself.'

'I'm hoping to take these home with me on Saturday so they will be clean on Monday,' Marjorie explained, looking down at her oil-streaked overalls.

'Well, when you're here a bit longer and if you have an old pair of curtains, I'm happy to run you up a pair.'

Marjorie went back to her bench, grateful that she now had two people to talk to, three if you included Harry. At least that was a step in the right direction. At five to six Harry announced they could all go home.

'Mind you're back at your bench before eight in the morning,' he warned them. 'Lotta work tomorrow.'

Marjorie managed to catch both buses in time. The girls on the bus still watched her to see if she put a foot wrong. She didn't and was glad as Irene was still at work, so she was on her own if there had been any nastiness.

Mrs Harrison had left dinner for her but as her parents were still eating dinner, she joined them at the table. Her father was surprised to see her home so early and she explained that tomorrow was going to be a long day as they began to produce the new guns. She also mentioned that she was now a kind of supervisor and would be demonstrating to twelve girls how to put together the pieces of the guns which would form the sights that the gunners looked down from their aircraft.

Her father found it very interesting but her mother demanded that things like guns not be mentioned at the dinner table, or at any time in the house. Marjorie was too tired to argue and gratefully received her father's offer of a bedtime brandy.

As she cleared the table and stacked the dishes, Marjorie thought of the incident that had occurred in the morning. She was grateful to Gloria for telling her about the girls' circumstances. She would remember that and help if there was any way she could.

When she had left the kitchen ready for Mrs Harrison in the morning, she thought about how fortunate she was with her life, being able to live at home with wonderful dinners made for her and lunches prepared in the morning. She really wasn't sure why the world was so divided. She knew now she was actually helping with the war effort, that pleased her, but so many young girls had given up better lives to do what they had to do now.

She hoped she could encourage them tomorrow but right now all she wanted was a warm bed. She hung up the tea towel and went to join her father for a night cap.

12

Having managed to be one of the first off the bus that morning, Marjorie was in her overalls and taking last-minute instructions just as the other girls were arriving. An ancient chair had been placed at the end of the table so Marjorie could watch each of the girls as they worked. First though, Harry introduced her simply as Marjorie who was there to help them assemble the new parts. Each girl received a box full of the bits necessary.

Knowing that the two girls who had tried to make a fool of her yesterday were at the table, she tried to concentrate on all of them at once. She took the pieces out one by one on the table and then laid them out the way they would be put together. As she demonstrated each piece individually the way Harry had taught her, she asked them to hold them up in front of them to study before they moved on to the next bit.

'Speed is what we're aiming for, but safety is of the essence. If we get these wrong, men will die, so it's important to put every bit together as they ought to be.' She said it in a voice that was factual, then sat back to watch as they got on with it.

She noticed a few of them looking baffled and went over to see what the problem was, doing it as discreetly as she could.

She was sure some of them would have headaches with concentrating, but fortunately she had aspirin in her bag should that happen.

At teatime, she took out the mug Mrs Harrison had given her yesterday, from her own house so it wouldn't look too new. When she took out her packet of biscuits, she passed them round as she would have done anywhere else. She watched as the two girls so nasty to her yesterday ate the biscuits like they hadn't eaten that morning. It was obviously true what Gloria had told her.

By the end of the morning, just before lunch break, it was obvious some of the girls were having a lot of difficulty. Only three completed items were handed back to her. The mood was quiet at the table and looking round Marjorie was horrified at some of the lunches which appeared on the table. A couple seemed to have sandwiches carefully made, a few appeared to have bread and jam but two of them seemed to have one slice of butter folded over and filled with Spam.

She felt too uncomfortable asking if anyone would like one of her sandwiches but tomorrow she would ask Mrs Harrison to make her an extra round. She knew there was an ample supply of cheese and eggs at home and she was sure her family would be happy to help people in need. When she went up to go to the toilet, no one bothered her. Irene was there and greeted Marjorie cheerfully.

'All right, Ducks? Everything hunky dory?'

'Yes thanks, all seems to be going to plan. Did you get the bus this morning? I didn't see you.'

'Yeah, I was there all right, but you was at one end and I was at the other. See you tonight? You was early last night.'

'Back to normal tonight,' Marjorie replied. 'Yes, I'll see you at the bus stop.'

The two girls who had been so awful to her yesterday appeared quite contrite although not friendly. Marjorie noticed the dark rings under their eyes and the pallor of their skin. She would have to think of some way she could take down the barrier between them.

When everyone was back sitting at their places, Marjorie told them she felt awful that she didn't know their names. 'How are we expected to work together if we don't even know each other's names?' she asked.

'Who are you?' she smiled at the first girl on her left.

'Edna,' she replied, turning to the girl on her left.

'Susie,' the next to her called out and then each one round the table called out her name. Joan, Joyce, Jackie, Linda, Eva, Gloria, Sadie, Theresa, Kate and Lizzy, called out.

'Thanks, everybody, you all know I'm Marjorie, so let's carry on. If you're finding it difficult, please ask me. I'm sure we can work out a way to remember the parts.'

Hands went up after that and Marjorie did her best to show them in the simplest ways she could. The metals were different colours and the first three parts looked like copper, silver and gold, so she suggested they place them as to their value, copper coming first, silver second and gold the third. This seemed to help and by teatime they were getting much better although not yet quick enough. When the tea came she put the biscuits on the table and told everyone to help themselves as she wasn't very fussy on them. In three minutes, they had gone.

Harry came round to see how they were doing, checking

the wooden crate beside Marjorie to see how many there were. At that stage there were eleven completed. Marjorie was well aware that she managed that many by herself before lunch the day before but she explained that she wanted to make sure they were all done accurately. 'I'm sure by tomorrow we will have a production line going, but considering it's our first day, I don't think we're doing too badly,' she told him, out loud in front of the girls.

'Make sure you do,' he replied, but Marjorie was sure his mouth turned up as he left.

She now knew the names of the two girls who obviously didn't like her, were Joyce and Sadie. She made sure she used their names when she spoke to them, encouraging them by telling them they were doing much better.

By five o'clock, she felt she didn't need to keep such a tight eye on them and got on with assembling her own parts. By seven o'clock, there were thirty-six completed parts in the wooden crate beside Marjorie. She thanked them for all their hard work and then hurried off to get her coat and run to the bus.

Irene didn't arrive for another few minutes but managed it just as the bus pulled in. Somehow they were able to stand beside each other just as the bus pulled out.

'Seems like you was a bit of a star today by all accounts.'

'Really, Irene? Are you sure it was me?' Marjorie asked her. 'I'm not exactly popular. I did ask their names though.'

'Nah, they didn't say that, they said you thanked them for all their hard work and nobody has ever done that before. Most they get is a grunt from Harry.'

'Oh well, I'm sure he doesn't mean to be so abrupt, it's just the way he is,' Marjorie replied, trying to defend him.

'That's as well may be, but it's nice to know you're appreciated. Harry's a fair boss and all that, but it's nice sometimes to know that your work matters.'

Marjorie made a mental note to remember that. As they walked from the bus stop, Marjorie asked Irene what she had done before the war.

'You really don't wanna know,' was the reply.

Marjorie laughed, 'Oh come on, it can't be that bad.'

'It was luv, believe me. I don't think you would ever have spoken to me if we'd met back then.'

'I doubt that very much. You are so friendly and you have such a lovely smile, I know I would have spoken to you,' Marjorie told her.

'Believe me, you wouldn't.' She took a long pause and then, looking at her feet, she said, 'I was on the game, know what I mean? I sold myself to anyone who'd pay me. Then I met a bloke I really liked, but I knew he would drop me like a hot brick if he found out. I decided there and then I was going to leave it all behind me and would get a new life and put those years behind me.

'Then the war came and I volunteered for something that would make a difference, and here I am, in bloody Reading, scared every day that someone will walk in and recognise me. That's why I dyed me hair,' she explained, pulling back her turban to expose her peroxide blonde curls.

'Irene, I'm so sorry and please believe me, I wouldn't judge anyone. There, but for the Grace of God go I is my motto. Thank you for telling me. Your secret is safe with me, I promise. I'm still sure I would have spoken to you though,' she replied with a smile. 'I think you have a lot of guts. It must have been awful for you,'

'It was, Ducks, but I've escaped and I ain't going back.'

'And your young man, are you still seeing him!'

'Lordy no, I scarpered before he could find me. He was far too good for me. I'll maybe meet someone someday, but I'd have to tell them the truth. It's one thing my mother taught me, "always tell the truth, Irene."'

'And you have obeyed her. Do you see much of her?'

'Nah, she died when I was eleven, then the old man ran out on us. My gran looked after us, but after she died we were on our own. It seemed the easiest way to make money. Hey, love, you better run, your bus will have left.'

Marjorie had completely forgotten the time, but shouting goodbye to Irene, she ran as fast as she possibly could.

When she got there, she couldn't believe her eyes, the bus hadn't left. She jumped on, out of breath and saw it was the same lady driver.

'I knew you'd make it,' she told Marjorie, 'Mind, I couldn't have waited much longer,' she said as Marjorie handed her fare.

'Thank you so much, I'm so grateful to you. I honestly thought I'd have to walk,' Marjorie said, accepting her change.

'Grab a seat and catch your breath. No harm done.'

Marjorie got a few dirty looks from some of the other passengers but she smiled at them and walked on. Dinner was waiting for her and she hadn't realised just how hungry she was. It had been quite a day in so many ways.

The following morning Marjorie set off with an extra round of sandwiches and another packet of biscuits. She thought she must have somehow missed Irene, but she concentrated on how she would go about giving the sandwiches to Joyce. She wasn't sure what way she was going to approach it, the last thing she wanted to do was to insult them. She would just have to wait and see if the opportunity arose.

Production was slow first thing but increased as the morning went on. At teatime once again she offered the biscuits round and once again the packet came back almost empty.

'How do you manage to have so many bloomin' biscuits?' Jackie shouted down the table. 'We haven't had a packet in weeks.'

'Ah, that's a secret,' Marjorie replied. 'My mother was stocking up on them for quite a while before war broke out. They have to be used up before they go mouldy. She doesn't even like biscuits, and especially not Garibaldi.'

Marjorie hoped her lie sounded better than she felt. The truth was Mrs Harrison knew someone who knew someone who could get them from a factory. She knew they wouldn't last forever. At lunch time, on her way to the toilet, she put down a round of egg sandwiches on the table next to Joyce. 'I can't manage this, but I'm sure you could,' she said quietly as she walked off without waiting for an answer. When she got back it had disappeared and she noticed the greaseproof paper had been neatly folded.

When Harry did his rounds that afternoon, he could hardly believe his eyes when he checked the box. It was almost full to the top and would need to be emptied very soon to make way for more.

'Blimey,' he said, 'don't know what's got into you lot, but I'm not complaining. Just need to make sure they're all done proper or there'll be hell to pay.'

'I think you will find they are all faultless. I check each one before they top part goes on so I can see down the middle and I know they're not missing anything.'

She didn't mention she had had to have a few rebuilt as they weren't fitting together properly.

'Okey dokey, I'll see if you're right. I can tell just by running my hands down them.'

'Oh saucy, you can check me out anytime,' Edna called out and the rest started to laugh heartily. Harry turned on his heels and left.

Half an hour later one of the guys in a brown coat came down with a trolley to lift the box and five minutes later he came back with an empty replacement. Marjorie was delighted as she hadn't imagined they would have managed to fill a box before they finished for the day. 'Well done, girls,' she said to them as the tea arrived again. In the toilets, Sadie saw her and actually walked over towards her.

'We just wanted to thank you for the sandwiches,' she said. Before Marjorie could utter a reply, Sadie continued, 'I don't know why you gave them to us but we're very grateful. Our landlady says she can't afford the bread to give us, but I know she gives our rations to her kids. She knows we can't find digs any place else, so we have to put up with it until we can find somewhere which ain't likely. We get a slice of bread, a spoonful of jam and a cup of cold tea for breakfast. That sandwich was the nicest food we've tasted in a long time, weren't it, Joyce?'

The other girl stood beside her, looking at Marjorie. 'Sorry about the other day, we wasn't very nice to you. We thought you was all hoity toity, looking down your nose at the rest of us. As it happens, you're dead on, you are.'

Marjorie looked at them. They reminded her of her first formers back in Jersey who had been caught on being naughty. She smiled broadly at them. 'That's ok, I've forgotten all about it. Look, I'm happy to bring you a sandwich each day. Because we're out in the country, we get plenty of eggs and my mother often bakes our bread, so it's no bother, it really isn't,' she lied, hating herself for it but knowing that explaining their housekeeper was the one who got the eggs would make matters worse.

Gloria came up to Marjorie, just before quitting time. 'Don't you forget, if you need any sewing done, I'm happy to do it. You've made such a difference to us girls. Thank you goes a long way as my old mum used to say.'

'How nice of you to tell me that, Gloria. I'm glad it has all gone so well, I can hardly believe tomorrow is Saturday. This week has flown.'

And it had, it really had, Marjorie thought to herself as she headed off to the bus that night. I suppose you could say I have two more friends now, three if I count Gloria.

It was the hardest work she had ever known in her life before, but she'd made the best of it and she felt that she had really achieved something. However, nothing was as sweet as knowing she was going to have time off at last. Might not be for long, but she'd make the best of it.

'Hey, Irene, wait for me,' she called, seeing her friend just ahead of her. Irene turned round and looked surprised to see Marjorie.

'I didn't think you'd want to see me after what I told you,' she said quietly. 'I thought you'd go on without me.'

'Oh Irene, how could you think that?' Marjorie asked her, taking her arm, 'you were the first person who spoke to me and you told me you'd look out for me. How on earth could I forget that?'

Irene laughed, her face full of relief. Then arm in arm, they ran for the bus.

13

Marjorie's group production line reached a high the following morning, so much so that Marjorie asked Harry if she could have ten minutes of his time. He immediately said yes and invited her into his office. 'What's all this about?' he asked. 'Nothing wrong, I hope.'

'No, nothing at all to do with work, 'Marjorie replied, 'it's after work that worries me.' Seeing Harry's hesitant look, she quickly smiled, 'Not me, Harry, it's the girls' digs which worries me. It's obvious Joyce and Sadie are not getting enough to eat, nor enough sleep given the state of their bedroom. I can't believe, with a war going on, that people aren't prepared to offer spare bedrooms for a reasonable price.

'I would be happy to open my house up if I had one but as my home doesn't belong to me and is too far out, I can't do that. I'd like to see if I can find some though. The happier the girls are, the better they will work. Could I try walking round some houses on Monday morning? The girls are doing so well and I'll put Gloria in charge. After all, you do have some new equipment arriving you need us to work on, and fast, I believe.'

Harry was sitting back in his chair, fiddling with a pencil and looking at Marjorie with a curious expression. It was true some new parts were coming and he'd only trust Marjorie with them.

'How long do you think you'd need then? I can't spare you for too long, you gotta understand that. Like three hours, four?'

'Two if I find somewhere quickly and four at the most.' Marjorie gave him an earnest look and crossed her arms as she waited.

'Ok then, just don't tell anyone what you're up to, can't have everyone having you find them digs. Be back here by noon sharp on Monday.'

'Ok then,' Marjorie gave him her best smile, 'and as there are only enough parts today to keep us for another hour and a half, can we get out early enough to catch the first bus at lunch time?'

'Right, that's it. Only if they're finished and the crates collected, mind. And no more favours! Go on, get out of here.' Harry's head was pointing down at his desk, but Marjorie knew he was smiling.

When she arrived at Reading station, Marjorie decided to have a stroll round town, not for long but maybe to go to her favourite bookshop. She was walking past an art gallery which had been there for years when she noticed a painting which was totally different to the kind of paintings she normally saw there. She walked closer and stood, just looking and studying it.

It was a portrait of an Asian boy with dark skin. He was young, maybe ten or twelve years old, standing under a tropical plant. There was something about it which encouraged her to take a closer look. She decided to go inside so she could enquire who painted it. She had met the gallery owner before and he smiled in recognition. 'How are you, how is life treating you?' he asked.

'Well, you know, the same as everyone else, doing one's best. I've had to give up teaching for a while. I'm working in the munitions factory in Theale.'

'That is very different for you, very different indeed. One of the advantages of being as old as I am is that I'm considered too old for war work. Sorry, your time is precious, is there anything you'd like to ask me about?'

'I'm rather intrigued by the portrait in the window. The one of the young boy standing beside an exotic plant.'

'Ah yes, by David Paynter. He studied at the Royal Academy and exhibits every year there. This was his entry this year and he allowed me the privilege of selling it for him. He lives in Ceylon and is known internationally for his religious paintings, but it's now the thing to have your portrait painted by him. You have good taste, Miss Fitzpatrick.'

'Thank you, but sadly my taste is not matched by my budget. I have my savings but I don't know how long this war is going to last.'

'Come and see me at the end of the month. If it hasn't sold by then, we will work something out.'

Marjorie thanked him and after she closed the door, she gazed at the painting again. She couldn't quite understand why but something attracted her to it so strongly. Although he was an Asian boy, he wasn't Indian, but it triggered something in her early memories of Madras.

For another hour she walked around Reading looking to see if there were any houses big enough to be able to take in lodgers. She wandered down one road and discovered a cul de sac running off the bigger street. It was called Hawthorn

Gardens and she could see why. There was a row of hawthorn trees running along a small piece of waste ground.

She counted there were eleven houses in total, four pairs of semis and three detached houses. Although they were close to the heart of the city, they could have been in the country. She imagined it might have been because the trees sheltered the houses from the noise of traffic. They were pretty houses, built long before the First World War, with stained glass windowpanes and fanlights over the door.

In the last of the semis, an elderly lady was brushing the path up to the front door. She was dressed in a warm tweed coat with a knitted hat that covered her head. A shock of white hair had escaped from the front and it bounced as she swept the ground. Seeing Marjorie look at her, she called across, 'Can I help you, are you looking for someone?'

It was a genteel voice and Marjorie smiled at the lady who had called her. 'I'm actually only looking but thank you.'

'Oh, are you looking to buy somewhere? I don't think anyone's selling just now. Not with the war and everything.'

'Oh no, I'm not looking to buy, I was just wondering if anyone might be taking in lodgers,' Marjorie replied.

'For yourself?' the lady asked.

'No, not for me. For two girls I work with. They have awful digs at the moment and I feel so sorry for them.'

'Come inside and have a cup of tea, why don't you? You can have a look and see what you think of these houses inside. They're all the same, even the detached.'

'Well, I don't know, I'm supposed to be catching the three o'clock bus, but never mind, I'd love to come in and thank you for inviting me,' she added following down the path after closing the gate behind her.

'It's changed times we're living in now. So many people away to war. Now close that door and come into the living-room. I'm Elsie by the way, Elsie Armstrong.'

'And I'm Marjorie Kirkpatrick, very nice to meet you.'

'Lovely to meet you too. I don't have many visitors these days. My daughters are both in Canada and my boys are both doctors, one with the army and one with the navy. My husband died five years ago, so I'm on my own now. Strange times as I said. What way would you like your tea?'

'Just a little milk, no sugar,' Marjorie replied. 'What a comfortable room.'

'Well, it's just me as I said, but I light the fire as soon as I come down in the morning.'

The room was comfortably furnished with a sofa and two armchairs. A dining-room table sat in the corner and the fireplace had a brass canopy which was sparkling as the flames burnt brightly beneath it. A matching coal scuttle stood in the corner, its brass lid bruised and bent, but polished until it shone.

The kitchen ran off the living-room and Marjorie could see Elsie setting up a tray, taking china cups from the dresser in the corner. The kitchen was spotless, the tiled floor, although quite old, hadn't a blemish on it. The dresser in the corner was full of colourful china and looked as though it was much loved.

'Here we are then, I've put out the china as it's so nice to have a visitor. You're not from these parts, are you? I can tell,' and she smiled, tapping her nose with her finger.

'You're right, I live in Sonning with my parents. I was

teaching in Jersey but I had to come home due to the occupation there. I don't think of it as home though. I was brought up in India but I came back to England to go to boarding-school, then University. I'm a bit of a nomad I think,' Marjorie told her, accepting a slice of cake from Elsie.

'Baked it myself, force of habit. When my husband was alive and four growing children, I baked twice a week. Now it's just once and I mostly give it all away.'

'It's delicious,' Marjorie tried to tell her, her mouth full of sponge, 'and so is the tea.'

'One thing I've always indulged in is good tea, I prefer Indian, but it's not easy to get good tea these days, nothing is. Now, tell me about these girls looking for lodgings.'

'Well, and I'll speak frankly if I may, they didn't have the best childhoods and now they're in digs and the landlady practically starves them. They're not terribly refined but I've discovered they have warm hearts and they're so grateful for anything they're given. That's why I'm looking for them. I think it's terrible that they have to work eleven hours a day only to go home to cold food and share a miserable bedroom. We all work at Theale, in the munitions factory as you have probably guessed.'

Well,' and Elsie filled Marjorie's cup, 'I was a nurse before I got married, that's how I met my husband when he was a patient. He was in the navy and had lost part of his arm fighting in Germany. We got married as soon as we could and lived in a house much smaller than this. Then Richard, that was my husband, he got a job with the Admiralty and we were able to buy this house. My four children have all grown up here.'

'How lovely,' Marjorie replied, refusing another slice of cake, 'you must have very special memories here.'

'Indeed, I have, but I didn't expect my girls to join the WRNS and leave home so early. Now, it's only me, rattling around while my children are all over the place. So, are you trying to tell me these girls are a bit rough?'

'Oh well, not exactly, a little rough around the edges, but they are good girls when you get to know them.'

'Here's how it is. I have four bedrooms. The girls shared one and the boys had one each. I need to keep bedrooms ready in case any of them come home, but if they don't mind sharing a biggish bedroom with twin beds, I'm sure we could come to some arrangement. I'm up at seven every morning, out of habit, and I make myself a proper dinner each night. Come and see the room and see what you think.'

Marjorie followed Elsie up the stairs and into a room which looked out over the back garden and more trees.

'The garden is full of colour once the daffodils start, then it's tulips and after that roses and all sorts of colour.'

The room was large and bright with a pink carpet and pink damask curtains. The two beds had fitted coverlets to match the curtains. There were two sets of drawers, a large wardrobe and a dressing table with three mirrors. It was very much a girl's room.

'Oh Elsie, I imagine they wouldn't be able to believe their luck. I doubt if they have even seen a room like this,' Marjorie told her as Elsie opened the door of the bathroom, which had a large bath and a hand wash basin with a large mirror over it. There was a set of open shelves filled with towels and bowls of soap and bath cubes.

'Lavatory next door,' Elsie said, pointing to a door in the landing.

'I really don't know what to say,' Marjorie told her. 'Never in my wildest dreams did I think I would find anything like this. I just wanted to find somewhere they would be warm, clean and safe.'

'Well, between me and you, I've been praying for an answer to my loneliness and I think you've just answered it for me.'

'Oh Elsie,' and Marjorie spontaneously threw her arms around her new friend, 'you have answered my prayers. But,' and she drew back, 'will they be able to afford it?'

'They can give me what they're paying now plus their ration books to help me get the things they'll need. I have my husband's pension and he left me comfortably off. It will be nice to be able to help girls who haven't had what I or my children had. And there's something about you, Marjorie, I know I can trust. I hope we can be friends.'

'But of course we will, and if it's ok with you I'd like to come back another Saturday. As long as there's cake,' she added with a big smile.

Walking back to the station, Marjorie thought to herself that if she hadn't believed in answered prayer, she did now. She made the bus just in time and found herself wishing for Monday to come quickly so she could tell the girls that their luck had changed. She knew that Elsie would be the best landlady ever and she prayed the girls would behave. Somehow she knew they would.

It was dark when she hopped off the bus. She walked

swiftly towards home, the night air chilly round her face. Her mother was not at all pleased at her being late although Marjorie couldn't imagine why. Her father smiled as he saw her walk into the drawing-room. 'Been shopping?' he asked.

'Not really, just browsing, but it was nice to have leisure time.'

'That's understandable. Well, I'm glad you're back. I have a rather nice wine for you to try tonight. There's a duck casserole, I believe.'

'Oh lovely, I'll go and look and turn the oven on, then I'll go and get changed.'

'Righty ho,' her father called after her. 'A letter came for you. It's from France, I believe.'

Marjorie thrust it into her pocket as she investigated the casserole. When it was finally in the oven, she pulled the envelope out of her pocket. It was from France. She turned it round and her heart missed a beat. It was from Celeste.

14

U p in her room, sitting on the edge of her bed, Marjorie's heart continued to beat rapidly. She was so afraid of reading the words she dreaded most that Nicolas was dead. She straightened the page and read.

Chère Marjorie,

You must forgive my English. It is not good when I write it down. I want for you to know that I am well and my grand-mère is good also. We are living together and it is very nice, we are both happy. She is doing cooking very much with me. It is nice to see my cousins who live close my grand-mère. Nicolas is well, he is with my father. They are making a new house and they do many things together. You must not worry. They make a very good house. I hope you understand. They work very hard together but that is good, is it not? I will write and tell you how well the house is coming. We never forget you and one day we want to talk with you again. I hope you are well.

Your friend
Celeste

P.S. You must not worry. I will tell you how Nicolas goes.

Marjorie read it again and again. She realised that Celeste was afraid her letter might be opened. She wondered what she was trying to tell her, that Nicolas was working with his father. He was building a house, but what else was he doing? Was he working with the French underground? Yes, that was it, of course. He was building a house during the day but working with the resistance movement. He said he would fight the Germans and keep the French free from them. She would write back when she came to bed that night. There was no post until Monday. She would ask Mrs Harrison to post it for her.

Dinner was delicious and her father's new wine, a gift from a grateful patient, was just what she needed. She explained to her parents what she had done that afternoon. Her father congratulated her but her mother didn't understand it at all. 'Why would anyone knock a stranger's door and ask them to take people in they didn't know? They could be murderers or thieves for all you know, Marjorie.'

'No, Mother, I know them, I work with them. They don't have families of their own, it's the least I could do.'

'Good for you, Marjorie, we all have to work together to get this war over. The poor lads I'm operating on every day would agree with that. Have some more wine, dear, it's good for your health,' he told his wife, topping up her glass.

That night, back in her room, Marjorie wrote to Celeste, in French.

My dear Celeste,

How lovely to hear from you. It's wonderful that you are with your grandmother. You will be good company for one another. It's good also to hear about Nicolas, he must be so happy to be working with your father. He will learn so much from him. I remember him talking about how much he was looking forward to building a house with him. It is wonderful that you are all safe and well.

I hope, when this horrible war is over, that we can all visit one another. Give my love to your grandmother and tell Nicolas to keep safe. It can be very dangerous building houses. I hope he has a hard hat in case anything falls on him. You must feel the same. I will write soon. And always remember you can phone me if there is anything you need. It is hard to get anything these days.

With my love,
Marjorie

She hoped Celeste would realise that she understood what she was saying. She hoped Nicolas would not do anything too crazy. She would pray for his safety every night.

In the morning Marjorie appeared at the bus stop at the same time as usual. Irene was amazed to see her.

'Hey, Ducks, what are you doing here? Weren't you

supposed to have this morning off?' she asked.

'I was,' Marjorie agreed, 'but as it happens I was able to do what I needed to do on Saturday, so here I am.'

'Good on you girl, you get things done, that's for sure.'

Marjorie smiled as the bus arrived and there was the usual scramble to get on. Irene squeezed up the queue until she got beside Marjorie. 'I never asked you,' she said in a quiet voice that no one else would hear, 'where you live. I know it's near Reading and out in the country, but where exactly?'

'I live with my parents since I had to come back from teaching. We live near a village called Sonning,' Marjorie replied, in an even quieter voice.

'And your old man, what does he do?'

Marjorie really didn't want to answer this question, but she had only two choices, to lie or refuse to say. She decided to do neither.

'He's an eye surgeon in London.'

'I knew it, I bloody knew it,' was Irene's reply. 'There's a bloke came in the pub last night, I work there some nights to pay for my lodging. Anyway, he comes in with his head all bandaged up. We was ribbing him like, asking what the other fella looked like. He says he's in the army and had gunshot wounds in his head. He said he's had an op and the doctor what done it was called Fitzpatrick. Said he saved his sight, he did.'

Marjorie wasn't quite sure how to react so she just said she hoped he would recover quickly and was delighted when the bus stopped. She hopped off and started walking ahead. Irene had to run quickly to keep up with her. 'It's all right, I'm not going to tell anyone, am I? I just thought when he said the name that it might be your old man. I mean, you're a clever gal, chip off the old block!'

'I don't think so, but I'd be awfully glad if you wouldn't mention it to anyone else.'

'Scout's honour,' Irene replied, 'it's between you and me and no one else.'

Marjorie believed her and remembering what Irene had been through in her own life, she would never think ill of her.

Harry couldn't believe his eyes when Marjorie walked in. 'Blimey, that was quick. You up at five or something?'

'No, nothing like that,' she laughed, 'I sorted it on Saturday afternoon.'

'You told them yet?' he asked.

'No, not yet, I'm keeping that till break time. When do we start the new job?'

'Soon as you and me has worked it out. Come into the office after tea break. Make sure them girls has plenty to do.'

Back in her seat she told the girls to collect their boxes for the day. There were only enough left to last the morning so she was hoping Harry would have the next lot sorted by lunch time.

When the tea trolley came round, she filled her mug and walked over to Joyce's chair and beckoned for Sadie to join them.

'What's up then, what have we done wrong?'

'Nothing, nothing at all,' she explained. 'I just wanted to ask you a question.'

'What's that then?' Sadie asked, looking slightly uncomfortable.

'Well, on Saturday I took myself for a walk. I ended up on a place called Hawthorn Gardens which is just off Oakley Road,'

'Never heard of it,' Joyce said anxiously.

'They're lovely houses,' Marjorie continued, 'nice gardens, big bedrooms.' The girls were looking even more puzzled now. 'I met a lady who owned one of them. She invited me in for a cup of tea.' Marjorie took a sip of tea from her mug, and then went on. 'It's a lovely house, four bedrooms and only her living in it.'

'Blimey, she's bleedin' lucky, I couldn't imagine having even a bed to myself,' Sadie said, wondering where this was going.

'Well, her two sons and two daughters are away fighting for our freedom, and as her husband died five years ago, she's quite lonely.' Marjorie took another sip of her tea. 'So, I mentioned I knew two girls who would give anything to live in that house, so she took me upstairs to look at one of the rooms. It was very big with twin beds, a huge wardrobe and dressing table and a lovely pink carpet. It's just beside the bathroom as well.'

'So why are you telling us this?' Joyce asked, her eyes wide.

'Well, she said she'd like you two to come and live with her. For the same money as you're paying now.'

'Marjorie, you're not having us on now, are you?' Joyce asked.

'You can't be serious. Us, in a place like that?' Sadie asked.

'Yes, it's all yours, provided you behave yourselves. Elsie is a really lovely lady.'

'Oh, my Gawd! When can we see it? When can we move in?'

'Let me arrange that, but just for now, get back to work or Harry will be shouting into my ear.'

'Marjorie,' Joyce shouted, 'I bleedin' love you, I do.'

'And I love you too. You're a marvel, you are, and that's for sure,' Sadie told her, 'I never met anyone like you before but I'm so glad I did.'

Marjorie, who had always disliked being the centre of attention, finished her tea and left Joyce and Sadie to tell the rest.

'You told them then? Seems like a bit of excitement over there. They better get on with their work.'

'They will, Harry, they will, but let me see what comes next.'

'This job's top-secret, Marjorie, straight from the top. For the navy this time. Battleships to be exact. Guns with sights so they can see where they're directing fire to. The big guns upstairs didn't know if they could trust anyone here to handle it, but I told them about you. Someone's coming up to meet you this afternoon.'

'Blimey!' It was out before Marjorie knew it.

Harry laughed. 'Blimey is right, but I told them you was the brightest I've met since coming here, so they said that sounded good, but they'd like to meet you.'

'Ok then, but I can't tell the girls about this. Might be best just to say it's just a bit more of the same so they don't think they're handling anything different.'

'That's the idea. I know you'll handle it well, but we got to get it right. Can't afford any mistakes or men will die.'

'I'm with you,' Marjorie assured him. 'I'll be standing over every bit. It's going to take a while, so what do we do in between?'

'I've got it covered. They'll be going back to what they were doing before you started. They could do it blindfolded, then we'll say you're learning yourself before you pass it on.'

'Righty ho, but Harry, you have a car don't you?'

'Course I do, I can't bleedin' walk too far. But what's that got to do with it?'

'I thought you might be able to give Joyce and Sadie a lift to their digs tomorrow night. They can't exactly afford a taxi now, can they? How does Wednesday sound?'

'Blimey, Marjorie, I don't know what's coming next with you. I'll have to tell the wife I'll be a bit later, war work and all that.'

'Super, I'll let them know. Ok if I go with you. I need to make the necessary introductions.'

'In for a penny, in for a pound. Get off with you now and tell them girls there's plenty of work coming their way.'

Marjorie told the girls to start packing, that they were getting a lift to their new lodgings on Wednesday night. They couldn't believe it was with Harry but they were so excited, everything delighted them. Marjorie would telephone Elsie tonight and tell her to get ready for the onslaught. She couldn't wait to see the girls' faces when they saw their room. She would get Mrs Harrison to bake a loaf to take to Elsie and maybe some eggs if there were enough.

But now she had to prepare for the man from the Admiralty coming this afternoon to meet her. So much for thinking all she had to do was stand there and screw things together, not that she minded in the least. It would be nice to use her brains, even if it wasn't to teach languages. She thought again of Nicolas and the dangerous work he was involved in. She hoped that what she was helping with, would keep the English Channel safe for both of them.

15

Marjorie was back working when one of the men who collected the crates tapped her on the shoulder.

'Harry wants you in his office, miss. Two gents with him, city types, briefcases an' all. Hope you ain't been up to no good,' he added giving her a big wink.

'Righty ho,' Marjorie replied, 'I'll go now. Gloria, can you take charge please.'

'Okey dokey, Marjorie, I'll keep them busy till you get back.'

Marjorie ran up the steps to Harry's office and found the door shut which was unusual. She tapped it gently and Harry answered. 'Come on in Marjorie. These gentlemen would like to talk to you.'

The two men stood up as Marjorie walked in; she had almost forgotten what it was like in polite circles. Harry introduced her to them, only as Mr Vaughan and Mr Burke. Harry had had several chairs brought in and he indicated for her to sit down.

Mr Vaughan spoke first. 'Miss Fitzpatrick, Harry has mentioned how quickly you have picked up things and how you have been able to teach the girls how to do it. We've taken the liberty of checking out your credentials and it would appear you are unusually bright, double first at

Oxford. We think you might be rather wasted here. Would you be interested in moving to the Admiralty?'

Marjorie hesitated before replying. After all, Harry had only told her that the next job would be quite secretive.

'Well, to be honest, I wouldn't really. My sister is in the War Office but I wasn't interested in that. I'm really quite happy here.'

Mr Burke spoke next. 'Miss Fitzpatrick, it's very important that the work we are authorising here must be carried out in strict confidence. We don't want news leaking from here that indicates we are furnishing a new ship with some of the best guns ever seen before. War at sea is quite different from war on land, but these guns will give the navy a great advantage over the Germans.

'We know that your father is Lieutenant Colonel Henry Fitzpatrick, so we know you will have been brought up in a certain way. We also know your father has a connection with the King and you, therefore, can be trusted with matters of State. Mr Johnston here, told us that you knew how to put your last job together instinctively, almost without the need for instruction. That kind of intuition is valuable to us. Might I suggest you come along to the Admiralty for a day or two and then come back here to start production on the new guns? It will mean a proper salary for you, of course, we know what you earn here.'

Marjorie was still feeling confused about it, but as long as they didn't intend for her to leave altogether, she would certainly think about it.

Mr Vaughan sat forward in his chair to address her. He seemed a kindly man in comparison to Mr Burke.

'The other thing, Miss Fitzpatrick, is that you must not let any of the people working here know what the guns are for. They must continue to think of them as 'parts' and could be for army jeeps or aircraft. Nothing must be indicated that might make them think of anything other than run of the mill, if there is such a thing in war. These are early days but the navy is going to be at the forefront of many battles we foresee in the future. So, if you come on board with us, you will be helping us to literally win battles.'

Marjorie looked down at her stained brown overalls, her ugly shoes and compared herself with the gentlemen talking to her. Both wore pinstriped suits, white shirts and silk ties, their polished shoes shining despite the rain outside. But then, if they were from the Admiralty they probably had a driver outside.

'When would you like me to come and visit you?' she asked. 'I'll have to think up some excuse to tell the girls.'

'How about next Monday and Tuesday?' Mr Vaughan asked. 'Carry on with whatever you're doing now and you can make up some excuse as to why you are not in work at that time. It will be useful for you to see the plans we have in our office. Before that, you will have to sign the Official Secrets Act of 1939 of course.'

Mr Vaughan stood up as he finished speaking to her. 'Harry here is one of the best men we have working for us. It was he who spotted that you might be useful to us. Sorry you had to leave Jersey. I believe you were very happy there.'

Marjorie raised her eyebrows; they had obviously checked her out before they came here. It seemed like Harry was well known to them also. He wasn't just a supervisor, that was for sure.

'Thank you, Miss Fitzpatrick, I'll look forward to seeing you on Monday. You will receive a letter on Friday morning giving you instructions. Until then, thank you for cooperating with us, it is much appreciated.'

When Marjorie came back down the steps, she was met by a sea of expectant faces. 'Blimey, that was more than a cup of tea and a biscuit. What you done?' Gloria asked.

'I didn't do anything really. It seems they were very pleased with the work we're doing and one of them recognised my name. His daughter was at school with me and apparently I visited their house for a birthday party. Such a small world. Now, come on, girls. We have to keep up the good work.'

Thankfully her excuse was accepted without further question and she was delighted when she saw the tea trolley appear. Joyce and Sadie were both so excited about going to their new digs but were working hard to make the time go in more quickly. Then a miracle happened. Harry sent word that he was leaving at six o'clock and the three of them had better be ready.

This was practically unheard of from Harry, but it transpired that he had to be back home by 7.30 for his daughter's concert and his wife had put her foot down.

Joyce and Sadie had brought their belongings with them in two battered suitcases, one held together by string. It really pulled at Marjorie's heartstrings that people could have so little to show for their lives. It made her even happier that she had found somewhere for them.

Harry threw the cases in the boot of his car before setting off. Marjorie was so impressed by how he drove, considering his injuries. Sitting beside him she directed him around Reading until he came to Hawthorn Gardens. The girls looked up incredulously from the back seat when they pulled up at the house.

'Blimey, is this really it, Marjorie? It looks so posh.'

'Yes, this is it,' Marjorie replied. 'Wait till you see inside. Come on in, Harry. Elsie's expecting to meet you.'

Elsie had been watching out for them for the last hour. She answered the door and immediately gave Marjorie a hug. 'Come on in girls, and you must be Harry, lovely to meet you all. Now, I have your room all ready for you. Why don't you girls run upstairs and have a look while I make Harry and Marjorie a cup of tea. Your dinner's in the oven.' As the girls ran excitedly up the stairs, she shouted after them, 'It's the room at the back with the door open.'

Marjorie wished she had been able to see their faces when they saw their room, but Elsie took her into the living-room where Harry was already sitting down. There was a cake sitting on the table along with china cups, saucers and plates. 'I baked it specially for you, Marjorie, to thank you for changing my life for the better,' she said, carrying a large teapot from the kitchen.

'But Elsie, it's you who are changing peoples' lives,' Marjorie protested. 'You have no idea how excited Joyce and Sadie have been.'

'That makes me so happy to hear, but it's given me a purpose instead of sitting here on my own night after night. It's going to be lovely having the girls to cook for. Oh, here they are. Sit down, girls. Now which of you is which?'

'I'm Joyce and this is Sadie and we ain't never seen a room

like that before. It's bloomin' massive, it is. We don't know how to thank you, do we, Sadie? I can't really believe it. It's so warm as well.'

'Well, I'm very pleased to meet you both. I hope you'll both be very happy here. I'm not going to offer you a slice of cake as there's a casserole in the oven for the three of us but have a cup of tea.'

The girls both seemed in a daze as they looked around them. Everything was so welcoming, the flames from the fire reflected on the brass canopy, warmed the room.

'There's a gas fire in your room you can use going to bed and getting up in the morning, as long as you always remember to turn it off,' Elsie told them, 'and there's an alarm clock beside the bed. It's a seven-minute walk to the bus station. I timed myself this morning.'

'No excuse then for being late,' Harry told them. 'And you'll work better with food in your belly.'

'Yes, I will make you porridge and toast every morning, except maybe Sunday when we'll have a fry-up after church,' Elsie told them.

Marjorie had never seen the girls so lost for words before. She knew Harry needed to go home, so finishing her tea and cake, she stood up to button her coat. 'Thank you so much, Elsie, you really are the kindest person I've come across for a very long time.'

'Come and see me as soon as you can. Lovely to meet you and Harry. I'm so sorry you can't meet my husband. He worked for the Admiralty, you see. He would have wanted to do his bit for the War Office. But now I have the girls to look after, that will help me to stop missing him so much.'

Marjorie kissed Elsie goodbye, warned the girls to behave well and told them she'd see them in the morning. She glanced over her shoulder as she left and thought she would never forget their faces at that very moment.

Harry offered to drive Marjorie all the way home but she refused, knowing he had to be home on time.

'No, I don't, not really,' he replied, 'I just made that up for the girls. I knew how excited they were and it gave me an opportunity to talk to you about the meeting we had earlier. Vaughan and Burke are bigwigs in the Admiralty, so it was quite something for them to want to meet you. You see, I just knew the way you looked at parts and immediately knew how they fitted. It takes a certain kind of intelligence to do that.

'I also know you have a way with you, so that even though you're a bit posh and all, people like you. What's more they trust you and you get the best out of them. From now on you're going to have about fifty under you, although they won't know that. You'll be showing them what to do and watching them as they do it,' he explained.

'But that means four more tables, I can't get around everyone at once,' she argued.

'You don't have to; each table will have someone you trust to look after them. This ship's going to be ready in a couple of months so our work has to be done in time. I know what those lads will be going through and all I can do is to make it as safe as can be for them.'

Marjorie was so busy listening to Harry, she had forgotten to give him directions, yet here they were, on the road to Sonning. 'Harry, how on earth do you know where I live?' she demanded to know.

'I had to make it my business once I'd recommended you. Nice houses, very nice indeed,' he said, lowering his head and looking out the window. 'Your old man must have quite a job. Eye surgeon to the King and all.'

'Honorary Eye Physician to the King,' she corrected him, 'we don't exactly dine at the palace.'

'Looks like a bleedin' palace to me,' Harry laughed. 'Seriously though, it's a nice place to live.'

'It's not even ours,' Marjorie pointed out, observing her home from the passenger window. 'It's convenient for my father's work. We should have moved by now but this war seems to slow everything up.'

'It does, but we have to bleedin' win it. Well, here you are, Marjorie. I hope you sleep well, 'cause I know those two girls will. That was an amazing thing you did for them, especially as they weren't that nice to you.'

'You really do know everything, don't you, Harry? You're a man of mystery.'

'And you're a lady with a lot of talents. Night, Marjorie, see you in the morning, don't be late,' he shouted after her. Marjorie stood in the driveway, thinking over the events of the day. She couldn't have imagined it in her wildest dreams. Bleedin' mad, she thought, and laughed out loud as she turned the key in the door.

16

On Monday Marjorie felt as though she was back teaching again. Dressed in a smart grey suit, cream blouse and black court shoes, she felt as though she was ready to meet the people in the Admiralty. She travelled with her father until they had to go to their separate ways, she to Whitehall and him to the hospital. She hadn't been in London for quite a while and she really could detect the tension in the air as people prepared themselves for the Luftwaffe bombings at night.

The Admiralty building itself was dark and airless and Marjorie felt rather apprehensive when she was led into a small room with a desk and four chairs, another desk which housed a typewriter in the corner and a settee against the wall which looked as though it had been slept on.

She stood up when she heard the door open. Mr Vaughan and Mr Burke entered with a third man behind them. Marjorie shook hands with the two men she knew and was introduced to a third man, Commander Grieves, who was dressed in a smart naval uniform. He was a man of early middle age, she imagined, with steel grey hair and eyes that matched. His handshake was firm, but his eyes twinkled as he spoke, 'Delighted to meet you, Miss Fitzpatrick.'

Feeling more at ease, Marjorie sat and waited for the

briefing she had been promised.

It was the commander who opened the conversation. A fourth person had entered the room. She was not introduced but sat at the typewriter and took notes in shorthand. 'Miss Fitzpatrick, I am about to take command of a new aircraft carrier which is being made ready as we speak. This ship will have new, highly technical radar equipment which will enable us to prepare for battle ahead of the Germans.

'The guns will be the best ever produced but we cannot allow their details to fall into any other hands other than ours. It's imperative no small comments of what we are making can be let slip in any kind of conversation, be it the local pub or amongst family. The Royal Navy is the largest in the world and we intend to win the war and save the British people. Are you with me, Miss Fitzpatrick?'

'But of course, sir, I know exactly what you mean.'

'The important parts of our equipment are to be made in your factory. We are aware it's smaller than most munitions factories but that's a bonus for us. What we need to do is ensure that there are no mistakes made. Mistakes cost lives, so that is why we're anxious to talk to you. You must test every single part to see that they are all interconnected and in place.

'There is also a great degree of urgency in this. I've known Harry for a long number of years. Before his accident, he was the best man under me. He may not have had the education you have had, Miss Fitzpatrick, but he has a built-in intuition and he's a thinker. If he says you're the one to do this, then I take him at his word.'

There was a silence in the room for a few seconds as the

stenographer took notes. It was interrupted by Mr Vaughan. 'Miss Fitzpatrick, I'm sure you understand all of this but I would be grateful if you could advise us as to how you think this could be done within the factory.'

Marjorie straightened her back as she prepared herself to speak to the gentlemen present.

'I presume you're asking me how quickly I can do this and how I could ensure that no one in the factory, with the exception of Harry, will know what an important job this is. That in itself is a difficult task. The first job I worked on was guns for bomber planes. We were told how important it was that there were no mistakes or men would die. I see no reason to let them know anything else other than that this is the next batch with the rules the same.

'The girls I work directly with are good workers, some quicker than others at picking things up. I think it would be impossible for me to watch over more than twenty people at a time to ensure the accuracy. Obviously you need to start this as soon as possible, so if I may ask for direction today, I should be able to have a good team together by Wednesday or Thursday. But first I need to acquaint myself with the procedure so I can see the best way of explaining it to the others. I will certainly emphasise the urgency and the safety element needed but provided they are happy, they will work well.'

'Thank you, Miss Fitzpatrick, I'm sure these two able gentlemen will get you started as soon as possible. If you foresee any difficulties arising, please contact them immediately.' With that all three men rose from their seats and the commander shook hands with them before coming over to Marjorie, looking at her intensely with his steel grey eyes and shaking her hand again. Then he left without another word.

'I think that went well, don't you?' Mr Vaughan asked Marjorie. 'He seems satisfied that you will have it under control, as are we. Now come with us to the canteen. The coffee is pretty dreadful, but it is guaranteed to be hot and wet.'

In the canteen Marjorie looked around her in amazement. There were so many people, men and women, some in uniform, the rest in civvies. Mr Burke explained that many of the men in uniform would be working on the aircraft carrier, so were being taught about radar equipment and weapons. 'I'm going to introduce you to Captain Melville, he's one of the naval officers and he will explain to you how the guns work. After that he will show you what you will be assembling and explain how it's put together and in which order. He's an engineer as well as an officer.

'Should you not feel totally satisfied about any of it, you must come back tomorrow. If not, you can begin to prepare within the factory and organise it how you think it will work best. If it goes well, everyone who satisfies you can look forward to some kind of reward for good service. Ah, here's the coffee. You may judge for yourself the quality.'

For once Mr Vaughan smiled and in that instant looked ten years younger. The coffee was indeed hot and wet but they had failed to warn her of its bitterness. It took three heaped teaspoonfuls of sugar to make it drinkable. The scones on the other hand, were freshly made and most acceptable.

Tristan Melville turned out to be a graduate in engineering

from Oxford no less. Although they didn't manage to find anyone they both knew, they agreed that tutorage was incomparable with anywhere else. He was very patient as he demonstrated the order the parts fitted together.

'You should have studied engineering,' he told her, 'you're a natural.'

She did rather astonish him when she managed to complete each anti-aircraft gun in record time. The guns themselves were heavy to lift when completed and Tristan demonstrated the position the gunners would be in as they fired. He slipped his arm around her shoulder to demonstrate and as he did this, Marjorie felt her cheeks burn. He didn't seem to notice, or if he did he certainly didn't refer to it.

They had lunch together in the canteen and when, at six o'clock, she was preparing to leave to catch her train, he suggested that he might walk with her. Although she originally told him there was no need she was secretly pleased when he did. London was in darkness as they walked away from Whitehall towards the railway. When she discovered she had missed her train, he insisted on taking her into the station bar for a drink. The brandy he brought her was warming and she lessened her hold of the heavy coat she had worn over her suit.

'I've really enjoyed today, Marjorie. I'm not used to working with women and I'm certainly not used to women as obviously intelligent as you are. Are you due to come back to the Admiralty?'

'No,' Marjorie replied, 'they seemed pleased with the report you gave them telling them I'm "highly competent" as you put it. So, it's back to the factory tomorrow for me, I'm afraid.'

'What are you doing on Saturday?' he asked.

'Working until two, then I'm off until Monday.'

'May I take you to dinner on Saturday night.? I can pick you up if you like, it will give us more time. Shall we say six o'clock? May I have your telephone number just in case anything goes wrong?'

Marjorie scribbled down her home telephone number on the back of his hand with the pen he gave her, and then leapt up when she realised the time. He walked her to her train and as she was about to board, he kissed her lightly on the cheek, then stepped back to wave goodbye.

Marjorie's head was full of figures, component numbers and variations, but now there was another task to add to the list. What would she wear to go out with a rather attractive naval officer? She would have to confide in Aunt Margaret. She would definitely know. Meanwhile, she had to work out in her head what to tell the girls tomorrow. First, she needed some sleep.

She was grateful when she saw the bus driver wave to her, meaning she was in time. She prayed that her mother would not be waiting to question her about her day. Her prayer was answered. Only her father was downstairs. He was sitting in front of the last embers of the fire. He had obviously nodded off but sat up abruptly as she entered the room.

'Did you get the dinner Mrs H left for you?' he asked.

'No, I'm too tired. I just made myself a sandwich with the leftover ham. I wouldn't say no to a glass of wine.'

'Reach me a glass from the cabinet and I'll pour you some of this,' he asked her, holding up a bottle of red wine from his side table. He poured her a glass and she sat down beside him.

'I know you can't talk about things, Marjorie, but are you happy with how things went today?'

'Yes, Father,' she replied, 'I think we understood each other. I really don't want to work in London, so I'm happy that I can still do a good job within the confines of the factory.'

'Excellent. I'm proud of you.'

For a second Marjorie almost displayed signs of emotion, but said instead, 'Thank you, Father.'

Father and daughter sat side by side, watching the flames of the fire get greyer as the ash burnt out. He was wondering about the young soldier he would operate on in the morning in the hope of restoring his sight in the remaining eye; she was wondering how she would put her team together.

Then her thoughts changed to her date on Saturday night. She hadn't gone out with anyone since her disastrous romances at Oxford. Tristan was quite different. He wasn't trying to test her intelligence, he was simply respectful of what she achieved. She wondered if he would have asked her if he saw her in her revolting brown overalls. She had noticed raised eyebrows from Mr Vaughan and Mr Burke, almost as though they didn't recognise her at first glance. She smiled at the thought.

'Time for both of us to climb the stairs, my dear. We both have busy days tomorrow.'

'You're right, thank you, Father,' Marjorie replied.

'What for, the wine?' he smiled.

'That and the fact you told me I've made you proud.'

'Oh dear, then I haven't told you often enough,' her father replied quietly. 'I haven't been around enough, I know that.'

'It's fine, Father, it's nice just to hear you say it.'

In bed, after her prayers, Marjorie thought again about Saturday night. Her heart missed a beat thinking about the kiss on her cheek. It was just like the flutter of a butterfly, but it was enough to make her fall asleep with a smile.

17

On Tuesday morning Marjorie had prepared her story, that her mother was taken ill and her father could not get home from work, so she had to stay with her until her father came home. She hated lying, she wasn't good at it, but she hoped the girls believed her.

They were pleased to see her when she got on the bus and seemed relieved to find out she herself wasn't ill. It made Marjorie feel even worse as they were so genuine towards her, particularly Joyce and Sadie who couldn't wait to tell her about their weekend in their new home. 'Home' is how they referred to their new digs and it was obvious that all had gone well with Elsie.

'She even makes our packed lunches for us and they're bleedin' lovely,' Sadie told her, and then seeing Marjorie raise her eyebrows, she corrected herself, 'I meant bloomin' lovely. Wish there was something we could do for her,' she added.

'I'm sure you just being there will help her,' Marjorie replied, 'as long as you are on your best behaviour,' she added with a smile.

'Blimey, Marjorie, I've never been so well behaved in all my bleedin', bloomin' life,' she corrected herself. 'It would be hard to be anything else 'cause Elsie's so lovely.'

'She is,' Marjorie agreed, 'I'm so glad we met as we did.

Wartime has changed so many things, but not people like Elsie.'

Marjorie could hardly believe the change in Sadie. It was as if all the worries in her life had dropped off her shoulders. Her hair was shining, and she explained the wonderful joy of washing her hair in warm water. Joyce was looking equally well and they explained that they'd been doing each other's hair and were going to give Elsie's hair a bit of a wave on Saturday. They had asked Marjorie about her mother and were assured when told she had just had a weak turn and made a bit of a drama out of it.

When they arrived at the factory, Harry also enquired about her mother, with a wink no one else saw, but let Marjorie know there was a lot of work waiting for her. Back in her brown overalls, washed almost spotless by Mrs Harrison, her comfortable shoes and her hair back in a plait, the two of them sat on opposite sides of Harry's desk and discussed how best to find a structure which could convey the urgency and the need for meticulous accuracy. Marjorie said, having thought it over, that having twenty girls around two tables pushed together would be the best way for her to check every single component being put together.

'You know, Marjorie, I thought you might have accepted the offer to work in the Admiralty, so it's pretty decent of you to refuse and stay here in this dingy warehouse which is basic to say the least,' Harry told her. 'You're a good egg, make no mistake.'

Marjorie, never comfortable accepting compliments of any kind, laughed it off and reminded him that the Admiralty offices themselves were not exactly bright and luxurious.

'Tea's good though, and the scones are edible.'

Harry agreed before suggesting they got working. 'Let's get this moving. You go and get the tables together and I'll give you the lowdown on the girls who'll be joining you.'

The rest of the morning was one of great activity, several men being drafted in to get the tables together. The girls sat on forms beside each other, Marjorie was the only one with a chair. She explained to groups of them how urgent the guns were as more and more fighting began in Europe. 'It's our chance to do our bit and although we are merely the background workers, our jobs are incredibly important. If we get it done in time and with a hundred percent accuracy, I'm sure we'll get some form of thanks. Now, I need you to gather round me, four at a time so I can explain just how everything fits together. If more of you can see me, that will be even better.'

Marjorie could hardly believe the excitement the girls displayed at the thought of creating a different environment and they certainly showed enthusiasm for getting on with the job. It really couldn't have gone any better.

In the afternoon, after lunch break. Marjorie sat down to demonstrate how to put the first components together. She decided, to ensure accuracy, that half of the girls would prepare the first half and the other ten girls would complete the guns. Not all of the parts were there, Marjorie would complete them herself, but it meant that no one would see the completed gun and therefore would not be able to tell others.

Harry agreed the plan and rang Whitehall to get the go-ahead. They agreed completely and it was arranged the final parts would be assembled in Whitehall once a week by Marjorie. Irene was now part of the team and Marjorie was pleased about that as she trusted her and felt that if anything untoward was going on, she would tell Marjorie. Irene also felt pleased at the prospect of working with someone she now thought of as a friend.

Although the rest of the afternoon did not go entirely well, Marjorie decided that the mistakes were better to be made at this stage. She was quite astonished how fast some of the new girls worked and noted that they were quick to show the other girls how to rectify their mistakes.

When she left to catch the bus, she had that happy feeling of having achieved something. She also felt exhausted in that she had rarely sat down and now her back and the backs of her legs were aching.

After dinner that night, Marjorie had a soothing bath made up with Epsom Salts at her father's suggestion. He told her that in India he had a bath every evening with the salts after he had spent a full day operating while standing on his feet. She could tell her father would have loved to know what exactly his daughter was doing, but as a surgeon, had enough knowledge to know some things simply cannot be shared. He was waiting for her when she returned downstairs and handed her a glass of brandy as soon as she sat down.

'Damned awful thing, war. I've been through it all before and although things are different nowadays, too many lives are altered forever. I'm proud you and Daphne are doing your part.'

'We are, Father, but I'm very aware of the huge part you

have saving young men's sight. I'm very proud of you.'

Her father smiled shyly but she was glad she had told him. While he had his ear glued to the radio, Marjorie telephoned her aunt, in the hope that she might have a suggestion for what Marjorie should wear on Saturday night.

She had! 'Darling, I know exactly where you must go. I saw a wonderful dress in Reading a week ago and I immediately thought of you. It's the colour of Bordeaux wine, fitted to the waist and a skirt that falls to the knee. It has a buttoned bodice and a sweetheart neckline. Perfect for you and you have such beautiful legs. Now tell me about this young man. Is he good looking?'

'My dear aunt, you know I'm not good at these things, but I do remember thinking he was rather handsome in his uniform. He's very bright though, and I find that much more attractive. He's not competitive like some of the men at Oxford.'

'Then you must tell me how you met him. How about we have lunch at my favourite little restaurant. Say two o'clock on Saturday afternoon? How exciting, I'm happy for you.'

'Don't get too excited, and don't forget I will have to tell the parents that a man is collecting me on Saturday night.'

'Don't you worry yourself about that. I've a feeling they will be delighted, as long as he's an officer, good family and all that.'

Lying in bed after turning off the light, Marjorie tried to visualise the dress. She had a rather lovely necklace a great-aunt had left her and wondered if that would be appropriate. She was so unused to this kind of thing, she hoped she wouldn't make a fool of herself, but they had got on awfully well together at the Admiralty, so why would they not get on even better in more relaxed surroundings?

Wednesday was a lot easier than the previous day. Most of the girls had got the hang of it and she liked the fact that each one of them was concentrating, speaking to each other only at tea break or lunch.

It was all going even better than she had anticipated and when she discovered that several of the girls had held down really good jobs before the war began, she became more confident. She actually invited four of the girls, including Irene, to check up on all the work done by the others around them. She warned them not to be too conspicuous about it and they didn't let her down.

By Friday there was so much work done, she was able to tell them that she would be taking the first crateloads to the depot on Monday to have them checked out and she would be leaving some of the girls in charge until she got back. There were several questions as to where the depot was but she told them it was in another munitions factory, much bigger than theirs, but that Harry reckoned wasn't nearly as good as they were. They seemed satisfied with that and worked hard right until the minute the bell rang on Saturday.

Marjorie had brought a skirt with her to slip into before she met her aunt in Reading. She also had a pair of smart court shoes tucked into her bag, hoping none of them noticed. When they did as she walked towards the bus stop, they suggested she must be going to meet someone.

She totally agreed that she was, but it was her aunt, who was always very particular about clothes. They didn't tease her any more about her accent and simply accepted that she was clever and a bit odd. Sadie and Joyce had helped a lot by telling them all that she might be posh but she had a heart of gold. 'Proper lady she is, not in the slightest bit stuck up.'

Her aunt was already at the table when Marjorie arrived. She had the waiter pour Marjorie a glass of wine while she studied the menu. Aware that she was having dinner that night, she chose the simplest dish on the menu.

'Darling, you haven't got butterflies, have you? How exciting.'

'No, Aunt, I don't. I'm simply aware that I can't eat two big meals in the same day,' Marjorie insisted, 'so Dover sole grilled with a side salad will be perfect.'

Her aunt accepted that and asked a few more questions about what exactly Tristan did in the Admiralty. Marjorie reminded her that she wasn't supposed to discuss those things but that he would shortly be going to sea.

'Then you must make sure that tonight is very pleasant for both of you.'

After lunch they crossed the street and walked until they came to the shop that was one of her aunt's favourites. The assistant hung the dress up in the dressing-room and Marjorie undressed to try it on. It fitted like a glove and from the second she tried it on Marjorie loved it. 'My dear, it's perfect, as though it was made for you,' her aunt remarked as Marjorie stepped out from the dressing-room. 'But perhaps there's something else you would like to try on before you decide.'

'No thank you, Aunt, I love it and I think Great-Aunt Bella's necklace and earrings will go perfectly with it.'

'Wonderful, I'm so glad you like it as much as I do. Now pass it out and I'll have it parcelled for you.'

Seeing the price had made Marjorie slightly nervous, but she did have enough in her account to cover it. When she had finished dressing and went to pay for it, the assistant assured her it was already paid for. When Marjorie protested, her aunt merely put her finger to her lips and shook her head. 'My dear girl, it's one of the few pleasures left in my life, to go shopping with my niece. Please don't spoil it for me. Now, let's get you home and I'll help you with your hair, you simply can't go to dinner with your hair in a plait.'

Marjorie laughed seeing her aunt shudder at the very thought of it. But then again, Margaret had never worked a day in her life. She never needed to wear a plait.

Now that she had the dress, she did actually feel quite excited. While her aunt took afternoon tea with her parents, Marjorie ran upstairs to have a bath and wash her hair. She used her best body lotion that had been a Christmas present. She then took out the silk stockings she was glad she had bought. Pulling her dressing gown over her underwear, she went downstairs to let her aunt know she was ready to have her hair dressed.

In three hours, she would be leaving for her date. Despite her previous protests, she did have butterflies and she was excited. The only man she had been alone with since she left Oxford was Nicolas. She hoped wherever he was that he was safe and not in danger. Sitting by her dressing table, her hair wrapped in a towel, she waited for her aunt to climb the stairs.

18

Aunt Margaret announced she would be delighted to stay for dinner, much to Marjorie's indignation, but when she explained that she would do her best to distract Marjorie's parents from asking questions, she thanked her with a smile.

She had done a wonderful job with Marjorie's hair, so that it was full of waves on top with curls on her shoulders. She had to admit that it did look very feminine and flattering. Her dark hair looked quite dramatic against the dress and the jewellery was perfect with it. Even her parents gave her admiring looks when she walked into the dining-room just as her parents prepared to go to the dining-room.

Her mother enquired what coat she was wearing over it and Marjorie replied that she was going to wear her black coat with the raised shoulders. Her mother said a fur jacket would look much nicer and gave her permission to look in her wardrobe to choose one. Aunt Margaret gave her a wink and suggested she would come up with her to decide. They both agreed the dark mink three-quarter length looked best.

Marjorie lifted the curtain to look outside and saw a rather smart black coupe sitting outside on the road.

'Oh, my goodness, he's early, it's only ten to. What should I do?' she asked her aunt.

'Take your time, darling, it means he's keen, so let him wait a little longer. Have a spray of your mother's perfume. That lipstick really suits you.'

When Marjorie went to say goodnight to her parents, she really did have butterflies in her stomach for some reason. Her father got up from the table and congratulated her on how she looked. 'Next time you must ask him in for a drink before you go out,' he told her.

'I have no idea whether there will be a next time,' she replied.

'Of course there will, after he sees you tonight. You look wonderful, doesn't she?' he asked her mother. Her mother replied that the fur coat looked very good.

Closing the door behind her on the dot of seven, Marjorie heard the unfamiliar click of her heels against the pavement. Seeing her arrive, Tristan jumped out of the car to open her door for her. He looked a little surprised at seeing her but gave her a friendly smile.

'You look amazing,' he told her as she sat on the passenger seat while he made sure her skirt was well tucked in before he closed the door. As he climbed into the driving seat, he remarked that she smelt wonderful also.

'My mother's scent and my mother's coat,' she confided. 'I do rather think I'm too young for fur, but she insisted as it's so cold this evening.'

'Good for her. I've booked a table at the Country Club, I hope that's ok with you. My father's a member so it was easy to get a table. I thought a little bit of music might be pleasant.'

Marjorie replied that she would like that and admired the car. It was a roadster, quite close to the ground, and must have been quite new as it still smelt of leather.

'My brother's,' he laughed. 'He's a doctor and has gone off to France with the army, so he does allow me to borrow it from time to time. My own car is an old Austin but perfectly roadworthy I assure you.'

It was quite a sensation sitting in such a low car as he dealt with the twisting country road with precision. They seemed to have plenty to talk about so there were no awkward silences. 'The shoes and coat are my own,' he laughed.

'As are my dress and shoes,' she replied, 'and I do have all my own teeth.'

Tristan laughed out loud at that and before she knew it, they were pulling up in front of the Club House. She remained in her seat until he opened the door and offered his hand as she came out sideways. She congratulated herself on that as she wasn't altogether confident in high heels. As they walked towards the entrance, they could hear the music drifting out of the doors. Tristan signed them both in then took her coat with his own to give to the girl in charge of the cloakroom.

A waiter in white shirt and tails came over to greet them and take them to their table which turned out to be a rather intimate table for two close to the window but not close to any of the other diners. The waiter seemed to know Tristan quite well and bowed slightly before he left to find them a menu.

'How about a martini?' Tristan asked and Marjorie agreed that it would be lovely, although she hadn't the slightest clue what it was. She was familiar with wine and brandy, and of course sherry, but a martini was not something she would have drunk, even at Oxford.

Looking round the room, Marjorie was so grateful that her aunt had insisted on buying her the dress. The younger women were very glamorous and the older women elegant to say the least. The waiter arrived back with the menus which he handed first to Marjorie, then to Tristan.

'I would recommend the beef, sir, and the salmon is excellent and caught locally. For your starter I might recommend the chef's pâté or the fish soup. Feel free to ask any questions you might have, madam.'

'Thank you,' she replied, 'I shall take your advice and have the pâté followed by the salmon.'

'A good choice, if I may say so. And for you, sir, your usual steak?'

'I think so and the pâté for a starter.'

'Thank you, sir, madam,' and with another small bow, he left.

Their martinis arrived immediately after and holding his glass up against Marjorie's he proposed a toast. 'Here's to a very enjoyable evening, Marjorie. I must say I've been looking forward to seeing you again.'

Marjorie smiled, but as she lifted the glass to her mouth, she prayed that the cocktail stick holding a cherry would not poke her eye. Fortunately, it didn't, much to her relief.

The band had taken their break so there was only the sound of conversation coming from the tables around them.

'So, how did the week go for you? I'm told you are coming back to Whitehall on Monday,' Tristan asked.

'Much better than I expected actually. Some of the girls are remarkably quick and that has helped a lot. I've quite enjoyed it, and it feels as though what I'm doing is actually worthwhile.'

'Indeed it is, more so than you even realise. We've been really lucky stumbling across you.'

'But you have to remember that languages are my subject although I must admit I wish engineering had been regarded as suitable for women. I'm quite intrigued by it all.'

'I can see that,' Tristan smiled, 'you took to it like a duck to water. Not that for one second do you look like a duck I hasten to add.'

Marjorie laughed and as she did so she noticed that Tristan looked even more attractive when he smiled. At that moment the wine waiter arrived and handed the list to Tristan. Without really looking, he asked whether Marjorie would prefer red or white.

'I really don't mind,' she replied. 'I'm happy for you to choose.'

'Well as you are having the salmon, we shall have the Chablis and I will have a glass of Beaujolais with my steak. Thank you,' and he handed the list back.

'Now where were we?' Tristan asked. 'Ah, I remember, I was telling you what a natural you were. You must have been good at maths at school.'

'I was actually, I was tempted to go down the science road although I had no intention of following my father. In the end, languages came to me rather easily, and I loved English so I took that route.'

'It's funny, but my brother never wanted to be anything else other than a doctor whilst I found the idea quite appalling. I thought engineering was a bit of a doddle to be honest, but of course it's a lot more complicated. Then when we saw war coming, I joined the navy. Oh dear, here comes our starter, we'll finish this conversation later.'

The pâté was delicious as was the melba toast that went with it. Marjorie and Tristan smiled at each other across the table, wondering if they should restart the conversation. Just as Tristan began, their main course arrived and they resorted to small talk, something which Marjorie was never comfortable with. However, the Hollandaise sauce was so good she decided just to enjoy it.

When they finished their meal, the head waiter returned to the table to see if they had enjoyed their meal. They assured him they had. Before he left he asked Tristan, 'If I may be so bold, sir, have you heard from the viscount?'

'Well, my father has and I understand he's quite safe and established in a small hospital there,' Tristan replied. 'Thank you for asking, Thompson.'

Seeing Marjorie's enquiring look, he told her quietly that the viscount was his brother, the one who owned the car. 'The staff here have known us since we were born practically, and everyone loves my brother. He's just that kind of chap,' Tristan explained.

Then, as the band began to play, he asked Marjorie if she would like to dance. Marjorie had, of course, learnt to dance at boarding-school, as all young ladies did, but that was with girls, not with boys. However, as the music played out a beat, she discovered it was rather pleasant to be led by a man a head taller than her. She noticed some of the older ladies watching Tristan with interest. She imagined they must be friends of his family.

After the second dance Tristan led Marjorie back to the table, holding on to her hand. He held it until she sat down again, at which stage he poured her another glass of wine. This was her second glass and on top of the martini which she thoroughly enjoyed, she noticed that she felt much more relaxed.

The band began to play a blues number and Tristan grabbed her hand again and guided her on to the floor. This time he danced much closer, his hand firmly around her waist. She allowed herself to go with the music and felt quite disappointed when it stopped.

Again, he led her back to the table where the waiter came to see if they would like a desert. Marjorie chose a simple dish of ice cream while Tristan ordered the apple crumble. 'And bring us two glasses of dessert wine, please.'

He said to Marjorie, 'It's so easy to forget there's a war on when we're sitting like this. Because I'm at the Admiralty and not on my ship, it seems almost like normal. Where were you when this war started?'

'In Jersey, having the time of my life, you might say,' she replied. 'I was teaching in a rather lovely school overlooking the coast. I had my own apartment within the school but had all my meals made for me, except if I chose not to. I was very sad leaving.'

'I can just imagine. Did you make good friends there?'

'Oh yes,' she replied. 'The matron was just wonderful and then there were two locals, Nicolas and Celeste, who used to take me round the island as they had practically been born there. They are in France now,' and Marjorie's expression changed. 'I believe Nicolas is working with the resistance.'

'And his girlfriend, has she gone there too?

Marjorie replied, 'No, Celeste is his young sister. She is safe with her grandmother now.'

'You look concerned. Are you worried about Nicholas, were you and he.....? and the question hung in the air.

'He was not my boyfriend, if that's what you were thinking. I believe we were fond of each other, but Nicolas was intent on getting back to fight. I pray every day that he will be safe.'

'That must be difficult,' Tristan said quietly.

Marjorie was relieved when their desserts arrived and she could finish the conversation. The dessert wine was perfect with her ice cream and she was grateful that it made her relax once more.

'Let's dance again before our coffee arrives. I've noticed a few raised eyebrows as some of my mother's friends admire you,' Tristan told her, once again taking her hand.

The band were playing 'Only Forever' as they danced slowly around the floor. Marjorie was only aware of Tristan's hand holding her hand and his arm around her waist as she experienced feelings she hadn't had before. She wasn't sure if she enjoyed them but on the other hand she was keen for the music not to stop. When it did, Tristan walked her back to the table with his arm around her waist.

When they sat down, he reached for her hand across the table. 'I'm enjoying tonight very much. I trust you are too? It's been quite a while since I've had the privilege of bringing someone I really liked to the Country Club. I suppose because it's all so familiar and yet with you, it feels quite different.'

Marjorie couldn't stop her mind from thinking: Who does he usually bring? But she managed to look back at him and say, 'I've had a lovely evening, thank you.' She pulled away her hand as she lifted a cup and saucer and asked, 'Coffee?'

He nodded but he didn't smile the way he had done earlier.

She wondered if she had said something wrong, but she did not want to make a fool of herself with the first man she had been out with since her university days. It was best, she decided, not to get too involved and therefore less likely to be hurt.

On the drive home Tristan was much quieter than he had been on the way there. Eventually she asked him, 'Will I see you on Monday at the Admiralty? Will you be there?'

'Yes, I will. Did you have something you needed to ask me?'

'Not that I can think of right now, but there's bound to be something.'

Instead of driving to the front of her house, he pulled into the side of the road, quite a distance from her home. She hoped he wasn't going to leave her here. Not with all the lights on and wearing high heels surely.

'Marjorie, can I be straight with you? It's wartime and I don't think anyone has time not to be. I told you how much I enjoyed this evening. You didn't sound so keen. If this chap Nicolas is on your mind, then I'll step away and leave you in peace. I will respect your wishes.'

'What on earth are you saying? Nicolas is a dear friend. Of course I care about his safety, but I am not his girlfriend nor would he wish me to be. And you are the one telling me how many girlfriends you have taken to the Country Club. I am sure they are much more interesting than a language teacher who knows how to put a bomb together.'

She stopped for a second and then all she heard was Tristan laughing. 'Why are you laughing at me? What is so funny?'

'You are,' he said between laughs, 'thinking I take lots of girls to the Country Club. I don't, I'll have you know. I did take a couple of girls who were just friends I'd grown up with and whose parents knew each other.' He was serious now as he took her hand and looked at her.

Marjorie put her head down and then raising it she looked him straight in the eye. 'And I suppose you're going to tell me you're a lord or something. I mean, I haven't a clue who you are.'

'My dear girl, I am not a lord, my father is an earl, my brother being the eldest son is a viscount and I am merely The Honourable. Not a useful title at all. What you see is what you get. And I am very happy looking at you,' he told her gently, running his index finger along her cheek. 'Am I forgiven?'

'Nothing to forgive really, I suppose,' and Marjorie did manage a smile. 'Misunderstandings, shall we say?'

'Yes, let's leave it at that, forever.'

Tristan removed his hand from hers and leaning forward he wrapped his arm around her neck and pulled her close towards him. Then he kissed her, not a long and lingering kiss, but long enough for Marjorie to be totally silenced.

'May I see you tomorrow? If you're not busy I mean. I thought we could go for a walk. If you agree, please don't wear those shoes. They're very pretty, but totally impractical.'

'Yes, I'd love to,' was all she said, but suddenly she was

being kissed again, this time longer and even more enjoyable.

He suddenly looked at the clock on the dashboard. 'I'd better get you home. Don't want your parents blame me for keeping you out late.'

He pushed the car into gear and drove slowly to her home, this time to the front door.

'I shan't kiss you goodnight, just in case your father is standing behind the curtains with a rifle.'

The thought made Marjorie laugh out loud.

'Till tomorrow. Shall I pick you up at two?' he asked.

'That will be perfect. Thank you for a lovely evening.'

Closing the door quietly behind her, Marjorie removed her shoes and crept up the stairs. She could see a light still on in her parents' bedroom. Was he really hiding behind the curtain? she wondered. Well, she didn't mind if he was.

Throwing her mother's coat over a chair, she lay on her back in the darkness of her bedroom. She thought this kind of thing happened to other people, not to her. Marjorie the blue stocking was even surprising herself. Darn, she didn't want to undress, she just wanted to remember all the nice moments of the evening.

Dragging herself up slowly, she switched on her bedside lamp and headed for the bathroom. She was pleased to see parents' room was in darkness. She wondered what the conversation would be in the morning. Her mother would be very disappointed that he wasn't an earl.

Giggling at the thought, she prepared herself for bed.

19

Marjorie woke so late she had to excuse herself from church. Her mother gave her a very strange look while her father raised his eyebrows. As they left, with one hand on the bannisters, she turned to them and said, 'Tristan is calling for me at two o'clock. Would you mind us having lunch at one please? If it's inconvenient, I can skip lunch and just have a sandwich.'

Again, they both looked at her oddly and her father said lunch was at one anyway, and Mrs Harrison's niece would be here at eleven to prepare it. Marjorie felt very relieved as she could have a long soak in the bath before deciding what to wear. Her hair had stayed in good shape so she would just have to decide whether to wear boots or shoes. She decided on a herringbone pleated skirt with a cream blouse and camel jumper. Her brown brogue shoes were comfortable for walking but still looked smart.

She had thoroughly enjoyed her bath and was sitting at her dressing table, about to do her hair when the phone rang. She threw on her dressing gown and ran downstairs in her bare feet. She had a feeling of dread that Tristan couldn't make it, so was delighted to hear her aunt's voice on the other end. 'Darling, I thought you might have stayed behind this morning if you were home after midnight, and I was dying to hear how last night went. Do tell.'

Marjorie smiled, knowing her aunt meant well and had been partly responsible for her having such a good evening.

'It went really well, Aunt, in fact he's coming at two o'clock so we can go for a walk and to a pub for a drink after.'

'Oh, how exciting,' her aunt replied, 'he certainly is keen.'

'I suppose he is,' Marjorie agreed, 'but then again, he's not sure how much time he will have before his ship is ready for sailing.'

'Of course, this damned war changes everything. So where did you go?'

'To the Country Club. It was lovely and the band were really good. I found out his brother is a viscount, so he is just an Honourable, but that should please Mother.'

'If she can be pleased, I suppose. My sister continues to surprise me after all these years. Your father has her thoroughly spoilt, but then I've told you that many times before. It's lovely that you're seeing him again and it's nice you're getting to know him properly.'

'He's very easy to talk to,' Marjorie told her aunt. 'He's so much easier than those wretched Oxford boys, even though he was there also, but I think engineering must have been so much more down to earth. I'm seeing him tomorrow as well. I have to go up to Whitehall for the day, so we'll maybe have tea together. Thank goodness I don't have to wear those wretched overalls.'

Her aunt laughed at the thought, told her to have a wonderful afternoon and she would speak to her during the week.

Marjorie finished dressing, applied a little make up and

stuck a couple of clips in her hair so that it wouldn't blow away. It was a chilly day, but the sky was quite blue and there was no sign of rain. She ran downstairs and into the kitchen to see if she could help with lunch.

She found Elizabeth making some custard to go with the apple pie. The roast was in the oven and smelt gorgeous. Marjorie made herself a cup of tea and a slice of toast before her parents arrived home. She went into the dining-room with the tray of cutlery to set the table for lunch. Elizabeth had already seen to the fire in the drawing-room and it was already burning brightly in the grate.

She wondered if her father would want Tristan to come in for a drink before they left. She thought it would probably be the polite thing to do, after all they weren't teenagers. The Sunday papers had been delivered and she left them on the table in the drawing-room ready for her father.

Her parents returned just minutes after twelve. She heard them hanging up their coats in the cloakroom before her father called her name. She came out of the drawing-room to greet them and once again was treated to her mother's questioning look.

'You'll have a sherry, of course,' her father stated, pouring three glasses from the drinks table. Marjorie accepted her glass and remained standing in front of the fire before her parents sat down.

'So, young lady, what time did you get home at last night?' her mother asked.

'I believe it was after twelve,' she replied. 'We went to the Country Club. They had a dance after dinner and we left not long after it finished.'

'I see, well as long as it wasn't later. You don't want to give him the wrong idea, that we would approve of you being out till the small hours of the morning.'

'I can assure you he thought no such thing, he has impeccable manners. His father is the Earl of Hargrove, his brother is the viscount as Tristan is the younger. His brother is a surgeon, Father. He signed up and is in France now with the army.'

'Ah, young Hargrove, yes indeed, I remember him. He came to a few lectures but went on to do general surgery. I met his father a couple of times in the club. Nice chap.'

Marjorie thought she might be imagining it but she noticed her mother taking more interest in the conversation than she had been. Her father suggested she invite him in when he called and she agreed, secretly hoping her mother would be pleasant.

She was and Marjorie felt rather pleased at how well Tristan spoke with both of her parents. He seemed quite at home in fact, as her father told him how he often thought he might have liked to do engineering himself. 'I suppose I am in a way, it takes quite a bit of engineering sometimes to work on an eye under a microscope. Do tell your brother I was asking after him. I rather thought he might be tempted to study eye surgery, but I'm sure he chose the right thing. Hope the lad stays safe in France. Do give him my kindest regards and wish him well.'

'I will pass on your greetings next time he rings. He's in a makeshift hospital in a chateau, so he does have access to a phone occasionally.'

They politely said goodbye to her parents and Marjorie

slipped into her warm coat with a scarf and gloves.

'I know a rather nice walk around a lake and it just happens to end up at a village with a particularly nice pub, complete with log fire. How does that sound?'

'Pretty perfect, I'd like that,' she replied as he leant over and kissed her cheek.

'Right then, let's go,' Tristan replied as he steered the car out of the driveway.

They shared easy conversation as he drove along the country roads. He told her his mother had been rather curious to know who he had taken to the Country Club. 'I'm sure some of the old dears we saw last night had great pleasure in telling my mother at church this morning, you can't keep anything secret in a village like ours. Anyway, she was quite happy when I mentioned your name and my father asked if you were the daughter of the renowned eye surgeon Henry Fitzpatrick. I told him you were and my mother smiled at that. What about you, did you get the third degree?'

Marjorie laughed out loud. 'Yes, I did, and when I told my father your brother was a doctor, he immediately told me he knew him and had met your father a couple of times.'

'Well, thank goodness we've got that over with. Now we can just get on with enjoying ourselves. I was so looking forward to seeing you again. I'm glad you agreed to come today.'

Marjorie felt herself blushing as she was just thinking how glad she was that he asked her out today. When they reached the lakeside, Tristan reached over to the back seat and pulled over a brown paper bag. 'Bread for the ducks,' he explained. 'They seem to be always hungry.'

As they walked around the lake hand in hand, they stopped several times as the ducks and geese swam over to meet them and were rewarded with handfuls of bread.

When it was finished, he stuck the paper bag in his pocket and put his arm round Marjorie's shoulders. Whilst she enjoyed the feeling, she was furious at herself for blushing again and found herself with nothing to say. Tristan broke the silence by asking if she fancied dinner after work on Monday. 'Just something casual on the way home,' he explained. 'I shall leave you back home, I'm not required to stay on Monday night.'

'Well, if you're sure, I'd enjoy that as it's my last night off until Saturday again, I'm afraid.'

'Ah, I meant to ask you about that. Do you think you might like to have dinner at the Naval Club on Saturday night? I have to sit with the commander, my boss, and I rather think you two would get on.'

Marjorie looked at him and actually stood still. 'But wouldn't I be in the way? I mean, do you need to have someone with you?'

Tristan turned to face her. 'Most of the guys will have their wives or sweethearts with them. I don't have to have someone with me, but since I've met you, I'd rather like to have you with me. Is that a problem?'

'No, no, not at all,' Marjorie stammered. 'I mean, I'd love to come, but please don't feel you have to invite me.'

Tristan turned to look at her directly. 'Marjorie, since I met you I've wanted to see more of you. I love how humble you are about your cleverness and you make me laugh. You're not silly like so many other girls, you're not even slightly vain although you should be. And as I told you already, there's a war on and I don't know how much time we can have together before I have to sail. Even then I'd want to write to you. Right now, there's something else I'd like to do.'

'What's that?' Marjorie asked, in a very small voice.

'This,' he said as he took her in his arms and kissed her. At first she pulled back, then she found herself kissing him back. It seemed to go on forever, but eventually Tristan stopped and bent down to lean his forehead on hers. 'Now do you believe I want you to come with me?'

Marjorie's answer was to wrap her arms round his neck and kiss him before she whispered, 'I do.'

The skies were clouding over as darkness descended and hand in hand they walked back briskly to the car. They were silent for a while as he drove to the village with the pub. Marjorie was silent because she was so happy. She could hardly believe the emotions she had felt were real.

Tristan was quiet because he was praying that he would have more time before he had to sail again, this time not knowing when he would return. He had met the girl of his dreams and he didn't want to lose her. He knew that if she spent more time at the Admiralty there would be plenty of men who would ask her out. And they hadn't seen the way she looked last night, he smiled to himself.

'I think we both deserve a whiskey, or a hot toddy. What do you think?'

'I think I feel quite cold on the outside but warm inside,' she replied.

'Couldn't have said it better myself,' he smiled, 'I know I'm being greedy but I want to see you as often as I can.'

'Thank you,' she replied demurely. 'I do have one major worry though.'

'What's that?' he asked, turning his head to look at her.

'Will my mother lend me a fur coat again, and will your brother approve of you using his car again?'

'You really had me there,' Tristan laughed. 'I've a feeling your mother might approve, and as to my brother, what he doesn't know, won't hurt him.'

Tristan pulled into the pub car park which was in total darkness before pulling her towards him to kiss her once more. He noticed with pleasure that this time he met with no resistance.

20

Knowing that she would have practical work to do, but also knowing that she would be seeing Tristan, Marjorie was in quite a quandary as to what to wear. Aunt Margaret suggest she wear a simple blouse and skirt with a cardigan, but to take a pretty scarf and brooch so she could dress it up in the evening going to dinner after work. She eventually decided on a blue silk blouse with a navy cashmere button-up cardigan and a navy pleated skirt. She did have navy shoes and a rather battered but much-loved shoulder bag.

Once again she travelled with her father which gave them the opportunity to discuss Tristan without her mother's interference. Discussing a boyfriend with her mother was simply out of the question. Her father, though, was quite matter of fact about it. 'Very nice chap, Tristan, good family and if he's like his brother, very bright. You seem to get on well together, you must do to see him two days in a row, three when you see him tonight.' Her father smiled and looked happy as he said this, which helped Marjorie to relax.

'Well, we're certainly not short of things to talk about. I'm going to the Navy Club with him on Saturday night. He wants me to meet his Commander.'

'Oh, that will be interesting. Now listen, Marjorie, if you need a new frock for the occasion, don't hesitate to ask. I don't want Margaret paying for anything more although I know it gives her pleasure.'

'Thank you, Father, I'm sure I'll manage something as it must be rather smart.'

'Indeed, it will be. Well, here we are at Euston. I doubt if I'll see you tonight, but I will see you in the morning, so goodbye for now.'

'Thank you, Father, I'll see you then.'

Marjorie had to get to City of London and then to Whitehall, so she had some time to think alone. She was excited to be going to dinner, but she wanted to keep work quite separate. She hoped that it would work that way.

Mr Burke was waiting for her when she arrived. He informed her the final part of the guns had arrived from another munitions factory. 'It's best that no one else sees the finished gun so neither factory knows about the other. Follow me and I'll take you to where the final assembly will take place.'

Marjorie followed him down several narrow staircases until they came to a large room which must have been in the bowels of the building. The doors were made of heavy steel and she was grateful that Mr Burke held them for her. There were lots of people, men and women, standing around long metal tables which had been joined up.

'All we need you to do is to make certain everything is put together accurately and safely. Everyone here is employed by the Admiralty so they're aware of the need for secrecy. This is April,' he said, standing alongside a girl dressed in navy overalls. 'She will fill you in and introduce you to whoever you need to deal with. Lunch is in the canteen at one o'clock.'

And with that he was gone.

April was very friendly and helpful but it was obvious it was heads down and no conversation till the job was done. The final parts were intricate and she was grateful it didn't have to be carried out back at the factory. However, the people working here appeared to be very efficient and aware what an important job they were doing.

Marjorie walked around, checking every single piece and helping where there was any confusion. She had thought how much she would miss having a tea break, but before she knew it, they were all told to finish up and head to the canteen. April asked if she would like to sit with her and Marjorie gratefully accepted.

The canteen was already humming with people as they stood in line to collect lunch. There was only one choice on offer, chicken in a white sauce with potatoes and carrots. Marjorie was so hungry she wouldn't have cared what it was. She followed April to a table and sat down beside her. The other people at the table obviously knew April well, so Marjorie asked if she had worked here before the war started.

'I'm actually in the navy, I'm a WREN, but for some reason they asked me to come and work at the Admiralty for a while. I've been involved with the guns since they were designed, so it's been good to be able to see it through. I'm a radar operator and I'm hoping to be allowed to go to sea. Do you mind me asking what you've been doing?'

Marjorie thought for a second or two before answering. 'I'm actually a teacher but I volunteered for something to do with the war effort. I started in a munitions factory close to where I live. I'm not quite sure how it happened, but someone seemed to think I would be better employed supervising and advising on how these guns should be put together.'

April looked at her with a curious expression on her face. 'Really? I don't think it's as simple as that. I heard you had a photographic memory and could put things together after a glance.' She stopped and waited for Marjorie, who was blushing, to reply.

'Oh dear, I'm afraid that's an exaggeration. I think it would be fair to say I pick things up quickly and I do understand the urgency involved.'

'After watching you this morning, I'm inclined to believe what I was told. You can spot what fits where with only a glance at it. Anyway, let's go and get ourselves some jam sponge. It's actually really nice even though the custard's a funny colour.'

Back at the table April told Marjorie that her boyfriend was also in the navy. He was away at the moment and she didn't know where, but he sent letters whenever he could.

April was a very pretty girl, even in her navy overalls. She had wavy. blonde hair which she kept out of her eyes with a red spotted scarf. Her eyes sparkled when she talked about her boyfriend which made her even prettier.

She was the same age as Marjorie but hoped to get married as soon as she and her boyfriend had leave together. 'There's no point in waiting until the war's over, is there? His Mum has a nice big house with only her in it, so we will have somewhere to live. We can't tell what's going to happen to us with him being out in the middle of the fighting, so if we only have two weeks together, it will be worth it. I'm mad about him to be honest and it seems he feels the same way.'

Marjorie's heart missed a beat when she heard that. She was so happy living in the present, she hadn't stopped to think about what could happen. Then she told herself off for being silly, after all they'd only just met. But even in such a short time she knew there was something very special about Tristan. She jumped when she heard April ask if she had a boyfriend. 'Well yes,' she replied, 'we haven't known each other very long, but I already think about him a lot.'

'That's all right, it's a good thing,' April told her. 'What does he do, is he a teacher like you?'

'Oh, my goodness no, he's in the navy too, but on shore at the moment.'

'Lucky you! Wish Teddy was, but I have to be patient. Golly look at the time. Back to work, but we do get tea at three, believe it or not. To wake us up I think. Come on, let's go.'

They were walking towards the stairs when she heard her name being called, 'Marjorie, hold on.'

She turned around to see Tristan running towards her. April stopped too and stood beside her as he reached them, a smile over his face. He was in uniform so Marjorie knew he must be working in the office.

'Just to say I'll see you outside at six o'clock in case I hadn't already said that,' he said quietly.

'You already told me,' she replied, smiling up at him, 'I'd better go, we're going to be late. Oh, this is April, she's been helping me.'

'April, delighted. I'll not keep you. See you later,' and he walked away from them.

'Well, you are a dark horse, Marjorie. Half of the girls in the WRENs are in love with him. By the way he looked at you, I would say no one else has a chance.'

Marjorie felt a thrill hearing that. They were always in their own company so it was nice to hear how other people saw them.

After an incredibly tiring afternoon, even with a cup of tea, Marjorie was delighted to finish work. She had been told to come back the following morning just to check everything was in order.

In the ladies' toilet upstairs, she took out her powder compact and applied a touch of powder to her face, followed by a soft pink rouge. She added a fresh coat of lipstick and then took the scarf out of her handbag and draped it around her shoulders. She fastened it to one side with the brooch and, satisfied it looked as good as it should, she pulled on her camel coat and headed for the side door of the building.

Tristan was there, his navy overcoat over his uniform. He slipped his arm around her waist and kissed her cheek. 'Busy day?' he asked.

'You could say that,' she answered. 'Quite honestly I'm exhausted, but it went better than I expected. They're a really good bunch. Very few mistakes so I'm not sure why I was there.'

'To make sure there were no mistakes made and to fix any that were, I imagine. Ah, here we are, I thought this would be a good place as it's not far from my car.'

Tristan held open the doors and they walked into a pub that was already almost full, many of them in uniform. 'Let's

166

grab a drink, then we can go into the dining-room. I've booked us a table. What would you like to drink?'

'A glass of red wine would be nice. You choose and I'll stand by the fire and thaw out. It's not really warm in the dungeons.'

Standing by the fire with her hands behind her, Marjorie glanced over to where Tristan was standing at the bar. He was taller than anyone else and she could see his face in the mirror behind the bar. She smiled at his reflection and felt so glad to be with him. She watched as he came towards her carrying two glasses of wine.

'Here we are, and here's to us,' he said as he touched her glass with his. 'Did you sleep well?'

'I did, thank you. Did you?'

'Quite well, but I had something on my mind I couldn't get rid of.'

'Oh really, what was that?' she replied with an anxious look on her face.

'You,' he answered as he bent over and kissed her forehead. 'I was thinking what a lovely weekend we had together and how I hoped there would be many more.'

'That's very strange,' she murmured, taking a sip of the wine, 'for I was thinking just the same thing.'

Tristan laughed and pulled her towards him with his free arm. 'Then we must make sure we do. I had very good news today.'

'You did? Please share.'

'I've been granted Christmas leave, so it looks like we will be able to see quite a lot of each other.'

'That's wonderful news, I'm so happy,' she told him, barely

able to keep from throwing her arms around him.

They looked at each other for a minute and then he said, 'Let's go and find our table. You must need to sit down.'

The dining-room was only half full so they were able to hear each other speak even when they spoke quietly. Marjorie didn't really care what she ate and allowed Tristan to order for her. He ordered lamb cutlets which came with mint sauce, carrots and potatoes. She wasn't overly hungry having had lunch in the canteen, but the food was pleasant and she was eating it with Tristan.

He entertained her with stories of his childhood when he and his brother were sent to stay with his grandfather in a cold and dark castle. She told him about India, about her Amah, about boarding-school and then they shared their experiences at Oxford.

When they finished dinner and ordered coffee, they held hands across the table. She didn't notice the other diners and she was sure they didn't notice her. When they finished their coffee, Tristan ordered brandy for both of them. Sipping brandy with one hand while Tristan held her other hand was a whole new experience for Marjorie. She had stopped questioning why he was with her and instead concentrated on being together.

Driving home, as they approached her house, Tristan once again pulled into the side if the road and drew Marjorie to him. 'You do know that I am totally and utterly happy when I'm with you, don't you?'

'I suppose I am,' she replied demurely, 'but I'm not totally and utterly sure why.'

'Because you are the most amazing woman I've ever met

and I just want to be with you all the time.'

Marjorie smiled as he leant forward to kiss her gently.

'Well, let me tell you that whilst I enjoy every minute with you, I am definitely not seeing you before Saturday. There is no way I could allow you to see me in my ghastly brown overalls with my hair in a plait. I adamantly refuse, but I shall be very happy to see you on Saturday night.'

'Well, that's that then, I guess. I'll just have to learn to be patient. Until Saturday night, I'll leave you with this.' He wrapped his arms around her and kissed her for a very long time.

Marjorie really hoped her parents had gone to bed. She didn't want anything to disturb her thoughts. As she walked quietly into the hall, she saw all the doors were closed, indicating that her parents were indeed in bed. She locked the door behind her and quietly climbed the stairs.

When she lay down in bed, tired but utterly happy, she wondered what Christmas would be like now that Tristan was in her life. She hoped it would be one she would remember for the rest of her life.

21

At the Admiralty the following morning, Mr Burke congratulated Marjorie on the speed and accuracy at which the job had been completed. He referred once again to her coming to work full time at Whitehall and this time she said she would consider it.

She had found April trustworthy and likeable and enjoyed working with her. She also enjoyed the fact she was more intellectually challenged than she was at the munitions factory. In the Admiralty offices she would work from nine until six and that idea appealed to her compared to the long and unsociable hours she had been working. It also meant she would see more of Tristan and that aspect was becoming more and more attractive.

After discussions with her father and Tristan, she decided to go back to the munitions factory until Christmas and start in the Admiralty in January.

Back in the factory on Wednesday morning, she was met by a crowd of anxious faces at the bus stop. Irene was the first to hug her and tell her she was glad to see her back safe, followed by Joyce and Sadie in hot pursuit. She told them she had missed them too and that it was good to be back. As she was only going to be with them for another three weeks, Marjorie felt an awful sense of guilt. She had to keep telling herself she was doing the right thing for her country, but it didn't feel any more convincing when she was back round the table.

Harry thought that joining the two tables was the best way to go and the next job which had been delivered in her absence was given out to twenty instead of ten. The job was monotonous, one the girls were very familiar with so the atmosphere was relaxed but busy. Marjorie realised that it was the company of the girls she missed most. The work itself, sorting out boxes of ammunition and putting them into the pockets of gun belts, was not what she wanted to spend months doing.

At tea break she was delighted to hear that Joyce and Sadie were unbelievably happy with Elsie and that Elsie was missing her and had invited her to join them for dinner on a Friday night. She told them to tell Elsie she would be delighted.

Harry was far from pleased that Marjorie was leaving but not unduly surprised. 'It was all right when you were working on important weapons, but ammunition isn't going to use much of your grey matter,' he told her. 'Just keep it under your hat until Christmas, will you? I need them to think they are working with you until then. You've done a smashing job with them, even though you ain't exactly one of them.

'They really respect you, they do,' he added. 'Could have gone two ways so I took a bit of a gamble bringing you here, but even though you're so posh, you're down to earth, you are.'

Marjorie smiled and thanked him for that. 'I will miss all of them, and you, but I shall keep in touch with you as best

I can. I'm not far away if you ever need me.'

'Yeah, but I'll have to go through the Admiralty for that,' he smiled back. 'Now get out of here and get on with your work,' he told her and laughing, she did just that.

The next few days passed slowly at work and she found herself counting the hours until home time. Tristan had told her he would ring her at nine each night and after she spoke to him she went to bed happy and slept well.

Only the worry about what she would wear bothered her. She decided to go back to the shop where her aunt had taken her, by herself this time as she didn't want her aunt to pay for it again. She had enough in the bank to pay for it without disturbing her savings and if her father insisted on paying for it, that would be even better.

On Friday night Marjorie got off the bus with Joyce and Sadie and, arms linked, they walked to Elsie's house. She had asked Mrs Harrison to bake a fruit cake for Elsie and she was happy to, so she had a brown paper parcel under her arm as they arrived at the door.

Elsie answered and immediately hugged Marjorie with both arms. 'Come in, come in, I'm so pleased to see you. I have your dinner all ready, so come and sit down by the fire. I was just thinking, girls, we should go and buy our Christmas tree tomorrow after you finish work. I pulled out our old decorations from the attic, so you two can dress it nicely.'

Joyce and Sadie's faces were such a joy to see. Marjorie realised that they probably had never had a proper family Christmas in their lives.

With her coat off, she gave the parcel to Elsie and

explained that Mrs Harrison had baked it especially for her. As she removed the brown paper, then the grease proof paper underneath, the smell of freshly baked fruit cake filled the room. Elsie couldn't thank her enough and asked for Mrs Harrison's address so she could write her a thank-you letter.

'Just give it to the girls to bring to me and I'll give it to her personally,' Marjorie replied. 'In the village, everyone seems to know someone who can get hold of flour or butter. I'm never quite sure how, so I don't ask questions.'

Elsie told her she didn't mind where it came from, she and the girls would enjoy every slice.

The evening was spent around the table, relishing Elsie's chicken pie and roast potatoes. Marjorie enquired after Elsie's family and was told they were all safe and well.

'And what about you, Marjorie? Haven't you found yourself a nice young man yet? You'd be a great catch for any man,' she added, smiling warmly.

'Well, if you two girls can keep a secret, I am seeing someone,' Marjorie replied and waited while there were gasps of happy surprise around the table. 'He's in the navy, waiting for his next ship but he's been told he has leave at Christmas.'

'How lovely,' Elsie proclaimed, 'then it's going to be a happy Christmas for you and I'm so pleased for you. He's a lucky man.'

'I rather think that I'm the lucky one, but he seems to feel the same,' she replied, her cheeks pink from blushing. 'I'm actually going to the Navy Club with him tomorrow night.'

'Oh, my Gawd, what's you going to be wearing then?' Sadie gasped. 'Have you got a new dress?'

'Is it long or short?' Joyce piped in. 'What colour is it?'

'Well, that's just it. I don't have anything suitable, I haven't worn an evening gown since I was at Oxford and they would be far too girlish. I'm going to have to buy something new tomorrow afternoon.'

'That's cutting it a bit neat for time, Marjorie,' Elsie said. 'Have you anywhere in mind?'

'Well, I have actually. It's just off the High Street in Reading. Walton Street I think it's called. I've been there with my aunt so I think I should get one there without too much trouble. My father has said he will pay for it. He likes Tristan very much.'

'Tristan! What a lovely name,' Elsie sighed.

'Never heard it before,' Sadie said.

'Sounds like a film star. I'd love to see you in your dress Marjorie. I bet you'll look blinking marvellous,' Joyce added.

Marjorie thought for a second or two, then said, 'Look, how would you three like to come with me to buy a dress. You're going to be in Reading anyway.'

The two girls were speechless. It was Elsie broke the silence. 'Why don't you all come here after work tomorrow, then you can get changed and we'll all go. You can't go somewhere like that in your overalls,' and they all agreed.

'But would they let us in, me and Joyce I mean, to a smart place like that?' Sadie asked in an anxious voice.

'Of course they will. You two will dress up smartly and look just great, I know.' Elsie assured them. 'That's it then. What a lovely time we're going to have.'

Seeing Marjorie to the door later, Elsie took a step outside. 'Marjorie, that's a lovely thing you just did. Those girls will be beside themselves. I'll make sure they look neat and tidy, me too. They've made a world of difference to my life. I can never thank you enough.'

On Saturday afternoon four ladies stared into the window of 'Arabella's' of Walton Street. In the window was just one dress. It was royal blue crepe with a sweetheart neckline. The skirt was full and hung in folds down to the ground.

'That's it! You couldn't get anything nicer than that,' Sadie sighed.

'We won't know that till we get inside,' Elsie told them.

'Are you sure they will let us in?' Joyce asked.

Marjorie pushed the door and walked inside. The assistant recognised her and walked out from behind the counter.

'Miss Fitzpatrick, how lovely to see you again. Your aunt isn't with you?' she asked, looking curiously at the three ladies standing beside Marjorie.

'Not today, these are my friends Elsie, Joyce and Sadie. May I see the dress in the window. You know my size,' Marjorie asked her.

'Well, as a matter of fact we got three new dresses yesterday, let me show you all of them,' she replied. 'We're very lucky with all the rationing of fabric.'

While she went into the back to collect the dresses, Sadie and Joyce looked down the row of cocktail dresses in awe. They didn't dare touch them, but Marjorie took a couple off the rail to show them.

'I don't think I'll ever get to wear anything like that. Not ever,' Sadie said.

'Me neither,' Joyce added, 'but don't cost nothing to look at them, does it?'

'Girls, you have no idea what lies in front of you. You're very young, there's plenty of time,' Elsie told them.

Both girls were dressed in their best coats, one in blue and one in purple. They were made of thin wool which wouldn't have kept them very warm, but they looked nice and Marjorie told them so.

'These are the other two and the one in the window is your size so I'll get it out for you,' the assistant told her. 'If you'd like to start trying them on, the fitting-room is free. Would you like a seat, madam?' she asked Elsie, pulling one out for her.

Marjorie stripped down to her underwear and tried the first dress on. It was turquoise tulle, strapless with a full skirt. It fitted perfectly but needed shoes. She saw a pair of silver shoes in the corner and tried them on to see if the dress looked better. It did and she stepped nervously into the shop.

'Oh, my Gawd, that's bleed........just gorgeous,' Sadie corrected herself.

'It's amazing, I never seen nothing like it. You look like a movie star,' Joyce said in an unusually quiet voice.

Marjorie looked to Elsie for her opinion. Elsie asked her to turn around and then nodded. 'I don't think you'll better that one, Marjorie, but do try them on.'

The next one was red satin, tight on the bodice and swathed round her hips. It was beautiful but she felt like someone else wearing it. The girls were not so ecstatic this time and Elsie shook her head.

The blue one was the last one she tried on. It fitted beautifully and she felt quite sophisticated in it. The girls said it was a pity she couldn't have both, but if they had to choose, they would choose the turquoise one. Although Elsie agreed, she said the blue one was beautiful on her also.

Marjorie took the turquoise dress but quietly asked if she would leave the blue one over and it would be collected later that week. Marjorie had worked out that she could afford to buy the turquoise one herself and her father could buy the blue one. She knew she would have more events over Christmas and by having two dresses she didn't need to panic.

After treating the girls to tea and scones in the tea rooms, Marjorie left to catch her bus home. She needed to prepare her hair and get ready for the evening. The girls and Elsie headed off to find their Christmas tree and they hugged her warmly before they parted. Marjorie knew they were overjoyed to share the shopping experience with her and she was delighted to have thought of it.

Tristan arrived shortly before seven o'clock and Marjorie's father brought him into the drawing-room for a drink.

When she called out that she was ready, three pairs of eyes followed her as she made her way downstairs. Her hair hung loosely on her shoulders and she held the skirt up with one hand as she held on to the bannisters with the other. She was wearing the silver shoes and an embroidered evening bag which her aunt had given her. She had chosen long, diamond earrings and a diamanté bracelet as her jewellery.

Tristan offered her his hand as she reached the bottom step. Her father looked proudly at her. 'You look wonderful, doesn't she, dear?' he asked his wife.

'Yes, Henry, but you'd better go upstairs and fetch me my silver fox stole. The gal will be frozen if she doesn't have it.'

Marjorie knew that was as close to a compliment as she would ever get from her mother, but as her father placed the stole around her shoulders, she thanked her mother profusely.

Getting into the car with Tristan, making sure her dress was safely inside, she waved goodbye to her father in the doorway. 'Well, I didn't think you could make me speechless, but you just did,' Tristan told her, gazing at her with his eyes lit up. 'You look so beautiful, Marjorie.'

Marjorie knew she wasn't beautiful - she had great bone structure, good hair and a neat figure, her aunt had assured her - but right now, with the man beside her gazing at her with such admiration, she felt beautiful, more beautiful than she had ever dreamed.

22

Walking into the Navy Club, while the cadets at the door saluted Tristan, made Marjorie feel so happy she had chosen the dress she was wearing. The tulle skirt floated out behind her as she walked arm in arm with Tristan up the stairs to the reception. She felt rather like Cinderella going to the ball.

More cadets were serving champagne and canapés. Lifting a glass from the tray for her, Tristan told her he felt like the luckiest man in the room. Smiling and blushing at the same time, Marjorie looked round the room which was full of a mixture of ages, the men in uniform and the ladies in a dazzling array of evening dresses with lots of precious jewellery on show.

Placing his hand on her back, Tristan guided her over to a group of people standing together by the bar. 'I have to introduce you to a few people, but don't worry, they're all very pleasant.'

Marjorie was very aware of the ladies in the group running their eyes over her while the men were more appraising, each one waiting to be introduced. 'Marjorie, let me introduce you to the boss, Commander Christopher Grieves and his lovely wife Giselle.'

'Ah, Marjorie and I have met before.' Commander Grieves

took her hand and kissed the back of it. 'We have been wondering who the mystery lady is who has kept this man's mind off his job,' he told her. 'Now we know, I'm not surprised.

Giselle smiled at Marjorie in such a warm way that she could only smile back. 'Don't listen, he's only teasing, but I have to say Tristan was a little distracted last night when he came to dinner.' She smiled again. 'How pretty you look, what a gorgeous dress.'

'Thank you so much, it's very nice to meet you,' Marjorie replied, shaking her hand.

Giselle was very tall and elegant. Her black dress was fitted and fell to her ankles. Her shoes were silver, the same colour as her silver blonde hair which was dressed in silver diamanté clips. Marjorie felt quite in awe but Giselle's friendly demeanour had helped to make her feel at ease.

Her husband, the commander, was even taller than his wife and complemented her beautifully with his sparkling blue eyes and handsome face. Marjorie guessed him to be in his early fifties whilst Giselle looked younger. Commander Grieves now introduced her to the other officers and their wives who varied in age from just a little older than herself to much older.

The eldest lady, who leant on an ebony cane with a jewelled head, stepped forward to speak to her. 'I've a feeling I might know your papa. Lieutenant Colonel Henry Fitzpatrick?'

'Why yes, that is my father. May I ask how you knew him?'

'Well, apart from the fact he removed my cataracts, I knew your parents in India. We lived there for a short time and our paths crossed. I believe you and your sister were away at boarding-school.'

'Yes, Father thought we needed to go to England for a proper education,' Marjorie explained.

'I heard you were a bright little thing. Can't have been easy, but to be honest, I found your mother a difficult woman, not at all maternal. Our boys didn't go to boarding-school until we all came home. How is your mother by the way?'

'She's quite well I think, but she misses India and the life she had there.'

'I'm not at all surprised. Personally, I felt it quite stifling. I was delighted to get home again. But we're all different. Now, young Tristan here, he's a thoroughly decent chap. Lovely parents, have you met them yet?'

'Not yet, but I will soon I'm sure,' Marjorie answered.

'I should imagine you will. The boy's quite smitten. Now I must let you circulate. Give my regards to your father.'

'Indeed, I will, he will be pleased to know your operation was a success.'

'We're going through to dinner now. May I escort you?' Commander Grieves asked, offering his arm to Marjorie.

They walked through double doors to a large room with tables set for dinner, cadets waiting to assist the ladies to their seats. 'Ah, here you are. I've altered the rules a little to let you sit beside Tristan. I don't think he'd appreciate it if I didn't.'

Marjorie was delighted to find she was sitting beside the commander on her other side as his easy manner made her feel comfortable.

Tristan was delighted she was sitting beside him. 'I'm so sorry Marjorie, it must all feel very boring for you, but it will get better when the dancing starts. The Admiral's wife seemed quite taken by you,' he added.

'Only because my father operated on her eyes here in London, but they met my parents in India,' Marjorie explained.

'I'm not surprised she remembered. She's very astute.'

'She said she found my mother difficult,' Marjorie laughed, 'I didn't tell her I agreed wholeheartedly.'

'I'm very fortunate then, that she approves of me.'

At that moment they were called to stand for the National Anthem. To her amazement, Marjorie saw Lord and Lady Mountbatten standing by the centre of the top table. The realisation that this was an important evening suddenly hit her. When they sat down, Marjorie whispered to Tristan, 'I had no idea they would be here. I'm feeling quite overawed.'

'Well, don't be, we won't be in their company. Just relax and enjoy it all. Did I tell you, you look amazing?'

'Just once or twice,' she smiled back and he reached under the table for her hand and squeezed it.

Marjorie felt quite relieved when the wine was poured. She sipped it gently in the hope it might make her feel more at ease.

'Giselle used to hate all of this when we first met.' Commander Grieves leant over to speak to Marjorie. 'Now she takes it all in her stride. But even after all these years, she's never got used to me being away at sea. It will be worse now with the state of the war. At least we still have two children at home. The boys are in the air force, much more exciting than being at sea. They're both flying Spitfires now. Another thing for Giselle to worry about, but we have to win this bloody war, if you'll pardon my language. Damned if we can let Hitler win.'

'If I'd been a man, I would have done just the same thing,' Marjorie assured him. 'I hope I can feel useful when I move to the Admiralty in January. It was all quite a shock having to leave Jersey where I was teaching.'

'I think the young man sitting beside you would admit to being grateful that you did come back. It seems like old Burke is delighted to have you with us. Otherwise you might have ended up in Bletchley Park!'

Marjorie wasn't quite sure what he was referring to but she was pleased to hear that Mr Burke was happy with her. It was difficult to hear the conversation from the other side of the table and she was so pleased to be beside Tristan. He had continued to hold her hand when the opportunity presented itself. However, her conversation with Commander Grieves had alarmed her slightly. He made it feel as though his ship was indeed about to sail and of course, Tristan with it.

'Would you like to come to the cloakrooms with me?' Giselle asked when they finished dessert. 'I doubt if Tristan showed you where they were.'

He hadn't, so Marjorie was grateful to accompany Giselle.

'How are you managing?' Giselle asked her. 'At least you don't have to try and remember everyone's names.'

'Your husband has made it very easy for me and I'm grateful that Tristan is beside me. I had no idea the Mountbattens would be here,' Marjorie confessed.

'Oh, didn't he mention it? Personally, I don't have much time for either of them, but he will do a good job when he goes to sea. He has plenty of experience. I hear he will have command of one of the new aircraft carriers.'

Marjorie's ears picked up when she heard that. She

wondered if that was where 'her guns' were going.

'You do know that Tristan will be Christopher's next in command, don't you? Thank goodness it won't be for a few weeks yet. Don't worry, Chris will take excellent care of him. All very hush hush though.'

Marjorie took out her compact and examined her face. She dabbed a little more powder to her nose and applied her lipstick. She applied a little of the perfume from the phial she had brought with her and combed her curls carefully.

Some of the women from her table came in and immediately headed for the mirrors. They were young, about her age, glamorous and confident. They smiled at her but not, she felt, sincerely.

'You've put their noses out of joint, I'm afraid,' Giselle whispered to her as she applied her lipstick. 'First of all, you have the man they all want and then you turn up looking amazing. But the rest of us more mature ladies have to compliment Tristan on his choice of girlfriend. He didn't seem to be interested in anyone until he met you. Too busy studying to get on and he's doing just that,' Giselle explained.

Marjorie felt a wave of affection for the woman smiling at her. She had always felt out of her depth with glamorous girls like that. She also had studied rather than buy clothes. Meeting Tristan had changed that.

'You know, Tristan and I haven't known each other very long and it's hard to explain, but it just feels right,' she found herself confiding to her new friend. 'I certainly wasn't looking for anyone. I was just concentrating on my job and working impossible hours.'

'That's how it goes: when you're not looking, love finds you.'

Marjorie looked surprised. Love? Was this love?

When they got back to the ballroom, the men had disappeared from the table. Giselle and the Admiral's wife sat on either side of her.

'Have another glass of wine, my dear,' the older lady advised. 'They've all been called into another room, but they won't be long, they'll be back for the cheese and brandy. Don't look so worried, it's quite normal behaviour. In wartime anyway.'

Giselle nodded to the cadet with the wine bottles and told him to fill their glasses. 'Isn't it wonderful we have Christmas to look forward to? I was so worried that Christopher would be away. I'm hoping the boys will get home, if only for a couple of days. At least the girls are here. You must come and meet them, Marjorie.'

'Thank you, I'd like that. I was dreading Christmas at home this year but I know it will be much nicer for me knowing Tristan will be around. My mother can be difficult and my sister's not easy either, although I'm very proud of her doing her bit in the War Office.'

Suddenly they heard footsteps as the men returned and they walked back into the ballroom. At the very same moment, the band began to play. Tristan sat down beside her and reached for her hand. 'I'm sorry, darling, for leaving you like that but I had to, I'm afraid. We just had the lowdown from Mountbatten on the state of play. Why are you looking at me like that?' he asked.

'You called me darling,' she replied.

'Did I?' he asked, smiling broadly.

'You did. I rather liked it.'

'Then I shall have to make a habit of it. Would you like to dance, my darling?'

'Darling, I'd love to,' she replied.

Laughing, though both their hearts felt a little heavy, they walked to the floor together.

Marjorie was amazed at how easily they danced together, how natural it felt to lay her head on his shoulder as the lights went down. The younger officers swept their girlfriends round the floor while the older couples stayed in the centre. The music changed to a slow, blues number with the female singer in the band crooning into the microphone. Tristan tightened his arms around her and Marjorie wished that time could stand still.

It seemed that all too soon they were standing again for the National Anthem. The younger members headed off to find taxis to take them to nightclubs. Christopher invited them into the private bar for a night cap. The admiral and his wife bid their good nights and soon there were only the four of them left to say goodnight. Giselle reminded Tristan that he must bring Marjorie to meet her girls and he promised he would.

When they finally headed to their car, Marjorie pulling her mother's fox fur tightly around her, Tristan pulled Marjorie towards him and kissed her gently. 'I've been dying to do that all night. Now, come on, let's get you back to the car.'

After he tucked her dress around her and got into the driver's seat, Tristan reached into the back and pulled out a tartan rug which he wrapped around her legs. Then they set off to drive to Marjorie's parents' home. As they approached the road, Tristan ignored it and drove straight ahead.

Ten minutes later he parked in the gateway of a farm. The sky was bright with stars and empty of aircraft. The nightly bombing appeared to have stopped. Tristan stopped the car and moved closer to Marjorie, wrapping the rug around them both. 'Marjorie, I have something I need to tell you,' he whispered.

Dreading him telling her he was joining his ship soon, her body became tense and she made fists with her hands. 'What is it?' she asked in a very small voice.

'I have to tell you that I've fallen hopelessly in love with you. I know it's only been two weeks since our first date, but I haven't been able to stop myself. Forgive me, please, if I appear to be going too fast.'

Marjorie's shoulders relaxed, her fingers unfurled, she took a deep breath. 'I don't think you're rushing me at all,' she told him, 'for I rather think I've fallen the same way.'

Tristan gave a sigh of relief and then took her in his arms. 'My darling girl, I didn't dare hope. I think this must be the happiest day of my life.'

'Mine too,' she whispered back. 'I didn't know what love was until I met you. Now I don't know how to describe it, but it's the nicest feeling I've ever known in my entire life.'

'You're amazing, the most amazing woman in the world,' he told her as he pulled her towards him and they kissed as though time didn't exist.

It was after two in the morning when Marjorie crept upstairs. She needed to sleep before Tristan called for her tomorrow. She was going to meet Tristan's parents.

He wanted to introduce her as the girl he intended to marry.

23

M arjorie's mother was delighted to hear that Marjorie would be meeting the earl and countess later that day. She was actually very pleasant with Marjorie at breakfast and although Marjorie was tired, she tried her best to be pleasant. Her father, who already knew the earl, thought he was a decent chap who Marjorie would enjoy meeting.

Marjorie decided to wear her navy dress which always made her feel confident. Her mother suggested she should borrow her sapphire earrings and matching brooch. Marjorie had to admit they were a perfect addition to the simplicity of the dress. Thankfully her hair looked well even after a night when she had tossed and turned, thinking of the perfect night when Tristan told her he loved her.

She wondered whether to tell her parents that Tristan had mentioned them getting married. She decided against it thinking that she would wait until it was official. She imagined that Tristan would want to speak to her father first. Everything was happening so quickly she could hardly believe it was only weeks since they had met each other. However, she had no doubt in her mind that Tristan truly loved her and she herself knew the feelings she had for him were real.

When Tristan called for her, her father answered the door and invited him in for a pre-luncheon drink. From the hall

Marjorie could see that Tristan was dressed immaculately in a dark grey suit and white shirt with a blue tie. She smiled when she realised his formality was due to the fact he was introducing her to his parents.

Marjorie's father had poured him a glass of sherry and he was talking amiably with her parents when she entered the room. Tristan turned around to smile at Marjorie and then to her surprise he leant forward and kissed her cheek. Her mother looked quite surprised but pleased. Her father asked if she would like a glass of sherry and she thought it was probably what she needed as she was quite nervous about what was ahead.

Her father asked Tristan if he had any news of his ship being ready to sail. Tristan replied that there was indeed talk of it being ready in the new year but he would not know until Christmas was over. He said how grateful he was to have such generous Christmas leave and he hoped to spend more time getting to know Marjorie's family better. Her mother said she hoped he would have time to call in and meet her sister when he left Marjorie home that evening. Tristan replied that he would be delighted to meet Aunt Margaret as he had heard so much about her.

Looking at his watch he said they would have to forgive them for leaving so early but he knew lunch was being served at two o'clock. 'My father is a stickler for time especially mealtimes, and Sunday lunch in particular. They are very much looking forward to meeting Marjorie,' he added.

'We shall look forward to seeing you again when you call later. Enjoy your lunch both of you,' her father replied.

Tristan bent forward to shake her mother's hand before

ushering Marjorie out of the room.

'You manage them so well,' Marjorie told him as they got into the car.

'Your father is a delightful man,' he replied, 'very pleasant and likeable. I imagine your mother will just take a little more time.'

'I think you have won her over already, she seemed delighted to see you today.'

'And I, my darling, am even more delighted to see you again. Please don't be nervous about meeting my parents, they want to meet the person who has made their son so happy.'

'I will make sure they know how happy you have made me,' Marjorie replied. 'Last night was one of the happiest of my life.'

'And you have no idea how happy you made me. Knowing my feelings were reciprocated was the greatest relief I could imagine. I meant every word I said. I really do want us to get married as soon as possible. I hope it doesn't frighten you, how quickly this is all happening, but it is wartime and none of us are promised tomorrow.'

'Oh please, Tristan, don't talk like that. It makes me so sad and I already know how much I will miss you when you are called to join your ship.'

'Sorry, my darling, the last thing I want to do is make you sad. If it was not wartime, I would still have fallen in love with you just as quickly. I might not have mentioned marriage but I would still have known that you are the only girl I would ever want to marry.'

'Tristan, I do not for a minute doubt my feelings for you

and I want to marry you, but it's so sad that we will be parted so soon.'

They were both silent for a while until Marjorie suddenly noticed they had entered some very large and impressive gates and were driving up a narrow road bordered on each side by poplar trees. Beyond she could see grassland stretching as far as the eye could see. Ahead of her she could see a large and imposing house. Standing outside the main door were two very large dogs, standing as though they were guarding the door.

Tristan smiled seeing them, 'Oscar and Gertrude waiting to meet you. Don't worry, they're very friendly despite their size. Come on, let's go and introduce you.'

As he opened the car door for her to get out, he took her hand and kissed it. 'They are going to love you,' he said.

As they walked up the steps to greet the dogs, the door opened before they got to it. Standing in the doorway was an elderly man dressed in a black suit, white shirt and bow tie.

'Sir, madam, your parents are waiting for you in the blue room. Can I take your coat?' he addressed Marjorie, 'It's particularly cold today, but nice to see some winter sunshine.'

'Thanks, William, this is Miss Fitzpatrick,' Tristan explained, handing William his coat before helping Marjorie out of hers while the dogs sat patiently.

'Thank you, William,' Marjorie said as he led them down a long corridor before opening a set of double doors and leading them in.

An elegant-looking woman rose from her armchair when she saw them enter, her husband beside her. 'So, this is Marjorie,' she said, her hand outstretched.

Marjorie took it and smiled when she saw how alike Tristan and his mother were. She had dark grey hair with streaks of white, caught back in a twist of curls at her neck. She was wearing a very simple dress of green and black tweed with black stockings and black high heels. Marjorie could tell she had been a beautiful woman and still was.

'We're delighted to meet you. Tristan hasn't told us much about you, and we have never seen him quite so happy before. Call me Annabelle and this is my husband, Julian.'

Standing tall, Julian bent his head towards Marjorie and shook her hand warmly. 'Pleased to meet you, m'dear, I've met your father of course. Damned fine surgeon, he fixed Annabelle's eyes perfectly. Couldn't see a thing before she saw him.'

'A slight exaggeration, darling, but I have to say it has made a great improvement to my life,' his wife interrupted.

'What can I get you to drink?' Julian asked Marjorie. 'I have to tell you, I make a really good martini.'

'Father, I refuse to allow you. I will make Marjorie a gin and tonic.' The dogs settled themselves in front of the fire, closing their eyes almost immediately.

'Please, Marjorie dear, do sit down. This is the warmest room in the house, but you still need to sit near the fire,' Annabelle explained.

Marjorie looked around the room and soon understood why it was called the blue room. The ceilings were high and heavily ornate, painted in white and gold. The walls were painted in a deep Wedgwood blue. The heavy curtains were made of midnight blue velvet. Around the walls hung paintings she imagined to be family portraits, all in heavy gilt frames. There were four candelabras hanging from the ceiling, while along the walls, table lamps sat on various antique side tables.

In the corner was a very large grand piano. In any other house it would have dominated the room, but here it seemed almost diminished in size. Above the fireplace hung a gilt framed mirror which reflected the candelabras.

'Here you are, darling, I can assure you this is safe to drink. My father's, however, would not be.'

Marjorie found herself drinking rather than sipping her gin. Perhaps it was the vastness of the room, but she felt very small sitting in front of what appeared to her to be very grand people. She noticed now, as she turned her head slightly, that there was a matching fireplace on the other side of the room.

'So, my dear, Tristan tells us you are very bright and have come to work at the Admiralty,' Annabelle addressed her.

'Well yes, but not until January. I've been working in a munitions factory and I've promised to stay there until Christmas.'

'A munitions factory?' Annabelle looked quite shocked.

'Yes, I was teaching in a school in Jersey but I had to come home because of the German occupation, 'Marjorie explained. 'I needed to do something to help the war effort, so I joined the factory.'

'Good Lord,' Tristan's father said, sitting up when she mentioned the word 'factory'. 'But you weren't trained for that kind of thing, were you?'

'No, I wasn't,' she replied smiling. 'I was at Oxford the same time as Tristan although we never met. I studied languages, but I was also reasonably competent with maths.'

'Slightly more than competent, darling, you are quite brilliant. I have never seen anyone do something quite so quickly,' Tristan replied, looking over at her.

'How many languages do you speak then?' his mother asked.

'Four reasonably well and I can read in Italian and German,' Marjorie replied. 'I considered studying Mandarin or Russian, but it would have meant longer at Oxford and I didn't want to do that. I shall probably teach myself.'

'You gals are so different today to what we were as gals,' Annabelle said. 'I was only taught how to embroider and dabble with water colours. All very boring. Then we were sent to Switzerland to finishing school before being presented to the King. That's where I met my husband and ever since I've been here.'

'I imagine that must have kept you pretty busy,' Marjorie remarked, looking round the room again.

'I don't suppose Tristan would ever want to marry someone who'd stay at home,' Annabelle sighed. 'Most of the gals he met seemed to bore him and he lost interest after meeting them. You must be rather special, I can tell you.'

Tristan smiled at Marjorie when his mother finished speaking. 'She is, Mother, very special.'

William had opened the doors and was standing waiting by them. 'Lunch is served. May I take your glasses for you?'

'No thanks, William, we'll leave them here and enjoy our wine with lunch.'

'Thank you, my lord, the wines are ready.'

Tristan took Marjorie by the hand as he led her into the dining-room, the dogs following at their feet. This room was smaller but more ornate. The table was huge, the chairs seemed endless.

Marjorie was grateful when they were led to the end closest to the fire where once again the dogs made themselves comfortable. The room was predominantly gold, the curtains thick gold brocade, the same as the seats of the chairs. More portraits hung on the walls, but there were still lifes hanging over the sideboards.

'Sit down, my dear, you'll have a little white?' Julian asked.

'Yes please,' Marjorie replied and William poured wine into her glass. A younger woman poured water into her glass. She then returned leaving a tray with a large tureen and small bowls on the sideboard from which William then served.

'Leek soup, I trust it's to your liking, Miss Fitzpatrick?' William asked, placing the bowl in front of her, and Marjorie assured him it was.

'We're so lucky to have a large vegetable garden here,' Annabelle explained, 'it's so hard to get anything these days.'

'We are fortunate also that our cook is well acquainted in the village and seems to be able to get most things, although not plentiful supplies,' Marjorie replied.

'We're quite self-sufficient normally,' Annabelle explained, 'but of course so many of our men have left to go and serve in the forces.'

Marjorie was seated beside the earl himself but thankfully opposite Tristan, even though he was such a distance away. Although lunch was very pleasant, Marjorie was secretly amused that Mrs Harrison's cooking was even better. The conversation over lunch was not particularly interesting for her as a lot of it was about people and places unfamiliar to her. Somehow Tristan managed to turn it around to their time at Oxford where they had a few things in common.

'Tristan was telling us that old Mountbatten was asking a few questions about you last night,' Julian said to Marjorie. 'Personally, I haven't much time for him but I do believe he knows how to command a ship.'

'Really? This is news to me. You didn't mention it to me, Tristan,' Marjorie said, looking directly at him.

'I expect there were more important things to tell you,' Tristan smiled and Marjorie lowered her head. 'The old boy was just asking who you were, but it turned out he already knew what you were doing and had been informed of the adjustment you had suggested which put us back on time.'

'Oh, what suggestion was that then?' Annabelle asked.

'It was really very simple,' Marjorie replied. 'By replacing a seal with a small metal ring, the two main parts fitted together more smoothly. It was obvious really.'

'Obvious?' Tristan laughed. 'None of the great brains worked it out before you.'

'So, a pretty gal with a brain. An unusual combination. Shall we have coffee by the fire?' Annabelle asked.

When they returned to the blue room, Marjorie asked about the portraits and Julian offered to show her round. He showed her the first dukes in the family, down to the present-day earls and lords. Whilst Marjorie recognised the likeness amongst some of them to both Julian and Tristan, some of them looked decidedly stern and she would not have wanted them in her home.

Julian also showed her around some of the rooms, the green room and the library amongst others. The library was the one where she would have loved to have spent time.

It was getting colder as the light began to fade and Julian suggested they return to the warmth. Marjorie wished they could have been in the smaller, more intimate drawing-room with its chintz furnishings and floral wallpaper Julian pointed out to her. It was, he told her, the room they spent most time in when they were on their own.

'We don't entertain much at the moment, doesn't seem right when so many are experiencing hardship. Tristan seems very taken by you,' he said, changing the subject. 'He's always been a bit of a loner and not at all interested in the ladies he met through friends. I'm very glad he has met you. You're an unusual young woman if you don't mind me saying so, but very interesting. Not at all airy-headed as so many young things are these days. If you choose to get married, you do it with my blessing. War changes everything and you need to grab all the happiness you can get.'

By now they were standing in the wide corridor in front of the blue room doors. As if by magic, William reappeared to open them. When Julian and Marjorie entered the room, Tristan and his mother appeared to be in deep conversation. They looked up as Marjorie and Julian walked towards them.

'Ah, there you are, we thought you'd got lost. Not easy for my husband of course, but rather puzzling for you, Marjorie. Come and sit down. Tristan tells me you have to be on your way, but please, have a glass of brandy before you leave. It's very cold outside I hear.'

Marjorie sat on the velvet sofa and Tristan sat down beside her, unashamedly holding her hand. William had poured them all a glass of brandy and Marjorie enjoyed the warming sensation as she swallowed it.

'You have a very beautiful home,' she addressed Annabelle. 'I have to tell you how envious I am of your library. We have a small one at home, mostly full of my father's medical books. He does, though, have some interesting books by Irish authors he knew while at Trinity in Dublin.'

'I have more time to read these days, now that there are so few social engagements,' Annabelle said. 'You must recommend me some titles. I do love a good romance.'

'Indeed I shall, I can't imagine life without books.'

'And I can't imagine what your father will say if we don't get you home soon,' Tristan said. Standing up, he took Marjorie's hand. 'Please, Father, Mother, don't get up. It's so cold outside. Stay in the warmth and I'll see you when I get home.

'Goodnight, Marjorie, it has been wonderful to meet you. Please take care of Tristan's heart. He rather appears to have given it to you,' his mother called after her.

Back in the car, Tristan drove a little further down the avenue before stopping to take Marjorie in his arms. 'You did terribly well, my darling. I couldn't be more proud of you.'

'I think perhaps, if it wasn't wartime, your mother might not approve of me so much. Your father perhaps just might.'

'I think you might have got that one wrong. My mother has suggested that on Christmas Eve, your parents and Aunt Margaret join us for our annual Christmas party. She has also suggested that on that evening, you and I might join her in her bedroom first so that you can choose a ring from the family jewels. Then we can announce the engagement immediately after. What do you think?'

For once, Marjorie was speechless. If the countess had not approved of her in some way, she would not have made such a suggestion. 'Well, please tell me. Will you marry me? Will you wear my ring?'

Marjorie's reply was to reach towards Tristan to whisper a very quiet 'Yes' before sealing it with a kiss.

As they set off on the drive home, Tristan looked across at her. 'My turn to be nervous. Time to ask your father for your hand in marriage.'

24

Aunt Margaret's face lit up when she saw Marjorie and Tristan appear. Her father jumped up to introduce them.

'Ah there you are, Tristan, I'd like you to meet my sister-in-law Margaret.'

'Margaret, I'm delighted to meet you,' Tristan said, shaking her hand. 'I've heard so much about you, Marjorie talks about you all the time, and it's always good. Mrs Fitzpatrick, I hope we didn't keep you back from tea.'

'Not at all, we finished half an hour ago. Did you enjoy lunch?'

Marjorie had never seen her mother so pleasant and smiling in front of her before.

'We had a lovely lunch,' Marjorie replied. 'And Tristan's father very kindly gave me a tour of some of the rooms. The library was amazing, Father.'

'Oh, I can just imagine you in the library,' Aunt Margaret laughed. 'I can never get her past a book shop, Tristan.'

'I gathered that,' Tristan smiled back. 'I'm sure my father would be delighted to let her run free in his library. We did use it a lot on rainy days as children. Not so much nowadays when we're all away from home a lot.'

'I haven't offered you a drink, very remiss of me,' her father said, standing beside the drinks cupboard.

'Thank you, sir, but on this occasion I shall say no. I need a clear head for the morning.'

'You are working in the Admiralty at the moment?' Margaret asked.

'Yes indeed, until my ship is ready to sail, which won't be before January,' Tristan replied. 'A new ship is always exciting, but there's no such thing as a safe ship nowadays. However, this ship will be one of the very best in the Royal Navy. We have a great Commander who it's a privilege to work with.'

Marjorie felt a wave of nausea when he mentioned his ship for it would be the ship that would take him away from her.

Tristan had sat down beside Margaret and was soon chatting away to her as though he had not just met her. He tried to include Marjorie's mother and she responded well. Her father looked comfortable, listening to the conversation while he sipped his brandy. After a while Tristan looked at his watch.

'Sir, do you think we might have a word?'

'You mean now? Oh, but of course. Come into my study,' her father replied with obvious surprise in his voice.

When the men left the room, Marjorie's mother and aunt looked at her. 'Well?' her mother asked.

'That's for Father to tell you,' Marjorie replied, 'but there is something I'd like to tell you. You will be receiving invitations from the earl and countess to their annual Christmas supper on Christmas Eve.'

Their faces were so full of surprise, Marjorie wanted to laugh. 'I imagine it will be very grand, so you will both need special outfits.'

'Well, I shan't be purchasing anything new I can assure you,' her mother replied. 'I have some wonderful gowns from India and I shall wear one of them. I presume you will need a new dress, Margaret.'

'Oh, I'm sure I have something in my wardrobe, but I rather think it might just be the perfect opportunity for you and I to go shopping, Marjorie.'

'That would be lovely but I do have a dress I haven't worn but couldn't resist buying, from your special shop, Aunt Margaret. In fact I've rather been hoping you could collect it for me.'

'Gracious me, so that's where the wonderful dress you wore last night came from. I'm told you looked amazing and yes, of course I will do that. I'll collect it tomorrow.'

'I was very pleased with it and it was the right dress to wear,' Marjorie agreed.

'I must say, your young man is quite delightful. I imagine he must look very handsome in his dress uniform,' Margaret remarked. 'You must have made a very handsome couple.'

Just as Marjorie was about to answer, Tristan and her father came back into the room.

'You'll stay and have a brandy, won't you?' her father asked him.

'I'd love to sit here chatting some more, but I do have to get back as I have a very early start in the morning, as does Marjorie,' he added, smiling over at her.

He rose to shake hands with them all. 'Please, sir, Marjorie will show me to the door. Thank you so much for your advice. It was very much appreciated. So lovely to meet you, Margaret, and delighted to see you looking so well, Mrs Fitzpatrick.'

Her mother and aunt sat with beaming smiles as he waved goodbye.

'Well?' Marjorie asked Tristan once they were out of earshot, 'what did he say?'

'He was perfectly amiable and said that while it was all happening so very quickly, he understood why. He gave us his blessing and told me to make sure I looked after you for the rest of my life. I told him that was the plan, but there were no guarantees for anything at the present time. I assured him there was no one else in the world for me.'

'Well that's a relief,' Marjorie sighed, 'not that I would ever have dreamt of him refusing, it is all very rushed.'

'Let's get engaged first and the rest will fall into place.'

He reached over and embraced her, pulling her close and kissing her. They stood like that, holding on to each other for a couple of minutes before he pulled back and took her hands. 'When will I see you?'

'How does Wednesday sound?' she asked.

'It sounds perfect, where shall I see you?'

'How about close to the station in Reading at seven-thirty? We can go for a drink if that suits you.'

'Of course it will suit me. Any night I don't see you is a miserable night for me, but we both have jobs to do. Goodnight, my darling, until Wednesday.'

When Marjorie returned to the drawing-room, her father, mother and aunt gave her a knowing look.

'Well?' her aunt asked. 'When will it happen? Don't be coy, your father has told us Tristan has asked for your hand in marriage.'

'Only if you can keep a secret. I am to choose one of his

mother's rings. They have been in the family for many years. Then the earl will announce it at supper.'

'Oh, how thrilling,' Margaret looked ecstatic. Her mother looked rather like the cat who had just had the cream.

Even her father was beaming. 'I must say, young Tristan is a jolly good chap. He's already thought about what he'll do after the war. He'd like to start his own company building bridges as he reckons this country is going to need a lot of new ones. I don't think you could ask for anyone more suitable, my dear.'

'Thank you, Father, I don't think I could either. Now, if you'll excuse me, I really do need an early night.' She kissed them all goodnight before making her way upstairs.

Lying in bed, thinking over the events of the last couple of days, she never thought that only months after returning from Jersey, she had met the man she was to marry. He was simply the most wonderful man in the entire world. And very soon, he would be hers.

Going to work on Monday morning was the hardest day since she had started in the munitions factory. She felt as though she was living in a totally different world now. At the bus stop Irene was waiting for her. Her face lit up when she saw Marjorie walk towards her. 'You made it! I was getting worried you might have decided to stay at that other factory you were working at.'

'Of course not,' Marjorie smiled brightly, 'I would never do that and if I was, I would tell you and that's a promise.'

'Thank goodness for that. I don't mind you telling me what to do but that Gloria's doing my head in.'

'Hey, Marjorie, you back for good this time?' It was Joyce and Sadie now, coming to stand with them.

'I never said I was going to be away every Monday and Tuesday, that was only until they got their problems sorted. They're not anything as good as you girls.'

'Ha! Bet you sorted them all right.' Sadie laughed. 'Look how you sorted us lot out. Poor old Harry would be lost without you.'

Marjorie was so grateful that Joyce and Sadie kept their promise and didn't mention Saturday. Even though she wasn't looking forward to getting to work, she was really happy to see these girls again. Somehow they managed to see the bright side of things no matter what was going on.

Harry was waiting by the door when the girls arrived. 'Ok you lot, no hanging about, there's a lot to do and I got a bit of a surprise for you. Come on in.'

They followed him through the door and there, in the centre of the room, sat a huge Christmas tree, covered in decorations and balloons. There was an angel on the top, dressed in white with silver wings. Paper decorations hung from every branch.

Harry said, 'The kids made them at school and their friends came round on Saturday night and made some more. Only had to pay them a bag of chips each. Now, get back to your tables please if you don't mind.'

Marjorie smiled to herself. Harry was forever grumbling and telling them off for not working hard enough, but he had a heart of corn. Getting a Christmas tree was such a lovely gesture.

'Harry, you need to be careful. The girls will start to think you like them,' she told him, 'but it was such a nice thing to do.'

'Gotta have something to cheer us up,' he replied. 'It sure as hell won't be like any other Christmas's we've all known. Lots of houses with no father and no money for a bag of mince, never mind a bleeding turkey. The earl offered me a tree from his estate when I met him in our pub *The Jolly Earl*. I took him up on it and not only did he cut it for us, he delivered it right to the door. He's a decent bloke is the earl.'

'That's nice to know.' Marjorie said quietly. 'Makes Christmas seem a lot closer,' she added, looking at the tree.

'Don't tell me that,' Harry sighed, 'we ain't even got the kid's toys yet. Come on up to the office, I've work to show you,'

Back in the office Harry showed her the letter he'd had from the Admiralty. 'Seems like we won't be having you for long then.'

'Yes, I'm sorry about that, Harry. I didn't want to go, but they weren't taking no for an answer.'

'Can't say I blame them, your brain's wasted here. I shall miss you and so will the girls when they hear. Anyway, here's your worksheet for the week. Mind blowing it ain't, but it's a job as has to be done.'

Marjorie looked at it and saw what he meant. It was boring, monotonous work, but there was a huge need for ammunition, so she'd better get on with it.

Sadie and Joyce managed to find a quiet spot for them to talk with Marjorie at lunch time. 'Well, how'd it go?' Sadie asked. 'Did his eyes pop out when he saw you in the dress?'

'Well, I wouldn't say that, but he did seem pretty impressed.'

'Did everybody look at you? Joyce asked. 'Did you wish you'd bought the blue one?'

'No, quite the opposite. It was exactly the right dress to wear.'

'Bet he fancied you something rotten,' Sadie said, 'bet he was dead proud an' all.'

'I think I could say that yes, he told me he was proud.'

'Blimey, he'll be asking you to marry him next,' Sadie said.

Marjorie felt herself blushing. 'It's a bit early for that, we've only known each other a few weeks, but he does make me very happy.'

And he does, she thought to herself as she tried to concentrate. He made her happier than anyone else in her entire life. She couldn't wait to see him again on Wednesday night. To hold him again, to kiss him, to just be close to each other. Finding herself looking into the air, her hands still, she jumped up and put her head down. Only two more days.

25

The week before Christmas Eve was so hectic, Marjorie had no choice but to take three days off work. Harry wasn't pleased at first, but realising that there was nothing too important happening, he agreed. Marjorie suggested he put Irene and Gloria in charge. In fact, Irene had come on so well over the past weeks that Marjorie suggested that he might consider her for promotion.

Irene cried after Harry had called her in and told her he was making her a supervisor on par with Gloria. 'No one has ever told me I was good at anything before and I have you to thank for that Marjorie,' she said tearfully. 'Means the world to me it does.'

'You deserve it, Irene, your accuracy with everything you do is always one hundred percent and you're always willing to help anyone who's struggling. You're an asset to the factory and don't forget that.'

On Wednesday Marjorie visited Elsie, travelling there with Joyce and Sadie. The house was transformed with decorations and there were brightly wrapped parcels under the tree.

Over dinner, she told her three friends that she wouldn't be back to the factory after Christmas as she was being transferred. Joyce and Sadie were both really sad about that but cheered up when Marjorie told them she would continue coming to see Elsie whenever she could. She also told them something very exciting was happening to her on Christmas Eve but she couldn't say until after then. Their excitement for her was as though it was happening to them.

Marjorie was so pleased she had asked Tristan to call for her at Elsie's and she smiled as she heard the doorbell ring. 'Who on earth can that be at this time of night?' Elsie asked as she left to answer the door. Her face was a picture as a very handsome young man in his naval uniform stood at her door.

'I'm here to collect Marjorie,' he explained. 'You must be Elsie.'

As the realisation hit her, she ushered him inside where Joyce and Sadie were sitting, eyes wide with curiosity.

'As you've probably realised, this is Tristan,' Marjorie explained. 'Tristan, this is Elsie,' pointing out the lady standing beside him, 'and these two are Sadie and Joyce.'

Elsie's reaction was to reach up and hug him while the other two appeared to be in shock. 'Blimey, Marjorie, this is a bit of a surprise, but a bleedin' nice one at that,' Sadie eventually replied. 'Very nice to meet you.'

'I'm delighted to meet you all. Marjorie talks about you all, in a very fond way I assure you,' Tristan replied, 'and thank you all for helping her choose her marvellous gown.'

Elsie made them all a cup of tea and a slice of Mrs Harrison's fruit cake. She told Tristan with pride about her husband and her family's part in the war. They were all sad when Marjorie announced she had to get home but hugged them both warmly when they left.

'Thank you for doing that, Tristan,' Marjorie said as they

drove off. 'It means a lot, especially to Joyce and Sadie who haven't had the best starts in life.'

'I know, darling, but look at the home they have now, it couldn't be any more comfortable. And anyway, it meant I got to see you one more time before Saturday,' Tristan replied.

'I can hardly believe it's just three more days. I get flutters in my tummy every time I think about it,' Marjorie confessed. 'I can't imagine what I will be like by Saturday.'

'I get flutters every single time I think of you, makes me look a bit stupid in work, 'Tristan laughed.

'Thank goodness I have a dress I can wear, my mother changes her mind every day. Oh, you don't mind Daphne coming, do you? I really can't leave her out of it.'

'Of course not, darling, she will probably have loads to talk about when she meets my mother's sister, if they don't already know each other. Vivienne is horse mad and loves to talk about them to anyone who'll listen.'

'That's comforting to know, but I do wish it was all over, don't you?'

'Of course I do, and it will be soon,' Tristan assured her. 'Let's look forward to Monday. I thought we might take a drive somewhere and have a lovely, long walk. I'll get cook to make us some sandwiches and a flask of tea. The party is really for our families and friends.'

'That sounds like heaven,' Marjorie sighed.

After Tristan drove off, Marjorie hoped she would be able to go to bed, but found her mother waiting for her in the drawing-room.

'Marjorie dear, what do you think of this?' Her mother was holding out a plum-coloured dress, embroidered in rich colours and scattered with sequins. 'I have a matching wrap to go with it.'

Marjorie looked carefully as her mother held the dress up in front of her. 'It's beautiful, Mother, and the wrap is a wonderful idea as I can't imagine it will be overly warm.'

'Well, if you're sure, dear. Your father loves this dress so I'm glad you like it too. Your sister is wearing a black dress which I didn't think was entirely appropriate but she assures me it's very smart and she has only worn it once to a formal dinner in the War Office.'

'I imagine it will suit her very well with her colouring. She's so much more like you than I am. Now, Mother, if you'll excuse me, I'm very tired, it's been a long day.'

In bed, Marjorie thought over what Tristan had said. He was right, the party was for their families. For once her mother was excited about something to do with her and her father appeared to be very pleased. Aunt Margaret was, of course, delighted.

She herself was excited about choosing the ring and announcing to the world how they felt about one another, but after that, she just wanted it to be the two of them. In January he would be away with no idea when he would return. She would seize the moment and cherish every memory.

26

On Friday Aunt Margaret collected Marjorie to take her to her hairdresser. They would discuss what they would do with her hair and on Saturday the hairdresser would come to the house to style it before she dressed. After that they would enjoy a leisurely lunch before collecting Aunt Margaret's dress which was being altered.

It was a treat for Marjorie getting out of the house without her mother. Mrs Harrison had promised to have dinner ready for them when they got back. She had been a life saver for Marjorie who was able to escape to the kitchen when her mother got too much for her.

The hairdresser was very glamorous and made Marjorie feel rather dowdy in comparison. Her blonde hair was immaculately coiffed and her scarlet lipstick suited her porcelain skin. Despite her sophisticated appearance, Marlene had a very warm personality and made sure Marjorie felt relaxed.

While Marjorie sat in the chair, Marlene stood behind and pulled her hair this way and that until she was satisfied she had it to the right side. 'You have a very strong profile and a very good jawline, we want to emphasise that. I suggest we dress your hair to the side and have soft curls on the nape of your neck. Now, describe your dress to me.'

Marjorie explained that it was made of heavy crepe which fell like a column from the waist down. The sweetheart neckline was not too deep and the sleeves came to just above her elbow. All in a rich shade of blue.

'Right, I got it. Perfect. I think we should have an orchid among the curls which you will see from the front as your hair will be dressed to the side. Right, let's get your hair washed. I'll style it for you now, but I'll dress it up tomorrow. How does that sound?'

Marjorie explained that it sounded wonderful and agreed to all of it.

'I'll bring my make up with me tomorrow and we'll make those eyes of yours shine,' Marlene told her.

Marjorie emerged from the salon feeling like a different person. Marlene had assured her that it would be looser and more natural on Saturday night, but for now it felt very unlike her usual self.

Margaret, however, was delighted. 'You are going to look fantastic, Marjorie, and every eye in the room will be upon you. You have such unusual looks, but you don't value them as you should. You like to fade into the background, but love has changed you and I'm very grateful to Tristan for bringing about the change. Head up, my dear, this is the best time of your life, believe me.'

Over lunch, Margaret told Marjorie something she had never heard before. 'I was engaged in 1916 to a very handsome young army officer. We met when he was home on sick leave and we both attended the same party. Clive was twenty-five years old to my twenty-one. He had already been injured in France and was returning there after he recovered.

'He went back and wrote to me to tell me how much he thought of me when he was lying in his bunk at night. We wrote to each other for six months so I really felt as though I knew him when he got back. He came home in July and in August he proposed.

'By then two of my brothers had been killed and I was scared to love any man and then lose him. But we were so in love, we went ahead and got engaged. Only our parents knew, we didn't celebrate, but we had the most wonderful month of my life. We went to Cornwall for a week and we were never apart for the whole time.

'Two days after we came home, he was sent back to France. A week later he was killed in battle. The last letter I received from him said that if he were to die, he would die happy knowing I loved him.'

Tears dropped from Margaret's eyes as she finished her story. She dabbed at them with a lace handkerchief she took from her handbag. Marjorie felt tears stinging her own eyes. She had had no idea. She knew her mother and father had brought Margaret to India to find her a husband but her mother had said that Margaret was simply too fussy.

'I wasn't too fussy. I simply never found anyone who could ever compare with Clive. I didn't want anyone else, I had known real love and nothing could replace that. So, you see, my darling girl, that is all I have ever wanted for you. Things are not as bad in this war, no filthy trenches to lie in. Tristan is a great chap, I've no doubt he will return.'

27

Marlene zipped Marjorie into her dress and sat her down at the dressing table. Her hair, Marjorie thought, seemed incredibly different this time. The curls were looser and more natural, the orchid was small and its deep maroon colouring suited her dark hair. Marlene applied a little foundation to Marjorie's face and touched her high cheekbones with a little rouge. The blue eyeshadow was very subtle, her eyelashes merely kissed with mascara. Her only jewellery was a simple pearl choker.

'Now, you really are ready for the ball,' Marlene announced, standing back to admire her handiwork.

The deep rose lipstick, Marjorie had to admit, was very flattering.

Helping Marjorie into the silver fox stole her mother had lent her once again, Marlene admired Marjorie's silver shoes and matching evening bag. Then they were ready to go downstairs. Marlene slipped quietly out the back door while Marjorie stepped into the drawing-room. Her mother, father, aunt and sister were all waiting for her.

'Darling, you look magnificent,' her aunt told her. 'Doesn't she?' she asked her sister.

'Well, I have to say I am most surprised,' Marjorie's mother replied. 'You look very well, dear.'

'You do look smart, old thing,' Daphne nodded.

'To my beautiful daughter. Here's to your happiness, my dear,' her father said, lifting his glass towards her. 'How about a little brandy for the nerves?'

Marjorie accepted the glass gratefully. The butterflies were turning somersaults in her tummy already.

Her father helped his wife into the passenger seat before opening the doors for Marjorie, Margaret and Daphne to get in. The drive, although not a long one, seemed to last forever. At last they were driving up the avenue and the house came into view. There were so many cars, men were helping with parking and the house was brilliant with lights.

Standing by the door with William was Tristan, who ran down the steps to greet them as soon as he saw them. 'Welcome everyone, thank you for coming. Mrs Fitzpatrick, you look wonderful, as do you, Margaret,' he said, kissing each of them on the cheek. 'And you must be Daphne, delighted to meet you.'

Marjorie had to admit that Daphne did look exceptionally well. Her black dress was very simple but flattered her figure and her blonde hair. She felt suddenly very proud of her family who all looked so well.

Tristan hadn't let go of her hand since he helped her out of the car. In his dress uniform he looked even more handsome than usual. Ushering the others ahead of him, he whispered to Marjorie, 'I didn't think you could look more beautiful, but you do. I didn't think I could love you more, but I do.' He brushed a kiss on her cheek as he drew her closer to him.

His mother and father were standing at each side of the ballroom doors. An enormous Christmas tree stood in the bay window, and holly decorated the windowsills. A small band stood in the corner playing Christmas music. The log fires crackled, guarded by fire screens big enough to sit on.

Tristan's father was the first to welcome Marjorie. 'My dear, you look just beautiful, my son couldn't have chosen better,' he said, kissing the back of her hand.

Tristan's mother raised her eyebrows in surprise. 'Well, I must say, you look absolutely delightful, Marjorie. You must tell me who styled your hair, my daughter must use her. Now, give me half an hour to greet everyone, then the three of us can go to my room.' With that she was gone.

Tristan took a champagne flute off one of the waitress's trays and gave it to Marjorie before taking one for himself. 'Let me show you something,' he said, taking her by the hand and pulling her gently down the hall. He opened a door, brought her in and locked the door behind her. 'I wanted to give you this,' he said, taking a small velvet box from his pocket. 'Open it, I chose them for you today.'

Marjorie pressed the stud, and the box opened to display a pair of sapphire and diamond earrings.

'I did ask Elsie what colour your dress was going to be,' he explained. 'Try them on.'

Marjorie stepped forward to the fireplace of the sitting-room and looked in the mirror, then lifting them out, she clipped them onto her ears. The flames of the fire reflected on the diamonds making them a myriad of colours. 'Tristan, they're beautiful, I really don't know what to say.'

'You don't need to say anything. I wanted you to have something from me to mark our engagement, something personal that I chose for you. The sapphire is from Sri Lanka which is why it's such a pale blue.'

'I love it and I love you so much for thinking of something so surprising and lovely,' Marjorie replied.

'I did it because I love you more than words can say,' he told her and pulled her closer to him before he kissed her.

They stood like that until the clock over the mantle struck.

'Oh Lord, we'd better go or Mama will have sent for a search party.'

Marjorie replaced her lipstick and powdered her nose before Tristan unlocked the door and they made their way back to the ballroom. Marjorie searched for her family and to her relief saw each of them engaged with other guests. Daphne was talking animatedly with an older, striking-looking lady.

'Vivienne,' Tristan laughed. 'Didn't take them long to find one another.'

'There you are, I thought you'd disappeared,' said Tristan's mother, who was beckoning to Marjorie and Tristan to follow her. 'Come along, we want to make the announcement before supper is served.'

Marjorie and Tristan climbed the stairs together and followed Tristan's mother until she led them into her bedroom. 'Now, you just sit there by my dressing table and I will bring the rings to you,' she said, opening the doors of a black, ebony cabinet. 'Here we are. Now, look at each one and don't worry about size, we can always have them adjusted.'

Tristan stood behind Marjorie, watching as she opened the first box. Inside the ancient velvet box, frayed at the edges, was a diamond ring, the centre stone oval, the shoulders of the ring covered in small diamonds. It was beautiful, Marjorie decided, just not for her. The next box, equally battered, contained a large emerald, surrounded by diamonds. It was exquisite, but too big for her finger.

The third was ruby and diamonds, a large ruby in the centre and a diamond and a ruby at each side. It seemed too wide for her finger. The next box, covered in black velvet, had three large diamonds of equal size, side by side. Marjorie loved their simplicity.

The final box, covered in blue leather, opened to display a sapphire, pale in colour, like her earrings, surrounded by sparkling diamonds. It fitted perfectly. She met Tristan's eyes in the mirror and they smiled at each other.

'I think she has found it, Mama.'

'I think she has too,' his mother replied, smiling. 'Are you quite sure or would you like to try them on again?'

'I'm quite sure,' Marjorie replied, 'I really love it.'

'Then you are its new guardian. Enjoy it and guard it well,' she said, bending over to kiss Marjorie's cheek. 'Right, I will leave you two for no longer than five minutes. Your father will make the announcement as soon as you come down.'

As soon as she left, Tristan got down on one knee. 'Will you marry me? Will you make me the proudest man in the country? Will you be my wife?

'Yes, I will, I will be proud to be your wife,' Marjorie replied as he took her in his arms.

'Never, ever forget how much I love you,' he told her, their foreheads together. 'I love you more every time I see you, every time I think of you, I don't know where it's all coming from, but I do.'

'Tristan, I couldn't love you any more if I tried. Thank you for making me happier than I ever dreamt possible.'

As they walked downstairs, William nodded to the earl who nodded to the musicians to stop. Walking over to where the band played, he began his announcement.

'Ladies and gentlemen, on behalf of the countess and myself, it is with great pleasure I can announce that my son Tristan has tonight proposed marriage to the love of his life, Miss Marjorie Fitzpatrick, and she, in turn, has accepted. We simply could not be more delighted. May I ask you all to raise your glasses to the happy couple, Tristan and Marjorie.'

A cheer went up as Tristan led Marjorie up to where his father stood. William handed them both a glass of champagne while his mother came towards them, shaking their hands and kissing them both on the cheek.

Tristan managed to thank everyone, telling them that this was the happiest night of his life. Marjorie's parents were next and then it seemed as though the whole room was around them. The band leader announced that supper was served and they slowly walked towards the supper room, each one pausing to congratulate them.

The rest of the evening passed in a blur. So many people to meet, Tristan's sister first who said how jolly it was to have another girl in the family. Aunts, uncles, school friends of Tristan's and friends from Oxford.

Her father had managed to track down Louisa and her parents and Louisa's husband too. They couldn't believe the change in Marjorie and Louisa's mother was ecstatic about her appearance. 'I always knew there was a beauty in there, waiting to get out. It seems that love did just that. I'm so happy for you, darling girl,' she told her.

Louisa and her husband were both working as doctors in the hospital where they treated injured soldiers. They knew of Tristan and Louisa assured her that all of it was good.

'How did I get so lucky?' Marjorie asked her.

'Isn't that funny? I was just thinking that about Tristan.' Louisa replied.

It seemed as though Marjorie and Tristan were drifting in a sea of well wishes. There was barely a moment when Tristan left her side.

Towards the end of the evening, they danced together as the band played 'Have I told you lately that I love you?' Neither of them could stop smiling.

Tristan had invited Marjorie to join him and his family on Christmas night, but both of them knew that it was Monday, when they would be alone, they looked forward to most. It had been a magical evening though, one neither of them could have dreamed of just weeks ago. Everyone seemed so happy for them, it had been an incredibly happy night for everyone.

'Love makes the world go around,' Aunt Margaret told them both. 'You two are made for each other.'

Marjorie's mother looked as though she had grown taller as she accepted congratulations from people as they passed. Her father and the earl enjoyed a glass of vintage brandy together and Daphne and Vivienne agreed to meet up together for the Boxing Day Hunt.

Marjorie and Tristan managed one goodnight kiss outside before Marjorie joined her family. Her ring sparkled in the moonlight and Tristan kissed it, then touched her lips with it.

She fingered her earrings and smiled, and he kissed her again.

Then she was driven down the avenue towards home, Tristan waving until she was out of sight.

28

That Christmas was Marjorie's happiest ever. Waking up and looking at her engagement ring, she jumped out of bed to retrieve the earrings Tristan had given her. On opening it she found a piece of paper, folded over several times, at the bottom of the box they came in. He had told her to look there on a Christmas morning and she had resisted the temptation to open it the night before.

Unfolding the paper, she discovered it was a handwritten note from Tristan.

My dearest Marjorie,

As you read this, it is Christmas morning and I wanted you to know that it is the best Christmas of my whole life, even better than when Santa came. Having you in my life has been the greatest gift I have ever received. I can hardly believe it has happened, that someone as beautiful, gentle, kind and lovely as you have agreed to be my wife.

No words can adequately describe my love for you. It hasn't happened because there is a war on, it has happened because I have met the love of my life and no one else could ever compare to you. Just remember that no matter where in the world I am, or even if I am no longer in this world, the love I have for you is forever.

Happy Christmas, my darling.

Yours forever,
Tristan

Tears filled Marjorie's eyes as she read the words he had written to her. They were tears of joy, but also of sadness as she knew he would be leaving soon to take his part in the war against Hitler. Wiping away the tears, she promised herself that she would not allow the sadness to ruin what was the happiest time of her life. He had promised to ring her this morning, so she prepared the clothes she would wear that day before she bathed.

She met Mrs Harrison in the kitchen, preparing breakfast. The turkey was in the oven already, together with the ham. Breakfast would be simply tea and toast as Marjorie had insisted that Mrs Harrison must leave immediately after lunch was ready. Her niece Daisy was coming in to help serve lunch and to wash the dishes before going to her aunt and uncle's for their own Christmas dinner.

Mrs Harrison was so excited to see the ring and she gasped when she saw it. 'Oh, my word, what a beauty!' she said, holding Marjorie's hand. 'I don't suppose I'll ever see a nicer one. I wish you both all the happiness in the world, you know I do,' and she hugged Marjorie warmly. 'He's got himself a treasure and I do believe you've found gold as well.'

Her mother and father had breakfast with Marjorie in the morning room, both of them looking tired, but very happy. 'I hope you're going to spend the day with us, my dear, for after all, it will be the last Christmas we shall have you. Next year you'll be a married woman,' her father said, happily.

'Tristan has asked me to visit him tonight, but I'm going to tell him I'd like to spend it at home. He's going to ring me soon, so I'll tell him then.'

'That's very considerate of you, Marjorie. Do tell Tristan he's always welcome here with us,' her mother added, 'He will be the son your father never had.'

'Steady on, dear, let's get the wedding over first,' her father laughed. 'Have you any idea when that will be?'

'We just don't know yet, Father,' Marjorie replied. 'We will certainly get married when he comes home on leave, we just don't know when that will be.'

'As long as we have a little time to prepare,' her mother added quietly. 'I do understand these are difficult times, but I'd like to think your father and I can contribute in some small way, but the countess said it will be their pleasure to host the reception and they have a family church on the estate. So kind of them.'

Marjorie noticed her mother's eyes clouding over as she thought about it.

Upstairs again, Marjorie wrote a card to include with the present she had bought Tristan. She had had so little time, but Marlene the hairdresser had given her an idea. She had taken some photographs of Marjorie in her blue evening gown last night. She was going to have them developed after Christmas.

Knowing this was going to happen, Marjorie had bought a silver frame when she went shopping with Aunt Margaret. She intended giving the frame today with a note saying that she would give him the photos to choose from so he could take it with him when he left.

Aunt Margaret arrived, followed by Uncle John, her father's only brother who had survived the First World War. He was a bachelor who lived with his housekeeper just a mile or two from Aunt Margaret. He was quite a jolly man, always very kind to his nieces. Daphne as usual was late but arrived just in time as lunch was about to be served.

The atmosphere over lunch was the happiest Marjorie could remember. Even Daphne joined in wholeheartedly, especially as she was joining the Boxing Day Hunt with Vivienne. She was quite animated about the engagement party and the countess had invited her to visit their stables with Vivienne.

When Tristan rang, Marjorie explained it would be difficult for her to leave the family, so he suggested he would come and join them, sometime after eight. Marjorie's mother and aunt were delighted and Uncle John said he was glad to have the opportunity to meet the young man who had swept his niece off her feet.

Marjorie found herself with flutters in her tummy when she saw that it was almost eight. Daphne had left to feed the horses, and her father had brought out his best brandy and some liqueurs for the ladies. Mrs Harrison had excelled herself with their Christmas cake this year. She had iced it beautifully with a group of tiny Christmas trees and Santa on his sleigh, pulled by Rudolph. Everyone confessed that they couldn't eat another bite, but they would slice the cake when Tristan arrived.

He arrived just one minute after eight and Marjorie ran to the door to welcome him. He was wearing what he called his 'Christmas jumper' as was the family tradition on Christmas night. It was dark blue, and round his neck was a rather ridiculous scarf, much too long, which a great-aunt had knit for him. It made him look particularly boyish and Marjorie's heart melted.

'How good it is to see you. We had a perfectly lovely Christmas Day,' he told her, 'but all I could think about was seeing you again. You look gorgeous,' and he wrapped his arms around her and kissed her.

'Shhh, they'll hear you,' Marjorie giggled.

'I don't care if the whole world hears us. I love you, Marjorie Fitzpatrick. And how could I not?' he asked, holding her away from him and looking at her appraisingly. With Margaret's help, Marjorie had bought an unusual outfit, unlike anything she had worn before. A full skirt, made from midnight blue velvet, trimmed round the edges with pink roses, and a pink polo neck cashmere sweater to match.

'But don't you think my earrings are the best bit?' she teased, 'except, of course, for this,' and she flashed her ring under the light. He agreed and kissed her once again.

The men stood up when they walked into the drawing-room, Uncle John to introduce himself and her father to shake Tristan's hand. Tristan kissed Marjorie's mother and her aunt before sitting down next to the fire. He fitted in so naturally and Marjorie felt so proud of him as he talked to her uncle like he had heard all about him. The conversation was surprisingly jolly and her father offered the men his prized cigars. Even though her mother despised cigar smoke, especially in the drawing-room, she smiled amiably at Tristan as though it was totally acceptable.

Marjorie and Margaret made a pot of tea and they sliced the Christmas cake. It was pronounced as the best Christmas cake ever, congratulations to be passed on to Mrs Harrison. When they had finished eating, Tristan insisted that Aunt Margaret sat where she was, and he accompanied Marjorie to the kitchen with the empty plates. 'Just an excuse of course, but it's very hard being in the same room as you and not being able to touch you.'

Marjorie confessed to feeling the same and melted into his arms.

When everyone had gone to bed, Marjorie and Tristan sat on the floor beside the fire. Marjorie produced her Christmas present, apologising that it was so small, but promising he would have the rest of it before New Year's Eve. He was delighted and told her he couldn't wait to see the photos.

Then Tristan produced another box from his pocket, bigger than the last one but only by a margin. Inside was a gold locket, engraved on the back with 'Yours always and forever, Tristan'. Inside was a tiny head and shoulders photo of him in his naval uniform. He was smiling in it and she felt as though he was smiling at her. 'And I am,' he whispered as he slipped it round her neck.

Then he told her that the commander and his wife had invited them to dinner on New Year's Eve. 'I'd like to go if you would Marjorie. They're very easy company and I know you will get on really well with her,' Simon explained. 'They've invited us to stay, separate rooms of course, if that's agreeable to you.

'Well, yes, that's very kind of them,' Marjorie agreed, 'and I did like her very much.'

'That's settled then, and there's something else.' Tristan was sitting with his back to an armchair and he pulled her close to him. 'My father has suggested we start our married life in his townhouse. It's very safe as there's a wonderful basement should there be an air raid. I'd like to show it to you before you make up your mind. What do you think?'

'Well, yes, it's very generous of them, and it makes sense if I'm still working at the Admiralty. I'd love to live in the country though when this awful war is over.'

'And we shall, I promise you. Shall we go and see it on New Year's Day? We'll be very close to it.'

'Yes, that will be lovely. I'd love to see it.'

They sat like that until Tristan thought it would be sensible for him to leave before her father came down with a shotgun. 'I'll pick you up at twelve tomorrow. Cook has promised to make us up a picnic with some hot soup and a flask of coffee.'

'And I shall supply the Christmas cake,' Marjorie laughed. Neither of them wanted him to go but Marjorie insisted he get some sleep as it was only twelve hours before he'd be back.

Marjorie fell asleep clutching the locket close to her heart. She had so many things to look forward to, but always, at the back of her head was the reminder there was a war on. She fought it off as she remembered the words *Yours always and forever*.

And she would be his, forever. Of that she was sure.

29

The days after Christmas were the happiest either of them had ever known. Each day Tristan would call for Marjorie and they would drive miles into the country or out onto the coast. Whatever the weather, they walked, found little pubs to lunch in and sometimes they would just sit planning their lives together.

They both wanted children, two, maybe three, and they would not send them to boarding-school, unless the children themselves actually wanted to. They would like to live in the country with access to beaches not far away. Tristan would find work in engineering and Marjorie would teach until the children arrived. They agreed on everything.

Each day they would find out something new about each other and delight in it. Every day Tristan would find Marjorie more beautiful and she would marvel at his handsome face. Saying goodnight was painful and they looked forward to the time when they wouldn't have to.

On New Year's Eve, they only saw each other until lunchtime. Marjorie was going to see Marlene to have her hair dressed, and Tristan insisted on taking her and waiting for her in the café next door. Marlene hugged Marjorie when she saw her coming in and asked her to have a seat while she went to fetch some clean towels. She returned with the towels and a large white envelope.

'These are for you, and though I say it myself they are much better than I thought possible. You take such a wonderful photograph, Marjorie.'

Marjorie opened the envelope and pulled out the contents.

'My uncle developed them quickly especially for you,' Marlene explained. 'He said they were very professional but it was his camera after all.'

Marjorie could hardly believe her eyes. They were all beautiful, she couldn't believe she looked so glamorous. But one stood out above the rest. Sitting down, she had turned her head to talk to Marlene and unknown to her, Marlene photographed her at that precise moment. Her eyes looked bright and her mouth was just slightly open but it was so natural, even Marjorie smiled looking at it.

There were others taken full length showing off her dress to perfection, some were head and shoulders but this one looked as though she was just about to say something. Marjorie remembered talking about Tristan at the moment it was taken, so she knew the joy in her eyes was because of that. There were also small proofs included which would fit perfectly into Tristan's wallet.

'I don't know how to thank you, I really don't,' Marjorie told Marlene, 'but I couldn't be more pleased. I showed you the silver frame I bought, this will fit perfectly.'

Marjorie joined Tristan in the café and sat down to enjoy a cup of tea with him. He admired her hair. This time Marlene had set it in loose curls, less formal than she had done it for their engagement party, but pretty and feminine. 'I have something special for you,' she told him, reaching into the envelope and removing the photograph. 'This is the one Marlene and I thought the most suitable for the frame I bought you.'

Tristan accepted the photo from her and smiled broadly as he studied it. 'I wonder what you were saying. You look as though you are saying, I love you.'

'Well, I was talking to Marlene about you when she took it so I was probably thinking, *I love you*,' she replied.

'I shall treasure it and it will go everywhere with me,' he said as he looked through the rest of the photos. She gave him some of the small proofs for his wallet. She noticed the habit she had got into, of fingering her locket, even when she was with him, knowing the photo of Tristan was inside.

She had decided to wear the dress she had bought for their first date together. The party wasn't going to be formal and she thought it was the most appropriate, especially with the way she was wearing her hair. Once more her mother had insisted she wore her silver fox and this time she would wear her silver shoes with the dress as it was going to be a party.

She had explained to her parents they were staying with the commander and his wife and that they were going to look at his father's house on New Year's Day. Aunt Margaret had come to spend the night with Marjorie's parents, and Tristan joined them all for a drink before whisking her off to the party. They all wished each other a Happy New Year and the atmosphere in her house was warm and happy as they left.

The commander and his wife lived in a large London terrace which was spread over five floors. It had been gifted to them by his father when they married, but when the commander's ship sailed, his family would go back to their country house which was better and safer for the children. Inside it seemed like every light in the house was on when they arrived, but the blackout curtains were drawn and a fire glistened in the heart of the large drawing-room.

Giselle came forward to welcome Marjorie with a warm hug. 'Let me show you your room. It's rather far up, but it's the quietest part of the house.'

Tristan carried their bags until they came to the third floor. Giselle said, 'Here you are, not too far to come down if there's an air raid, but far enough up to be quiet. This is yours, Marjorie, it's where our eldest daughter sleeps when she's in London. Not often these days, I'm afraid.'

The room was obviously a girl's room with pink wallpaper and curtains and a pink satin eiderdown. Tristan left her suitcase beside the dressing table as Giselle explained he was sleeping in the room next door. 'The bathroom is just opposite and do use the electric heater in the morning, Marjorie, the boiler is on its last legs. I'll leave you two to get sorted and I'll see you downstairs.'

Marjorie was wearing the dress beneath her winter coat and had discarded the fox stole. She had just opened her suitcase to fetch her silver shoes when there was a tap on her door. 'Sorry, darling, I thought you were ready,' Tristan said.

'Just changing my shoes. I need to comb my hair and put on my lipstick but I won't be a minute,' Marjorie replied.

'Mind if I wait?' Tristan asked, 'it seems stupid standing outside.'

'Of course you may,' Marjorie laughed, buckling her ankle straps. She ran the comb through her hair and applied the rose lipstick she loved. 'There, I'm ready.'

'You look good enough to eat,' he told her, 'but if I kiss you, you'll have to put on more lipstick, so I'll resist the temptation.' Then he took her hand and they went downstairs together.

There was some lively music playing from a gramophone in the corner. The drawing-room was already quite full and a young cadet in uniform was carrying glasses of white and red wine on a tray. Marjorie accepted a glass of white and Tristan a glass of red.

The commander was standing in the corner talking to a couple who Marjorie recognised from the Navy Club. Seeing Tristan and Marjorie, he came over to greet them, kissing Marjorie on both cheeks. 'Looking even more gorgeous, Marjorie, it's so good that you could join us. Have you had a good Christmas? Tristan obviously has.'

'It has been lovely, we've enjoyed it so much. Hard to believe I go back to work on Monday.'

'Of course you do. Well, that will take your mind off this lad, sailing on the high seas.'

'But not on Monday?' she asked fearfully.

'No, not on Monday, but pretty soon after. Don't you worry yourself, he's got me to look after him,' he added, 'and you must keep in touch with Giselle. Spend a weekend in the country with her, she would love that.'

Marjorie's heart sank at the thought that it might be just days before Tristan would have to leave. They had been inseparable over the holiday period and now it could come to an abrupt end.

Tristan put his arm around her and kissed her cheek gently. The commander had gone on to welcome some guests who had just arrived. Tristan took her hand and led her into another room where there was only one other couple. They were sitting close together, the girl dabbing at her eyes with a handkerchief.

'Darling, almost everyone here tonight, with the exception of some family members, are going to be sailing with us,' Tristan explained. 'I was going to tell you tonight, as I got the call this morning. It's painful and the last thing on Earth I ever want to do is leave you, but it's my job and a very important one. I know you know that too, but the pain is just as bad for me. Only the single men are anxious to get on with it.

'But please, can we celebrate tonight? Can we be thankful for what we have, which is so special I thank God a hundred times a day? I'm with you now, I'll be with you tomorrow, so please, let's not waste a single moment by being sad.'

Seeing his face, Marjorie realised how equally painful it was for Tristan and felt guilty for being so selfish, thinking of herself. She reached her hands up to his face and slowly kissed him, then blinking back the tears she whispered, 'I will cherish every moment, I promise.'

'That's my girl, now let me introduce you to some of the guys I'm going to have to live with,' Tristan replied, and Marjorie could see his eyes were also fighting back tears.

The evening was unbelievably full of laughter and music, some of the young officers singing along, everyone drinking just a little too much, but all of them hoping that the new year would be a better one than this. 'Auld Lang Syne' was so meaningful and emotional for all of them, as they clung together to see the new year in.

Tristan and Marjorie were oblivious to everyone else in the room when they kissed and held each other tight. At one o'clock, Marjorie was overwhelmed by tiredness and emotion and Tristan said he would see her to her room.

As she kissed Giselle goodnight and thanked her for the wonderful hospitality, Giselle took her into a corner. 'Marjorie, I know how you are feeling, I'm feeling the same way, but I'm determined to be brave for Christopher. I just wanted to say that I understand and I know there was no time for you to get married, but if you and Tristan want to be together tonight, we totally understand. This bloody war is causing so much heartache and people do things they wouldn't do in peacetime, but I've never seen a couple so much in love with each other. I'm always here for you and I hope you know that.'

Marjorie didn't know quite what to think but she did know she felt completely sober at that moment. 'Thank you, Giselle, I will remember that,' was all she could manage.

Upstairs, Tristan and Marjorie stood on the landing, holding on to each other as though they couldn't bear to part.

'I'm sorry, darling, you must be so tired. I should let you go to bed,' Tristan whispered. 'Please go and sleep well. No one could ever love you as much as I do,' and with that he opened her door and left.

Lying in bed alone, Marjorie allowed her tears to flow. She knew they had only a few days left before Tristan would sail for as long as three months. She prayed that God would keep him safe and bring him back to her. She was restless, tossing and turning, tired but unable to sleep.

She thought of Tristan, lying in bed at the other side of the wall between them. She thought of what Giselle had said to her, and suddenly realised her meaning. If she knew that her fiancé was definitely coming back in three months when they would get married, things would be so different. Tristan was such a gentleman, he would never shame her or do anything to hurt her. But they were not promised tomorrow.

She sat up in bed and wrapped her dressing gown over her shoulders. She walked quietly over the bedroom floor and opened the door. She could hear the sounds of people downstairs but they sounded very far away. She quietly opened Tristan's door and stepped into the room closing the door behind her. Then slipping out of her dressing gown, she got in beside Tristan. He wasn't asleep but was lying there with his eyes closed.

Opening them, he saw Marjorie climbing in beside him and he opened his arms to receive her. They didn't speak. They lay there in each other's arms and nothing else in the world existed. Marjorie didn't feel at all wicked or evil, she simply felt as though she'd come home, where she belonged.

30

Marjorie woke to the sound of the curtains being pulled. As she stirred herself awake she saw Tristan standing by the end of the bed smiling down at her. She smiled back and then, with a start, checked her watch.

'It's ok, darling, it isn't eight o'clock yet and I doubt if there are many people up. I've been awake since seven, but I didn't want to wake you, you looked so peaceful.' Tristan moved over to sit on the bed beside her. Stroking her hair gently, he lay down beside her. Sleepily, she stretched out her arms to hold him. 'Is it all right to tell you last night was the best night of my life?' he whispered. 'I hope it was for you too, my darling, I hope you never regret it.'

'I never will,' she replied, and he pulled the bedclothes over them.

When they went downstairs an hour and a half later, Marjorie thought everyone would recognise that she was different, but no one seemed to notice. Giselle was in the kitchen making coffee. Dressed in a midnight blue velvet dressing gown and with her hair tied back, she was taking bread out of the oven. 'It's yesterday's, I'm afraid, but I was very lucky to get it,' she explained. 'Tastes much better just out of the oven. Please help yourselves.'

Marjorie poured coffee for Tristan and herself and forced

herself to eat a bowl of cornflakes.

'We really weren't expecting breakfast,' Tristan assured Giselle, 'but the coffee is very welcome. Are you staying on here for a few days?'

'No, we're going home so Christopher can say goodbye to the children properly, then we'll come back here tomorrow so I can see him off when he leaves,' Giselle replied. Her voice was sad as she uttered the last sentence and Marjorie concentrated on buttering her toast so as not to cry herself.

'You know I'll be at the Admiralty if you need company at any time,' Marjorie managed to say.

'I do and I shall take you up on that,' Giselle replied and headed off upstairs to bring her husband a cup of coffee.

Tristan and Marjorie left shortly after ten and drove the ten minutes to Mayfair so that Marjorie could see the house. It was empty but Tristan had asked the housekeeper to turn the heating on for a few hours to warm it up. Marjorie was delighted to see that the Aga cooker in the kitchen was still on, and she quickly stood with her back to it to warm up.

Tristan took the opportunity to wrap her in his arms before pulling her into the nearest sitting-room where he directed her on to the sofa. 'I will remember last night for the rest of my life,' he said quietly as he nuzzled into her neck. 'You are the most gorgeous, warm and generous woman I could ever have asked for. When I'm lying in my horrible bunk on board ship, I will stare at your photograph and remember every detail.'

'Can we go upstairs and see which room will be our bedroom when we come to live here?' Marjorie asked.

'Well yes, of course we can,' Tristan agreed and took her by the hand.

There were two large front bedrooms which overlooked the square. One had been used for decades by his parents and the other was used mostly by guests.

'This is the one I would like,' Marjorie told him. 'I love that you can lie in bed and gaze at the sky,' she said, jumping on the bed and lying down. 'Yes, this is perfect,' she announced. 'Aren't you going to come and try it out?' she asked.

'I thought you'd never ask,' he laughed. 'Marjorie, if it was possible for me to find someone to marry us today, I would give anything to do just that. In my eyes, we are married already. I have never been closer to anyone in my life.'

'And in my heart, you are my husband.'

That day Tristan and Marjorie lived as though it would be their last time together. They stayed there until dusk when they both discovered they were hungry.

Sitting in the London pub they had sat in after they met and which Tristan knew served fish and chips, even on New Year's Day, they sat together by the fire. The atmosphere in the pub was optimistic. A new year heralded another year closer to peace being declared.

With a new intimacy between them, Marjorie felt as though Tristan was hers forever. Tristan didn't think it was possible to love Marjorie any more, but he felt as though he did. They had discovered a closeness nothing could take away.

When he left her home, he didn't know when he would be able to see her again. His ship sailed on Wednesday and as second in command he had to check every man on board. Marjorie didn't think she could bear the pain of saying goodbye to the man who meant everything in the world to her. So they agreed that he would ring her and he would write every day that he was away.

It was agonising having to watch him say goodbye to her parents. Her father held Tristan's hand in both of his as he left. Tristan looked into his eyes and said, 'Sir, your daughter is the most precious being in the world to me. Please look after her for me until I can come back and marry her.'

'You have my word,' her father said.

There was nothing more to say as Tristan turned to leave.

Marjorie felt as though her heart would break. As she lay awake, she thought of their last hours together. Nothing could take that away from her. She knew it was impossible for her to love any other man in the same way. What she couldn't deny to herself, was the feeling she had, deep in her soul, that she would never see him again.

Just two weeks later, Marjorie's father received a telephone call from the Admiralty to inform him that his daughter's fiancé had been fatally injured whilst on duty. The following morning, he read the following notice in The Times.

'On the tenth of January 1941, HMS Illustrious was attacked by dive bombers in the Mediterranean off the Italian island of Pantelleria. Captain Tristan Melville, younger son of the Earl of Hargrove, was fatally injured whilst trying to carry some injured sailors to safety. Commander Christopher Grieves described it as a selfless act of bravery by a man who looked out for everyone with little regard for his own safety. Captain Melville was to be married to Miss Marjorie Fitzpatrick, older daughter of Lieutenant Colonel Henry Fitzpatrick, on his next leave.'

It was his duty to give the news to his daughter. It was the most painful thing he had ever done as a father.

Marjorie had never known such grief as she experienced after Tristan's death. She lay in her room, unable to sleep or eat. The only person who could comfort her was Aunt Margaret.

A week later, she realised that she could not lie under her grief for ever. Tristan would never have wanted her to do that. She returned to the Admiralty where she continued to work for the duration of the war. During that time, she helped with designing weaponry for use on aircraft carriers. Her work on the guns of the aircraft carrier HMS Illustrious saved many lives.

She continued her friendship with Elsie, Joyce and Sadie, often spending Saturdays with them. She spent weekends with Giselle and her family in their home in the country.

She managed to purchase her painting of 'The Burmese Boy' that Tristan hadn't been able to see. Her mother was horrified when she brought it home. She thought it out of the question to hang a painting of a coloured person in her home, so it remained under Marjorie's bed until she would one day find a home of her own.

Her friend Nicolas survived after years of helping hundreds of prisoners to escape the Nazis through the French resistance. When the war was over, she visited him and his sister in Brittany. She spoke to them of Tristan, and Nicolas put his hand on his heart to show he understood her pain. She returned to Jersey just once to visit the friends she had made there.

Marjorie confessed to Elsie that she never felt totally alone, she felt Tristan's presence everywhere. She could never replace him and she never tried. She wore the locket he gave her with his photograph and a lock of his hair she had cut off when he was sleeping on their last day together. She never took it off.

Shortly after Tristan's death, Marjorie returned her engagement ring to the countess. She knew she was its only custodian and it belonged to the family. She heard that his brother, the doctor, married after the war and provided his father with an heir. She was invited to the christening but replied saying she was unable to attend.

She coped as best she could with her grief. She continued to work for the Admiralty for several years after the war. It was only when Giselle and Christopher relocated to Cornwall that she began to think it was time for her to move on.

She had loved the little flat the Admiralty had arranged for her close to Whitehall, but she knew it was time to move back in with her parents, who by now had moved from Sonning to a new home in Hampshire. They were both frail and Marjorie felt it was her duty to look after them. She resigned from the position she loved and moved in with them at the beginning of summer. From there she would apply for a teaching position as close to their home as she could find.

And thus, the most precious and meaningful chapter of her life ended and a new one began.

31

Marjorie's bedroom in Hampshire was not as large as the room she had in Sonning, but there was an alcove where she was able to put her desk. She spent her first week with her parents mostly applying for jobs in local schools. She was delighted when she received a letter from the headmistress of St Augusta's, a girl's school with an excellent reputation, inviting her to attend for interview the following week. It was just a half-hour drive from her parents' home which made it the most convenient of the schools she had applied for.

She chose a simple grey suit to wear for the interview which she wore with a plain, cream blouse. Since Tristan's death, she hadn't any interest in clothes, but Aunt Margaret had done her best to cajole her into buying feminine clothes for her work in the Admiralty. It was such a male-dominated world, she had felt better in plain suits and court shoes. Although she had some men friends, it didn't occur to her to think of any of them from a romantic point of view.

The headmistress of St Augusta's, Mrs Hardcastle, was a pleasant, no-nonsense kind of woman whom Marjorie rather liked. She had Marjorie's letter in front of her and after studying it for a moment or two she began to ask some questions. 'I note that you haven't actually taught since before the war. Do you think of that as a disadvantage?' she asked.

'No, Mrs Hardcastle, I don't. Language doesn't change, nor does English and of course I have been using both in my work for the Admiralty. Teaching is my vocation and I am anxious to return to it as soon as possible.'

'We have some very bright girls here, girls from families who believe their daughters should be taught in the same way as their sons,' Mrs Hardcastle explained, her glasses held in her hand as she concentrated on Marjorie's answers. 'We also have scholarship girls, selected for their intelligence and because we believe their education here will benefit them in later life. We pride ourselves on our exam results and quite a large number of our girls are going on to university. It's something we encourage, and I note you have a double first from Oxford. That should enable you to share your knowledge with them.'

'I should be delighted to,' Marjorie told her. 'It's something I feel quite strongly about. So many women with degrees were able to contribute to the war effort hugely through their education.'

Mrs Hardcastle smiled at her reply, making Marjorie realise she was much younger than she had previously imagined. 'My late husband often praised the women in his department for their amazing abilities. He was killed during a visit to the troops in France in 1944, but he was a great admirer of the women who worked behind the scenes.'

'I'm glad to hear that,' Marjorie replied, 'but very sorry to hear of your loss. I lost my fiancé at the beginning of the war; he was killed at sea.'

'Then we both understand the meaning of grief. I find

teaching a great way of working through it. You tend to concentrate so much on the girls, you forget about yourself. I'm glad we've had this conversation Miss Fitzpatrick and I am pleased to tell you that I shall be recommending you to the board of governors as our new language mistress.'

At that she stood up to shake Marjorie's hand. 'I hope you'll be very happy here. I have a feeling you will fit in very well.'

Marjorie drove home with the feeling that a huge weight had been lifted off her shoulders. The fact that she would be away from home during the day meant it would be a break away from her mother. They had an excellent housekeeper who would look after them while she was at school and all their meals would be taken care of. She would try and have Aunt Margaret to visit on Sundays as she was also becoming less able although she remained as good-humoured as ever.

She felt as though things were fitting into place very gradually and that was giving her great peace of mind. Even the fact that Mrs Hardcastle had also suffered a loss during the war gave her a feeling of comfort, that someone else understood.

Her father was delighted with Marjorie's news and decided it might be just the right time to open a rather good bottle of claret he had been saving. Her mother appeared less pleased, but that was something she was used to living with. Maeve, their new housekeeper, congratulated Marjorie and assured her she didn't need to bother her head about her parents, she would take good care of them. She had also made a steak and kidney pie for supper, so she told Marjorie to go and do whatever she needed to as she had all at hand.

Marjorie missed Mrs Harrison terribly, but it wouldn't

have been possible for her to travel, and sadly Marjorie's parents hadn't found a suitable home to retire to anywhere near Sonning. Her father assured her that the house would be hers when they passed on as she had given up such a lot to look after them. Daphne had her own very comfortable home with a large stable for her beloved horses, so would not need the family home.

Sitting in her room after supper having shared a glass of brandy with her father, one of his few pleasures, she sat at the desk which she had used to write to Tristan. She talked to him about her new position and how much she was looking forward to it. 'It's a different life to the one that we planned together,' she told him, 'but I know you are pleased for me.'

Marjorie found it comforting to talk to him in the silence of her room. She talked to him during the day in her head but it was here that she really felt close to him. She wished he had been in this house, that she could imagine him sitting with her father, enjoying a glass of brandy, but she could still conjure up those pictures in her mind. She simply couldn't imagine going on with her life without him with her. She could never have anyone replace him.

She lifted up the photograph she placed beside her bed each night, Tristan in his officer's uniform, his handsome face smiling at the camera. 'I was saying I love you, when I had it taken for you,' he told her when he saw her for their very last time together.

'I love you too Tristan,' she said, 'now and forever.' She placed it on her bedside table, the last thing she saw at night and the first thing she saw in the morning. Then she went and prepared herself for bed.

32

Marjorie and Claude

Marjorie settled into life in St Augusta's with surprising ease. The girls were just as Mrs Hardcastle had said, hard-working and keen to go to university. They were mostly girls from prosperous families, but the brightest of them all, a girl small in stature but large in intellect, was one of the scholarship girls. She reminded Marjorie of a little mouse, a pale face with freckles and mousy coloured hair, parted in the middle and tied back. She had, Marjorie noticed, amazing grey eyes, which were mostly unnoticed behind wire rimmed spectacles.

Marjorie found out from Mrs Hardcastle that her mother was a widow and worked in a shop to make ends meet. Deidre walked each day to pick up her little brother from primary school and looked after him until her mother came home from work. Her appetite for books was endless and she visited the library twice a week.

Marjorie had started bringing some of her books, which were now in packing cases, from her home, the ones she had read at the same age. She handed them to her discreetly, when she taught her for the final class of the day. Deidre blushed with pleasure each time she received them and Marjorie told her to keep them as there were plenty more at home.

'Thank you so much, Miss Fitzpatrick, my mother has

given me my father's old trunk to keep my books in.'

'What a lovely idea, that's a wonderful place for them,' Marjorie assured her.

'My mother says I'm just like my father as he read books all the time.'

'Well, he would be very proud of you. Now time for you to go and collect your brother. Good afternoon, Deidre.'

'Good afternoon, Miss Fitzpatrick,' and sticking her beret on top of her head she ran off.

Marjorie chose to correct homework in her classroom after the children had gone home. She enjoyed the solitude of an empty classroom and it was preferable to trying to do it at home in her father's study as her mother was more likely to interrupt. 'Honestly, Marjorie, I don't know why you have so much work to do at home. All those books, you will ruin your eyesight.'

Even though Marjorie's father assured her mother that her sight would not be affected, her mother seemed glad to have something to complain about.

That afternoon, just as Marjorie completed the third form's French homework, Mrs Hardcastle opened the door and asked if she might come in.

'I've had a letter from the headmistress of a school in Rouen asking if we might like to take some of our fifth formers over for a week. They can stay at some of her pupils' homes or in a small *pension* close to the school. I wondered if you might agree and we could do the same thing for them next year. It means you'll miss out on your time off for half term, but I'm sure we can manage a couple of days off in lieu.'

Marjorie thought it would be a splendid idea and she was perfectly happy to arrange the trip.

And so, in February of the following year, Marjorie set off with fifteen pupils, aged between fifteen and sixteen. She had been invited to stay in the home of the English mistress, Claudette Gilbert.

Mademoiselle Gilbert turned out to be an utterly charming lady, twelve years younger than Marjorie. Although from the outside it looked as though they might have nothing in common, they found that they got on incredibly well, spending hours chatting in a mixture of French and English on every subject under the sun. Claude, as she preferred to be called, had the same regard for her pupils as Marjorie had, and although the French girls did not have the same affluence as the English girls, they got on remarkably well.

During the day they met in the school and were encouraged to speak each other's language. At night they gathered in one of the classrooms where they listened to music and danced. The went to the local cinema one evening and had lots of giggles after, wondering if the English girls had understood any of Elvis Presley's dubbed French lyrics.

The night before the English visitors flew home, they went to a French restaurant in Rouen where the English girls were told they had to order their meals in French and the French girls were eager to assist their new friends. Claude and Marjorie found a table for two in the corner where they could hear themselves speak but keep a discreet eye on the girls.

They both had a keen desire to travel, Claude being particularly keen to see Ireland. This suited Marjorie as she had always been fascinated by her Irish connections. She knew there were cousins of her father's living in Dublin. So Marjorie and Claude promised each other that they would travel to Ireland together when the time was right. It was the first time since she worked in the munitions factory that Marjorie had felt close to anyone.

Claude was gregarious, petite and always impeccably dressed. Marjorie was thoughtful, tall in stature and dressed in clothes she regarded as both sensible and in keeping with her position. She was uncomfortable wearing trousers whereas Claude wore her high waisted narrow pants with flat healed, ballerina type shoes. Marjorie's hair, with the first signs of grey, was permed three times a year and set in a severe style behind her ears. Claude's rich, black hair was worn up in a chignon for school and down on her shoulders at night.

The girls seemed to be genuinely sad to say goodbye to each other and although Marjorie was relieved to get them safely home in one piece, she, too, felt sad leaving behind her new friendship. But they had agreed to write to each other and perhaps make the odd phone call.

Marjorie had the weekend to attend to her laundry and prepare herself for the following week. Maeve had looked after her parents so well that Marjorie felt she could safely go away for a few days whenever she needed a break.

Marjorie loved walking round Reading on a Saturday afternoon after she attended to her parents' needs. One afternoon she passed by a street she hadn't been on before. She noticed people coming out from what appeared to be some kind of walled yard. Reaching the gates she looked in and saw five white ambulances parked beside each other. She knew they had nothing to do with the Royal Berkshire Hospital which was several miles away.

Curious, she walked towards them and realised they were the kind of ambulances which were driven round the streets during the war. The back doors were open and as she looked in, an idea sprang into her head. She looked round to see if there was anyone looking after them. She caught the eye of a man who was in the process of putting a SOLD sign on the windscreen of one of the ambulances.

'Can I help you, darlin?' he asked with a look that said, 'I know I can't.'

'Yes indeed, are you selling these vehicles?'

'That's the idea,' he replied with a grin, 'but what on earth would a lady like yourself want with one of them? Sam's the name, by the way.'

'You'd be surprised,' she told him, looking at him with her steely gaze. 'I'd like to convert it.'

'Convert it to what?' he asked.

'A motorised caravan,' she laughed. 'Bed here, sink here, store cupboard there. All I need is a good carpenter.'

'And I know the very man,' was the reply.

Having agreed that day to a price that suited them both, Marjorie promised to come back the following week with drawings and her specification. If the conversion was finished in time, Marjorie's hope was to take that trip to Ireland she and Claude had talked about.

She wrote to Claude that night, explaining what she hoped to do and inviting her to come with her. She didn't think either of them would enjoy camping as such, but the camper-van would allow them to go where they liked and stay wherever the notion took them. She was excited at the very thought of it and prayed that Claude would also love the idea.

She did! Just three days later she received confirmation that Claude would be delighted to come with her.

True to his word, Sam found a master carpenter and by the beginning of June, Marjorie inspected the conversion and pronounced it even better than she had ever imagined it. The table, which sat between two upholstered benches, folded away to enable the benches to convert to twin beds at night. The draining-board beside the sink flipped over to become a preparation area for food. A two-burner primus stove tucked away under the sink beside a large container to hold water for cooking and washing up. Every single bit of available space was used for storage. Marjorie could not have been more delighted and even Sam had to admit it was 'bleeding marvellous'.

Marjorie spent her weekends storing sheets and blankets, towels and saucepans into their places. Her mother, of course, thought it the most ridiculous idea she had ever heard of and demanded that Marjorie keep 'that van' round the back of the house so no one would see it. The van had been sprayed white and two windows had been set into the back of the van. The driver and passenger cabin opened straight into the rear with a curtain that could be pulled across at night.

Marjorie reckoned she was as excited as a small child at Christmas as she prepared her road trip. On the first of July, in what was one of the warmest summers of the 1950s, she drove to the airport to pick up Claude before setting off for the ferry to Dublin.

Their journey had begun.

Marjorie's father had written to his cousins in the South of Ireland to inform them of Marjorie's arrival. Back then Marjorie had taken to wearing trousers, a bit of a surprise for her much more elegant cousins all of whom lived in large, fashionable mansions around both Dublin and Cork. To her disappointment, she felt no affinity with them at all. They were strangers to her, and although they were kind and hospitable, they seemed to lead different lives in comparison to the world she inhabited.

She was much more comfortable in the city of Cork where she met Rose, an elderly cousin of her father's. Although Rose was not nearly as well off as the Dublin cousins, her welcome was much warmer and her homemade scones absolutely delicious. Marjorie and Claude felt quite emotional when they said their goodbyes. As she was in her nineties, it was unlikely that Rose would see them again.

The most enjoyable part of the holiday was when they sat at night, close to beaches and rivers, drinking wine and eating local bread and cheeses. They would discuss their childhoods, their student days and the hopes and aspirations for their adult selves. They were so relaxed in each other's company that Marjorie felt she could confide in Claude without any fear of not being understood. One thing though that Marjorie simply couldn't discuss, was her love affair with Tristan. One day she knew she would tell Claude, but for now she still kept it as her closely guarded secret.

After enjoying their travels round the Lakes of Killarney,

the amazing Ring of Kerry and the majestic Cliffs of Moher, they decided to head towards the Mourne Mountains and finally the famous coastal drive on the North Antrim Coast before taking the ferry from Larne to Stranraer. It was there, one glorious night as they parked in a place called Whiterocks, that they looked down on a tiny hamlet where a row of houses looked out over the bay. Marjorie told Claude that that was the kind of place she'd like to live when she retired. It seemed like a dream that night, with the moon reflected on the water and a million stars in a perfectly clear sky.

It was just two days later that Marjorie discovered, on a trip to Bushmills to purchase fresh fruit and vegetables, that the bay was known as Portbradden. When they saw one of the cottages up for sale in the window of the only estate agency, Margaret could hardly believe her luck. Claude was convinced it was simply meant to be and when they drove out that afternoon, down the steep road leading to the bay until they parked outside the house which didn't even display a For Sale sign, Marjorie was convinced. She had never felt more excited or sure about anything else in her life.

'Honestly, Claude, I'm not sure right now how I'll be able to afford it, but I'm going to have a darned good try,' she declared.

Two days later, in the middle of August, as Marjorie rang home, she heard the news that her Aunt Margaret, her mother's youngest sister had passed away. She was instructed to come home right away.

With an incredibly sad heart, Marjorie began the process

of packing up the camper-van to return home. Her father had kindly made travel arrangements for Claude to return home by train and ferry. Claude had suggested she might stay for the funeral, but Marjorie felt they were not the circumstances she would want to introduce her friend to her family. She was sad that Claude would not have the opportunity to meet her dear Aunt Margaret, but even sadder that she had lost the one person in her life who fully understood her love of Tristan. The excitement of finding the house in Portbradden was set aside to be replaced by the grief of losing someone she cared for so deeply.

As they said their goodbyes at the train bound for Dover, Marjorie promised Claude that they would meet up again as soon as possible. The holiday they had both longed for had come to a sad and abrupt end. They both had tears in their eyes as the train left the station. The only comfort Marjorie had was knowing how much stronger their friendship had become. For someone who had mostly lived a solitary life, the friendship was one of the greatest gifts she could have received.

33

Marjorie was grateful that by the time she arrived home in Hampshire, her father had made most of the funeral arrangements. She was surprised to find her mother quite distraught at having lost her sister. Although they argued a lot and agreed on little, Aunt Margaret had been her mother's only remaining sibling. She had been the one she had shared memories with of their childhood and the loss of their brothers who had died in the First World War. Margaret had also spent time in India and was familiar with her sister's friends at that time.

Now that the reality had hit home, that she had no one else in the world who shared those memories, Marjorie's mother made a sad figure, dressed in black and sitting beside a side table which displayed her family photographs. Marjorie longed to reach out to her, to comfort her, but felt unable to make physical contact with the woman who had never encouraged it. Instead she pulled a chair closer to her mother and held her hand. To her surprise, her mother did not withdraw it.

'We will all miss her terribly,' Marjorie said quietly, 'but you more than any of us; you knew her all her life.'

'We shared the same nursery, you know,' her mother replied tearfully. 'The boys had the bigger nursery next door, filled with toy soldiers and forts. Margaret and I had dolls and doll's prams. Margaret loved dressing and undressing those dolls, but they never appealed to me in the same way,' she whispered. 'I preferred the doll's house, moving and rearranging the furniture. Once Margaret was old enough, we shared the same bed.

'Margaret was always much braver than me. I used to get scared at night when there were strange noises coming from the attics or when there were storms that felt as though the roof might come off. Margaret always said we would be all right and put her arms round me. I've never forgotten that, you know,' she added, dabbing her eyes with her lace handkerchief.

Marjorie had never seen her mother so sad and vulnerable. She had been a distant figure in Marjorie's childhood, not comfortable with children and more attuned to her own needs, it had appeared.

'She was very good when I stayed with her during the school holidays. I never felt afraid of anything when Aunt Margaret was around, so I do understand what you mean,' Marjorie confided. 'What lovely memories we both shall have of her.'

To Marjorie's total surprise, her mother nodded and held her hand a little tighter.

The funeral was in the church that Aunt Margaret had attended for most of her adult life. A few of her neighbours arrived, followed by her housekeeper, the gardener and the cleaning lady. Some distant cousins arrived, none of them familiar to Marjorie but whom her mother seemed pleased to see. The local doctor came, accompanied by his wife and three ladies who had known Margaret from her wartime work. The service was simple and comforting, the words coming from a vicar who had known and respected the deceased well.

Marjorie's father had arranged for mourners to cross the road to the small, local hotel opposite the church. Although it was August, there had been a cool breeze in the burial ground beside the church. The sky was quite grey with the promise of rain as they gathered in the reception area where tea and coffee were served. Some of the men went into the adjoining bar where her father offered them something a little stronger.

Marjorie tried to support her mother and was grateful when the cousins suggested she sat down on one of the comfortable sofas where they joined her. Marjorie was familiar with all of her aunt's friends and neighbours and was grateful for the opportunity to meet them again. Just as she walked towards another group, a formal-looking gentleman introduced himself to her as Paul Archer, Margaret's solicitor.

'I'm delighted to meet you in person. Your aunt spoke often of you and I know she held you in very high esteem,' he told her. 'I will require you to come to my office along with your father who is executor of her will. I can't go into details right now, but I can tell you, you are the main beneficiary, along with your sister, of course. All will be disclosed when you come to my office. My sincere condolences to you my dear, you meant a great deal to your aunt,' and with that he bowed his head and left.

Daphne had taken time off, away from her horses, to attend her aunt's funeral and, in her own way, had been quite upset by her aunt's passing.

'Great that the old girl didn't suffer,' she told Marjorie, 'she wouldn't have wanted to hang around for long. Hope I go the same way.'

'I don't suppose we will have much choice in the matter,' Marjorie said, 'but yes, I'm very grateful she didn't have to go through a long illness. Her solicitor has just told me that you and I are the main beneficiaries of her will. I had never really thought about it, but I have to say I'm touched to say the least.'

'I say, that's a bit of a surprise. A very welcome one I can tell you, I've just made an offer on a few fields beside me, so the money will not go amiss. But in fairness, you were much closer to her, you spent time with her while I was always busy with the horses. You deserve it much more than me.'

Marjorie stood back a little to look at her sister more closely. They didn't talk much, she and Daphne. They didn't really have enough in common, so this is the closest she would get to a compliment from her sister.

They were joined at that moment by their father who said he felt it was time he took their mother home. Marjorie agreed and together they said goodbye to the last of the mourners before her father instructed his driver to wait outside.

Back home, Marjorie and Daphne sat with their parents in the drawing room discussing how well everything had gone.

'You bore up incredibly well, it can't have been easy for you,' Marjorie told her mother.

'One has one's duty to perform,' her mother replied. 'I'm relieved that it's over, but pleased that my sister was so highly regarded. Thank you, girls, for your support, I'm very grateful.'

Marjorie and Daphne exchanged surprised looks, but it was Daphne who replied.

'Least we could do. Delighted it went so splendidly. Now, I'm awfully sorry, but I really do have to get back. I never fully trust the grooms to settle the ponies for the night.'

Marjorie and her father sat together after her mother had retired for the night. Her father poured them both a glass of brandy before sitting down opposite his daughter.

'I take it Paul Archer told you that we have to go to his office to discuss the will? Daphne too, if she can spare the time.'

'Yes, he did. I was very surprised that she and I are to be the main beneficiaries,' she replied.

'Well, mostly you, I have to say. The house and contents have been left to you although Daphne has to choose anything she would particularly like. She has also been left a substantial amount of money and your aunt's car. There's money for you also and I will be happy to provide any advice you may need. Her jewellery will be divided between you girls and your mother. You meant a great deal to your aunt, Marjorie. She appreciated that you allowed her to be quite a large part of your life.'

Marjorie felt the tears rising from her eyes, listening to her father's words.

'Oh Father, I wish I had done more, but I'm so grateful she saw the camper-van and that I sent her postcards from places we visited in Ireland.'

'Yes, she told me you had, last time I spoke to her. She was enormously proud of your spirit and independence. She has left very generous amounts for everyone who took care of her, but you are going to have a very healthy bank balance when it's all sorted.' Then he asked, 'Have you thought of anything you might like to do with the money?'

'Well yes, there is something,' Marjorie told her father. 'You see, there's a house I would like to buy, a cottage in a tiny place called Portbradden on the North Antrim Coast of Ireland.'

34

The weeks seemed to drag as Marjorie went about her normal day-to-day business. By now, her father had given up teaching in the hospital. During his time back in England he had written and published two books on cataracts using his massive knowledge from his time in India. Now fully retired, he continued writing but he and Marjorie's mother were now depending even more on her.

Their housekeeper Maeve looked after them during the week but at the weekends Marjorie had to do all the cooking. Longing to be back in her dream house, she persuaded Maeve to move in over the Easter holidays to allow her to travel back to Portbradden. Meanwhile, she was busy preparing her pupils for their Christmas exams.

On Christmas Day they were joined for dinner by Daphne. It was hard for Marjorie to cover her resentment towards her sister who was able to live the life she had chosen with no particular regard for her parents. However, her good nature successfully overcame her less-than-Christian thoughts. Seeing her parents relax in front of the fire with their glasses of brandy compensated for any desire she felt to be alone.

Her father had mentioned several times his surprise at Marjorie choosing to buy a home in the North of Ireland rather than near Dublin, the place he had known as home. He had studied Medicine at Trinity before joining the Indian Army where he rose to the rank of Lieutenant Colonel. 'Marjorie dear,' he asked her time and time again, 'Why not reconsider? If you want to live near the sea, why not go to Killiney or Howth, if you must?'

'Father, if you would only come and see it for yourself, you would understand.'

'Well really, Marjorie, how do you expect us to travel to Ireland at our time of life? I do think it's rather selfish,' her mother interrupted.

Marjorie looked to her sister for support, but all she got was her sister's hand outstretched. 'Pour me another brandy, old girl.'

Holding a knife in her hand as she sliced into the Christmas cake she had made herself in October, Marjorie conjured up a picture of her holding it up to her sister's neck, but instead smiled sweetly as she offered her a slice.

Despite the opposition, Marjorie spent the evenings of the last week in term shopping for food and other necessities to store in the camper-van in preparation for her trip away at Easter.

'Really, dear, I do think it's peculiar that you should go on sojourn before Holy Week. I don't even know how we'll get to church on Easter Sunday,' her mother told her as Marjorie folded the tea towels she had bought to take with her. She had also purchased pairs of Wellington boots for herself and Claude, hoping to make a start on the garden.

'Mother,' Marjorie replied, politely but firmly, 'Father managed to drive himself to and from the hospital in London for years. I really think he can still manage to drive the mile to the village. After all, you often go to play bridge during the week while I'm teaching. What's the difference?'

Her father's face did not appear from behind his copy of *The Times* during this conversation, but as her mother tutted, he lowered his newspaper and giving his wife a stern look said, 'Are you complaining about my driving?' winking at Marjorie before her mother had time to answer.

And so, on the Friday before Easter week Marjorie set off for Stranraer having picked up Claude from the railway station in London. Claude had also fallen into the unfortunate position of having to look after her parents, but her brother and sister had agreed to keep an eye on them while she was away. 'Really, Marjorie, it seems so unfair that it is we who have to take up this position whilst the rest of the family are able to do just as they wish.'

Marjorie smiled at her friend, realising that she had not spoken anything other than schoolgirl English since they last saw each other. As time went on they spoke a mixture of French and English, catching up on all their news and sharing their difficulties over the long journey through Scotland. The weather was beautiful and when they reached the sea, it filled them with anticipation for their first view of the Atlantic.

They arrived on board in time for dinner in the cafeteria of the Antrim Princess. The best choice they decided was the plaice and chips. Although it was in no way up to the standard of Claude's fine cooking, the early start that morning and the long drive had made them so tired and hungry, they ate every bit, even the slice of bread and butter which was served with it. Marjorie laughed out loud at

Claude's expression when she was served the slice of bread. 'Butter up, Claude. tomorrow we will have proper bread, but for now I intend to eat it all.'

As Marjorie drove down the ramp of the ferry and on to Irish soil, she felt a shudder of excitement at the prospect of almost two whole weeks in the place she thought of as heaven. She wasn't disappointed as they made their final stage of the journey from Ballintoy to Portbradden. The fields were full of new born lambs and the primroses grew everywhere in the hedgerows. It was just as Marjorie had imagined, even better because of the blue skies.

Finally turning left to the road which led to her house, she turned to Claude and said, 'Wasn't this worth waiting for?'

'*Mais oui*, a beautiful house in a beautiful place with my beautiful friend. What more could I ask for?'

They enjoyed a late supper of buttered fruit loaf and a pot of Earl Grey tea. The house was cold so they decided to light the fire in both rooms to circulate round the house to air it. Marjorie carried the electric heater she had purchased that week up to the bedroom. She switched on the immersion heater for her bath and once again was grateful for this modern convenience.

Claude meanwhile had brought in their suitcases and the box of newly washed towels Marjorie had brought. Then, placing the fire guards they had bought in Bushmills on their last visit, they switched off the lights and headed to bed.

Tomorrow Marjorie would start on the garden.

35

On Easter Sunday Marjorie and Claude drove to the church in Ballintoy for the morning service. It was easy for everyone to see them for the camper-van was still very much a novelty in the area. There wasn't a great deal of room in the car park, but Marjorie skilfully reversed into the corner which was slightly out of the way.

Claude was wearing a smart navy suit with a navy and white blouse, a navy hat which sat at an angle to her forehead and a small, navy clutch. Her hair was pulled into a chignon which sat at her neck. Navy shoes with a small heel completed the outfit.

Marjorie knew she could never compete with her friend for elegance, but she had made an effort with a grey flannel suit and white blouse. Her hat was a grey trilby circled at the crown with a strip of black leather and a small gathering of grey feathers at the side. Her hair, in its usual plaited style, was almost invisible under the hat. She carried a sensible black leather handbag and wore a pair of black brogue shoes.

As they walked into the tiny church every eye rose to look at them. With a small nod of acknowledgement, Marjorie sat down and took out her prayer book from her handbag. Claude, brought up as a Catholic, shrugged her shoulders as she hadn't the slightest idea what to do next. However, she took her friend's lead and followed her to the altar where they took communion, particularly relevant for them on Easter Sunday.

Shaking hands with the vicar after the service, Marjorie explained that for now they were only able to visit during school holidays but that sometime in the future she hoped to live in Portbradden permanently.

As a special treat Marjorie had booked the Beach Hotel in Portballintrae for lunch. Once again the car park was difficult, but she managed before making their way to the front entrance, and being shown to their table. After the lunch of vegetable broth, roast lamb and sherry trifle, they were invited to sit in the lounge to enjoy their coffee. Claude said the view certainly compensated for the total lack of flavour in the coffee. Marjorie smiled but had to agree. It was so nice to be somewhere else just for a while.

She noticed the appraising looks Claude received as gentlemen passed where they were sitting. It always amazed her that Claude would find herself, Marjorie, in any way attractive. Claude insisted that Marjorie's strong bone structure made her stand out in a crowd, but whilst she appreciated the compliment, she had not felt really attractive since Tristan died.

Marjorie drove home the long way, stopping off at Dunluce Castle to admire the amazing situation. She had learned the whole history of the castle, remembering the cook setting fire to the kitchen and the huge drop to their death the poor servants took. Marjorie and Claude vowed to come back soon to enjoy a picnic in the grounds. They couldn't remember a more beautiful Easter Sunday when every part of the coast was illuminated in sunshine. When the gardens were completed they would have time to enjoy the rich scenery around them. The Glens of Antrim was listed as a must for their next visit.

By the time they got home, there was a chill in the air and Marjorie pulled her comfy Aran sweater over her head after removing her jacket. Claude grabbed a cardigan from her room while Marjorie lit the fire in the drawing-room. As they sipped a glass of sherry later, they both agreed it would be an enormous wrench leaving this time but assured each other there were years ahead to enjoy it. Already they were thinking about Thursday when they had to sail back, but they agreed to make their last few days a time to remember. And they did.

On Monday morning Marjorie was standing in the middle of what she now referred to as her sea garden. The small area was covered in long grass with weeds coming up in abundance. She was deep in thought when she heard a voice behind her.

'Miss Fitzpatrick, I presume? I'd like to introduce myself. I'm one of your neighbours. Connell Auld is the name.'

Marjorie turned to see a kind and handsome face smiling at her. She recognised the man she and Claude had seen mowing the grass in his front garden.

'Marjorie, please. I'm delighted to meet you. Yours is the first house in the row?'

'Indeed it is. I've been here for a number of years now, but my main residence is in Holywood in County Down. I teach in Belfast, you see.'

'And I too am a teacher. Oh, and here is my friend Claude coming to meet you.'

Claude had come to tell Marjorie her coffee was ready, but after meeting Connell she suggested he join them. They made their way into the sitting-room where the fire was now burning brightly and the aroma of coffee was drifting in from the kitchen. Claude had brought a French style cafetière which she used on the ancient stove. As she busied herself producing another cup and saucer, Marjorie invited Connell to have a seat by the fire.

'Well, this is utterly charming,' he announced, looking around the room appraisingly. 'You have worked wonders as the house had sat empty for quite a while. It's delightful to see it lived in again.'

Marjorie was delighted to hear from Connell which flowers flourished best in the soil and where best to plant the shrubs that she hoped to purchase in the nursery they had passed on a drive round the countryside. Both she and Claude found him to be excellent company, an interesting man who had travelled quite extensively and shared many of their views on teaching. He was in Portbradden all of his free weekends and would be able to keep an eye on the garden when they were back home. Before he left, he invited them to his house for dinner, an invitation they readily accepted.

The weather remained bright, sometimes warm enough to sit outside, other times when they enjoyed cups of hot chocolate round the living-room fire. They had followed Connell's advice and bought bulbs and seeds in preparation for their summer trip. The gardens were taking shape and Connell promised to keep an eye on the yellow daisies she planted in the seaside garden. She was promised by the gardener she bought them off that they would grow effortlessly even in windy situations, as long as they got some sunshine. She had traced out the area for the paths in the back garden and was looking forward to arranging them.

On the Wednesday evening before they left, Connell cooked a superb dinner of roast pork cooked in cider, with fluffy potatoes and some early carrots. He confessed the months before they returned would not be the same without them, although he himself led a very busy life. He even had to conduct the wedding of a past pupil in the month of August in his little church. In between times he would occasionally have pupils from his school's Scripture Union for the weekend.

Still, he would look forward to seeing the lights in the cottage again.

After packing all their belongings into the back of the camper-van, Marjorie and Claude drove away from Portbradden in a much more thoughtful mood than when they had travelled there two weeks before. The ferry proved an uneventful voyage and they passed on the fish and chips this time, eating instead the lunch Claude had made the night before. The drive between Stranraer to London, although neither were anxious to say goodbye, was long and arduous.

When they reached the station where Claude would board the ferry from Dover to Calais, Marjorie unpacked Claude's luggage.

'Just remember, my dear friend,' Marjorie said as they embraced, 'this is not goodbye, it's *au revoir*.'

'I know, my darling, but I shall miss you so much.'

'And I you. Now, go quickly and buy your ticket. I'll write next week.'

And with that Claude was gone. She disappeared into the doorway of the station without turning to wave goodbye.

Marjorie put her foot on the clutch, went into reverse and, with tears running down her cheeks, made her way to Hampshire where her duty lay.

36

By the end of September the cottage at Portbradden was signed for, and Marjorie spent the next month arranging for furniture from Aunt Margaret's house to be packed and delivered to her new home.

At half term, Claude flew to London where Marjorie picked her up. Together they drove the camper-van full of her own personal bits and pieces, including the portrait of 'The Burmese Boy'. They took the ferry from Stranraer to Larne, stopping at Bushmills to collect the keys.

Marjorie couldn't believe the excitement she felt driving down the steep road from Ballintoy to Portbradden. This was the first place she had ever had that was totally her own. Turning the key in the front door and surveying what was to be her home, forced her to catch her breath and hold on to Claude.

It was October and although the sea was a startling blue, reflecting the cloudless sky, there was a nip in the air which led them to set the fire in the empty grate. They hauled in two old, well-worn leather chairs and set them on each side of the fireplace. The furniture had all been delivered, but with the exception of the beds and wardrobes, all of it had been stacked together in what Marjorie always referred to as the 'drawing-room.' It was what she was used to and so she pulled out the furniture needed for the sitting-room on the left-hand side of the cottage.

The removers had kindly left the circular dining table by the window and that is where it stayed until Marjorie's death many years later. Between them they arranged the dining-room chairs around it and, too tired to do anything else, they made a pot of tea and had some fresh wheaten bread from the bakery in Bushmills, spread with butter and home-made raspberry preserve. Marjorie retrieved the fruit cake she had made the previous weekend, carefully wrapped in greaseproof paper, and cut it into generous wedges.

The following morning, after sleeping as soon as their heads touched the pillows, Marjorie rose and immediately switched on the immersion heater for her bath. Then, whilst Claude was still asleep, she went to the kitchen and set the table for their breakfast. She was like a child with her first doll's house, pulling out a tablecloth and napkins and tenderly unpacking her aunt's favourite china.

On impulse she stepped barefoot out of the kitchen door and into the garden. The very last of the summer roses were still blooming and she picked the best of the pink blossoms and brought them inside. She found a milk jug and filled it with water before arranging the roses. She then gathered up the sticks from the previous night and set the fire, separating the ashes in the hearth.

With the fire glowing, the sun coming through the window lighting up the table, set with the china and the roses in the centre, Marjorie allowed a tear to land on her cheek. It was really the happiest she had felt in a very long time. Good things never really happened to Marjorie; she knew she wasn't

274

pretty and although she worked hard and her pupils achieved great results, she had never really had anything that was her very own. It was a long way from India where she was born, but looking out the window, she believed nowhere else could be so beautiful.

The bathroom felt freezing cold as she pulled her nightdress over her head, but the water was blissfully warm and she allowed herself to lie back and relax her body. Deep in thought, she was startled when she heard the tap on the bathroom door. 'Marjorie, I am so sorry, I have slept too long, but it was so cold outside and so warm in the bed that I did not allow myself to open my eyes. Are you all right, *ma chérie*?'

'Of course I am and you thoroughly deserved to rest. I will be out of here in five minutes. You may bathe whilst I make our breakfast.'

Ten minutes later, Marjorie was filling the kettle and trying her best to make the ancient gas cooker work. It was the first thing she would replace, she decided. There was still a considerable amount in the bank left over from the sale of her aunt's house. For now she made the best of the grill to make some toast and unpacked her silver spoons to put in the preserves she had brought with her.

When Claude arrived downstairs ten minutes later, she smiled broadly at the scene as she opened the door. The fire was burning brightly, the silver was glinting from the sun coming through the window and there was her beloved Marjorie with an apron tucked round her waist and an oversized brown teapot in her hand. Although they allowed themselves to enjoy a leisurely breakfast, they quickly washed the dishes after, before sorting out the furniture in the drawing-room.

Marjorie decided that she would paint the dining-room chairs, each one a different colour, and Claude suggested some stencils might make them even more unusual. By the end of the week, four chairs were painted in pink, blue, green and lilac. A chaise longue was pulled into the sitting-room and placed opposite the fireplace. Like the armchairs, it was also made of faded leather, but they dressed it with cushions and draped one of Aunt Margaret's painted silk shawls over the back.

'The Burmese Boy' took pride of place above the sitting-room fireplace. That is where Marjorie wanted it, so it would be the first thing she saw in the morning.

By the time Marjorie and Claude climbed back into the camper-van, they left behind a fully furnished house. The beds were made up, the curtains drawn and the fire set for their return.

Before they left, Marjorie took one last look in the drawing-room. She had almost copied her aunt's own room. There was an old but beautiful sofa, covered in a tapestry rug. Two matching chairs sat each side of the fireplace. The watercolours painted by her aunt stood out against the cream walls. The windows were dressed with rose velvet curtains and an armless nursing chair sat beside the book case. Marjorie was reminded of the lovely holidays she spent with her aunt and the kindness she experienced from the woman who was more than just her aunt.

Those memories were swept aside as Claude stepped in

behind her. '*Mon amie*, I hope you will have many, many happy years in this wonderful place.'

'With you here too,' Marjorie assured her. 'This is for both of us.'

Marjorie took one last look behind her before firmly closing the door.

37

The following two months seemed to be the longest ever. Marjorie dutifully took her mother shopping, drove her father to his club and arranged their meals with Maeve who, once again, had agreed to stay for two months in the summer. This didn't please her mother even though she had to admit the girl was a wonderful cook and looked after them well. Her father was more sympathetic and urged Marjorie to enjoy herself while she could.

In school, preparations were on for the end-of-year exams. Marjorie often sat up very late marking papers and writing suggestions for her pupils to take up. Her results were always good, perhaps because she tried to encourage the girls to do their very best and to appreciate the freedom education would give them.

It was a different world to the world she came from but girls were still being advised to make good marriages and become mothers. For some of them Marjorie knew that would be their outcome but for some of them going on to Oxford or Cambridge, Durham or Bristol Universities, the world was their oyster. They could marry a little later, but many could hold down good jobs and still have families. It hadn't happened that way for her, but she knew it was right for many of them.

It was still the most delightful feeling to turn the lock in her school study. With a spring in her step she headed home to start packing.

Marjorie decided that this year, instead of driving the camper-van she would drive her new estate car to Portbradden. It would be easier to park around Bushmills, but still have plenty of room for peat and wood and, of course, gardening supplies. Both she and Claude had packed their summer clothes this time as the weather forecast told them they were in for a long, hot summer.

When they eventually arrived in Bushmills, they were told that the pilots flying in and out of Ireland referred to it as the 'Spanish run'. Her father assured Marjorie when she rang home that the summer was pleasant but not particularly hot. The girls couldn't believe their luck when they arrived at the cottage to find it really warm inside. The garden had started to blossom and it was obvious Connell had done more than keep an eye on it.

The days quickly formed a pattern. Every morning started with work in the back garden and afternoons saw some planting, watering and nurturing the plants and bushes in the seaside garden. Connell helped enormously with his labour, pushing his wheelbarrow to an area he knew was safe to dump the weeds. Marjorie had worked out a series of paths which zigzagged horizontally round the steep back garden. She had taught herself how to make cement and then imbed the stones she had collected laboriously over the weeks.

The result was very pleasing to the eye and all three of them agreed it was a labour of love which deserved awards. These came in the form of glasses of white wine, French of course, which they carried out to the seaside garden on the evenings the weather permitted. Other evenings they sat in the drawing-room of the cottage gazing out to sea at the ever-changing landscape.

Each weekend they took it in turns to cook dinner, Connell one week and Claude the next. On the evenings in Connell's, Marjorie and Claude held each other up as they made their way back. Connell insisted on brandy or whiskey after dinner and Marjorie, unused to such large measures, became so relaxed she found it impossible to walk in a straight line afterwards.

They found out a lot about each other on these evenings. They learnt that Connell's ambition was to buy back Clanbrassil House where he had been brought up. Whilst he owned a perfectly nice bungalow in Holywood, left to him by his parents, he much preferred the grandeur of his childhood home. He also learnt the history of all the big houses in Holywood and had prepared a sketchbook full of his own drawings of them.

Marjorie also shared her story of her life in India, how she and her sister Daphne used to hide on the landing with their Amah while guests arrived for dinner. They were fascinated by all of it, the evening dresses encrusted with beads and sequins and the hairstyles where the hair was gathered up with ostrich feathers caught inside the French pleats. The men were incredibly smart, some of them in military jackets of scarlet and navy, some all in white and some in black tails.

She explained to Connell and Claude how the staff in the house had worked endlessly preparing the table, arranging flowers and the delicacies prepared in the kitchen. Cook always made sure there was some dessert left aside for the girls which the Amah brought up to their room after the guests had retired for dinner. Sometimes, when they visited their mother for afternoon tea, some of the leftover cake was given to them as a special treat. Their mother always wore long dresses in cool cottons and linens and held a lace-trimmed parasol over her head.

On very hot days, a marquee was set up on the lawn where her mother, and any guests who called, would sit on gilt-edged sofas and chairs which were kept for the occasion. On the afternoons their mother visited friends, Cook would prepare a picnic for the girls which was served on a large rug on the lawn. Although it meant they didn't see their mother, they really enjoyed feeling quite grown up.

Most of the army personnel who came to see their father on the days he was not at the hospital arrived on horseback. Daphne was a great deal more interested in the horses than she was in the riders. When her father presented her with her own pony, she began her lifelong commitment to all things equine. Marjorie instead spent long hours with her tutor learning languages which also set her path for life.

One night when Claude and Marjorie returned home to the cottage and lay on the beds with the window open and the curtains not pulled, Claude begged Marjorie to tell her more about her life in India which seemed so glamorous compared to her own in a small town in France. It ended with Marjorie shedding a tear, thinking again of the woman who was really her mother for the first thirteen years of her life. Marjorie never saw her again. She couldn't even write to her as the poor woman had never been taught to read or write.

Claude held Marjorie's hand and said, 'Oh *ma chérie*, it wasn't right to treat a child that way. She should have come with you.'

Marjorie assured her that could never have happened for, as soon as they had settled in, she and Daphne were sent to a boarding-school for the next five years of their lives.

As the end of August was fast approaching, Marjorie and Claude became quite melancholy at the thought of leaving what had become for both of them their dream home. They tried hard not to think about it, but at the same time they were preparing the cottage for winter. Mothballs were placed amongst the bedding and among the few clothes they had decided to leave there.

As Marjorie stood in the door of the drawing-room, she wondered what it would have been like at Christmas. She imagined where she would have put the tree and how she would have brought in armfuls of holly from the garden. She knew, however, it would be some time before this could ever happen. She needed to spend Christmas with her parents, they depended on her to provide for them. Half terms were too short in the winter, so realistically it would be Easter before they would be back.

In February Marjorie was planning to fly to Paris where she and Claude could spend a few days together. In October she would drive her parents to Brighton so they could meet up with some old friends from India. So for now she would focus on Easter, when they would have two weeks together in the cottage. Less than a term later they would be back for another blissful summer.

With that thought in mind, she pulled the curtains closed for the last time that year.

38

S itting outside the station waiting for Claude, Marjorie
turned round to assure herself there was plenty of space
for Claude's suitcase. Having seen that there was, she turned
back in time to see her friend emerge from the station just in
time for her to get out to greet her. They embraced tightly,
each one knowing that the time they had both dreamt of had
at last arrived.

Standing back to look at her friend, Marjorie quickly noted
that there was something a little different about her. While
her smile was warm, there was something dull about her eyes.

'*Mon amie*, it is always so good to be with you again, but
please, there is no room in the back of your car,' Claude
remarked, having stood back and looked towards the boot.

'Don't worry, I have left you plenty of room on the back
seat. Now give me your suitcase and I will sort it for you.'
Marjorie smiled, ushering her friend into the passenger seat.
'I thought it would be a good idea to bring some of Aunt
Margaret's bits and pieces to make the cottage more personal.
I'm sure you will like them.'

Selecting the gear and releasing the handbrake, Marjorie
steered the car into the traffic.

In half an hour they had left the city behind and were
headed for Scotland. They chatted about their respective

schools, how the exams were going and how their families were getting on. Claude explained, with a pained expression, that her father had had a stroke just over a week ago. He was at home but now her mother was having to look after him.

'He can no longer walk with the right side, if you understand, so he has to drag his foot along the floor, so now Maman has to walk with him everywhere, even to the *toilette*. I felt very bad about leaving them but my sister has promised to be there every day until I come back, and my brother also.'

Marjorie looked lovingly at her friend, understanding now the pain in her eyes she had noticed earlier. 'Well, then, we shall just have to make the best of it and of course you must telephone often from the post office in Bushmills, as often as you like,' she smiled encouragingly.

Claude acknowledged her friend's smile with a nod before turning her head to look out the window.

They stopped at the little restaurant they preferred, just over the border to Scotland. Claude insisted she wasn't very hungry but was persuaded to have a sandwich with her tea. Marjorie's mood had dropped just a little, recognising her friend's sadness. This was not how they had planned it, but they would jolly well have to make the most of it.

Claude was trying her best to be cheerful but it was only when Marjorie explained the surprise she had arranged for her that she cheered up a little. 'Ah, this is the hotel we always wondered about when we walked past it. Having lunch there will be *magnifique*.'

Marjorie assured her that they would have a very easy time once they had removed everything from the back of the car.

'You can really relax, feet up, reading a book or just gazing out to sea.'

'Oh *mon amie*, I think this is the medicine I need,' Claude replied with a happy smile.

The crossing was uneventful and the traffic coming off the boat was not quite as bad as she had imagined it would be. The journey to Larne was pleasant, only a short shower marring an almost perfect day.

When they arrived at the cottage they were amazed to see smoke coming out of the chimney. Inside the fire was burning brightly and the smell of peat was so welcoming. Although it was not cold outside, the cottage had not yet warmed up so the fire was a delightful surprise.

On the table was a note propped up against a bottle of Cote du Rhône. It read:

> *Welcome, ladies. Hope you had a good journey. I took
> the liberty of lighting the fire to provide you with
> warmth as it's not quite summer yet. Have a good
> night's sleep and I'll see you in the morning. Connell*

'Oh how kind of him,' Marjorie said after reading the note out loud. Why don't we just bring our suitcases in from the car and leave the rest for tomorrow? I'll make us a light supper and we can enjoy the wine in front of the fire.'

An hour later, with hot water bottles in the bed to air and warm it, they sat down to a splendid supper of fresh bread, duck terrine made by Maeve, a generous slice of brie and a bowl of grapes served on the table close to the fire.

The two friends relaxed with a glass of wine. Although

Claude no longer had the look of sadness in her eyes, she remained slightly on edge as though something was still troubling her. Marjorie spoke gently to her, then her intuition told her that Claude had something she needed to get off her chest. 'Do you want to tell me about it, Claude? I know there is something troubling you.'

'You know me too well, *ma chérie*, and you are right. I have something to tell you that I have never spoken of before. Always we have been honest with each other, but you see I carry a secret with me in my heart.' Claude's beautiful eyes filled with tears and she dabbed then away with the handkerchief she took from her pocket.

'My dearest girl, you must know there is nothing you cannot tell me, nothing at all.' Marjorie held her hand over the hand Claude rested on the table.

'I suppose the best way I can tell you is to go way back when I was just sixteen years old. That summer a family came to stay in our village. They were Italian relatives of our neighbours, and they had come to stay so that their children could learn to speak French. The girl was my age and her brother Angelo was one year older. The friends arranged a big Sunday lunch which we all love to do and so we were four families altogether. The Italian mother and father already spoke very good French, the boy was also quite good but the girl had to try hard.

'Maman suggested that I should ask Isabella to come with me when I went out each day so I could speak to her and help her improve her French. So I took her with me into the village and into the shops so I could help her with the names. Her brother Angelo also came with her sometimes but he already spoke French quite well. He said he wanted to speak it better and he liked to listen to my accent.'

Realising this was going to take some time, Marjorie threw some more peat on the fire and poured more wine into their glasses. She couldn't imagine what Claude was going to tell her, so she encouraged her friend to take her time and carry on.

Claude continued, 'Well, after a while Isabella started playing more with my sister as she was young for her age and perhaps back then I was a little bit older. Angelo continued to come to my house each day and I would walk with him to the lake outside of the village or to the forest when the days were very hot. We became more than friends, we were boyfriend and girlfriend. I was very flattered because he was older and very Italian, very good-looking. His skin was much darker than mine and his eyes were almost the colour of his hair.

'Every morning I would look at myself in the mirror wondering why he found me so pretty. "You are *bella, bella*," he would say and then he would put his arm round my waist. Papa was not too pleased, he said we were seeing too much of one another, but Maman, she would laugh and say, "Pierre, are you too old to remember what it was like to be young?"'

Claude's face had lit up as she remembered all the details of that summer, almost like she was reliving them. '"Be careful, Claude," Maman would tell me when I was alone. "You don't need to spend all your time with Angelo. Just remember, after August he will go back to Milan."

'When August was half over, I became very sad. Angelo and I went everywhere together. At night we went to the cinema and sometimes we would sit in the café and drink milkshakes. He used to put money in the jukebox and play songs that were very romantic. Often we would just sit by the lake and talk about what we wanted to do after school. Angelo was already enrolled for university to study law. In one more year I would do my exams so I could study English, maybe in Paris.

'Then, on our last night together, we went to the lake. The moon was very bright and was reflected in the water. I started to cry because it was so beautiful and we would not be there again. Angelo, he cried too and then he kissed me very hard on my lips. I don't think, *mon amie*, that I need to tell you what happened next.'

Claude stopped, blew her nose and straightened her back. She took a long sip of her wine and steadied herself before continuing.

'So that year at Christmastime, I couldn't understand why my school uniform was feeling so tight. I wasn't eating any more, but all the time I get bigger. Maman saw this and she told me she was taking me to our doctor in the village. I was praying I wasn't going to be ill and miss my exams. After he examined me, the doctor and Maman went out while I got dressed. When she came in I could tell she was crying.

'"Maman, what is wrong, am I ill?" I asked her.

'"No, you are not ill, Claude, you are having a baby."

'I remember everything in the room was spinning. I held on to a chair to steady myself. "These things happen," the doctor told me. "Can you remember the date of your last period?" I could not, because they were never regular like my friends' but I knew Angelo and I had only made love once, on that night in August. It was so difficult to talk of this in front of Maman, but she said they needed to know. The doctor wrote in his notebook and then he told me, "Your baby will come in March, around Easter time."

'My mother was sobbing so hard and I could hardly see for my tears, but Maman hugged me and said we would work it all out.'

Once again Claude wiped her eyes and took another long sip of wine. Marjorie was exhausted for her, but although she herself was in shock, she needed to stay strong for Claude. 'Take your time, there is no need to hurry. This must be so difficult for you but please believe me, I know these things happen. I have taught in girls' schools for so many years and I know it does.'

'Thank you. I think perhaps that is enough for now. I can tell you that Maman was so marvellous. She told my father and she arranged for me to keep up my studies. That Easter I gave birth to a strong, healthy boy. I called him Philippe. I went to the hospital in a town far away from my village. Maman wrote and told the family of Angelo, but neither he nor his family wanted to know. His parents offered to send money, but my father refused it. Brigitte, a second cousin of my mother, who lived in Marseilles and whose husband Maurice was a lawyer, adopted the baby.

'I have never known such heartbreak as the day they came to collect him. I never stopped crying and even Papa would come into my room and tell me everything was going to be all right. Somehow or other, I don't know how, I passed my exams and the next year I went to university. Maman had cut a little piece of the baby's hair and she took photographs of him before her cousin came to take him away.'

She sighed again as she put her hands up to her neck. She pulled out a locket Marjorie had not seen before. 'From Maman,' Claude explained, opening it with her fingers to unfold two tiny photos of a new-born baby. In one he was sleeping, in the other he was looking up at the camera. Behind the glass of the sleeping boy was a tiny lock of dark hair.

'He's a lawyer now, practising in Marseilles. He's very handsome and very clever,' she added with pride in her voice. 'He's had a very good life and the year after he was born, my mother's cousin had a little girl even though she believed she could not have children. My mother hears every year at Easter time and now she has been told that Philippe is getting married in the summertime.

'I did the right thing, I believe. So you see Marjorie, I owe my mother so much. Now is the time I must be there for her to help with Papa. You know that I was married once after university. You know he was not a good man, he drank too much and when he drank he was cruel. When Maman saw how unhappy I was she brought me home and gave me back my room until I was able to afford somewhere of my own. I owe her so much.'

'Of course you do, my love,' Marjorie told her, putting her arms around her. 'I know you will do everything you can.'

'*Mais oui*, but I cannot spend the summer here as we planned. I had to tell you everything. Maybe for two weeks, but no longer,' she added.

Lying awake in the moonlight that night, Marjorie felt her sadness engulf her. Claude was asleep beside her, her breathing quiet and even. She had exhausted herself and now

290

she looked like a child with her pale skin and her dark hair hanging over her face.

Marjorie felt all her dreams were falling apart. Then she thought back to the war and the things she had put up with then. Right, she would make the best of it. If Claude could only manage two weeks, then she, Marjorie, would make sure it was the best two weeks ever.

With that thought, she too fell asleep.

39

Both Claude and Marjorie spent the next few days in the back garden. Because of the school holidays, thousands of people were driving up the North Antrim coast, many of them taking the road from Ballintoy down to Portbradden. Connell remarked how grateful they should be that there were no cafés or shops as they wouldn't be able to cope with the traffic.

As they worked, they reminisced over periods of their lives which had led them to follow their careers. Claude, they decided, was a 'nurturer' bringing out the best in her pupils who were timid of speaking another language in front of others. Marjorie was an 'encourager', bringing out the best in her star pupils. Coming from quite different backgrounds, they both admired what the other had.

Claude often had her friend laughing out loud at some of the things which happened to her when she was at University in Paris. It was so different from her own time at Oxford. She and her fellow students sat up late at night discussing literature and philosophy. Her only goal was to get a good degree and please her father. Her mother still believed education wasn't important for women. Often, when she listened to Claude, she wished she had dropped her reserve, but it simply wasn't in her nature.

By Wednesday the sun had returned and the day trippers had all gone home. Although neither of them spoke about it, they were both downhearted at the thought of packing the car the following day in preparation of an early start on Friday morning. They were already preparing the house for their absence. Marjorie felt sad that the idyllic summer they had planned was not going to be quite the same. Claude was thinking how difficult it would be living with her parents and missing Marjorie's company and the thought of how restricted her summer would be.

They were having dinner that night with Connell, and Marjorie had purchased a rather good bottle of brandy to thank Connell for all his help whilst Claude selected a French sauvignon blanc and a bottle of robust Beaujolais to eat with their dinner that evening. Their laundry had been completed, bar the gardening clothes Marjorie would wear in the morning.

Dressed in her pink outfit of pedal pushers and crisp cotton blouse, Claude sat at the table looking out to sea. She was going to miss the view but there would be many other things she would miss as well. The silence in the hall, with the exception of the steady ticktock of Aunt Margaret's grandfather clock, reminded her of how quiet it would be for Marjorie.

Within minutes Marjorie arrived downstairs, dressed in navy slacks and a pale blue polo neck she had bought, encouraged by Claude, at The White House department store in Portrush.

'Ah *chérie*, the colour is so perfect on you,' Claude remarked.

Murmuring her thanks, Marjorie found the bottle of brandy and headed for the door. She would never get used to compliments, Claude thought to herself, yet she was a woman who was beautiful on the inside and out.

Walking up the gravel path towards Connell's house, the front door opened wide and Connell stood, arms outstretched, to meet them. 'Ladies, come in, come in, the fire is lit and the gin awaits you.' He was dressed in his cream trousers, normally kept for cricket, with a blue striped shirt, and a cream sweater draped over his shoulders.

The fire was roaring up the chimney and on the sideboard, three glasses stood beside a bottle of gin and an ice bucket. Dropping a slice of lemon into their glasses, Connell reached a glass to each of them before raising his glass to toast them. 'Here's to both of you, I've enjoyed your company so much and here's to the three of us in the summer.'

'I will drink to that,' Claude replied 'and here's to you for all your kindness.'

'And I'll second that. Thanks awfully for all your hard work,' Marjorie added.

After dinner, which was a delicious boeuf Bourguignon, they sat round the fire discussing how kind the weather had been and how they hoped it would be an equally good summer.

'I jolly well hope so,' Connell assured them, 'I have rather a lot of visitors coming this year. If Claude can't make it in August, I should really appreciate your help at times,' he added, looking directly at Marjorie.

'Oh my dear Connell, I'm a useless cook, you really can't depend on me,' she added with a look of horror.

Connell gave a loud laugh. 'No no no, my dear lady, all I ask is a little of your time.'

'And I can recommend her as an excellent commis chef,' Claude laughed, 'and they are hard to find.'

Connell agreed and Marjorie wondered what kind of help he could possibly wish from her.

Walking back home in the moonlight, Claude and Marjorie linked arms and stood outside the cottage to admire the sky, before they went inside. 'I shall miss all this,' Claude whispered, 'the quietness and the tide. And of course the great big sky.'

Marjorie agreed, for although they both lived in the countryside, there was nothing quite like a night sky over sea.

'But I shall be back in June and really, it's not far away,' Claude assured her.

'Yes, we will appreciate it as it will make our time together more precious,' Marjorie added.

The fire in the living-room was still smoking just a little and Claude poked it enough to make room for two more lumps of turf. Marjorie poured them both a glass of whiskey from the decanter. 'We might as well drink this now, for tomorrow night we will need to be in bed early, ready to leave at seven-thirty in the morning.'

Claude took a sip as she threw her head back on the big, comfy armchair. 'You know, two weeks ago I was dreading having to tell you about Papa and the decision I had to make, but as usual, *mon amie*, you made it so easy for me by not judging me and just listening.'

'My darling Claude, there was nothing to judge. You were so young and you made the right decision for yourself and for your son.' Leaning forward to poke the fire, Marjorie gave her friend a gentle look. 'Does the boy know who his birth mother is?'

Claude took another long sip from her glass. 'Well, he knows of course that he is adopted and they told him his mother was a distant relative, but apparently he never asked. But now, it is a little different. He is getting married and he and his wife will want to have children. So now he asks my mother's cousin if it would be possible for him to meet me. I have agreed to that as he has the right to know that I am healthy and the reason I decided to have him adopted. In June, my mother and I will make the journey to Marseilles and he can meet me if that is his wish.'

There was a silence in the room disturbed only by sparks from the fire.

'I should imagine he will be very proud of you if he does decide to meet you,' Marjorie said. 'For you I imagine it might be a little more difficult, but you must also be curious to see what kind of young man he has turned out to be.'

'My mother has always passed on to me how he was doing in school, what sports he played and how tall he was, but never a photograph, so of course I will be always wondering. I have had my nieces and nephews to love,' she smiled, 'but I have been sad sometimes that I myself was never a mother. Do you not wonder, Marjorie?'

'I do sometimes. There was a time, though, when I really believed it might happen. Tonight you have shared with me the greatest secret of your life. Now I would like to share mine with you, Claude.

'You know that I worked in the Admiralty during the war.

It was there that I met the one and only love of my life. He was an officer in the Royal Navy, helping with the project I was working on, while he waited for his ship to be ready to sail. He was an engineer and had been at Oxford the same time as I was, although we had never met. He asked if he could walk me to the train station in the evening after I had finished work, and then, at the end of that week, he asked me to dinner. It was wartime, you must remember, a time when we grabbed whatever life threw at us and treasured it. He was very handsome, especially in his officer's uniform.'

Marjorie paused again and smiled at her friend. Claude was leaning forward in her chair, intently listening to everything Marjorie said.

'After we had dinner, he made it clear he wanted to spend all his spare time with me. I could hardly believe it, that he should choose me when he must have had his choice of women. When he invited me to the Navy Club, I wore the most beautiful dress I had ever owned, and Aunt Margaret had allowed me to borrow her jewellery. My mother insisted I wore her mink jacket. I had never ever believed I was beautiful, but that night, I felt as though I was. We had a wonderful night, we danced, drank champagne and he only had eyes for me. I believe it was that very night I discovered what it meant to be in love.

'We knew our time together was going to be short as his commander had told us the ship would be ready to sail soon after Christmas. It was then that Tristan asked me to marry him. His father was an earl and the family had a wonderful collection of jewellery. His mother, the countess, invited me to choose an engagement ring before they announced to their family and friends that we were to be married.'

Claude looked at her friend in amazement. It was obvious, by Marjorie's change of tone, that she was sharing something she had kept to herself for a very long time.

Marjorie continued: 'The night of our engagement was Christmas Eve. I wore another pretty dress and the ballroom of their house was lit up with Christmas trees and holly and mistletoe hanging from the chandeliers. My mother and father were there with Aunt Margaret and Daphne. The band were told to stop and the earl announced that we had become engaged. The champagne bottles popped and everyone in the room wished us well. I shall never forget the happiness in the room that night. My mother was positively animated with pleasure, her daughter marrying the son of an earl, even though he was the second son.'

Once more Marjorie paused, taking a sip of wine before continuing. Claude was both surprised and enthralled, listening to every word, not daring to interrupt.

'That Christmas was the happiest of my life, it was perfect really. We went for long walks, sat in little pubs in front of log fires, sipping whiskey and talking like I had never talked to anyone before. You see, Claude, I had never had a romance before, I was much too serious and studious and I really had no interest in men. Tristan changed all that. It was as though we were made for each other, we even finished each other's sentences.'

Again, Marjorie paused, gazing into the dying embers of the fire.

'When we learned that his ship was ready to sail, fear gripped me like I had never felt before. We were invited to his commander's London house to celebrate New Year's Eve. Giselle, the commander's wife, understood just what we were feeling. She arranged for us to stay the night in rooms on the top floor, next door to each other. Tristan was a true gentleman and led me to my room where he kissed me goodnight, then he retired to his room next door.

'I couldn't sleep, I tossed and turned, dreading the thought of saying goodbye to the man I had come to adore. When he tapped on my door, I welcomed him in and we lay together, planning our wedding for his next leave. His father had offered us a house in Mayfair to begin our married life. On New Year's Day, Tristan took me there and asked me to choose the room that was to be ours. It seemed perfectly natural to be together in that room and I have never, ever regretted it. We were man and wife for just a few hours. He left me home and that, Claude, was the last time I ever saw him.'

Marjorie rose from her chair and poured herself a glass of brandy, filling a glass for Claude. They drank silently, Marjorie gazing into the amber liquid as she told the last part of her story.

'He sailed a few days later, taking a photo of me that I had given him for Christmas, in a silver frame that Aunt Margaret had helped me to choose. He told me that he would wish me goodnight every night he was away and mine would be the face he woke up to. Four days later he was killed, trying to save some of his men from the fire of a German ship. The commander returned the photo to me, together with the letters I had written to him which he kept under his pillow.

'Tonight, Claude, I will show you the photos of me and

Tristan. They go everywhere with me and I don't know why I haven't told you before. I've been afraid to tell people as though it would break the spell of that wonderful short time we had together. Now that you have opened your heart to me, it has been a relief to tell you.'

As they settled down for the night, Marjorie took the photos from her drawer, wrapped in faded tissue paper and rolled inside a silk scarf she kept in her bedside drawer.

Claude gasped when she saw them both. 'Oh Marjorie, Tristan is a very handsome man, but you, my dear friend, were beautiful. Love shines from your face and oh, Marjorie, your hair, it was amazing. You look like a princess and Tristan was your prince.'

Taking the photo back from Claude, Marjorie gazed at the photo of Tristan, and Claude saw her face transformed. She wrapped her arms around her friend and they sat for a while just looking at the photos in their silver frames. Marjorie carefully wrapped them up, face to face, back in their tissue paper and the soft folds of the silk scarf. Marjorie felt so happy as she lay down to rest. She had shared her innermost secrets with the best friend she had ever had; there was nothing hidden between them, nothing they couldn't share.

Although she had her eyes closed, Claude lay awake for quite a while after the light was turned off. She thought again of everything Marjorie had told her. She thought about the photograph Marjorie had shown her, of her younger self, beautiful because she was loved. How tragic that the love affair they had ended in such a tragic way.

She wished she had been loved that way, but love had been

elusive in her life. She thought about Philippe's father, the love she imagined she had for him, but it wasn't real. She tried to imagine what her son must look like now he was a man. He was only sixteen years younger that she was; would he look like his father or would he look more like her family?

What if he asked about his father? What would she say? She had no desire to hear about Angelo, that part of her life was too painful, but he was a good-looking boy. Did her son know his father was Italian?

Her father's stroke had changed so many things for her and now another difficult time lay ahead. As she listened to her friend's steady breathing, she thought how blessed she was to have such an amazing woman as her closest friend.

With that happy thought, she fell asleep.

40

Back in Hampshire, Marjorie's father was delighted to see her. Drawing her into his study he confided that her mother had been particularly difficult in her absence.

'Well, Father, I don't imagine she missed me, she just hadn't anyone to complain to.'

Her father chuckled and had to reluctantly agree. 'I'm just not used to spending so much time with her. I do take refuge in my study but somehow she always finds me. Now how was Claude and how was the cottage? Sit down and tell me all about it.'

Marjorie explained about Claude's father and he thought it sounded good that he was recovering so well. 'A good sign,' he pointed out, 'is when patients regain their speech and mobility quickly. Means there's not too much damage.'

She told him about the garden and the new paths she was creating with cement and stones.

'But that's man's work, dear girl. Isn't there a gardener you could employ?'

'No, Father,' Marjorie laughed, 'there are somewhere, I'm sure, but it's very satisfying doing it myself.'

'You always were a strong-minded child,' he replied, smiling. 'Always very independent. Don't know where you got it from. Not me, I wasn't around much. I regret that now,' he added ruefully, 'you had an interesting mind.'

As she emptied her case, Marjorie thought over what her father said. She was immensely proud of her father and she knew the hope he had given to thousands of people in danger of losing their eyesight, but as a child he was a distant figure who appeared every now and then from the city to the hills where they lived away from the intense heat of Madras.

She was grateful they had had these years together in his retirement when she found he had such a pleasant sense of humour and found her mother just as trying as she did. She hoped Claude found her father in good spirits and that she would see a noticeable improvement.

After changing her clothes she went downstairs to join her parents for dinner.

In Rouen, Claude was exhausted, having had to go through two train journeys and two sea crossings in one day.

Her brother Thomas met her at the terminal in Calais and drove her the hundred miles to her village. On the journey where the traffic was thankfully light, he explained the progress her father had made, how he could practically climb upstairs on his own, taking his time while their mother walked behind.

'He was never ever going to sleep in a makeshift bed in the sitting-room,' Thomas explained. 'He was determined to sleep in his own bed in his own room. Much easier for Maman. He comes downstairs for his lunch and goes back to his bed around eight o'clock, which gives her some time on her own. She hates him in the kitchen when she's cooking, says he interferes too much.'

They both laughed remembering their mother cooking the big Sunday lunch, when their father would come in to remind her to put cinnamon in the torte and herbs with the lamb.

Their parents had the kind of marriage Claude would have loved, with mutual respect and a lot of love for one another. Her own marriage had been a disaster, with her husband Antonio drinking too much and then abusing her if she dared to say a word. When he didn't drink, he was courteous and polite, anxious for them to start a family of their own.

Claude was not going to have a child she would be forced to protect every time her husband drank too much wine, so one evening, when he was out drinking, she packed two suitcases and left. Her parents met her off the train and her mother had prepared her old room for her, just as she left it.

Thomas drove off home to his wife and children after he left Claude at her apartment. She left her suitcase on the bed, pulled out a warm cardigan and drove herself to her family home in the village.

Her mother was waiting for her, the smell of roast chicken with rosemary meeting her as she walked into the kitchen. 'Ah Claude, my little one,' her father cried, arms outstretched to embrace her. 'Let me see you, did the sea air help you? Yes I can see it did,' he said, releasing her and examining her face. 'Maman, what do you think. Is she looking better?'

'Papa, it is you I am worried about. How are you, are you much better?' Claude asked, standing back to look at her father.

'He must be,' her mother replied, 'he has been telling me how much garlic to use and how many sprigs of rosemary, like I had never cooked roast chicken before. Now, my child, sit down and enjoy your dinner before you tell us all about it. Papa is much better, stubborn as ever, but definitely getting better.'

Looking at her parents, Claude thought once again how lucky she was to come from such a loving family. As her mother opened the door of the range, the one she had cooked in since Claude was a baby, she realised that her mother was a little slower than she was but still doing everything she had always done.

Sitting at the end of the table, between her parents, Claude began to tell them all about the cottage and the garden, and of course about Marjorie.

41

After a good night's rest, Claude returned to her parents' home to see how she could help her mother. Her father was still in bed and after wishing him good morning, she was grateful to spend some time alone with her mother. The coffee was sitting on the stove and two large cups, a jug of milk, her mother's home-made raspberry jam and a plate of croissants sat on the table the family had sat around almost since she was born. It was such a comforting sight as she had felt so sad leaving Marjorie and Portbradden.

Claude's mother said, 'So, now you need to tell about Marjorie and your vacation. I know you were very downhearted when you left, but you see I was right. Papa is so much better.'

'Marjorie is very well and the weather was so good, I had a lovely time,' Claude replied, 'and Maman,' she paused to look at her mother, 'I told her about Philippe wanting to meet me. She understood, as I knew she would, but it was difficult to bring it all back again.'

'Of course it was, but Marjorie is a good person, a wonderful friend and she will give you the best advice,' her mother nodded, 'but soon we will have to decide if you are ready to meet him.'

Claude stared into her coffee, thinking back to how mixed

her emotions were when she first heard that her son wanted to meet her. 'I know, Maman, and I have thought about it ever since you received the letter. I am ready to meet him, but only with you. I cannot do it alone.'

'Well then, that is what we will do. When your father is a little stronger, I will ask your sister to come and stay here and we will take the train to Marseilles. We can go on a Friday night, stay in a little hotel there, meet Brigitte wherever she thinks is a good place and then Philippe can join us.'

'Thank you, Maman, that sounds perfect. Of course I am curious to see how the baby I gave birth to has turned out.'

'By all accounts he has been a very god boy,' her mother replied. 'As you know, I have only had an Easter card each year telling me he is well, but you and I agreed she would never have our interference and that is the way it has been. Now finish up your croissant and I will pour you some hot coffee so you can enjoy it while I help your Papa to get dressed.'

'But Maman, I came here to help you, let me come with you,' Claude replied, rising from her seat at the table.

'*Non, non*, Claude, your father is very private. He will dress himself and shave himself, but it is early days and I must be there just in case.'

Claude sat down again and tore open her croissant to reveal the soft pastry inside. She spread a little jam on the piece she had just pulled off and ate it ravenously, realising that she was in fact quite hungry. The coffee tasted just like it always did, her mother's own particular blend which she herself could never quite emulate. She had the whole month of May to help her mother and then in June she could travel to

Marseilles with her mother. This would mean she would have a lot to tell Marjorie when she travelled to Ireland in June or July. But first she would help her mother as much as she could.

Standing up to clear the table, she smiled when she heard her father whistle as he always did when he shaved. This had to be a very good sign. Turning the tap on to wash the dishes she whistled along with her father. Her mother was right, her father was much improved.

Just as she finished drying the dishes, she heard her mother and father coming down the stairs. Quickly drying her hands on the tea towel, she walked towards her mother who was standing almost at the bottom of the stairs. She was delighted to see her father manage to come down using only the handrail for assistance. As she reached the bottom step he called out to her, 'I hope that's a fresh pot of coffee on the stove,' and she reached out a cup from the dresser.

Sitting down at the table again, this time with both of her parents, Claude listened to her father, his voice strong as ever, tell her his plans for the vegetable garden. It was time to plant the tomatoes and if she could spare the time he would really appreciate her help in the greenhouse. Looking at her mother who mouthed it was ok, she told him she would love to help as it was years since she had handled tomato plants. Her father grew his plants from seed and it would make it easier if she simply put down the new compost.

Her heart had really lifted as she prepared to drive home later that afternoon. Although her father was noticeably slower than normal, he was able to give Claude very precise instructions for arranging the compost and his only concession to taking it easier was to transplant the new growth from their pots into the raised beds while sitting on his ancient stool. As they worked together, he warned her that she was not on any account to cancel any plans she had already made.

Whilst she would have loved to spend the long summer months in Ireland, she knew that her mother would still need her help. Neither of her parents were getting any younger and besides, she had promised her sister to give some extra coaching to her niece and nephew who were both studying English in school. She would go to Portbradden for most of the month of July but August would be time for her family. She would telephone Marjorie to let her know as soon as she got home.

In Hampshire, Marjorie was preparing some schoolwork for the sixth-formers. She had taken herself and her books into the conservatory which looked out over the quite expansive garden. The gardener had recently mowed the lawn and tended to the flower beds. She loved to work in the garden herself, so she promised herself that she would be out there as soon as she finished the work she was setting for her pupils.

The sun was shining brightly and she had to move to the side of the room where she had previously hung a huge embroidered parasol from India she had found in the attic. It provided just the right amount of shade needed when the sun was overhead. So involved was she in her books that she was surprised when Maeve shouted to her to tell her that lunch was ready.

Schoolwork all prepared, Marjorie headed to the boot

room at the back of the house where she changed her shoes and filled a basket with her gardening gloves, secateurs, small fork and spade. The gardener had made a great job of the flower beds but the raspberry canes and the strawberry beds needed a bit of loving care. It looked like they would have a good harvest this year as the gooseberry and blackberry bushes were looking healthy.

Scratching her arms on some thorns, Marjorie stood up to straighten her back and survey the work she had done. She decided to take a break and have a quick cup of tea before checking on the roses.

Her mother looked at her disapprovingly as Marjorie arrived, a little late and with the scratches on her arms quite obvious.

'Really, Marjorie, what on earth have you been doing? Don't we have a man to do that?' And without waiting for an answer she continued, 'And without a hat! You will destroy your skin.'

'We're not in India, dear, it's pleasantly warm outside but not at all hot,' her father intervened.

'It matters little,' his wife continued, 'a lady never goes out in the sun without a hat.'

Marjorie decided not to reply, she had learned it was best not to argue with her mother but she was pleased when her father gave her an understanding wink.

'The tea is Darjeeling, I'm sure I told that girl we preferred Earl Grey in the afternoon.' Her mother was off on another subject. 'And we could do with less butter on the fruit bread. So hard to get good staff in England.'

'Mother, I've told you a dozen times how fortunate we are

to have Maeve. Now, if I may be excused, I'd like to get back to the roses.'

And with that Marjorie headed back to the garden.

The rosebushes were in pretty good shape but she thought she must remember to tell Edward the gardener to order some manure from the neighbouring farmer. She noticed that Edward, too, was not getting any younger. None of them were and it was all a matter of doing the best one can, she thought to herself.

She had just bent down to remove some weeds that had grown between the bushes when she heard her father calling her from the door of the conservatory. 'Marjorie, telephone for you. It's Claude.'

Indicating that she was on the way, she quickly removed her shoes and gloves and rushed into the hall where Maeve was holding the telephone. Nodding her thanks, she took the receiver and sat down on the chair beside the telephone table. 'Claude, is everything all right?' She asked, slightly out of breath. 'Is it your father? Is he ok?'

Claude laughed, '*Mais oui, ma chérie*, everything is good. Papa is doing so well I can hardly believe it.'

Marjorie could hardly reply with relief. She let out a long sigh before replying, 'Well, that's jolly good news. I'm very happy for you.'

'Yes, I am happy too. He is washing and dressing himself and is just a little slower, but today we plant some tomatoes, he and I, and his head is perfect.'

Marjorie laughed now too. 'Such a relief for all of you.'

'Yes, it is great news and today he told me I must not cancel my plans. But I think I must a little. I think I will come for

July, but in August I think they will need me.'

'More good news,' Marjorie smiled, 'and you know, I have been thinking the same thing. My father needs me here too, he's finding my mother even more difficult and to be honest, I don't really like him driving any further than the village, so it is best if I am here for them in August also.'

When they finished their conversation, Marjorie went up to her bedroom. After changing from her gardening clothes, she put on her blue tweed skirt and one of her many cream blouses. Then she sat down at her dressing table to look in her diary.

They would have to make plans for their journey back to Ireland and it was going to be better than she had thought. They would be together in Portbradden for most of July and that was something they were both deeply grateful for. She would write to Claude after dinner with her suggestions. She would post it tomorrow on her way to school.

42

B ack at school, Marjorie threw herself into tutoring her pupils for the upcoming summer exams. This year over half of the upper sixth form were planning to go to university, three of them trying for Oxford. She gave every one of them the right kind of encouragement they needed to aim high in their education. Some of the others hoped to go into the Civil Service, others would go on to finishing school. Whichever path they wanted to take, she guided them as best she could. She was not always the most popular teacher in the school, but she was always well respected. Although she was, of course, a language teacher, she was also head of house and had an interest in every one of the pupils.

She introduced to her father three of the girls who were considering studying Medicine, and he delighted in quizzing their agile minds. She brought the three girls to her home for afternoon tea on a beautiful May Saturday. Maeve had gone out of her way to bake scones and cake and served her excellent cucumber sandwiches. Her father became quite animated when he explained how he came to study ophthalmology, but he urged them to find out what really interested them most. 'You'll know when you connect with the field of Medicine that's best for you.'

Seeing the girls respond so well to her father, she wondered if he missed having grandchildren of his own. She wished once again that life had been different, but she had never had the slightest interest in romance when she was their age, or even when she went to Oxford.

Eventually it was time to drive the girls back into town where their parents had agreed to meet them. They were quite excited in their conversation and she was grateful that her father had planted the right seeds to whet their appetite.

When Marjorie arrived back home, her mother, who had not joined them for tea but chose to have hers alone in the morning room, had obviously been peeping behind the curtains. She told Marjorie she had no idea how those girls were allowed to wear such clothes. 'Their skirts were disgustingly short and the tall one with the red hair should never have been allowed out in such tight trousers,' she complained. 'Parents these days are much too lenient. It would never have happened in our day, would it, Henry?' she asked as she looked at her husband.

'Unfortunately not, my dear, I hadn't seen a bare leg until I studied surgery. I think those girls were very serious-minded and never mind what they wore. They have good heads on young shoulders.'

His wife looked suitably unimpressed and excused herself to go and prepare for dinner.

Once again her father had surprised Marjorie and it made her quite sad. He had been so busy giving the people of Madras their sight back that he often didn't come home at all but slept in the hospital. When they came back from India he was too busy teaching his techniques to young medical students.

Daphne never minded; horses were her life from when she was eight or nine years of age. But books had been Marjorie's only solace. As she combed her hair before dinner, Marjorie wondered if her father had ever regretted not getting to know his daughters properly.

She had dutifully written to both her parents from boarding-school and received the replies from her mother. They were, Marjorie believed, very dull, talking only about flower arranging and bridge parties. She knew very little about her mother apart from the fact she had a very aristocratic upbringing where educating your daughters was frowned upon. She and her sister were encouraged to play the piano, embroider table cloths and, most importantly, make a good marriage. India had been perfect for her with servants to do everything for her.

Marjorie thought, thank God I escaped that and I have my father to thank for my education.

After dinner that night, she found herself writing about all of this to Claude. She told her about her interesting afternoon with her pupils which she knew Claude would understand.

She read again the letter she had received from Claude telling of her father's wonderful progress and how she was looking forward to, and dreading at the same time, her trip to Marseilles with her mother to meet her son for the first time since he was just one week old. Marjorie really couldn't begin to understand the emotions Claude must be feeling, but she was gratified when Claude told her she was getting through all of it by looking forward to spending time at Portbradden with her.

Once again, as she did so many times, Marjorie asked herself why Claude could find her, Marjorie, even slightly interesting. Claude, with her beauty and elegance, her sense of humour bordering sometimes on naughtiness, could have chosen a very different life, but she chose to spend her time with a companion who in comparison must seem very dull.

Opening her diary, she counted how many weeks before they would once again be together. Then, telling herself it wasn't long at all, she left her bedroom and climbed downstairs to join her parents.

43

Claude folded Marjorie's letter and placed it with the others in her dressing table drawer. The latest from her friend had made her feel so sad. Marjorie's life with her parents was very different from her own. She was fortunate to have her own apartment. Although it was small, she had a beautiful view over the lake. Outside on her balcony, she had a small, circular table where, on warm evenings, she would sit outside with a glass of wine or a cup of coffee, whichever she felt like.

Tonight she chose coffee and, for after, a glass of Pernod. She loved this time of night, not quite dark, not quite light. Later the moon would reflect on the stillness of the water. The lake was calming for her when she was worrying about anything but lately it held memories she didn't always choose to reflect upon. They had been more and more on her mind for it was beside the lake that she and Angelo bid their goodbyes, the night that resulted in the birth of their son.

As she grew older she no longer thought of it as a love affair. The feelings she had experienced that summer were more of enlightenment, the transition from girl to woman. For Angelo, she imagined, it had been a good way to spend a summer which might otherwise have been very boring.

She knew it wasn't love.

When she still believed it was, she had been devastated when Angelo didn't want to know about the baby. She was too young then to know the enormous happiness the baby had brought to the family who adopted him. It had all been legal and Claude knew what she was doing when she signed the forms of consent.

Feeling a breeze coming in from the lake, Claude cleared the table and went back inside. Once again she tried to imagine who her son would look like. Both she and Angelo had dark hair, both had similar colouring. Would Philippe look like a mixture of both of them?

In two weeks' time they would be coming face to face: Philippe the young lawyer about to marry his girlfriend of three years, beginning a new chapter in his life; and she, Claude, divorced, still living close to her childhood home, an English mistress in a local school. He would realise how fortunate he was that his mother had chosen to give him away. He had enjoyed a good education being brought up in a vibrant city in a very comfortable lifestyle.

She had made the right decision, she knew that.

The one thing she had control over was her appearance. She had bought herself a simple, but expensive, black and cream A line dress which came just to her knee. With it she would wear a silk scarf draped around her shoulders in shades of blue which she knew suited her. She would wear her cream coat over it with plain but elegant black high-heeled shoes. A smart black handbag completed the outfit which, she hoped, would be appropriate for a family lunch.

Family. She said it again. She and her mother were family, but she and her son were not.

Claude expressed all her fears to Marjorie when she replied to her letter. Marjorie of course had a very small family, none of them particularly close. She had noticed though how Marjorie referred more and more to her father; it was obvious they were becoming closer.

She thought of her own father who had worked for the same wine company for years. They gave him a gold watch when he left and held a dinner for him in one of the restaurants in town. He had been the manager when he left but he was always there at the head of the family table every night asking each of them how they had got on at school that day. He had driven her to and collected her from friends' houses and had done the same for her brother Thomas and her sisters Claire and Josephine.

Sometimes at night he would waltz her mother round the kitchen to the songs coming out from the radio. Her mother would tell him not to be so foolish, but then she would laugh and join in.

Claude hoped Philippe had a mother and father who were both there for him.

She folded the notepaper and put it in an envelope which she addressed and stamped. She would post it in the morning before school. She checked her calendar to see how many weeks it was before she would leave France, first for England and then the drive with Marjorie to Portbradden.

Climbing into bed she thought about their evenings together, talking about many things and watching the sun go down over the Atlantic Ocean. It was where she really felt free, away from all the worries of her past with a friend who never judged her. Marjorie was the kindest, most interesting person she had ever met and she was so blessed to have her in her life.

With that thought she switched off the light and drifted into sleep.

44

The day that Marjorie received Claude's latest letter, she sat in the garden of her parents' home, the letter in her pocket, wondering how the meeting between Claude and her son would go. It was Thursday, which meant that Claude and her mother would be making the journey to Marseilles tomorrow.

Marjorie tried to imagine what Philippe would look like. From what she knew, Angelo was tall and dark, Claude was slightly above average height, also with dark hair. She was sure the boy would indeed be very handsome. How would Claude feel when she saw him? She doubted that there would be strong maternal feelings for she had not seen him since he was a week old, but she was sure she would feel proud.

She heard the door open and Maeve's voice telling her dinner was ready. Another evening listening to her mother complaining, but she knew her being here helped her father enormously, so she put on her smile and went in to join them at dinner.

After asking to be excused, Marjorie made her way out of the house and into some outbuildings which had once been stables. It was where a lot of the furniture brought over from India was stored. Sometimes it was almost like revisiting her childhood home when she sat in there.

Lifting one of the dust sheets, she found the beautifully carved but ancient sideboard. She wondered how she could possibly transport it from here to Portbradden. Auntie Margaret's furniture had gone straight from storage by courier across channel. She was sure the same company could do this for her. Remembering that the sideboard had travelled safely from Madras to England, she was sure it would survive another journey.

Digging deeper she discovered the silver kettle and teapot with its stand containing the burner she remembered so well from her time in the hills above Madras. She remembered her beloved Amah brushing her hair and washing her face and hands. Her Amah would do the same for Daphne and then take the sisters by the hand to see their mother. They were seated together on a rattan couch with oversized cushions. One of the servants would place a small, carved table in front of them and then Mama would pour the tea into the small cups kept especially for them.

Often Mama had visitors and would talk to them, but when she was alone she questioned her daughters about their homework. It wasn't long before Marjorie realised that her mother knew very little about the girls' education. Papa had recently engaged a tutor to come three times a week to teach them basic science. Marjorie found herself looking forward to his lessons and before long she moved to a level way above her school age. Marjorie preferred it when Mama had visitors. This way they could eat as many sandwiches as they pleased and occasionally she even sneaked some of the cardamom biscuits and almond cake into the pockets of her pinafore.

Sitting now in an old stable in England, the things she was

looking at transported her back to all the memories she had cherished. Her Amah was the most important person in her world back then for it was she who woke her each morning and she who would tuck her into bed at night. When she felt ugly her Amah would stroke her beautiful hair and tell her how beautiful her eyes were. When she had a nightmare it was her Amah who jumped up from her mattress in an adjoining room to comfort her. When she cut her knees or grazed her elbows it was her Amah who applied the special ointment she mixed herself.

Leaving India it broke Marjorie's heart to wave goodbye to the only mother she had known. It would be perfect to have this furniture from the happy part of her childhood, in the drawing-room of the cottage in Portbradden.

That night as her father prepared to go to bed, Marjorie asked his permission to take it.

'Of course you may, take anything you want, for I doubt anyone else would want them.'

The following day she rang the removal company to ask if they could take the sideboard and a few more pieces to Portbradden for her. They assured her they could as they were doing a run to Belfast at the end of the first week in July. Nothing could have pleased Marjorie more as she and Claude would be there to receive it.

As she replaced the telephone receiver she allowed her mind to travel to the cottage and all that it meant to her. She almost forgot for just a few minutes that today was the beginning of Claude's new chapter of her life.

Offering up a silent prayer, she climbed the stairs to her room.

45

Claude looked out of the carriage window as the train raced through magnificent rural countryside. Her mother sat beside her, book in hand but not appearing to be reading. Both of their minds were focused on the next day when they would come face to face with Philippe.

Her mother's cousin Brigitte had arranged lunch at a restaurant close to their hotel and had suggested they meet up at 11.30 on Saturday morning. All sorts of scenarios flowed through Claude's head. Would Philippe even like her? Would Brigitte resent them meeting? But no, that was foolish because it was Brigitte who had arranged the meeting. Would he judge her harshly for giving him away, but no, Maman had insisted he wanted them to know he had the best childhood.

Leaning her head against the glass, Claude allowed the motion of the train to lull her into sleep. It was her mother who woke her to tell her they were almost there and to gather up her things.

Their hotel was within walking distance of the centre. Their bedroom was simply furnished but spotlessly clean. Claude took her new dress out of her suitcase and hung it up in the wardrobe. Her coat had thankfully not creased and she hung it beside the dress. Her mother had also, without telling her, bought a new, long sleeved dress in navy with a smart pinstripe jacket to go over it.

They both examined the other's choice and both agreed they were perfect. Although her mother's hair was now very grey, almost white, it looked elegant caught up in a French pleat at the back.

Waiting for her mother to finish unpacking, Claude gazed out the window onto the avenue below. The trees along the edge were now full of blossom.

'Right, let's go and have something to eat,' her mother said, 'and I don't know about you, but I would just love a glass of red wine.'

'I think that's a perfect idea, Maman, let's see what the bar below is serving.'

To their delight the bar had a small restaurant and they chose some of the charcuterie with pâté, cheese and a freshly baked baton. Claude surprised herself by discovering she had an appetite. Her mother had ordered a bottle of Côtes du Rhône which was light and fruity.

They kept the conversation away from the events of tomorrow and talked about family matters instead. Claude's niece and nephew were excelling themselves with English and her mother insisted it was all down to her, Claude. 'You are a born teacher, you have a special gift of making your lessons interesting. I know, because I hear people in the village talk about how glad they are that you are teaching their children.'

Taking a sip of her wine and setting her glass down gently, she leaned towards her daughter. 'You did the right thing. Teaching is a calling and if you had kept the baby, there would never have been time to study. It wasn't easy for your father and me either, to say goodbye to our first grandchild, but we knew that my cousin and her husband could give him everything he needed and more. You changed their lives for the better, you know that,' and she gently took Claude's hand and held it.

'I do know that, Maman, and you and Papa helped me to make the right decision for I could never have given him up for adoption to a stranger.'

Claude thought over what her mother had told her as she drifted off to sleep. Her mother snored gently beside her, exhausted after a busy day. She had left everything ready for her husband so her daughter would not have much to do, but she was glad she was able to travel with Claude who needed all the support she could give her.

Claude thought how blessed she was with her parents who did everything they could for all four of their children. She thought of Marjorie and her lack of a mother's love but she was glad she was getting to know her father.

Sighing, Claude turned on her side and prepared for sleep.

46

Claude and her mother sat down to breakfast at nine. Neither of them had much of an appetite but were grateful that the croissants were warm and fresh and the coffee was good. Claude was too nervous to make conversation and her mother did not push her. The dining-room was small but full and most of the guests were talking noisily.

'Would you like to have a quick look around the shops? It seems a shame not to,' her mother asked.

'Yes, I think that's a good idea. I was thinking I might look for a cream jacket as my coat seems a little warm for today.'

'Good idea, let's have a look. The shops seem to be down on our right.'

Just by chance they found just what she was looking for in the second shop they visited. It was cream, the perfect match for the black and cream dress. It was cut in a curve at the back, slightly short at the front and flattered Claude's slim figure.

They arrived back at the hotel in time to change before meeting Brigitte and Philippe. They had found the restaurant when they were out earlier and knew it was just a five-minute walk away. Claude complimented her mother on her appearance before stepping in front of a full-length mirror.

She felt satisfied with her reflection. The sleeveless dress would be perfect if she needed to remove the jacket and the length of the skirt accentuated her long legs.

'You look perfect,' her mother assured her, 'any son would be proud of a mother like you.'

'Oh Maman, thank you, I really hope he will. Now, time to go or we will be late.'

When they entered the restaurant, only a few tables were occupied. It was too early for lunch and too late for breakfast. As Claude held the door for her mother, the maître d' walked forward to meet them. 'Good morning ladies, how can I help you?' he asked.

'We are joining Madame Bernard,' Claude told him quietly, 'and her son.'

'But of course, they are waiting for you. Follow me please.'

Before she realised it Claude was looking straight into the face of her son. The waiter had brought them to a circular table by the window which had no other tables beside it. Philippe had stood up the moment he saw them, hand outstretched. Claude took a sharp intake of breath when she saw him. It was like looking at Angelo all over again.

Brigitte had come round the table to greet her cousin, 'Marie, you look wonderful,' she said, kissing her on both cheeks. 'And you are Claude, how beautiful you look. I don't think I have to introduce this fellow, Philippe is so like you. You can tell he has been nervous all morning.'

They all sat down and there was an awkward silence before anyone spoke. Determined not to make it awkward, Claude's mother spoke first. 'The last time we saw you, you were one week old. You must excuse us if we stare at you.'

'I imagine I've changed quite considerably since then,' he smiled. 'You must forgive me, I'm not sure how to address you.'

'Well, that's easy, I'm Marie and this is Claude, we're so pleased to see you again.'

Claude studied her son. He was extremely handsome but with a very easy smile. He was dark as she knew he would be and his eyes were almost black, like his father's. He was dressed casually in cream chinos with a navy striped shirt and brown loafers. She knew he was also staring at her and she felt herself blush under the scrutiny. The warmth of his smile though made her smile back and she was struck by what a surreal moment she was experiencing.

'Would you like coffee, a glass of wine perhaps? It's too early to order lunch just yet,' Brigitte asked, nodding at the waiter to come over.

Claude told her she would absolutely adore a glass of wine.

'Perfect,' Brigitte said, 'I'll order a bottle.'

Over lunch, Philippe and Claude asked each other questions while Brigitte and Marie caught up with all the family gossip they both had. They discreetly let the other two to get to know each other.

Claude told Philippe how difficult it was to find yourself pregnant at sixteen years of age with no one to support her other than her parents. 'The only reason I allowed you to be adopted was because my mother knew the home you were going to and how well you would be looked after, I hope you understand that.'

'Of course I do. Listen, when my sister was sixteen years old she could never have looked after a baby, she could hardly look after herself.' He paused, looking gently at her. 'My mother and father told me I was adopted when I was old enough to understand. Later they told me you were distantly related and that you were still at school when you were pregnant with me. I never, ever felt angry about it, I just hoped one day I would have the opportunity to meet you. The wedding seemed like the right time.'

'And I'm so glad you did. I can see what a good life you have had. And Brigitte also,' she added. 'Yes, my mother always told me that if she had not adopted me, she would not have had my sister. It did something to her hormones,' he laughed.

Claude found herself feeling happier than she had in quite a while. She was amazed by her son, by his easy manner, by the way he talked with so much wisdom. He had showed her photographs of his fiancée and appeared to be totally in love with her. 'I really want you to meet her. I have told her everything and she can't wait to hear all about you. Now I can tell her how beautiful you are and how brave you are coming to meet me.'

Brigitte interrupted their conversation to say that she had something important to tell Claude. Looking across the table she reached out and placed her hand over Claude's. 'You have given me the greatest gift any human being could give to another.' She stopped as her eyes filled with tears. 'You gave me my son and there has not been a day in my life since he was one week old that I haven't thanked God for you.'

Brigitte looked at Claude's mother. 'And for you, my dear cousin. Without you it could not have happened. Also for the way you allowed me to bring him up as my son without interference, that was another gift.' Then wiping her eyes with a handkerchief from her bag, she lifted her glass. 'To Marie and Claude.'

Even Philippe had tears in his eyes when he toasted his mother and his grandmother. 'This has been a wonderful day for me,' he said, 'now I know I have the two best mothers in the world and the sweetest grandmother.'

The rest of their time together was much more light-hearted and Philippe discovered his birth mother had a wicked sense of humour. Claude discovered her son had inherited her gift for languages and planned to become an international lawyer.

He asked nothing about his father, but Claude told him she would send all the details she had for him, so that if later in life he wanted to find him, he should be able to find the family at least. He strenuously denied he ever wanted to know the man who never wanted him, but Claude explained that he might change his mind if he became a father.

She told him all about Marjorie and about the house in Portbradden. He assured her he had always wanted to go to Ireland and maybe he and his wife could come and visit her there. She wanted to ring Marjorie immediately to tell her but that would wait until tomorrow.

Before they left, Brigitte told them she wanted them to come to the wedding. Marie said absolutely not, it was a day for Brigitte to show off her son and they would not complicate it. She told them she could not leave her husband and the journey would be too long for him. Brigitte turned to Claude and asked her, but she agreed it would not be right. They would continue to write to one another and to visit when the time was right.

Then it was time to go. Philippe hung on to Claude when he came to say goodbye. 'I've just met you and now I have to say goodbye,' he said. 'I feel very sad.'

'But isn't it wonderful that we now know each other just a little,' she assured him, 'and it is not goodbye, it's *au revoir*.'

As they left, Claude noticed the striking likeness between her mother and Brigitte, who was a little heavier but more glamorous, dressed in a pale turquoise suit which Claude knew was expensive. Her haircut was perfect. Standing back to observe them, Claude decided her mother was the prettier.

Two hours later, as Claude and her mother found seats in a quiet carriage, they both wept at the beauty of it all. Claude had found her wonderful son and Marie her eldest grandson. Both confessed they would love to be going to the wedding, but both agreed it would not be right.

Claude was delighted that Brigitte was such a perfect mother and Claude was glad she would be hearing from her cousin with more than a Christmas card.

They both knew they would sleep soundly that night. And they did.

47

The telephone call from Claude on Sunday afternoon really warmed Marjorie's heart. There could not have been a better outcome from the meeting with Claude's son. Even Marjorie's mother's constant complaining during afternoon tea couldn't dampen Marjorie's spirits. Maeve had left a wonderful fruit cake she had baked for them on Saturday but her mother complained there weren't enough cherries in it. Her father pronounced it as perfect, making his wife even more crotchety.

Marjorie was happy to do the washing up by herself in the kitchen. Maeve had left them a cold salad for tea and Marjorie only needed to make the tea, so there was plenty of time to write a short letter to Claude. Although she had been told everything during her conversation earlier, she wanted to let her friend know just how happy she was for her. As she folded the letter into its envelope, Marjorie was smiling. She knew she would have the whole month of July with Claude and could actually begin to pack in preparation.

She had already put some more items from India into the sideboard for collection. One particular wall hanging, which had been meticulously embroidered with silks of every colour and gilt and crimson thread in the tassels, she planned to hang in the drawing-room above the sofa. The room would always remind her of her happy times in India, and that pleased her as there hadn't been a lot of happy memories.

Thinking of Claude, she pondered over the part of her life she felt she had missed out on. She didn't make many friends at boarding-school, she was regarded as too dull and bookish. Her fellow students from Oxford had mostly married and moved to places all over Britain and abroad. She had never had a boyfriend as she never gave anything of herself to any of them. Everyone else had been talented or beautiful whilst she was merely clever. That had all changed when she met Tristan, but since his death she had not met anyone who had the same effect on her life.

How strange, then, that the moment she met Claude she found herself opening up. There was something about Claude that she utterly trusted. Her friend had actually been interested in her, admired her teaching and her impeccable manners. 'Oh Marjorie,' she would say, 'you are so utterly English.' And of course Claude had been so utterly French. She smiled again thinking of Claude with her style and her delightful accent.

Working at the munitions factory during the war had been one of the happiest periods of her life. Initially the other girls mocked her cut-glass accent, but when they got to know her and realised she was happy to do some of their work for them, they warmed to her. She was incredibly quick doing her job and when she finished her own work and was waiting for more to arrive, she would offer to help one of the other girls who was running behind, or just to let them go out for a 'fag'. Some of the brighter girls asked her to teach them a little bit of French and she did during lunch breaks.

She tried to keep her family life a secret until one day there was a phone call for her and the office boy shouted out in a strong cockney accent, 'There's a Left Tennant Kernal Henry Kirkpatrick on the blower for you, miss,' he said, carefully reading from the note he had written down, 'says he needs to talk to you urgent like.'

With a face as red as a beetroot Marjorie made her way to the office, worried that something awful had happened. It appeared that Daphne and her horse had been evacuated but were both safe and well. For some reason her father thought Marjorie might have heard and been concerned. Marjorie hadn't heard and probably wouldn't have been too concerned, but she had to walk back the length of the factory floor with everyone looking at her. 'Who was that, duck? Everything all right?'

'Yes, it was just my father with some family news,' she replied, 'everything is totally fine.'

'So your old man's a bigwig in the army then, luv?' another asked.

'Not really,' she replied, 'he's actually only an eye surgeon.'

'Blimey, luv, I thought my old man had a good job, but he's a warden on the air raid station.'

They all laughed heartily but to her enormous relief they continued to treat her as just a good worker. Although some of them invited her to go out with them any night, she had at first refused, telling them she couldn't leave her mother at night as her father often worked late at night. She could never have invited any of them home with her as she could just imagine her mother's horror. Elsie and the girls had been her true friends, women she would never have met in her teaching life.

Looking at the clock, she realised she had better start getting things ready for tea. Later she would start to make lists for Portbradden. She might even take a shopping trip soon to purchase a pale blue dress or blouse. After all, she told herself, the war's long over and I don't need to make excuses. Her last shopping trip had been so successful, she was encouraged to do it again. Another afternoon at The Northern Counties, the restaurant she loved, was called for and perhaps high tea at the Beach Hotel in Portballintrae. She had been told there was a great shoe shop in Coleraine, that could be another trip for her and Claude.

She felt positively elated as she called her parents for tea. Putting the apple tart in the oven, she took off her apron and went to join them.

48

Traffic was light as Marjorie drove into London to collect Claude from the station. Although the sun was not shining, it wasn't cold and she could see a little bit of blue sky in the distance.

She was so happy and relieved to have left Hampshire, but all the preparations she had had to make for her parents had left her exhausted. Fortunately a cousin of Maeve's had stepped in to help at weekends or whenever she was needed. She had also arranged for a driver to collect them if they were going further than the local village. The thought of her father hurtling along the narrow roads of rural Hampshire in his ancient Jaguar filled Marjorie with dread.

Pulling in to park outside the station she pulled on the handbrake and turned off the ignition. She was a few minutes early, so she lay her head back on the headrest and closed her eyes. She was always methodical in her planning but she still worried as her parents were really quite vulnerable now. Daphne had promised to pop in while Marjorie was away, but that wasn't something she could depend on. Thank heavens for Maeve.

Opening her eyes, Marjorie searched for Claude as travellers began to pour out of the station. And there she was, still looking chic and as though she had just stepped out of her own front door, dressed in a trench coat over a navy and white spotted blouse over navy trousers and carrying what Marjorie later learned was a 'vanity case'. Marjorie rushed out to meet her and take hold of the suitcase she was hauling behind her.

With all the luggage safely put away, Claude reached over to kiss her friend's cheek. 'Oh Marjorie, it is just a few months since I last saw you, but it feels so much longer. But now I intend to leave my pupils and my family behind and just relax. And what about you my friend, you must be feeling so tired after all you have had to do.'

'I shan't lie, I'm jolly well exhausted, but it's all done now, so we both deserve to relax.'

They discussed the school exams, both sets of parents, the books they wanted to read before they reached the subject of Philippe, Claude's son.

'Oh Marjorie, I think I could talk about him all the way to Scotland and all across the Irish Sea. He is such a perfect boy although, of course, he is a man now. He is very handsome, very tall and dark, so like his father, but he is so nice I cannot tell you.'

Marjorie felt the tension drop from her shoulders as she watched her friend's illuminated face describing the day they met.

'Oh I know I already tell you everything, but it is so much better when I can see you in person.'

'So you have spoken since? Marjorie asked. 'His job sounds very interesting.'

'Yes, I think perhaps he is very clever for he is doing things you do not expect a young man to do. You know what's really strange, Marjorie? You remember our neighbours are relatives of Angelo? Well, she has told my mother that Angelo is a lawyer in Milan. Can you believe that? Of course Maman did not say a word about Philippe, because really, he does not deserve to know.'

By the time they reached Portbradden, Marjorie felt that she had met Philippe himself while Brigitte felt like a friend. It was wonderful to see Claude so animated about her son while she continued rightly to give all the praise to Brigitte for having made such a good job bringing him up. She hoped that maybe, when the wedding was over and the fuss had died down, she might meet them herself.

Meanwhile there was so much to be done unpacking and opening curtains. But, as at Easter time, Connell had been before them, the house was aired, and in the kitchen there was a chicken casserole with a note giving instructions and an invitation for drinks at six o'clock the following evening. It made their arrival so much easier.

Claude took her suitcase upstairs while Marjorie unpacked the bits and pieces she had bought for the kitchen. It was Claude's idea to hang a rod above the kitchen window. They had found hooks just the right size and were able to hang the pots and pans from the wooden rod, leaving cupboards free for other things. Claude had tied the gingham curtains to each side of the window and tied them back with matching yellow ribbon. They had no need to pull the curtains as there was nothing beyond the garden but fields, and the saucepans provided privacy that wasn't needed.

Claude had gathered the first of the daisies they had

planted at Easter time and put them in a milk jug which she sat by the window. Surveying it later Marjorie declared it felt as though they had been there all year. Then the two of them relaxed and enjoyed the chicken in white wine which they both declared was delicious, washed down with a large glass of French white wine. Claude insisted on washing up and sent Marjorie to put her personal things away.

Marjorie hadn't told Claude about the Indian cabinet arriving on Tuesday. She had told her things were coming but not exactly what they were. Looking round the drawing-room before retiring for the evening, she imagined in her mind's eye how it would look sitting against the wall opposite the window and she knew it was going to be perfect.

Upstairs they removed the hot water bottles from the bed they had placed there when they arrived. The room with its wooden floors and wood-panelled ceiling had held the heat from the evening sun and the room felt cosy and welcoming. Putting away her toiletries in the chest beside the bed, Claude felt the exhaustion of the last week roll of her shoulders. She would not need to read a book tonight, she would just lie down and wait for sleep to overcome her.

When Marjorie returned after her bath she found Claude fast asleep. With her hair down round her face she could just imagine what her friend must have looked like when she was young. How Angelo had left her behind and forgotten about her would remain a mystery she would never understand.

She climbed into bed and switched off the light. She could hear the waves washing up gently to the shore and within minutes she too was asleep.

49

Waking the next morning, Marjorie was delighted to see there wasn't a cloud in the sky. They needed to go to Bushmills for some shopping but when that was over she looked forward to a day in the garden. She wanted to buy a bottle of Bushmills whiskey for Connell as he was always so kind to them so she could give it to him when they went for drinks before dinner.

She would go and prepare breakfast before calling Claude. She smiled when she heard Claude's footsteps above her. Breakfast would be very simple today, just some of Maeve's bread and homemade gooseberry and raspberry jam. Claude as usual had brought the coffee and Connell had thoughtfully left milk in the fridge. They would decide what to have for dinner tonight and it might be nice to ask Connell for dinner on Saturday night.

It was bliss, she thought to herself, not to have to consult with her parents about what they would like each day. Hearing Claude back in the bedroom again she filled the kettle and put it on the stove to boil.

'Good morning, *mon amie*, another beautiful day and I am feeling so good after such a wonderful sleep,' Claude said, measuring the coffee into her coffee pot before adding the hot water.

Marjorie had taken the kettle off the boil knowing that that was the way Claude made her coffee, never with boiling water and with warm milk at breakfast time. 'I thought we could pop into Bushmills this morning when you're ready. Have you any ideas for dinner? I thought perhaps we should ask Connell for dinner tomorrow.'

'But of course,' Claude replied, 'why don't I make quiche for you and I this evening and then maybe some lamb cutlets for Saturday? This is a perfect time for lamb, is it not?'

'That sounds perfect. Now come and sit down, the coffee smells delicious.'

They bought wheaten bread and a crusty loaf from the bakery, bacon and lamb chops from the butcher, parsnips and potatoes, some fruit and two punnets of locally grown strawberries from the greengrocer's. Claude volunteered to buy the groceries while Marjorie went to the off-licence which was part of the 'pub' in the square. She couldn't see any French white wine so she asked the young man who had come in from the public bar if they had any.

'I'll have to ask my da,' he replied, opening the door of the lounge bar. 'Hey, Da, the posh woman from up the road, you know the wan who's usually with the wee French woman, well she wants to know if we have any French white wine. I told her I didnae know.'

There was a silence before an older man came in carrying two bottles of wine in his arms. 'Good morning,' he said, putting the bottles in front of her. 'This is all we have but there's more coming next week. This seems to go down well with the ladies,' he told her, pushing the bottles towards her.

'Chardonnay will be fine, thank you, I'll have both bottles

and I'll have a bottle of Black Bush please, preferably in a box. Oh and two bottles of the Burgundy behind you.'

'Just hould on and I'll get you the Black Bush and I'll put them all in a wee box for you.'

After paying the man, Marjorie carried the box carefully back to the car. Trying her best to copy the accent of both the men in the pub, Marjorie recounted the conversation to Claude. The two of them laughed all the way home to Portbradden.

Connell was dressed in cream trousers with a white shirt and a smart cravat in several shades of blue. He had a fire lit as the evening had become cooler. He had a silver tray set with green and black olives, some blue cheese and some little biscuits with ham and pickle. 'Now help yourselves, ladies, please, while I pour the wine. White or red?'

They both chose red and settled back on the sofa while Connell regaled them with stories of the school play. This year they had apparently shared with a girl's school to produce *Oliver!* which had played to four packed houses. 'My dears, I cannot tell you how exhausted I was. Keeping the girls and boys apart was in itself not for the faint hearted, but somehow or other it all went down jolly well. We got write-ups in the local papers and they were full of praise. All wonderfully well, but it's going to take all the month of July for me to recover. Now, let me hear all of your news please.'

Marjorie told him of her hopes for her sixth-formers and how her parents were becoming more and more reliant on her. Claude told him about her father's progress and how well her mother was coping. Then she told him how well her nephew and niece had done but of course they had to wait until August to get their results.

The red wine, the heat from the fire and the delicious canapés had all contributed to making Marjorie and Claude quite tipsy but very relaxed. Having agreed that Connell would join them for dinner the following night, the two of them headed back to the cottage, grateful that they hadn't further to go. The cottage felt cool after leaving the fireside so Marjorie lit the living-room fire while Claude attended to their supper. They were both grateful to have some proper food to sober themselves and had only water to go with it.

Sitting by the fire later, they both agreed that life in Portbradden was lived at a slower pace than the rest of the world. 'Which is why we love it,' Claude said as she stretched her legs and feet towards the fireplace. 'I can't think of anywhere I would rather be.'

After settling the fire and switching off the lights they made their way to bed. Although both of them had new books to read, the sound of the tide lulled them both to sleep.

50

As the week ran on, Claude and Marjorie settled into the rhythm of the cottage. In the mornings Claude would read or write letters while Marjorie worked on her beloved garden.

The paths were really taking shape, and Marjorie imagined herself planting enough vegetables to be almost self-sufficient, when she eventually would be able to call it her home and not just her holiday home. For now the paths were wide enough for a wheelbarrow and the beds broad enough to grow any kind of vegetable she could imagine.

Claude would prepare lunch which they mostly ate in the garden under the shade of a striped umbrella when it was too warm. Afternoons were spent reading their books in the sea garden were Marjorie mentally planned how she could decorate it with shells and pretty stones they collected when walking along the nearby beaches. Afternoon tea was a must before Marjorie would retire to work for another hour or two while Claude prepared dinner and took a walk by herself along the road beyond the port.

After dinner one evening Marjorie suggested that after they did their necessary food shop the following day, they could drive along the coast to Ballycastle. It would also be a good time for them both to phone home from the post office.

Marjorie had somehow managed to stop worrying about her parents and concentrated instead on her plans for the cottage. Claude had no real anxieties about her own parents as she knew they were in safe hands. She had written to them trying to paint a picture of the cottage and the scenery around it. It would be nice though to hear her mother's voice.

Yet another lovely day lay ahead when Marjorie first set foot in the garden. She had listened to the early news on the BBC when she first went into the kitchen. It promised that the weather would remain warm and sunny but to expect rain on Sunday. She knew it had to come sometime and the farmers needed it badly but she would miss another day in the garden.

Smiling at her selfish thoughts, she reached their breakfast plates down from the dresser. Two days ago Claude had painted the dresser blue and with the white walls behind it and the pretty yellow curtains on the window, it really was a welcoming space to cook in. In the corner sat an old rocking chair which had belonged to Aunt Margaret. Claude had also painted it blue, put an embroidered cushion on the seat and hung a tartan rug over the back.

It was the perfect place to sit and study recipes, Claude had decided, and Marjorie had to agree. Claude had brought a few of her own recipe books from home, all in French of course, and they had bought a book published by the Women's Institute from the post office in Bushmills. Claude couldn't wait to bake the Irish soda bread scones on Sunday. Knowing that rain was forecast, Marjorie was delighted that they had also had a delivery of peat by one of the farmers near Coleraine.

Hearing Claude's footsteps on the stairs, she lifted the kettle off the boil.

It was still sunny and pleasantly warm when they reached Bushmills, so they parked the car at the top of the street and, each carrying a basket, they made their way to the bakery, the greengrocer's and the butcher before going into the post office on their way back. They were greeted warmly by the postmistress as they entered the shop.

'Ladies, it's always nice to see you. You've been doing the shopping I can see,' she said, nodding at their baskets.

'Just necessities I'm afraid,' Marjorie replied. 'May we use the telephone?' She took out her purse full of coins.

'But of course you can, go ahead now.'

Marjorie indicated to Claude that she should go first into the booth at the back of the room. She was looking at some writing paper when she heard her name being called.

'Miss Kirkpatrick, could I ask you something please,' the postmistress asked quietly. 'Would your friends name be Claud (she pronounced it as the male form) and would her surname be Gerard?'

'Claude Girard, yes it is,' Marjorie replied, 'but why do you ask?'

'Well, it's just that this wee letter arrived and the postman said he never knew anyone with a name like that in Portbradden. But I heard tell that your friend was from France and so is this letter,' she explained, holding up an Air Mail envelope addressed to *Mademoiselle Claude Girard, The Cottage, Portbradden, Irlande du Nord.*

She held it out to Marjorie who immediately looked for the

sender's name on the back, which was *Philippe Laurent, Marseilles, France.*

Marjorie drew in her breath seeing the name and quickly looked over at Claude who was happily talking to her mother.

'I hope there's nothing wrong. I was just glad I could get it safely to her, so I was.'

'No no, nothing wrong,' Marjorie assured her. 'Just a nice surprise.'

When Claude finished her telephone call, Marjorie ushered her out of the post office.

'But Marjorie, you have not yet called your mother,' Claude protested.

'I shall do it tomorrow, we have to get to Ballycastle,' Marjorie explained, seeing the postmistress's eyes following them both. 'See you tomorrow,' Marjorie called cheerfully, 'thank you so much.'

Marjorie began to walk briskly up the road in the direction of the car. Claude kept up with her but, grabbing her friend's arm, stopped her.

'Marjorie, what on earth is wrong. Did something happen when I was speaking on the telephone?'

Marjorie assured her all was well and she would explain when they got into the car.

When they were both seated and Marjorie had opened her window to cool the car, she turned to her friend. 'This came for you,' she said, handing her the envelope. 'I knew you would want somewhere private to open it.'

Claude's look of utter surprise turned to excitement when she saw the name.

'Well, aren't you going to open it?' Marjorie asked.

Claude's hands were shaking as she pulled the letter out of the envelope.

'Oh my goodness, I cannot believe it. He says Maman gave him the address and he hopes I don't mind him writing to me, but of course I do not. Let me read it to you.'

'No,' Marjorie replied sternly. 'This is your letter, meant just for you. I'm sure you will tell me all about it when you've finished,' she smiled, putting the car into gear ready for their drive to Ballycastle. Claude wanted to tell Marjorie what her son had said but Marjorie told her she would appreciate it more when they returned, over a cup of tea, and Claude held the letter next to her heart before putting it into her handbag. Her smile was so infectious that Marjorie smiled all the way along the coast until they saw the sign for Ballycastle.

They parked at the top of a very steep hill and walked down towards the sea. Marjorie was looking in a hardware shop window while Claude walked a little ahead of her. Turning her head to the right Marjorie saw that Claude was looking intensely at the window of a small art gallery and was motioning for her to join her.

'Look, Marjorie, look what I see, isn't it perfect?' she asked pointing to a painting in the middle of the window. It was a still life in oils of a silver teapot sitting beside a plate of scones on a yellow gingham tablecloth. Beside the teapot was a blue and white striped jug and a glass bowl of strawberry jam. 'Can you just imagine it on the wall beside the dresser in the kitchen? It would be so cheerful,' she exclaimed.

Marjorie had no doubt that it would indeed be perfect and she thought it was just the sort of thing that Aunt Margaret would have approved of. Marjorie pushed open the door of the shop and Claude followed her in.

Hearing the door open, the young man in charge of the shop came out to greet them.

'Would you like to look around? I'll be happy to tell you as much as I can about the artists. They're all local, all from North Antrim.'

'Thank you, we would,' Marjorie replied, 'but we'd like to see the still life at the centre of the window.'

'Ah, that's the James Turner you're looking at. He's a great painter and he brings us most of his work. I'll get it out for you.' Carefully reaching into the front of the display, he lifted the painting off the easel and brought it to them. 'It's beautifully painted, I can tell you.' And indeed it was.

'Well, I don't think there's any doubt about it,' Marjorie said. 'We'll take it. How much is it, please? Will you take a cheque?'

She was assured he would and he covered the painting carefully in tissue paper before wrapping it neatly in brown paper. Handing her a receipt, he gave her a postcard with a painting of another still life by the same artist with his details printed on the back.

'Lovely to see you, ladies, and I hope you'll call back whenever you're back in Ballycastle.'

They assured him they would and explained they were staying in Portbradden but were here for a while.

After buying ice cream cones from a shop on the sea front, they started the drive back to the cottage. Claude couldn't contain herself any longer.

'Marjorie, Philippe wanted me to know how wonderful it was to meet me and he hoped we could meet again soon so I could meet his fiancée Madeleine. He was sorry I was not coming to the wedding but agreed it was Brigitte's big day and he would arrange for me to meet Madeleine soon.

'But Marjorie, you will not believe it: Philippe and Madeleine are driving to Ireland for a short holiday before the wedding. He says they both need a break from it all. He says maybe, just maybe they will get as far as Northern Ireland to see the Giant's Causeway. He knows the cottage is not far from there. Oh, it's too much, I can hardly believe it.'

Hanging the painting on the kitchen wall later, they both agreed it was indeed perfect. Marjorie had a warm feeling, knowing that the cottage was looking so much more like her home.

'And every time I look at it, it will remind me of my first letter from my son,' Claude said, standing back to admire it, Philippe's letter clutched once more to her heart.

'I think we should drink to that,' Marjorie smiled at her friend, pouring a glass of wine for them both.

'And you know what I wish for even more, Marjorie?' Claude asked. 'For him to meet you and for you to meet him. It is most important for me.'

They both raised their glasses and drank to just that.

51

Claude found it hard to concentrate on reading for the next few days so she started helping Marjorie in the garden. On Sunday it rained as forecast and, being so close to the sea, the temperature dropped and the wind was cool. Claude had made a delicious chicken casserole cooked in red wine, and the aroma of the herbs rose into the living-room, making them look forward to lunch by the fire. As Claude lived in hope of Philippe calling, her head turned each time she heard a car outside. Being a wet Sunday there weren't many cars around and of course she had no idea when to expect him, if indeed he was able to come at all.

Marjorie was also a little on edge as she had not entertained in the cottage before and she wasn't at all sure what to expect. She turned the radio on after they cleared away their tea dishes, just to hear the news and the weather forecast. They were delighted to hear they could expect the sun to return later on Monday afternoon. It would be cooler, but would begin to warm up on Wednesday.

When the dishes were cleared away, Claude took one of her cookery books from the dresser and sat down to read it in the rocking chair by the stove. 'You know, Marjorie, I think it would be a good idea to go to Bushmills tomorrow and I can buy some flour, sugar and eggs to bake a cake and maybe some pastries. It would be nice to have some sweet things that will keep in the tins and I thought maybe some madeleines and shortbread. And a fruit cake,' she added. 'If I put some brandy in it, it will last all month.'

Marjorie smiled at her friend's eager face and knew exactly what she was preparing for. She just prayed very hard that Philippe did turn up, that Claude would not be disappointed.

'I think that's a really good idea. Let's make a list, then we can go early in the morning whilst the weather is dull. Then we can get back in time for you to bake and me to do a bit more digging.'

They were agreeably surprised to find there was no rain at all, and they parked comfortably in the square before setting off to do their shopping.

The bakery was selling eggs from the farm just out of the town and they bought those as well as some of the wonderful wheaten bread and sausage rolls. The butcher carried a small range of fresh fish and today he had some smoked salmon caught and smoked just outside of the town. It would be perfect with the wheaten bread. He also had some wonderful roast ham which he cut in thick slices.

Claude came out from the grocers with a cardboard box full of flour, icing sugar and everything she needed to bake with. Marjorie helped her to put everything in the boot of the car before they walked back to the post office, where Marjorie wished to telephone her father. They had just walked in the door when the postmistress appeared from the back the instant she saw them.

'Would you believe it, Miss Fitzpatrick - and please call me

Eileen, everybody does - but look what just arrived for your friend, Miss Gerard. Och sure, there you are yourself, this arrived for you this morning,' she shouted excitedly, holding a postcard in the air before handing it to Claude.

Claude took it, looking curiously at the postcard which was from Killarney in Ireland. When she turned it over, her eyes opened wide. In French she explained to Marjorie that Philippe was coming to stay with his fiancée at the hotel beside the Giant's Causeway. '*Oh mon dieu, il arrivera jeudi*,' she exclaimed again much to the amazement of Eileen behind the counter.

Oh my Lord, Marjorie thought to herself, the furniture arrives this afternoon.

'Oh my God,' Eileen said behind the counter, 'don't be telling me it's bad news.'

'Oh no, quite the contrary, a relative is making a surprise visit on Thursday. 'All awfully exciting. Now Claude, sit down while I phone Father.'

Marjorie learned that all was well with her parents. The weather was slightly inclement but would pick up by the weekend. Maeve was looking after them awfully well and he had booked the driver to collect them and take them out for Sunday lunch. And no, he wasn't driving, he had organised for *The Times* to be delivered every morning, so not a thing to be worried about.

Marjorie found her shoulders relaxing as she replaced her coin purse into the deep recesses of her handbag. 'Come along, Claude, we must be on our way. Thanks awfully,' she called to Eileen, 'see you soon.'

Eileen was in fact bitterly disappointed. The postcard

arrived in a foreign language which she couldn't understand and then the French woman had read it out to the posh woman in a language she couldn't make heads or tails of. One thing she knew was they were expecting a visitor on Thursday. Would it be a man? she wondered. Did the French woman have a lover? They always did in the films, that's for sure. She didn't have a wedding ring either.

She would ask Seamus the postman to have a good look when he went down on Friday morning. Mind you, she couldn't see Miss Fitzpatrick putting up with any hanky panky. But then again she was a Protestant and you never knew with them. The French woman was like something out of a magazine with those scarves and sunglasses.

Well, she would just have to see what happened. You never could tell with foreigners.

Marjorie and Claude were making plans for Thursday. They both agreed it was best that Philippe stayed in a hotel. Marjorie would feel very strange sharing a bathroom with people she didn't know well and of course they would need two bedrooms.

Claude was just so excited she kept reverting to speaking in a French. 'I wonder what she will look like,' she pondered, 'I'm sure she will be pretty for he is very handsome. Oh Marjorie, I'm so glad you will meet him for you are like my family to me.'

'You had better start baking,' Marjorie laughed. 'Hopefully it will be good enough to sit outside for afternoon tea. I will work hard on the garden while you look after inside. But first, Claude, I will have a surprise for you this afternoon, so don't start baking too soon'.

At two o'clock precisely, a lorry emblazoned with 'Thomas Jackson and Sons, Furniture Removers' pulled up in front of the house.

'Claude, could you make these gentlemen a cup of tea while I speak to them?' asked Marjorie before opening the door. Seeing they were both strong men, she pointed to where she would like the sideboard to sit and made sure they had an easy pathway to carry it over.

Half an hour later, once Mr Jackson and his son had finished their work, the silver tray, silver kettle and silver teapot sat on top of the ornate and beautiful piece of furniture. Seeing the china Claude had left out, Mr Jackson laughed. 'Those cups won't fill us. Please would you fill our thermos with tea?'

'Of course,' Claude replied. 'Would you like something to eat?'

'No thank you,' he said. 'We had a ploughman's lunch in the pub up the road.' Looking at Marjorie, he continued, 'Cracking place you got here. Bit different from Hampshire all the same, but you can't beat the seaside. Me and the missus love Blackpool.'

Marjorie thanked him for his work and handed him a cheque.

'Thank you very much,' he said. 'Pleasure to do business with you, Miss Fitzpatrick. Whenever you need anything shifted, just give us a bell.' Then he said to his son, 'Come on, lad, shift yourself. We've got a boat to catch.'

Claude could not believe her eyes when she saw the furniture.

Marjorie took out the tapestry from one of the cupboards. 'I had thought this might suit here, but I've had second thoughts; I think it will look fabulous in the bedroom. Such beautiful colours. It really couldn't have arrived at a better time. We shall serve Philippe tea from the silver teapot.'

'Oh Marjorie, it's perfect, everything is perfect and especially you, *mon amie*,' Claude replied, giving her friend a hug. 'Now we have two very busy days ahead of us.'

And with that they retired from the room, one to the kitchen and one to the garden, just at the very moment the sun chose to shine.

52

The following day was spent cleaning and polishing and making the cottage as welcoming as possible. Connell had offered to get them anything they needed from Bushmills so on Thursday morning he came back with a freshly baked wheaten loaf, still warm from the oven. They had explained to Connell that they were expecting visitors from France and would tell them how it went on Saturday night when he came for dinner. Claude felt guilty hiding the fact that it was her son and his girlfriend but Marjorie assured her there was no need to supply the intimate details, sufficient to say it was a visit of family members from Marseilles.

When Connell arrived at the door with a large bunch of flowers from his garden, Claude exclaimed it was just what they needed. He left wishing them a good afternoon. The drawing-room was looking as though it had been this way for years. The flowers sat in the middle of the circular table near the window and the silver on the sideboard was gleaming. The burgundy crushed velvet curtains from Aunt Margaret's drawing-room were pulled into the bay at each side to maximise the view. The fire was set with a mixture of peat and logs, but as it was pleasantly warm outside, they decided against lighting it.

When all was as ready as it could be, Claude and Marjorie

went upstairs to change. Claude selected a simple dress of pink and white with a white collar and a very full skirt. She wore her hair down on her shoulders and applied a pretty pink lipstick. Flat white open-toed sandals accentuated the golden tan of her legs. She left to leave Marjorie to dress in peace while she ran downstairs to watch for a car with a French number plate.

Marjorie was so glad she had gone shopping before she left home, and she pulled the dress from the back of the wardrobe in the spare room. She didn't know why she hadn't shown Claude the dress, but she wasn't comfortable with anyone, even Claude, about showing off. However, when she saw her reflection in the mirror, she was quietly pleased with what she saw. The dress was in a warm yellow with white daisies scattered over the material. It was buttoned to the waist and had a narrow, cream leather belt. The sleeves, which were elbow length, were very flattering against her brown arms. Her shoes were the same colour as the belt.

She pulled out her amber beads that had once been Aunt Margaret's from the dressing table and saw that the colour went beautifully with the yellow. Then, making sure there were no hairs pulling loose from her neatly combed hair, she went down to join Claude.

Claude's eyes opened wide when she saw her friend come down the stairs. '*Mon dieu*, you look magnificent, Marjorie. Your dress is beautiful and the colour is perfect.'

Marjorie, looking rather flustered from receiving such a compliment, suggested they fill the kettle in readiness. Everything had been set out on two trays, ready to carry in when the visitors arrived. There was little to do but wait.

They didn't have to wait long as Claude spotted the car, an open-topped Citroen Dyane, cream with a red roof. Philippe was driving and beside him sat Madeleine, her hair held back with a blue and white patterned bandana. Claude was already at the front door waving madly. She pointed to a parking space beside the sea garden and he manoeuvred the car expertly to take up as little room as possible.

Marjorie stood back in the hall waiting for Claude to greet them.

'*Entrez*,' Claude invited them, 'this is just the loveliest surprise.'

Philippe greeted Claude with a warm embrace before breaking away to introduce his fiancée. 'And this is Madeleine. Madeleine, this is my.....Claude!'

'Madeleine, it's so lovely to meet you and this is my best friend in the world, Marjorie.'

Marjorie stepped forward and shook hands with them both, before ushering them into the drawing-room. 'Now then,' she said, speaking in French, 'you three have so much to talk about and I am going to make us all a cup of tea. You are most welcome,' she added before leaving the room and making her way to the kitchen.

As she turned on the gas to heat the kettle, she thought about her first impressions, brief as they were. Philippe was every bit as handsome as Claude had described him. Tall and dark, but such beautiful eyes and a very kind smile. Madeleine was, as she expected, a very pretty girl, very natural and friendly looking. She couldn't imagine how Claude was feeling, from not having set eyes on her son to meeting him twice in a month. It must be such a big event for both of them.

She spooned the tea from the caddy into the silver pot, inhaling the scent of the bergamot. She poured milk into the milk jug and lifted the first tray to take it to the drawing-room.

Madeleine jumped up immediately when she saw Marjorie enter the room. 'Please, you must let me help you.'

Marjorie's first thought was to say she could manage herself, but seeing the girl's rather anxious face she suddenly realised that this must all be rather strange for her too.

'That would be most kind,' she answered, 'perhaps you would kindly bring in the teapot for me.'

'I'd love to,' the girl replied, 'I'll follow you, shall I?'

When they reached the kitchen, Madeleine spotted the garden through the kitchen window. 'Oh, what a beautiful space, so sheltered and sunny. My parents live in an apartment and I have always wanted a garden.' She smiled, placing her palms on the windowsills and gazing out the window.

'A work in progress, I'm afraid,' Marjorie said. 'Would you like me to show you round when we've had tea?' She lifted the tray and indicated the teapot.

'I should like that very much,' Madeleine replied, and in that instant Marjorie knew she would like this girl.

Philippe ate everything with great enthusiasm, Marjorie pointing out that Claude had baked everything herself.

'But not the wheaten bread,' Claude remarked, 'this is from the little town where we go to buy food, and the salmon is from very close by, so you are eating Irish bread and Irish salmon.'

'This cake is delicious,' Philippe said, taking another slice. 'Is it your own recipe?'

'Well, it's my mother's recipe, but I have been making it for years. It was her mother's before that so actually,' and she paused, 'it is your grandmother's also.'

'I have so much to learn,' Philippe said thoughtfully, 'there is a whole family of which I know nothing.'

'But Philippe, I have told you I will answer any questions that I can.'

'I know and I'm most grateful. Marjorie, could I trouble you for more tea?'

Marjorie had left a jug of hot water sitting on the silver burner and she poured some of it into the teapot before pouring it into Philippe's cup.

'Claude tells me you are going to be an international lawyer. May I ask what your speciality will be?'

'But of course, it will be property because each country has its own laws about property and it is good to have someone who knows the law and can speak the language.'

'What a wise idea. I'm sure you will be very successful.'

'This house is so beautiful and the view,' he paused, 'is breathtaking.'

'Philippe, you should see the garden, it's amazing,' Madeleine told him.

'Why don't you and I go and have a look?' Marjorie suggested. 'We can clear the table later. Why don't we start at the front?' She walked towards the door. 'Back soon,' she called out to Claude.

'Thank you so much for letting me come with you,' Madeleine said as she followed Marjorie across the road. 'I know there are things Philippe wants to ask his, um, Claude,' she corrected herself.

'I understand that completely,' Marjorie assured her, 'but it's very nice for me to have someone to show off my garden to. I'm very glad you came.' She gently stroked Madeleine's arm. 'I didn't know what to do with myself until you admired the garden.'

They both laughed, the tension broken and they spoke to each other in English and French as they strolled round the garden.

'You are so lucky to have all this, Marjorie,' Madeleine told her. 'I grew up on the second floor of an old building, which was very nice, and we have a very large balcony and a park just in front, but my happiest times were with my grandmother in the country. My brother and I could run wild there and we never wanted to go home. Now my grandmother is not able to care for herself so one day soon her house will belong to my mother, but of course I will miss my grandmother very much. Where did you grow up, Marjorie?'

'In India, in the mountains above Madras. It seems like a very long time ago.'

'Oh I would love to hear all about it, you must have had many experiences.'

'You could say that, but I think we should go inside now or they will wonder what we're up to.'

They had walked round the sea garden and Marjorie had pointed out what she intended to do with the paths. This time they came through the back door and the kitchen. Madeleine explained that the kitchen made her feel so comfortable.

'Well, most of it is Claude's ideas. She's very artistic,' Marjorie explained.

'Yes, and she's very pretty is she not, and clever too,' Madeleine said quietly.

'She's all of that, but she also has the kindest heart you can imagine. Now, let's go and join them or they'll wonder where we've got to.'

Claude and Philippe were laughing and smiling when Marjorie and Madeleine interrupted them. They both looked towards Marjorie and Madeleine as they entered.

'Marjorie!' Claude said excitedly. 'You are not going to believe this but tomorrow after Philippe and Madeleine see the Giant's Causeway, they are going to Londonderry and then Donegal. Then they will come back here. Philippe wants to take us out for Sunday lunch. Isn't that lovely? I said perhaps the Beach Hotel as they will be going on to Larne to catch the ferry.'

'That sounds delightful, doesn't it, Madeleine? A chance to get to know you better,' she replied, looking at Philippe.

'I'd love that,' Philippe replied. 'Claude has been telling me all about you and it's wonderful she could tell you about me, it's all been a surprise for all of us.' He stood up and walked over to Madeleine, wrapping his arm around her waist. 'This is a magical place. Thank you so much for having us. Now we must go and check into our hotel. We will see you on Sunday at twelve o'clock.'

After Philippe and Madeleine had left and the dishes had been washed, Claude and Marjorie sat down round the living-room table with a fresh pot of tea.

'Thank you, Marjorie, for making it so easy for me,' Claude told her friend. 'I was worried about Madeleine as it could have been very boring for her but you seemed to get on so well with her. You are such a good friend and sometimes I think I don't deserve you.'

'Now that's just nonsense,' Marjorie replied. 'Yes, I like Madeleine, she has a good heart and she adores Philippe who is, I have to say, very handsome indeed.'

'He is, isn't he?' Claude agreed with happiness in her smile, 'but he too has a very good heart. His mother should feel very proud of how she brought him up.'

'And you should be very proud for creating him. Now, come on, let's break the rules and have a gin and tonic. I think we both deserve one.'

And Claude certainly didn't disagree, so off they went to find a lemon.

53

'You know, Marjorie, you are full of surprises.'

'What on earth makes you say that?' Marjorie replied. 'In what way could I possibly surprise you?'

'First of all, the beautiful yellow dress you did not tell me about,' Claude told her, 'and then you knew the right moment to take Madeleine to the garden. I was so busy asking Philippe questions that I quite forgot poor Madeleine was sitting there.'

'That, my dear Claude, was intuition with no intent to surprise. She had mentioned that she would love to see the garden and it was exactly the right time. As for the dress, I didn't hide it, I had actually intended to keep it for the next time we went to The Northern Counties for lunch. As it is, I shall have to think of something else to wear on Sunday,' she added with a smile, 'although I think the Beach Hotel is less formal.'

'Ah yes, you are right but it will be so nice to see them both again. Philippe is charming, is he not? And I am not boasting about him because it was Brigitte who taught him everything. I am very grateful to her.'

'Yes, Claude, she did, but you did the right thing and by agreeing that your mother's cousin should adopt him, you also kept him within the family and yet you never once interfered with your decision. Your mother is a very wise woman.'

'Yes, she is, I know I am very lucky to have her and my papa of course.'

'I don't think it's about luck, Claude, I think you are very blessed.'

'You're right of course, Marjorie, but I felt bad not being able to tell him anything much about his father, other than his family are very nice people, but he understands how hard it was for me when they did not want to know anything about the pregnancy.'

Marjorie turned to look directly at Claude. 'You were right to do what you did. However, as Angelo grew up and became a man, he must be curious at least to know how his son turned out.'

'My mother told me that her neighbour did tell Philippe's parents that I had a boy, but that he had been adopted. My mother did not tell her neighbour anything else about it.'

'Very wise. And now, will you look at the time?' Marjorie added. 'Connell will be here in half an hour.'

The weather had become very dull and so Marjorie decided to light the drawing-room fire. Connell had not yet seen the new sideboard and she hadn't mentioned it, but she knew that he had seen the removal van as he had waved when she was outside talking to the removers. She wouldn't say a word until they retired after dinner.

Claude had made a hollandaise sauce to go with the fresh salmon they had bought that morning. It would be served with asparagus and some local potatoes cooked in their jackets. For dessert there was a flan made with apples and almonds. Marjorie's mouth was watering just thinking about it as she had passed on afternoon tea, choosing instead to finish the bed she was working on in the front garden.

At precisely 6.30 Connell stood at the front door and knocked. He was, Marjorie noticed, looking quite dapper in a blue shirt with cream trousers and some stylish navy shoes. 'Ladies,' he said, 'how are you both? You seem to have had a very busy week.'

'Yes,' Marjorie replied, 'it has been unusually hectic. Now, what can I get you to drink, a sherry, gin and tonic or a glass of wine?'

'Wine sounds perfect. Pity about the weather, I was getting rather used to the warmth so it's a bit of a shock to the system. However, I heard tonight that it will begin to improve tomorrow.'

Marjorie handed him a glass of red wine and motioned for him to sit down on the sofa.

'Ah, so perhaps the sun will be shining again tomorrow,' Claude said as she appeared from the kitchen, rubbing her hands on her apron before accepting Connell's kiss on the cheek.

'I do hope so,' Connell replied, 'everything looks so much better when the sun is out.'

After their first course of smoked salmon with a dill sauce, Claude brought the main course to the table before joining the others. All agreed that she had excelled herself. After the apple and almond flan served with local ice cream, Marjorie suggested they leave the dishes and retire to the drawing-room. Claude made them coffee served with tiny squares of shortbread and they lay back in their chairs with that feeling which is only experienced after the enjoyment of a really good meal.

Connell could hardly contain himself when he spotted the sideboard. Getting up to study the ornate carving, Marjorie explained how she had retrieved it from the old stables where it had rested under blankets for the past couple of years. She also explained to him the story behind the silver kettle and teapot. 'When the weather is more autumnal, we will prepare tea just the way it was served in India, but for now we will enjoy Claude's excellent coffee.'

'I shall look forward to that,' he said. 'Amazing piece of furniture, Marjorie, you would never find workmanship like that nowadays.'

They spent the evening reminiscing over their childhoods, all so different but each one interesting. They moved on to their favourite topic, discussing their experiences of teaching and they discovered they had far more in common than they had imagined. Although Marjorie was teaching girls who were often overprivileged and Connell's school was more mixed with scholarship boys as well, they found a lot of their experiences similar to Claude who taught in a smaller school in rural France. Children, mostly teenagers were the same the world over.

Connell said, 'The only difference is that when you're teaching boys from fifth form upwards, you are dealing with a lot of testosterone which I don't expect you ladies have experienced.' Warming to his theme, he continued to entertain them with stories from his recent school production of *Oliver!*. 'All those hormonal males having to stand alongside some of those teenage girls doing their best to lead them on, was an experience I don't care to repeat.' With that he took a gulp of the brandy Marjorie had poured for him, before asking if they would like to call in for coffee in the morning so he could show them some photographs which had been taken of the *Oliver!* production.

Marjorie, unused to discussing male hormones with a man, took a large breath before replying, 'Well actually, we're going out to lunch at The Beach Hotel tomorrow as guests of our French visitors. Otherwise we'd love to.'

'Don't worry, there will be plenty of time for you to see them. Ah, that will be the young couple in the French car I saw the other day. Very pretty young lady and her companion looked suitably handsome. Friends from home, were they?'

'Well actually, Philippe is the son of my mother's cousin and the girl is his fiancée,' Claude replied. 'It's their first visit to Ireland and of course the weather has been most kind to them.' She didn't want to put Marjorie in a difficult situation, and it was the truth, if not the whole truth.

'Ha,' Connell replied, 'they will think it's always like this. And how we wish it was,' he added, taking the final swig of his brandy. 'Now it's time I was going home. You ladies have things to do and another busy day tomorrow.'

'Well, yes,' Marjorie agreed, 'except we will have no cooking to do.'

'Indeed, and I'm sure you will have a wonderful time. Thank you so much for the delightful dinner and your wonderful hospitality of course.'

And with that he kissed them both goodnight and headed off home in the moonlight.'

'Well, I must say, he didn't spare our blushes,' Marjorie said, taking a drying cloth out of the drawer and grabbing a dinner plate. 'I'm so glad he didn't go any further.'

Claude laughed out loud remembering the conversation and fished to the bottom of the sink to pull out the cutlery from the suds. 'I suppose it must have been very strange having teenage girls in his school. We know all about that, don't we?'

'We certainly do,' Marjorie agreed, 'especially when they're out of school and into make-up which makes them appear five years older. Thank goodness we still have weeks to go before we're surrounded by them again. By the way, you handled the situation about Philippe very well. I was rather afraid you might find yourself confessing, but you didn't and you didn't lie either. Well done, Claude.'

With that they switched off the lights, locked the doors and headed upstairs for a well-deserved night's sleep. Marjorie fell asleep first while Claude lay awake thinking about Philippe and how amazing it was seeing him again. If only things had been different, maybe she would be looking forward to her role of mother of the groom. But pleasing as it might have been, she knew, deep down, she had made the right decision.

Calling his face up in her mind she fell asleep with a smile.

54

Marjorie and Claude both slept a little later in the morning, partly because of the wine and partly because it had been a very busy and, at times, anxious week. Marjorie was down in the kitchen first and took the opportunity to sit with a cup of tea and finish *The Times* crossword which she had started the previous morning but hadn't had time to finish. The paper reminded her of her father and she wondered how he was managing without her. Of course he would never tell her if he wasn't coping, he was much too stoic for that. However, she was sure Maeve would let her know if he wasn't, and Marjorie almost always spoke to her before she spoke to her father.

Her parents were still a bit of a mystery to her. Her mother, whose name was Sybil, had come from a very privileged background where she was expected to marry well. Her father Henry also came from a good family but they had a strong work ethic and he was expected to look after himself when he left Trinity. He had always wanted to be an eye surgeon and therefore India seemed a good place to study it further. He had recently met Sybil and when he was accepted as a medical officer in the army based in Madras, he suggested they might get married before he left as it would be quite a while before he returned to England. Sybil agreed, much to her mother's annoyance, but as she wasn't the prettiest of the daughters, her father though it appropriate.

From the day they arrived, Sybil didn't have to do anything other than mix with the other officers' wives and play bridge. Arriving back in England with only a housekeeper came as quite a shock to her system, causing her to take weak turns which meant she needed to rest a lot. On the odd shopping trip when Marjorie accompanied her mother to London, she noticed that her mother showed no sign of weakness whatsoever, running from one shop to another with what could only be described as gusto.

Claude interrupted Marjorie's train of thought. 'Oh Marjorie, I did not know you were sitting here. Let me make breakfast for us both.'

'Not at all, it's the only meal of the day that I do and honestly, I was sitting here daydreaming really.'

'I hope they were good dreams, happy dreams,' Claude replied, gathering the breakfast dishes together on a tray whilst Marjorie toasted some bread on the grill.

'Not really, in truth I was thinking about my parents as I often do. A simple breakfast will suffice, I think, as we are going to eat lunch relatively early.'

'Coffee, toasted wheaten bread with butter and marmalade is just perfect,' Claude said, reaching the coffee pot from a cupboard, 'It's part of Portbradden and I love it.'

Sitting at the table by the window, they were pleased to discover little patches of blue in an otherwise grey sky. 'I think it will be perfect by lunchtime,' Claude remarked. 'And the sea will be calm for Philippe and Madeleine's trip on the ferry. They have been so blessed by the weather.'

'It's always more pleasant to travel home in good weather, makes the memories last longer,' Marjorie agreed. 'I think they will take home lots of pleasant memories.'

'Ah yes, already they are talking about coming back for a longer trip, maybe next year. I am so glad they love the place that makes me happy.' Claude added, 'and also they will come to visit me in France sometime. Philippe is very anxious to meet his birth grandfather, and his cousins. Suddenly he has a big family,' she laughed, her face lit up with happiness. 'You know, Marjorie, I could never have dreamed of all this.'

'It has been rather jolly, but now I must go and decide what to wear. As you know, I don't have much interest in clothes, but I don't want your son and his wife to be thinking that your friend is an old frump.'

'Oh Marjorie,' Claude laughed, 'you always look well.'

'In my new clothes, I think you mean,' Marjorie smiled, 'not in my old gardening clothes. Right, let's clear the table.'

Back in her room, searching through her wardrobe, Marjorie decided to wear the pale blue skirt and blouse. She wished she had Claude's panache for clothes; Claude could make anything look good. But she herself did not possess style. She could if someone helped her but there had never been any great need for her to dress up. Smart for work, decent for church and twin set and pearls for Sunday lunch and that was just about the height of it.

Still, she was rather pleased when she saw herself in the mirror. It was, she decided, an agreeable result.

Driving down the hill to Portballintrae, the weather was just as they forecast. A few fluffy little clouds in an otherwise blue sky. In the car park they saw that Philippe and Madeleine had already arrived. The little white and red car was filled with luggage, ready for their journey home.

In the lounge they found the young people sitting close to the window at a table for four. Rising to meet them, Philippe greeted Claude with a hug and three kisses on the cheek. He held Marjorie's hand and kissed her once on each cheek. 'Oh my goodness, you both look so smart. We are dressed for travelling I'm afraid.' Philippe pointed to his shirt and navy chinos which were, of course, casually smart.

Madeleine kissed both ladies and then moved to sit beside Marjorie whilst Philippe and Claude sat on the other sofa.

'Now, what would you like to drink, ladies? An aperitif?'

Both Marjorie and Claude declined, opting instead for Britvic orange. Philippe laughed, suggesting that maybe they try the hair of the dog. Neither could be persuaded.

Philippe told them about their trip to Donegal, and Madeleine told them about their walk round Derry's walls. They both said it was something they would never forget and the time they spent at Dunluce Castle, having seen it in daylight and at night, was one thing they had both fallen in love with. It was the beauty and the history regarding it which made it so special.

Marjorie found herself very comfortable in Philippe's presence. He included her in the conversation in a way that made her feel almost like family. Madeleine was delightful, never drawing attention to herself as so many pretty girls did. She and Philippe, she felt, would make an excellent marriage. For two people she had only just met, they were very easy company.

'Ladies, gentleman, may I take you to your table?' The head waiter asked. 'I've given you a table by the window as it's such a good day to enjoy the view.'

They followed him in and their table was, indeed, right by the window. Looking out they saw that quite a few sailors were taking advantage of the weather. Children with buckets and spades were racing ahead of their parents, anxious to get to the beach. On the horizon they spotted a larger yacht, tall and majestic as it glided smoothly across the ocean.

'Philippe, you must sail, living by the sea,' Claude said. 'I have only been to Marseilles a few times but I remember all the beautiful yachts in the harbour.'

'Ah yes,' Philippe replied, 'but it is not possible for someone like me to sail there, it is much too expensive. I do sail occasionally in a small bay about five miles away, but to be honest, I rarely get time.'

'He doesn't, believe me,' Madeleine agreed. 'The law takes up a lot of time and he is very ambitious. I'm quite happy to be with a small law practice that mostly allows me time at the weekends. It is a rule that we always spend Sundays together,' she added with the sweetest smile for her fiancé.

'I'm very pleased to hear that,' Claude said. 'When I was married, my husband spent the weekend drinking and gambling, so of course the marriage didn't work. It was a huge mistake but it was a long time ago and now I'm so happy that you two always find time for each other.'

'How could I not?' Philippe asked, 'I know I am a very lucky man and I will always look after Madeleine, I promise you that,' he added, looking at Claude.

Having decided on seafood, grilled sole for Marjorie and

Claude, salmon en croute for Philippe and Claude, they all decided on local smoked salmon and home-made wheaten bread as a starter.

They discussed all kinds of things over lunch, Claude and Philippe anxious to learn more about each other and Madeleine telling Claude about the small house they had bought, five miles inland from Marseilles. 'I had to have a garden and that was not possible if we bought an apartment. The house is quite old, made of local stone, but my father checked that it was well insulated so it will be warm in the winter. I am going to do a lot of the decorating myself and although the salon is not large, it has a wonderful fireplace and will be a room to relax in. I like the colours you have in your kitchen, Marjorie, and I think I will copy them if you don't mind.'

'Well, as I told you, it was Claude who chose the colours and I think she will be very flattered when she hears you plan to use them.'

'And you know, Marjorie, there is a lake we can walk round and maybe, if one day we have a dog, it will be the perfect place to walk him.'

Before they knew it, they were finishing their coffee and it was time for Philippe and Madeleine to start their drive to Larne and the ferry. As Marjorie hugged Madeleine goodbye, she was very touched when Madeleine told her she really wanted Marjorie and Claude to come and stay with them.

Philippe held on to Claude tightly before he said goodbye to Marjorie. 'I am so happy that Claude has your friendship and I hope I have a little of it too.'

Whilst they smiled and waved until the little white car was

out of sight, Marjorie placed her arm around her friend as they walked back to the car. 'I know it is always sad to see people leave, Claude, you must remember it is not the end, it is the beginning of a beautiful relationship. I know he adores Brigitte, but it's in you he sees himself.'

'And you know, it's remarkable, for when I look at him I can see my father,' Claude replied.

'Which is just as it should be,' Marjorie added, but deep inside herself she knew she herself would never see her father, or her mother, in anyone but herself.

55

'What do you feel like doing tonight, Claude? I thought we might light the fire in the drawing-room and listen to a little light music while we read, or would you prefer to do something else?'

Marjorie stood at the sink emptying the teapot before washing the dishes. Claude had been noticeably quieter over tea and Marjorie felt she needed to do something to keep her mind occupied.

'That sounds perfect, but I think before I begin to read I will write to Maman and tell her about today. Do you mind, Marjorie? I thought I might write here by the window while the light is still good.'

'Of course I don't mind. You go and get your writing pad and I'll finish off here before I light the fire,' Marjorie answered. 'There's going to be a beautiful sunset,' she added, looking out the window to the far side of the shore.

'Thank you, Marjorie, you are always so thoughtful. You know I am not sad because I won't be seeing Philippe and Madeleine for a while. It's just that now I am beginning to get to know him, he is gone. I feel as though I have missed so much of his life, but I know I did the right thing as I was much too young to look after a child and I had not finished my education.

'He does not have any bad feelings because I gave him up and Brigitte was always honest with him. She told him when he was ready she would arrange for him to meet me, but it was not until he met Madeleine that he wanted to meet me. He really adores her and he's sad that his father did not love me. Now he realises that it would never have worked.' Claude sat down at the table, clutching a tea towel.

Marjorie sat down facing her and smiled fondly at her. 'I'm glad you got that off your chest, my dear, as it was lying heavily with you. The way I see it is you gave birth to a beautiful baby boy. The father didn't want to know and your parents had three children to bring up and educate, including you, so it would not have been right for them to bring up a new baby.

'Meanwhile, your mother's cousin was heartbroken not being able to have children of her own but with so much to offer a child. You made her the happiest woman in the world, she told you that, and you were from the same family, although distantly related. She has done a wonderful job bringing up Philippe and she is big hearted enough not to resent him wanting to meet his birth mother. She has a solid relationship with her son and now you have a relationship with him that is quite different, but is a beautiful friendship.'

Claude dabbed at her eyes with the tea towel, but although there were tears, she was smiling. 'Oh Marjorie, you are so wise and you are so right. I'm a silly, selfish woman who does not appreciate the gift I've been given. Brigitte is a wonderful woman and I am so grateful to her. Philippe mentioned again that he still wanted me to come to the wedding but he understands what I tell him, that on that day Brigitte is the only mother of the groom.'

'Well said and I'm glad to see you smiling. Now start writing and tell your mother what a wise woman she was and still is. I'm off to light the fire and fetch my book.' And with that Marjorie grabbed a box of matches and headed for the drawing-room.

When Claude began her letter, she decided to take Marjorie's advice and tell her mother just how grateful she was to both her mother and her father for their wisdom. She put pen to paper and began.

My dear Maman,

Today Marjorie and I had lunch with Philippe and Madeleine. It was a beautiful day after the rain stopped and we had a table looking out over the sea which was just perfect. Philippe is so well mannered, thanks to Cousin Brigitte, but he also has such a warm heart. He never makes me feel at all guilty for giving him up when he was born. Brigitte had explained to him that I had only just turned seventeen with another year ahead at school and the ability to go to university.

You know, Maman, he told me when he was the same age, he looked at all the girls he knew who were seventeen and not one of them was capable of being a mother. He said the only thing that made him sad was that his father did not love me. I told him that I was not in love with his father either, that it was just

a crush because he was so good-looking and flattered
me so much. He still believes his father and his family
behaved very badly and he has no desire to meet
them.

Claude paused to think back on that time, that summer long ago when the sun shone every day and she and Angelo were so carefree, swimming in the lake, having ice cream sodas, listening to the juke box, holding hands walking back home. She felt so grown up and Angelo constantly told her how beautiful she was. No one had ever told her that before and she mistook it for love.

That night by the lake, the night before Angelo left to go back to Milan, had frightened her at first, then she fell under his spell and was scared to act like a silly, immature girl. Now here she was, twenty-six years later, still alone but much wiser and thankfully content. She picked up her pen and continued to write.

You know, Maman, it is the strangest thing, but
sometimes when he turns his head a certain way, he
looks just like Papa. When I notice a mannerism, it
shocks me as it is so like me. I feel he is my son and I
feel a connection that is quite strong.

Marjorie says I will always have a relationship with
him which is different from the relationship he has
with Brigitte. It was Brigitte who sang him to sleep,
cleaned his knees when he fell, taught him how to tie
his shoelaces, just as I have seen my brother and sister

do with their children. I was not there when she wiped his tears and listened when he was upset.

I know that and I'm so grateful to be able to stand on the sidelines of his life. I am a teacher and it makes me very happy every day. That is because you and Papa gave me the opportunity to be what I wanted to be. Thank you, Maman, from the bottom of my heart.

Marjorie and I will do more gardening if the weather is good and it promises to be. She is making such a wonderful job of the garden and it will be beautiful when all her plans are in place. Tomorrow afternoon we will go to the beach for a swim. Of course it is not as warm as the beaches at home but it's beautiful and we both love it. I'm using lots of your recipes here and every one has been a success.

Philippe and Madeleine loved the cottage and have invited us both to visit their house after they are married. I think it would be very nice for you and I and Papa to go there one day. He really wants to meet Papa and he will come to visit soon.

Well, I must go now and join Marjorie by the fire. Night time can be cool here after a warm day. I shall post this in the morning and I hope you receive it before I telephone you again. I love and miss you both.

Claude signed her name, folded the letter and put it into the airmail envelope. She would give it to Eileen when they went to Bushmills tomorrow. She addressed the envelope and slipped it into her handbag. The sun had gone down but the sky was a beautiful shade of pink. It looked like tomorrow would be a wonderful day.

Walking into the drawing-room she found Marjorie fast asleep in her chair. Her glasses had slipped down her nose and her book had closed on her lap. The radio was on. Claude thought the best thing to do was to make some supper before waking her up.

Ten minutes later, she returned with a tray holding two mugs of hot chocolate and two slices of fruit cake. Tapping Marjorie gently she said quietly, 'Supper time.'

Marjorie woke with a start, saw the book on her lap and asked, 'Good heavens, did I fall asleep? How silly of me, but I have to admit Mozart often has that effect on me,' she smiled, nodding at the radio before reaching over and switching it off. 'Oh, hot chocolate, what a lovely surprise, I'm sure I didn't deserve it after falling asleep like that,'

'*Mon amie*, you deserve so much more. You really helped me to see things just as they were. I told my mother how wise she was and how grateful I am to her. I feel so much better now. Drink up, we have a busy day tomorrow.'

By eleven o'clock, the only sound was the gentle ticktock of the grandfather clock in the hall. Neither Claude nor Marjorie had any desire to read and, each thinking their own thoughts, they drifted into a perfect sleep.

56

Marjorie returned to Hampshire to a father who was delighted to see her, Maeve who seemed a little disgruntled, and a mother who seemed totally put out about everything.

'I was wondering if you might bother coming home,' said Marjorie's mother. 'Your sister Daphne wants us to visit her but we had to wait until you got home to take us.'

'Really, dear,' her father sighed, 'it's lovely to see Marjorie back again. Please don't complain. She's entitled to have a holiday. Don't you remember the holidays you had when you were her age?'

'I was entitled to them too, Henry, you forget that. All those years in India having to entertain,'

'Yes, dear, but Marjorie works for her living, just remember that.'

Marjorie didn't think she had ever heard her father so cross with her mother in front of her before. Before it went any further she decided to go upstairs and have a bath before dinner.

She was exhausted physically from driving so far and emotionally from saying her goodbyes to Claude knowing it would be quite a while before she saw her again. The thought of returning home was in some ways pleasant, but having to listen to her mother's constant complaints was tiresome to say the least. She knew she could never do anything right in her mother's eyes. She had been expected to marry, she and Daphne both were, but she had never met anyone she would like to marry after Tristan died, and Daphne much preferred horses.

If Marjorie had married, she would have lived a considerable distance away from home.

Returning downstairs in time for a glass of sherry with her parents, she found her mother rather contrite. Her father on the other hand was quite jovial and obviously very pleased to see her home. He suggested they might have a walk around the garden before dinner was served. Her mother declined, which, of course, they both knew she would.

The gardener had done a great job over the hot summer and the roses were glorious.

'Nice to see you with a bit of colour in your cheeks,' her father remarked and indeed she had become quite brown from all the days out digging in the garden.

'Thank you, Father,' she replied, 'Mother wouldn't approve at all.'

'Oh, don't mind her too much, my dear. She can't get around the way she used to since she stopped driving, and now that I'm not driving too far she doesn't get out as she thinks she ought to, but we both know she isn't able at all. I will be ninety-two next month, but the fact I can still read is a huge advantage. Her eyes aren't good enough to embroider any more. She's taken to watching quite a lot of television during the day which is good for me, I don't mind telling you.'

They both laughed, each knowing that he enjoyed his breaks away from her.

'Don't be too hard on her, Marjorie dear, her bark is worse than her bite, and strange as it might seem, she was looking forward to seeing you home.'

They wandered round the garden for another few moments before Maeve called out that their dinner was ready. It was a rather delicious steak and kidney pie with French beans and creamed potatoes. Maeve's rhubarb pie was always something to look forward to and although Marjorie knew she would miss Claude's French cooking, she had to admit that Maeve's was quite special.

Carrying dishes into the kitchen after they had eaten, Marjorie thanked Maeve for looking after her parents so well in her absence.

'Well, miss, it weren't always easy, I'll not lie about that, the colonel is a real gentleman and a pleasure to look after. As for your mother, well her's a little different.'

Marjorie smiled kindly at Maeve who had her sleeves pulled up and was scrubbing the saucepans. 'I do it for you, miss, 'cause I sees what you have to put up with and you deserve a break and that's the truth.'

'Well I'm back now and I'm so glad you're getting a holiday yourself.'

'Yes, miss, me and the hubby are off to Southend, to a lovely little B and B. We'll go to the cinema and listen to some of the outdoor concerts, it'll be a nice little break.'

Marjorie took a drying cloth out of the drawer and began to dry the saucepans. 'My father tells me your cousin did very well on your days off. I shall be glad of her help, I don't mind admitting it, but Maeve, this is from me, for you to spend on your holiday. I'm really very grateful.' She thrust an envelope into Maeve's pocket.

'No need for that, miss, the colonel's already been very generous, but it's really nice of you. Me and him will have a few little toots before bedtime. There's a lovely little pub just beside the B and B.'

Although she didn't think she would, Marjorie slept well that night. She realised just how tiring the journey was. Poor Claude had another train journey and a boat journey tonight before she got home. It was good to know she still had a few weeks more before she returned to teaching.

She thought about her own school, about the new girls coming into the sixth form. It was always a challenge getting them interested enough to want to do well. It was all part of what she did best. She would make the most of it.

After saying her prayers she fell asleep.

Claude's brother was waiting for her outside the ferry terminal. She was so pleased to see him and he told her how well her father was and how her mother was carrying on as usual.

He was curious to know how Claude had got on with Philippe. He and Claude's sister had not been told when it happened, they were so young, so it was quite strange to be talking to him now about Philippe.

'I wish I had known about Angelo, I would have given him a good run for his money, treating you like that. Arrogant prat!' He almost spat the words out.

'Thomas, there is no need to be angry about it. It's a long

time ago and besides, Philippe has had a wonderful life with Brigitte and meeting him now has made me so happy. I'm glad I didn't meet him when he was little for I would have wanted to scoop him up and take him home. Now he and I can be good friends. Did Maman tell you he looks quite like you and Papa? He is looking forward to meeting all of you. But please, you must tell me about my nephew and nieces. I cannot wait to see them again.'

Thomas's mood lightened as he began talking about his children. He was such a good father and Claude was sure Philippe would be too.

Back in her apartment she was delighted to find a letter waiting for her. It was from Philippe thanking her for the wonderful time they spent together. He also asked for Marjorie's address as Madeleine wished to write and thank her for her hospitality.

Claude smiled as she knew Marjorie would be delighted to receive a letter from Madeleine and they had quite taken to each other. But who could not like Marjorie? she wondered. She smiled again thinking about the first time she had met Marjorie. She had looked so severe in her grey, no-nonsense suit, ordering her pupils to stand in a row until they were introduced.

By the second day they felt as though they had known each other for ever. Marjorie had dropped her rather austere manner, and although most certainly in charge of her pupils, she became much more lenient and friendly towards them. Even her dress sense changed, with the jackets replaced by comfortable cardigans. Claude discovered they shared a rather wicked sense of humour, and their laughter became the basis of a lasting relationship.

Claude telephoned her mother and promised to join her parents for dinner. After sorting her washing out and putting away her suitcases, she lay on her bed, loving the familiarity of everything in her room.

On her dressing table there was a photograph of herself with Marjorie taken on their trip to Europe in the camper-van. Marjorie was smiling into the camera. Her hair had come astray and she had a scarf tied round her neck. She was brown from the sun and it accentuated her blue eyes. Claude was laughing too, squinting her eyes at the brightness. They looked like they hadn't a care in the world and at that time they were indeed carefree and comfortable in each other's company.

How things had changed in such a short time. Marjorie's parents were frail and elderly. Her mother had had her late in life. At the time of her life when she should experience freedom to live alone, she was tied down in the same house as her parents.

Claude hoped that the rest of the summer would not be too difficult for Marjorie. Well, she would bring her here next Easter time and make sure she had a wonderful time. But for now Claude just needed to close her eyes.

In one minute's time she was fast asleep, under the quilt her mother had made for her. It smelt of lavender and home.

57

Once Marjorie got back to school, she was so busy and involved with the girls that she couldn't believe it when Christmas decorations went up for sale in the shops.

Her father was becoming noticeably more frail but was stalwart, insisting he could still drive his wife to town to have her hair done and to meet with her bridge friends for afternoon tea. She was always much more pleasant when she returned, sharing little bits of gossip she had picked up from her friends.

Marjorie had driven them to Daphne's farm one Saturday. Her housekeeper had prepared an excellent afternoon tea for them, but Daphne had allocated them just an hour and a half as she had a pony club meeting that evening. She did, however, announce that she would be joining them for Christmas lunch.

'Darling, that will be lovely, so good of you when you're so busy,' her mother said, kissing her daughter on the cheek in a rare display of affection. 'And thank you so much for tea, it was delicious.'

Daphne excused herself and the housekeeper saw them to the door.

Daphne hadn't missed India and their Amah in the same way Marjorie had. From an early age Daphne was quite independent, preferring to spend time in the stables looking after her ponies and helping the grooms to muck out. When they arrived back in England, the first thing she did was to get her father to buy her a horse and after that any spare time was spent riding or mucking out. In truth she missed her ponies more than she missed people.

Daphne and Marjorie had always had an uneasy relationship and even at boarding-school they had different friends. Daphne only agreed to go away to school provided she could take her horse. Marjorie was much more bookish and was quite happy reading on her own. It was nice, however, to have her sister to travel home with.

Maeve had ordered the turkey and ham for their Christmas lunch from her local butcher and had made them their Christmas pudding. Marjorie ordered a Christmas tree for the drawing-room and a smaller one for the dining-room. It would at least make her feel more cheerful but once again she wished there were more of them gathered round the table. When Aunt Margaret and Mother's widowed brother John had joined them it had made things a lot easier, but now there were no aunts or uncles still alive so she had to make the most of it.

Two weeks previously Marjorie had taken herself to John Lewis to do some shopping and purchase some goods for her mother. For Christmas Day she surprised herself by buying a red dress. Not a bright red, much more subtle but she was surprised at just how well the colour suited her. Claude had lectured her on the telephone about being good to herself, so she smiled as the sales assistant carefully folded it in tissue paper, because she knew Claude would approve.

She noticed a kingfisher blue cashmere sweater as she passed through the department. An assistant had placed a silk scarf round the display model with wonderful shades of blue, turquoise and pink which matched perfectly with the sweater. She knew it was the sort of thing that Claude would wear so well so she bought it immediately. Asking if it was for a gift, the assistant folded the sweater and the scarf together in a beautiful Christmas box. It would be so easy to parcel up, she would be able to post it on Monday afternoon after school.

After that she chose a moss green waistcoat for her father and a warm nightdress with bed socks for her mother. For her sister she bought a Jaeger scarf with horses' heads which would look good with the Barbour jackets she seemed to favour. She was so pleased with her purchases, especially her red dress, that she carried her parcels around the store feeling more like the other shoppers laden with parcels. It would have been so nice to have gone shopping with Claude, but it wasn't possible so she would just have to make the best of it.

When she returned home, her father insisted on carrying her parcels from the car for her. She realised again how bent he was, not at all the dashing officer in his white uniform she remembered as a child. She smiled at him as she realised that it was only in the last few years since she came to live with her parents that she had enjoyed a relationship with him. He told her on more than one occasion how he wished he had spent more time with Marjorie and Daphne, but he was needed so badly in Madras helping to restore the sight of so many young people and children.

Now as she saw him leaving her parcels in the hall for her,

he walked over to the hall table and lifted an envelope addressed to Marjorie. 'For you, my dear, the postman came very late this morning. All the Christmas cards he was having to deliver kept him back. Looks like it's from Claude,' he added handing her the blue envelope.

Marjorie thanked him and put it in her pocket to read when she carried her shopping up to her room.

'Don't be long,' her father called to her as she started up the stairs, 'there's a lovely fire in the drawing-room and I have a rather nice malt I'd like you to taste for me.'

'I shan't be long,' she replied and continued up the stairs.

Leaving her parcels on top of the bed, she sat on the chair by her bedside lamp and took out the letter from her pocket.

My dear Marjorie,

I was going to telephone to tell you, but I know how you love receiving letters so I decided to write instead.

As you know, Philippe and Madeleine came to visit us here in Rouen after their wedding. It was so wonderful to see them so well and happy and it was so joyful to see Papa and Philippe together. The whole family joined us for dinner and Philippe was so wonderful with the children, I'm sure he will be an excellent father himself. Married life suits Madeleine so well and she is much more relaxed now the wedding is over. She told us all about their little house and what she has done with the kitchen, and Marjorie, she says she cannot wait for you to see it.

*And this is why I am writing to you. Philippe and
Madeleine have invited you and me to stay with them
the weekend before Easter. Isn't that exciting? They
have a spare room with twin beds and she says she
will love decorating it for us to stay there. Maman
and Brigitte talk quite a lot on the telephone and
Brigitte wants Mama and Papa to come for a visit.*

*So I think now you have to book your flights and I
will pick you up at the airport. You can stay in my
apartment and see my family before we travel to
Marseilles. Madeleine says she will pick us up from
the station. It will be so good to see you again, it seems
like such a long time since summer.*

The rest of the letter was news about Claude's school and
her family.

Marjorie folded the letter and set it on her bedside table to
read again later. Now she would tidy up and take the
shopping her mother had requested down to the drawing-
room for her inspection.

Saturday night was always one of Maeve's wonderful pies
which she just had to heat in the oven. She had left a salad in
the fridge and an apple pie for dessert. What would I do
without Maeve? Marjorie asked herself again. She could only
hope and pray that Maeve would be able to move in at Easter
time. She simply couldn't bear it if she couldn't go.

Marjorie put a smile on her face before she walked into the
drawing-room. Her mother was doing a crossword as she sat
before the fire. Marjorie gave her the bag with everything she

had asked for and her mother actually appeared to be grateful. The wind was beginning to build up outside and they could hear the throb in the chimney.

Her father got up and walked over to the table where he kept his drinks. Pouring the whiskey into the Waterford Christal glass, he held it up to the light to appreciate the warm amber tones. 'For you, my dear, for really, what would we do without you? Cheers,' he said, hitting his glass against hers. 'Here's to a great Christmas for us all.'

As she felt the whiskey trickle down her throat, Marjorie thought to herself: Oh yes, Father, but can you do without me for another while? Then she swallowed the rest of glass and thought: Please God, let it be all right.

Smiling warmly, she set off for the kitchen to prepare supper.

58

Christmas went by happily and even Marjorie's mother seemed to enjoy it. The Christmas trees really cheered the rooms up and the log fires crackled up the chimney, keeping the house warm and cheery.

When her mother went to bed and Daphne left to look after her horses, Marjorie and her father sat on each side of the fireplace drinking the brandy Daphne had brought with her as a gift. Her father had put his slippers on and was listening to some thirties music on the radiogram he had recently purchased.

Marjorie stood up to put another log on the fire and as she moved back to her chair her father raised his glass. 'Here's to you, Marjorie my dear, you have given us all a very happy Christmas and I'm very grateful to you, I hope you know that.'

'Thank you, Father, I'm so glad you enjoyed it and I believe Mother did too.'

Her father smiled, 'There's no doubt about it, she did very much. You know I can't imagine it's a lot of fun for you, stuck here in the country with two old fuddy duddies like us. I hope you don't find it too wearing.'

Marjorie smiled back at her father. 'I don't mind at all, but it is important for me to have the occasional break. I've been invited to France at Easter; do you think you can manage without me for two weeks? I'll make sure there is someone here for you.'

'Of course you must go, Marjorie my dear. It's the least we can do, for God knows you deserve it. I have an extra little present for you I didn't want to give you in front of your sister.' He reached over to the bureau beside him and pulled out an envelope from one of the drawers. 'You might want to convert it to francs, I'd like to make your holiday even more enjoyable,' he said, getting up from his chair to hand her an envelope. 'Now I think it's time I went to bed or your mother will be shouting at me, even though I imagine she will be fast asleep. Goodnight, my dear, see you at breakfast and thank you once again.'

After kissing her father goodnight, Marjorie looked inside the envelope and discovered a substantial number of twenty-pound notes. She could perfectly well afford the trip herself, but she would use some of it for gifts for Claude's family and perhaps first-class travel by train to Marseilles. Yes, that's what she would do but she would keep it as a surprise.

She lay back on her chair and listened through till the end of the record, then she placed the guard round the fire, switched off the lights and carried the brandy glasses into the kitchen. She was so grateful she had washed the dishes before she sat down with her father. Tomorrow Maeve was coming in to make lunch and tomorrow night she would make some turkey and ham sandwiches for tea. That and a few slices of Christmas cake would be all they could manage, she was sure.

But now it would be nice to read in bed and rest. It had been a long day but she was sure the brandy and the electric blanket would make sure she had a good night's rest. Christmas always brought back memories of the best Christmas she had known; the time she spent with Tristan would live in her heart forever.

As she always did, she kissed the photo of Tristan she kept beside her bed.

On Boxing Day she had a phone call from Claude asking about how her Christmas had gone and telling of the huge family celebration her family had enjoyed on Christmas Eve. She was back in her apartment and enjoying the peace and quiet. They would celebrate again on New Year's Eve but most of all she was looking forward to Easter.

'Philippe and Madeleine ask about you when they telephone and I spoke to them on Christmas Day. Madeleine says she has almost finished the room we will be staying in and she even managed to persuade Philippe to help her paint the ceiling. They spent Christmas Eve with Brigitte and her husband Maurice, and on Christmas Day they had lunch with Madeleine's parents. They sound so happy, Marjorie, and that makes me happy also.'

Marjorie smiled as she listened to her friend. Although this time they were speaking English to one another, Claude still pronounced some words with a strong French accent, so today she was 'appy and Marjorie thought that she too was very 'appy.

'Now, Claude,' she said, 'please leave the travelling arrangements up to me. I can book the train journey from here and I'm so looking forward to it. And I won't be taking no for an answer.'

They thanked each other for their presents; Claude was delighted with her sweater and scarf and Marjorie was delighted with her Breton top and slim navy cotton trousers 'especially for wearing in France'.

When Christmas was over, Marjorie's mother went back to her quarrelsome self and Marjorie began to look forward to getting back to school. She took a trip to the sales in John Lewis and took her place amongst the busy throngs all trying to find a bargain. After purchasing a few necessary bits of nightwear and a pair of smart boots for work, she headed to her favourite bookshop. It was down a little back street which ran off the main shopping area.

Marjorie adored it from when she opened the door and smelt the familiar smell of old books, to when she examined all the new titles just published. She had read an account of *Girl with Green Eyes* by Edna O'Brien, and having read *The Country Girls* by the same author, she took it down from the shelf and went over to the designated reading area. This consisted of a few armchairs and a battered sofa in front of an open fire. She chose an armchair and read the first few pages of the first chapter before deciding to take it.

The man at the counter recognised Marjorie and said he had missed seeing her and how was life since she moved to Hampshire. She assured him she was fine, had bought a cottage in Ireland and hoped to live there some day,

'Oh, please don't do that,' he said, 'then we wouldn't see you again.'

She remembered how shocked he had been when she bought *The Country Girls* from him as the book had been banned from Irish book shops and was considered quite shocking. Feeling slightly embarrassed, she told him she needed to get going to get home before dark.

'Well, please don't be too long until you're back, we've missed you.'

Walking back towards the High Street and the car park, Marjorie wondered if the man in the book shop had meant 'I've missed you.' Was he flirting? Had he missed her? She was unused to male attention she couldn't be at all sure. Maybe she would ask Claude. Not because she was at all interested in the man, but as she had so little experience in knowing what to say or do in a situation like that.

She stopped to look at a dress in the window of one of the small dress shops, now known as boutiques. Her eye was taken by a cornflower blue dress, with what they called an A line shape. On impulse she went inside and discovered they did have it in her size. 'Why not try it on?' the assistant suggested. 'I'm sure it will suit you very well.'

She tried it on and yes, it did fit and it did look rather well on her. Catching her reflection on the long mirror in front of her, she asked herself why shouldn't she buy it if it flattered her rather ordinary figure.

And so, on that day in January, Miss Marjorie Fitzpatrick, head of languages at St Augusta's School for Young Ladies, purchased her first dress with a skirt two inches above the knee. What would the headmistress say?

Well, to be honest, Marjorie didn't give a damn. She loaded her parcels into her car and sang all the way home.

59

Marjorie's father insisted on her travelling to the airport with the driver he used from the village. He had assured her that everything had been organised for her absence. Maeve would be there every day except Sunday when her cousin would come and cook the dinner she had previously prepared. Her cousin would also come in to do the cleaning so that Maeve could devote herself to everything else. There really was nothing for Marjorie to worry about and Daphne would call once a week to ensure all was well.

Marjorie was so grateful to her father's driver and she had to admit how much easier it was not having to park the car at the airport. When they arrived he found her a trolley and loaded it up with her rather heavy suitcase. He promised to be waiting for her on her return and not to worry, he would make sure the colonel was taken wherever he needed to go. 'And Mrs Fitzpatrick too, of course,' he added with a wink.

Marjorie was delighted to find that her flight was on time and she would have time for a quick look round the bookshop and a coffee before her flight was called. She bought a copy of *The Telegraph* to read on the flight as she much preferred it to her father's favourite, *The Times*.

She was actually rather excited. She had looked forward to this trip so much and it seemed like such a long time since she had seen Claude. She had brought quite a few changes of clothes, unusual for her, but she knew they would be out to dinner in Marseilles with Philippe and Madeleine and she was sure they would be smart restaurants. She was also looking forward to seeing Claude's apartment for the first time. The last time she was in her home town she was living in a rented apartment which was very pleasant, but now she had her real home.

There wasn't anything to interest Marjorie in the book shop so she bought a very nice bottle of brandy for Claude's father and a large box of chocolates for her mother. Just as she completed her purchases, her flight was called and she made her way to gate number fifteen.

The flight was uneventful and pleasant. She had ordered a gin and tonic and a small bottle of red wine to go with her lunch which was perfectly edible. The touchdown was very smooth and twenty minutes later she was making her way through the exit and into the terminal.

Claude was one of the first people she saw as she walked down the final hallway. 'Marjorie, Marjorie, over here, oh *mon amie*, it is so good to see you and how well you look,' she added, standing back to look at her properly. Marjorie was wearing a pale blue twin set and navy trousers under her latest purchase of a cream trench coat which she thought was very French. The two ladies embraced warmly, each delighted to see the other.

Claude said, 'Let us go and find my car and go straight to my apartment. I have some lunch ready for us and look, it's a beautiful day.'

Knowing the flight was on time, Claude had parked in the

short stay car park, and after loading Marjorie's luggage into the back of Claude's little CRV, they headed off towards the motorway.

Claude and her family lived near a small town close to the sea, Claude in a village on one side and her parents on the other side. When they came off the motorway, Marjorie was amazed at how like Ireland parts of France were, except, of course, the weather was warmer. As Easter was late this year, Claude was hopeful that they would be able to sit outside this afternoon.

Less than one hour later, they pulled up outside a small apartment block beside a lake. Claude lifted out Marjorie's suitcase and directed her towards the entrance of the building. She was delighted to see there was a small lift as it meant they didn't have to carry the suitcase up flights of stairs. Claude's apartment was on the second floor and there were only four apartments to each floor.

Unlocking the door, Claude pulled in the suitcase and opened the first door on the left. 'This is your bedroom, Marjorie, I hope you like it. It is nice and bright, no?'

'It certainly is,' Marjorie replied, looking around her. It was simply furnished but beautifully decorated. The window looked out on to the forecourt, but it also looked out over trees and a small view of the lake. 'It really is lovely, Claude, and this is wonderful,' she added, sitting on the bed. 'What a beautiful quilt. Was this hand-embroidered?'

'Yes, by my grandmother, Maman thought it would look lovely in this room,' Claude replied. Although the room was light and airy, it also felt warm and comfortable. Claude's eye for design was obvious. 'Would you like to leave your suitcase and come and see my salon?' Claude asked.

Removing her coat first, Marjorie followed Claude as she walked over to the balcony and opened the French windows. 'This is why I bought the apartment,' Claude explained, pointing to the view beyond. 'Even in autumn and winter it is beautiful, but spring and summer are the best. Why don't you sit down? I will go and prepare our lunch.'

Marjorie sat on one of the seats by the table. The view was remarkable and there were several small boats sailing already. The temperature was very pleasant, not hot, but comfortably warm. Claude had lots of plants round the balcony and some hanging from the wall. It was beautifully quiet with just the sound of some ducks quacking on the lake. It was even prettier than she imagined.

'Marjorie, lunch is ready,' Claude called from inside.

Closing the French windows behind her, Marjorie sat down at the table where Claude had everything laid out.

'Some French cheeses and some local hams,' Claude pointed out. 'The bread is from the village and is always good. Not as good as Irish wheaten,' she added, 'but I think you will enjoy it. Maman and Papa cannot wait to see you, so we are going there for dinner tonight. Now, would you prefer red or white wine?'

As they chatted, both of them talking at the same time, trying to tell each other all of their news and then laughing as they realised, Marjorie looked round the room. The wooden floor was painted white with two beautiful rugs in different shades of grey and blue. There was a large leather sofa in cream with rugs scattered over it. Two armchairs sat at each side of the fireplace, which Claude said she didn't light too often as the apartment was so warm, but it was a very nice focal point.

Claude loved the markets and she had picked up lots of objects which gave the room its character. Some lovely old paintings, mostly portraits, were grouped together on the wall and over the fireplace was a huge, antique mirror she had repainted silver. Rich, embroidered cushions sat on the sofa and on the chairs. In the corner a set of bookshelves were painted yellow and full of all kinds of books, old and new.

'So, Marjorie, what do you think?' Claude asked. 'I couldn't afford to buy new furniture after I bought the apartment but I have enjoyed going out at weekends to all the flea markets and picking up things like this.' She pointed to a wonderful floor lamp made of ebony wood with a large, gold velvet shade.

'I think it's perfectly enchanting,' Marjorie replied, 'you have such good taste, Claude. I don't think I would ever be able to do what you do.'

'But you have such wonderful ideas for the garden. I had to have Papa help me with the plants on the balcony, as I wouldn't have had a clue, I mostly end up killing all my house plants by not watering enough or watering too much,' Claude said, rolling her eyes. 'Why don't we take our coffee outside,' she suggested, beginning to clear the table. 'It's pleasant enough I think.'

Marjorie dried the dishes as Claude washed up and then she waited while Claude made the coffee. She had baked little biscuits to go with it and she carried them to the outside table. There they caught up with their news once again, Marjorie explaining how difficult her mother had become, but how much closer she was to her father. Claude sympathised but was genuinely pleased to hear about Marjorie and her father. They watched the sails of the little boats heading out to what Claude explained was a narrow channel leading to the sea.

Knowing that Marjorie had had a very early start that morning, Claude suggested she lie down for an hour so she would feel rested for the evening. Marjorie was surprised at just how tired she actually felt. She telephoned her father just to let him know she had arrived safely and to ensure all was well with him. He assured her it was and told her there was no need to call all the time.

Lying down on the feather pillows, she pulled the quilt over herself and within minutes was fast asleep.

60

Claude decided it was better that she didn't drive to her parents' house in the evening as she knew her father would have selected wines especially and he would want her to try them. Marjorie was wearing her 'daisy dress', as Claude called it, and had to fold her skirt before closing the taxi door. She also wore a little bit of make-up which Claude insisted on applying for her. Seeing herself in the driver's mirror, Marjorie had to agree it was very flattering. It had certainly given her more confidence to meet all the members of Claude's family, which had felt a little daunting.

As the taxi drove them to the front of the house, Claude's father Pierre was standing at the door waiting for them. He greeted them both by kissing them on the cheek before ushering them into the salon where a log fire was burning in the grate. 'It can get very chilly in the evenings and Maman insisted it was lit, so that you will feel welcome. Come now, we must go to the kitchen so I can get you a glass of wine and Maman can't wait to see you.'

Claude's mother Marie was standing over a saucepan, but turned round as soon as the door opened. She embraced Marjorie, holding her tight and telling her how good it was to see her. Marie was more rounded than her daughter, but had the same high cheekbones and pale blue eyes. She was wearing a brightly coloured floral dress, mostly covered by a large green apron, and there were traces of flour on her cheeks which Claude was attempting to remove with a tea towel.

'Before you start introducing her, you must let me offer her a glass of wine,' Pierre interrupted, 'What would you prefer, white or red? The chardonnay is very good I think before dinner.'

'Then that is just what I will have,' Marjorie replied, looking round her.

There were so many expectant faces looking at her and children were standing in front of her, vying for attention. Claude handed Marjorie the glass of wine Pierre had poured for her. Pointing to a little boy with blonde curls and very blue eyes, she said, 'This little monkey is Beau.'

'How do you do, Beau?' Marjorie said, 'I'm very pleased to meet you.' She reached out to shake his hand, and the little boy giggled as he took her hand.

Claude pointed out two other children. 'And these two are Remy and Jules.'

Marjorie shook hands with both of them.

Claude continued, 'They are the children of Thomas, my brother, who is standing by the window, and beside him is Gabrielle, his long-suffering wife. And beside them are Josephine, my youngest sister, and that is her husband Luis beside Papa. And this is my sister Claire and her husband Liam. Oh darlings, how could I forget you?' Claude laughed at the two children waiting to say hello to Marjorie, a little girl of about six years old and a little boy of about four years old. Claude said, 'This is Adeline and this is André, they are Josephine's children. Now, children, go and sit down at your table which Papa has prepared for you.'

The children ran off into the conservatory which ran off from the kitchen.

'And lastly,' added Claude, 'these are my prodigies, Charlotte and Charles.'

The brother and sister were strikingly alike and Marjorie knew they were seventeen and eighteen, for Claude had talked about them often. Charlotte stepped forward and took Marjorie's hand. 'How do you do? It is a pleasure to meet you,' she smiled, testing out her English.

'And I also am very pleased to meet you,' Charles smiled, kissing Marjorie on both cheeks.

Charlotte was quite striking, tall and slender with a thick mane of auburn hair which tumbled on her shoulders. Charles was taller, with a lock of dark hair almost covering his deep brown eyes.

'As you already know, these are Claire's children and I'm very proud of both of them for studying so hard,' Claude explained, speaking in English which, going by their laughter, both Charlotte and Charles understood.

'I hope we do as well as Aunt Claude expects us to,' Charles smiled, 'but she is an excellent teacher.'

'We shall see how well I have taught you soon enough,' replied Claude. 'Now, everyone, we must sit down, for Maman is looking anxious.'

Pierre was standing at the head of the table. 'Marjorie, you must sit here, beside Maman when she is ready to join us. Claude, you will sit opposite. Claire, would you like to sit beside Marjorie? Her English is very good. Sadly, Maman and I do not speak English at all. Everyone else can sit where you like but of course I must sit opposite Maman at the other end of the table.'

Claude excused herself to go and help her mother serve dinner, and Claire and Josephine joined her.

The kitchen table sat in front of a window overlooking the garden, which was full of bluebells and primroses in profusion. Marjorie looked around the room and saw that it was very obviously the heart of the home. There were photographs of all the children on the wall opposite the window. In the corner a large dresser sat, covered in all kinds of china, mostly in blue and white. The stove was cream and behind it the tiles were dark blue and white. Above the stove was a very old mantle, on top of which sat coffee pots and jugs and two brass candlesticks, one on each side. From the ceiling hung every kind of pots and pans hooked on to a wooden pole. All were very much used and it was obvious that Marie loved cooking.

Josephine smiled as she placed a plate in front of Marjorie. 'I hope you will like this, it is Maman's famous duck terrine and the sauce is made from orange and onion. *Bon appetit!*'

When everyone was served they all sat down, Marie wiping her brow as she sat down at the head of the table. Pierre was filling their wine glasses and when he had served them all he proposed a toast. 'To Maman, who spoils us all with her wonderful cooking.'

They all lifted their glasses and Marie raised her eyes to heaven. 'He always says this. It's to make sure I keep on cooking for him and of course, I do,' she laughed.

The terrine was delicious, as was the wonderful rustic bread that was passed around the table. When everyone was finished, Claire, Josephine and Claude helped to clear the table and load the sink with the dirty dishes. Pierre once more arrived beside Marjorie.

'Pauillac or St Emilion?' he asked. 'I think either will be good with the main course.'

'I shall try the St Emilion if I may. It's one of my father's favourites.'

From the opposite side of the table, Luis said, 'Pierre is never happier than when he is choosing wine. Since his illness, he is not allowed to drink too much himself, but he loves to see his guests enjoy it. Sunday lunch with the family is his favourite time.'

Pierre had now gone in to see the younger children, bringing them jugs of orange and blackcurrant juice. She could hear their voices calling out to him, 'Papa, Papa.'

'I can just imagine it with all of you round the table,' Marjorie replied. 'Marie must have her hands full cooking for all of you.'

'And this is one of our favourite dinners,' Claude said as she stood behind Marjorie, laying a plate in front of her. 'Coq au vin, made from our grandmother's recipe,' she added proudly. 'It's so much better than mine.'

By the time Marie joined everyone sitting down, the table was groaning with bowls of fluffy potatoes, green beans and roasted carrots. 'Help yourselves, there's plenty more,' she said.

When the main course was over, an assortment of cheeses was passed around, eaten with the crusty bread and home-made chutneys. The light was fading outside and Claire switched on the lamps which were sitting around the kitchen. It gave the room a wonderful glow.

Marjorie imagined what it would be like to be part of this family. So different from dinners at home with her parents. Even when Aunt Margaret and the uncles were alive, it was more fun, but still quite formal. Marjorie always felt her mother was trying to recreate the dinners they had enjoyed in India, without the servants of course. But the table where Marjorie was now sitting was full of love and warmth and she felt included, if only for a short time.

Dessert was a delicious raspberry mousse served with Chantilly cream and a bowl of fresh berries. Marjorie insisted on a very small portion and pronounced it delicious. Pierre arrived back at the table with small glasses and a bottle of Sauternes. Marjorie had to agree the two complimented each other beautifully. Throughout the meal Marjorie listened to the kind of conversation only siblings could understand. Charles had asked her if she would converse with them in English so they could listen to her accent.

'Oh Marjorie, I love your accent so much,' Charlotte exclaimed, 'it is just so English, like we hear in the movies we watch with French subtitles. You sound quite like Queen Elizabeth also. No?'

'Oh dear, I do hope not, I think only the Queen speaks like that now,' Marjorie replied. 'Your English is really very good you know,' she told them and they looked pleased.

Josephine announced that it really was time for them to leave as the little ones needed to go to bed. Gabrielle said they needed to go also and they all gathered around Marjorie to say their goodbyes. Although she hadn't got to talk to them, each of the children kissed Marjorie goodnight.

Claude suggested that she and Claire would help Maman

to clear up and that Marjorie should go into the salon with Pierre and Liam. Charles and Charlotte joined them in front of the fire and explained to Marjorie what they each wanted to do at university. Charles was going to study law while Charlotte was going to art school to study dress design. 'It's what I have always wanted to do,' she explained. 'When I was a little girl, I would make clothes for my dolls. Then Maman taught me how to use a sewing machine and I started to make skirts for myself. Now I make almost all of my clothes except my jeans.'

'And did you make the dress you're wearing yourself?' Marjorie asked. 'It really is delightful, what a talent you have. You are creative like your aunt, I think.'

'Aunt Claude told us you went to Oxford University. That must have been great fun.'

'I don't think I thought of it as fun,' Marjorie replied, 'I was much too busy studying. I was a very serious young woman and I often think I missed out on the fun.'

'Well, I intend to do both, work hard and have fun,' Charles told her. 'After that I must work. Our cousin Philippe told us about his time at university in Paris and he had a lot of fun I think,' Charles added. 'I'm hoping to go to the same university.'

Marjorie was quite surprised to hear Philippe's name, but then he had spent time with them after his wedding. It was nice to hear him being discussed as a cousin.

Having said their goodbyes and promised to return when they got back from Marseilles, Claude and Marjorie climbed wearily into the taxi that took them home. Although they were both tired and ready to sleep, they talked about the evening all the way home, Marjorie saying how wonderful she found Claude's family.

Once they were back at Claude's apartment, Marjorie said, 'I was especially delighted to hear Charles and Charlotte talk about Philippe as their cousin. It's almost as though they had always known him. Charles is hoping to go to the same university to study the same subject, it's amazing. So nice for your parents to see him included.'

'Yes, I have been very blessed,' Claude agreed, 'he behaved so naturally with all the children and Madeleine and Charlotte got on really well. It's hard to believe it all happened such a short time ago. Now we will see them again on Friday.'

'I'm really looking forward to it, but right now I need to go to bed,' Marjorie said, trying to stifle a yawn.

'Then you must go and I will be right behind you.'

Marjorie went up to bed, then Claude switched off the lights, locked the front door and made her way to her bedroom.

After Claude had changed into her pyjamas she thought about what Marjorie had said about Philippe being like one of the family. Judging by the reaction of her siblings, her parents and her nephews and nieces, she thought that the same could be said about Marjorie. For someone with such a small family herself, Marjorie had fitted in really well. Claude was so glad of that as she had been slightly concerned that her friend might be overwhelmed, but being the wonderful person she was, she had simply liked them all.

Claude was still smiling when she eventually fell asleep.

61

Marjorie was so pleased she had booked a late morning train to Marseilles. It meant they would not arrive until seven o'clock, but as they could have both lunch and dinner onboard, it would not inconvenience Madeleine and Philippe. They took a taxi to Gare de Rouen and arrived in plenty of time to board at their leisure.

Claude, unaware of the fact they were travelling first class, thought they ought to choose good seats before it became busy. Marjorie said nothing but walked instead towards the front of the train having been given instructions from a guard she had spoken to whilst Claude was buying a paper. Claude called Marjorie back, fearing she was walking too far, but Marjorie replied, 'Don't worry, our seats are reserved and the guard pointed me this way.'

It was hard to keep from smiling but when they did arrive at the first-class carriage they were booked into, Claude's face was priceless. A uniformed guard, complete with white gloves, introduced himself and led them to their seats. The seats were like armchairs covered in rich blue crushed velvet. When they were seated and the guard had seen to their luggage, he returned with two glasses of champagne. 'I will be back soon with your lunch menu, please press the button if there is anything you need.'

Claude was still looking round her in disbelief. 'Marjorie, I really don't know what to say, I have never travelled first class in my life and I never guessed when you said you would book it for us. This is… just amazing!'

'Well, it wasn't really me who paid for it,' Marjorie explained. 'My father gave me money at Christmas to thank me for looking after him so well and he insisted it was to be used for my French holiday, so this was what I thought of. It's a very long journey and we might as well travel in comfort. It is rather wonderful, don't you think?'

'Oh, *ma chérie*, it is one of the best surprises I have ever had. I can't wait to tell Papa and Maman, they will be so pleased.'

The waiter appeared with their menus and, aware now that there would be afternoon tea, Marjorie and Claude chose a smoked salmon starter followed by a salad served with a selection of breads. They decided not to have wine and had Perrier water instead, followed by coffee. 'I am sure Philippe and Madeleine will have wine for us and I think we must wait until then,' Claude said, 'but a little champagne later will not harm us at all, I think.'

An hour and a half later they were in Paris and had to change trains. Again their luggage was carried for them and they were led straight to their seats which were very similar to those they had just left. An hour later they were served afternoon tea. Tiny little sandwiches filled with pâté, chicken and cucumber were accompanied by vol-au-vents filled with ham and cheese. An assortment of tiny pastries, almost too beautiful to eat, and chocolates filled with mint and coffee cream followed.

'You know, Marjorie, today I feel like a princess,' Claude remarked, 'I am totally spoilt, thank you so much, it is all just perfect.'

'It's good to be spoilt every now and again, don't you think? But this is a rather special weekend for both of us,' Marjorie replied. 'I'm jolly glad I did it,' she smiled. It was something she would probably never have done for herself, but sharing the experience with Claude made it somehow perfect.

The rhythm of the train soon lulled Marjorie to sleep. It had been a very busy few days and she was glad of the little rest. When she woke again, they were passing through some wonderful scenery which made her lie back again to enjoy. Claude, too, had dozed for a little while but was happy now just to relax and enjoy the journey.

Marjorie also noticed that the passengers who had boarded in Paris were very stylish, and she was grateful that she had bought the trench coat and silk scarf which made her feel a little more stylish, if not exactly 'chic'. That title belonged to Claude, who always looked so well.

They chose to eat at 5.30 which would leave them plenty of time to get ready to leave the train. They had both brought small suitcases which wheeled along behind them. The food did not disappoint but they had chosen well as they did not want to arrive feeling as though they had eaten too much.

The guard entered their carriage to tell them they would arrive in Marseille St-Charles in fifteen minutes. Just time to freshen up and gather their things together before the train slowed to a halt. The guard once more carried their luggage to the platform and Marjorie thanked him and gave him the notes she had ready for him. He saluted them both as they said goodbye.

Marjorie and Claude walked together towards the gate and, passing through, Claude looked nervously for Philippe. It was Marjorie who spotted Madeleine running up the platform towards them.

'Claude, Marjorie, I hope I'm not late,' Madeleine called to them. 'Philippe is stuck in the office for a while but he should arrive just after we get home. It's so good to see both of you,' she smiled, kissing them both on the cheeks. 'I managed to park the car very close to the exit, so just follow me.'

They did and there was the same little white and red Citroen Dyane they had seen in Portballintrae. 'Just as well you have small suitcases, but actually, there is plenty of room,' Madeleine assured them.

After settling Marjorie in the front seat, at Claude's insistence, and Claude in the back seat with one suitcase beside her, the other in the boot, they set off towards the city which seemed incredibly busy to Marjorie although it was after seven. 'The traffic is always busy on a Friday night, people going to the theatre or the cinema or out for dinner,' Madeleine explained, 'but soon we will be on the quieter roads and then it is less than thirty minutes to our home.'

As Madeleine so obviously knew the roads so well, it was less than half an hour before they arrived. Turning into the driveway, Marjorie felt as though they were in the middle of the country. The house was more like a cottage with dormer windows in the roof and a very pretty arch over the front door. Madeleine went to get Marjorie's case from the boot and insisted on carrying it inside. Claude climbed out of the back seat, hauling her suitcase behind her.

Waiting for Madeleine to open the door, Marjorie and Claude noticed the smell of wood burning. 'I lit the fire just before I left so the room would be warm when you arrived,' Madeleine said. 'It still gets cool at night although we have had a lot of sunshine. Now, I'm going to make coffee, but first, let me see you to your room. I'm sure you will want to freshen up, it's such a long journey.'

Madeleine showed them to their room. 'Here you are, this is your bedroom and just across the way is the *salle de bains*. I have left towels for you on your beds.'

The room was charming with the beds under the eaves and a window in between. The floor was wooden and painted white with a large, well-worn but beautiful Turkish rug. The walls were white and the rafters painted in dark brown. The curtains and bedspreads matched and Madeleine confessed she had just finished making them two nights ago. She switched on the bedside lamps which created a warm glow in the room. 'Now there's the wardrobe with plenty of hangers and you each have drawers beside you. Take your time and I'll go and make coffee. '

Even though they had travelled in such luxury, both Claude and Marjorie felt travel-weary. Claude insisted Marjorie should use the bathroom while she unpacked her suitcase. Fifteen minutes later, having changed their clothes and unpacked, they made their way downstairs. Madeleine brought them into the salon to show them where the fire was glowing, before taking them into the kitchen.

Claude and Marjorie both smiled broadly when they saw it. The yellow gingham curtains at the window matched the tablecloth on the circular table. The bookshelves, which were painted blue, were full of cookery books and blue and white china. 'You see? I told you I loved your kitchen and now it is finished just in time for you to visit,' Madeleine said. 'Would you like to have your coffee here at the table?'

They did and the warmth from the stove made the kitchen even more inviting. Taking the blue and white cups from the dresser, Madeleine poured their coffee before producing a chocolate cake she had made the night before. 'I remember you both like chocolate, so I made this for you,' she said, cutting large slices and serving them on the blue and white plates.

Both Marjorie and Claude felt so happy they had not had dessert after supper. 'Your home is utterly charming,' Marjorie said, looking round at the paintings on the wall. 'The paintings are perfect.'

'They are not very good,' Madeleine replied, 'they are painted by me from photographs we took on honeymoon, but they are a nice reminder.'

'What a talented girl you are,' Claude told her, 'they are just perfect in here.'

'Thank you so much. I was just going to pour your coffee, but I think I just heard Philippe's car in the driveway. He has bought himself a Mercedes, not new of course, but much more suitable for his work as he is going to have to travel a lot. Ah, there he is,' she added as Philippe entered the room, and Claude's heart missed a tiny beat. It happened every time she saw her son and today was no exception. They rose to greet him.

He said, 'Claude, Marjorie, I'm so sorry I wasn't there to meet you, but it is so good to see you both. Madeleine and I have really looked forward to your visit, although it is she who has made the preparations,' he grinned, kissing Madeleine's cheek, 'but my welcome is just as warm.' Philippe hugged and kissed Claude and Marjorie. 'Do I smell coffee? Oh and chocolate cake. What more could I ask for?'

Madeleine suggested they go to the salon and have a glass of whatever they would like to drink. Carrying his plate with the chocolate cake, Philippe led them in and told them to sit wherever they liked. They sat together on the sofa opposite the fire whilst Philippe sat in the large leather chair by the fireplace. Madeleine joined them sitting opposite Philippe.

Whilst they all enjoyed a glass of brandy, Claude and Marjorie told Philippe and Madeleine about life at home, their first-class journey and how Charles was hoping to follow Philippe to the same university. Claude brought them up to date with the whole family and Marjorie made them laugh about Daphne and her horses.

'She sounds like a typical English eccentric, like something out of Agatha Christie,' Philippe laughed, and Marjorie admitted she was the sort of character you would expect to pop up in one of Miss Marple's adventures.

At ten o'clock Marjorie excused herself, explaining it had been a long day. She actually wanted to give Philippe and Claude some time together. Looking down from the stairway into the salon where the door lay open, she realised that they really did look like a little family. She was so pleased for Claude and for all of her family who had made her feel so included.

She thought herself to be a very lucky woman and thanked her Maker before snuggling down for the night.

62

Waking early in the morning, Marjorie felt that sense of unease, of being in someone else's house and not wishing to disturb them. Claude was still fast asleep and Marjorie knew she wouldn't hear a thing. At home she often got up early just to go and sit outside in the garden when it was mild enough. In Portbradden she would often start working in the garden at any time from six in the morning.

Having looked through the curtains she could see it promised to be a beautiful day. She would love to see the garden. Maybe if she just threw her coat over her pyjamas she might be able to sneak quietly downstairs. She put on her shoes and her trench coat and stepped gingerly down the stairs. She knew the door to the garden was through the kitchen back door so that was where she headed. The door was obviously locked but the key was hanging on a hook on the wall close to the window. The door opened silently and she made her way out feeling slightly like a thief.

The garden was alight with morning sunshine and she walked down a stone path to a garden seat she had spotted from the bedroom. She sat down so she could have a proper look round. Someone was obviously tending the garden with love. She noticed the beginning of a herb garden, and close to the shed which had been painted yellow and blue like the

423

kitchen, there was also a small vegetable garden. Already she could see some shoots coming through the earth.

From the seat she could see the side of the house. Marjorie found it very pleasing to the eye. It was an old building, a cottage more than a house and it oozed charm from every angle. The arched stained-glass window she had noticed the previous night was on the landing between the bathroom and another bedroom. Clematis had grown upwards from the flower bed so that it now covered the wall but had been carefully cut away from around the windows.

Marjorie got up and took the path to the back of the house. The French windows from the salon opened up to a circular patio in the centre of which sat a circular table and four metal and wood chairs. The sun was getting stronger now and as she lifted her face to the sun she felt the warmth on her face. She could just imagine what it would be like to sit round the table, perhaps under a parasol, with a good book and a jug of homemade lemonade.

Looking up at the dormer windows she saw that Claude must be still asleep as the curtains were closed. There was something quite comforting about enjoying a garden at this time of the morning, before the rest of the world was up. The birds were in full voice now and Marjorie perched on the stone wall to listen. Looking up to see which tree the birdsong was coming from, she noticed that a hammock had been hung between the branches of the largest tree, and under the chestnut tree she saw a child's swing made from rope with a wooden seat.

She imagined how lovely it would be to grow up in a house like this. Although the cottage was small, Madeleine had explained to her that there was planning permission for an extension, as long as the new addition was in tune with the original house.

Suddenly Marjorie heard a voice calling her name. She had been so engrossed in her thoughts that her heart missed a beat.

'Oh Marjorie, did I startle you? I'm so sorry.' It was Madeleine calling to her from the now open patio doors. 'I've made some coffee, come and sit down. Here, put this cushion on the seat,' she added, bringing out four cushions in different colours.

'How lovely, I do hope I didn't wake you,' Marjorie replied, 'I just couldn't wait to see the garden.'

'It's beautiful, is it not?' Madeleine said. 'I'm so glad you can see it in the sunshine. Last week it was a little cooler and we had rain. That's why everything is looking so fresh, but this weekend it is like summer, no?'

'It certainly is, much warmer than Rouen, but of course you are so much further south.'

'Yes, sometimes it is too hot, especially near the city, but out here it is so much more pleasant. I've brought some fruit for us,' she added, setting down a bowl of apples, oranges, bananas, peaches and grapes. She brought out two plates and fruit knives along with two blue and white coffee mugs. Pouring the coffee, she pointed to the milk and sugar before sitting down beside Marjorie.

Madeleine was also in her pyjamas, with a pretty floral housecoat wrapped around her. She was wearing pretty sandals and Marjorie noticed that already her feet were golden brown. 'From gardening,' Madeleine laughed, seeing

Marjorie glance at her feet. 'Most Saturdays Philippe goes to the office in the morning, so I like to work on my vegetables and herbs. I've also planted some flowers which will bloom soon. I loved your garden so much, Marjorie.'

'I only wish I could spend more time there, but that won't happen for a while yet, I'm afraid. My parents are very old, they weren't young even when I was born, so it would be unfair to leave them for too long, but someday…'

'I know you will, Marjorie, and we will come and visit you again.'

'Do I smell coffee?' Philippe stood, smiling at them from the open door of the French windows. 'Don't worry, I'll fetch a cup. Good morning, Marjorie, I hope you slept well?'

'Indeed I did, but I couldn't resist coming down to see the garden. It's so beautiful and I can see why you bought the house.'

'Yes, it's small I know, but big enough for now,' Philippe replied, pouring himself a large mug of coffee and pealing a banana.

Marjorie thought he looked so handsome in a blue striped shirt and a pale blue sweater draped around his shoulders. He really was so like Claude and her father.

'I hope you will excuse me this morning, Marjorie, but I have to go to the office to prepare some notes,' he said. 'I'll be back by lunchtime and then I'll be all yours.' He took a large bite of the banana. 'Madeleine is going to take you into our local town, then with a bit of luck, we can have lunch in the garden'.

Finishing his fruit and taking his last gulp of coffee, he put his arm round Madeleine, planted a kiss on her mouth and promptly left.

After the three girls had showered and enjoyed more coffee and some delicious croissants, Madeleine said they should go into town where she could buy some fresh bread and cheese for lunch. Claude was so disappointed she had not seen Philippe but Madeleine assured her he would be home in plenty of time for lunch.

The town they drove to was just as Marjorie had imagined it would be. There was a market in the centre of town and they walked between the stalls, Madeleine picking up two kinds of bread, some delicious-looking salami, ham cut from the bone and tomatoes which were bright red and juicy. It was lovely to see the local farmers with their fresh vegetables and their wives with homemade chutneys and jars of olives marinaded in oil. They greeted Marjorie warmly as it was not often British people spoke to them in French. Claude suggested to her that they could go to a market near to her parents' house where they could pick up everything they needed.

Sitting outside a coffee shop, they sampled the delicious small cakes the shop's owner made herself. They chose strawberry tarts with strawberries in a fruit jelly and topped with Chantilly cream inside pastry cases which melted in their mouths, meringues made with almonds and sandwiched with chestnut cream, and every kind of fruit made from marzipan and dipped in chocolate. The coffee was served in large wide cups and smelt delicious.

Marjorie really did feel a thousand miles from home. She explained to Madeleine that from May on it could get quite warm where they lived but certainly not as warm as this. Claude asked about Madeleine's job. Was it going well? Was she happy there?

Madeleine told them she was happy as she worked regular hours and had weekends off. 'The law is not my passion,' she explained. 'I like it, I'm good at what I do, but I am not ambitious like Philippe. He will go far, I know that, so it is better that we are not both like that. I have always wanted my own garden and now I have it,' she smiled warmly.

She did indeed look happy. Her hair tied back in a pony tail, her sleeveless blouse showing that already her skin was turning pale gold, her face without make-up other than her familiar red lipstick, she looked like married life was treating her well.

Watching the people coming and going from the market, their baskets full of food for the weekend, made Marjorie wonder why she hadn't chosen France as her second home, especially as she spoke the language so well, but Ireland had drawn her there like a magnet and France would be a place she would always visit, but it would never be home for her.

On the drive back, Claude was anxious to learn as much as she could about Philippe. Realising this, Madeleine entertained them with stories of Philippe at university in Paris, how he always had so many girlfriends, how they used to meet occasionally at parties and how, although he was always gallant to her, she never thought of him as a boyfriend.

'He was always surrounded by other people whilst I had a regular boyfriend. I was the studious one then,' she laughed, 'he was more interested in sport and parties, but he passed his exams with flying colours despite that. Philippe was always caring, always polite and kind to people but I needed to study a little bit harder.

'Then one day my friend rang and asked if I would go to a party with her. I was no longer with my boyfriend so I said I would. Philippe was there on his own and he came over to talk to me as soon as he saw me. We were both living back home by then and he told me he was going back to Paris to gain another qualification. He asked me where my boyfriend was and I told him we were no longer together, that he had moved to Spain and I had come home. He asked me was I going to see him again and I said of course not, it was just a university relationship which we enjoyed at the time.

'He said, "Then that means I can ask you out on a date. I always wanted to but Joseph had given me the impression that you were together forever." I really laughed at that; I mean, I had never even introduced Joseph to my family. So after that he went to Paris and I would visit him there every other weekend and then he came home alternate weekends. When he came back to Marseilles permanently, we were always together. And now we are married.' She laughed again, flashing her wedding ring.

Not only was Philippe home in time for lunch, he had set the table and had glasses of chilled white wine ready to greet them. He offered to take Claude for a walk around the garden and to show her the farmhouse of their next-door neighbour. Marjorie offered to help Madeleine in the kitchen.

'It is nice for Claude to have Philippe to herself, is it not?' Madeleine asked. 'She has missed all of his life so far which must be very sad for her, but believe me, Brigitte was a very good mother. She always said she would introduce him to his mother when he felt he wanted to meet her. It can't have been

429

easy for Brigitte, but she feels she can never repay Claude for the gift she gave her. She is still very much his mother, but Claude is the one he sees himself in. He is very lucky, is he not, to have two mothers.'

'Indeed he is,' Marjorie agreed, 'but I think Claude wishes nothing more than to be his friend and to tell him what his birth family is like.'

'And he adores them,' Madeleine assured her. 'We both loved meeting them. I could see for myself where he got his looks from, but then he is also a little bit like Brigitte because she is a relation of Claude's mother.'

'Yes, I can see it too,' Marjorie nodded, 'but there is nothing but love and good thoughts from all of them.'

'Yes, and you and I are the outsiders, are we not? We are on the outside looking in.'

Marjorie thought about that as she washed her hands before lunch. She was not family in the blood sense, neither was Madeleine, but the family had accepted them both and embraced them. She was so blessed to have them all in her life, perhaps never more so than this weekend.

63

That evening, as Claude imagined he would, Philippe had booked a table at a restaurant in Marseilles, which was situated above the Vallon des Auffes in the seventh arrondissement of the city. The little fishing port was reached after a beautiful drive along the coast of Marseilles. In total contrast to the drive through the city, the sight of the colourful fishing boats and the beach close by was like being in a different country.

The restaurant was very relaxed in keeping with the rustic scenery below. The food was limited by choice but Philippe assured them it was some of the best seafood in Marseilles. He ordered an assortment of starters with crusty bread and dips made from local herbs and butter. They chatted happily together as they ate and Madeleine suggested they try the local fish for a main course, brought to the table as it would be served at home. Philippe ordered a carafe of red and a carafe of white wine, again typical of the area.

After they finished eating the fish, which was so delicious they used bread to soak up the juices, they stepped outside to a table overlooking the sea. As the plate of desserts was cold, they had it brought to their table outside. It arrived with a bottle of champagne. Philippe had previously not been drinking as he said he needed all his senses to navigate some of the narrow roads on their way home. However, he accepted the glass of champagne the waiter poured for him.

Holding his glass up high, Philippe told them he had an announcement to make. Marjorie and Claude looked up with surprise, but Madeleine was smiling. With their eyes upon him, he reached his glass towards his wife, smiling broadly. 'Here's to my beautiful wife Madeleine who is going to make me a father this year.'

With gasps of astonishment, Marjorie and Claude joined in the toast, both of them looking at Madeleine. 'But when?' Claude managed to ask.

'November,' Madeleine replied, 'this Christmas there will be three of us.'

Marjorie observed that she was indeed looking wonderfully healthy and even more beautiful.

Philippe smiled at Claude. 'We told our parents during the week, but I wanted to tell you in person. I hope it isn't too big a shock.'

'It is a huge surprise,' Claude replied, 'but a very lovely one, is it not, Marjorie?'

'Indeed it is,' Marjorie said, 'I had not even thought of it, but then I'm not awfully good at this sort of thing, having no experience myself. But I could not be more pleased for all of you.' She lifted her glass to the three of them.

They decided to have their coffee and Pernod inside as it was slightly cooler and the seats were more comfortable. Marjorie was quite bewildered by the conversation concerning cots, prams and baby clothes. Claude had, of course, been very involved with the birth of her nieces and nephews although none of them were babies any longer. For

432

Marjorie it was a new language and a new experience she didn't feel entitled to.

But Madeleine, as though reading her mind, said she was looking forward to introducing the baby to her English aunt. Philippe said that one day they would bring him or her to Portbradden to build sandcastles. Marjorie had no doubts that Philippe would make an excellent father and Madeleine would be a wonderful mother.

After another lovely drive home looking down at the moon over the sea, they had another brandy as a nightcap before retiring to bed. As they settled down for the night, Claude whispered, 'Can you believe it, Marjorie? Just a year ago I discovered my son and now I am going to have a grandchild as well. And Maman and Papa are going to be great-grandparents.' Claude giggled. 'So many changes in such a short time. Tomorrow we will see Brigitte and of course she will be a grandmother for the first time. I am so happy for her. And you will be the English Aunt Marjorie, isn't that sweet?'

Marjorie couldn't imagine, but she loved the idea of it all. There was something about Madeleine that she had warmed to and she knew that she would be included in the celebrations, if only from the sidelines.

Next day at the home of Brigitte and Maurice, Marjorie was once again treated as one of the family. The fact that she spoke their language so fluently certainly helped a lot as they didn't have to stop and explain things to her. The house was quite grand, with a marble stairway running up the centre of the hall. The reception rooms on each side had double doors made of ornate, dark wood. The salon was wonderfully comfortable with oversized pink velvet sofas and Louis XV gilt-edged chairs.

Before they sat down they were shown around the gardens which led out from the kitchen. The kitchen itself was quite modern, large and roomy, but to the right Marjorie saw that there was another living-room suited much more to family activities. The garden was also quite formal with marble sculptures sitting on plinths.

The flower beds were already ablaze with colour and Maurice explained that he liked to have flowers for every season. 'Not by myself, you understand, but I tell the gardener what I would like and this is what he produces.' He pointed out to Marjorie the roses which were already in bloom, but because of the climate, it was possible to have roses for almost every month.

Marjorie explained that her family's gardener was getting old and she now did a little more herself, but it could be time-consuming.

Maurice replied, 'This is what I know, but it seems that Madeleine loves to do the garden herself and now she will have more time when the baby arrives. Philippe, he is always too busy. He tries to do too much, but he is young and has the energy I no longer have.'

Brigitte told them it was time for tea, that they should go inside as Philippe's sister Angelique had arrived. Angelique and her fiancé Victor were waiting to meet them in the kitchen. Angelique had already made the coffee and was making a pot of tea when they went back indoors. It was amazing to Marjorie how alike Philippe and Angelique were.

The same dark colouring and olive skin. Angelique was like her mother but had her father's height.

Soon the conversation turned to the subject of the baby and it was obvious that this baby would be much loved by so many. Angelique worked with her father, and Victor had also joined the company as a director. Maurice had built up the business from scratch and was proud of his success. He told Claude that he had wanted Philippe to join the company but Philippe wanted to make his own way which, Maurice explained, made him equally proud.

They were called into the salon where sandwiches, vol-au-vents and delicate little pastries were laid out. 'In honour of you, Marjorie,' Brigitte explained, 'we know how the English love afternoon tea.'

Marjorie blushed at the thought that anyone would go to the trouble of making all this because of her. She was relieved, therefore, when Maurice announced a toast to Madeleine and Philippe on their pregnancy. Angelique passed around the champagne and kissed Madeleine as she handed her a glass. 'Maybe next year it will be our turn to celebrate,' she whispered.

'Oh I do hope so,' Madeleine smiled, 'that would be just wonderful.' She explained to Marjorie that Angelique was getting married in September.

There was no awkwardness at all between Claude and Brigitte. 'Without you, there would be none of this,' Brigitte told her, indicating her family. 'Without you I would not have Philippe, and without Philippe there would be no Angelique, so we are all happy. What do you think, Marjorie? Marie has told me how you are just like family to them.'

'Well, I think it's all as perfect as it could be. I think Claude could ask for nothing more. You are both grateful to each other and Marie is grateful that she gets to see more of you, Brigitte.'

'Yes of course, we are enjoying gossiping again,' she laughed, 'we have a lot of history, she and I. You know what cousins can be like.'

Marjorie did not, but she nodded agreeably to Brigitte.

On the train early on Monday morning, both Claude and Marjorie were tired but elated - Claude because she had felt part of Philippe's life and now had a grandchild on the way, and Marjorie because for the first time in her life she felt part of a family she previously had not known existed. She, too, could look forward to the baby's arrival and next time she was in John Lewis, she could visit the toy department.

Smiling and laying her hand on top of Claude's, she realised she relished the thought and it would be three more days before she had to confront her mother's ungrateful nature. But even that had suddenly become much more bearable. She had another life to look forward to.

64

The rest of Marjorie's visit to Claude and her family flew by at an alarming rate. The first evening of their return from Marseilles they had dinner with Marie and Pierre at a charming family restaurant chosen by Claude. It was the perfect opportunity to break the news of Philippe and Madeleine's new arrival. Marie was delighted, as was Pierre as he and Philippe had got on so well together - not to mention the family resemblance, Marie had teased.

They told them about Brigitte and Maurice's home, about the gardens and the huge rooms. Marie was rather overwhelmed at the thought of staying there on the visit Brigitte was arranging for them to come and stay. Claude was quick to explain that although the house was large, Maurice was prouder of his garden and Brigitte could not be more welcoming. Marjorie assured them that she really was welcomed like one of the family and how much Brigitte was looking forward to gossiping with Marie.

The day she spent shopping with Claude was definitely the most fun. They went to Galeries Lafayette in the centre of Rouen. Claude chose several outfits for Marjorie and hung them in the dressing-room for her to try on. Some of them quite shocked Marjorie, 'Really Claude, what do you think my girls at school would think of this>' she asked, pointing to the length of the skirt.

'I think they would say, "Oh la la, we have a new French mistress,"' Claude replied and she laughed so much that Marjorie had to laugh as well.

They compromised by buying a suit in a fine black, white and grey check which Claude matched with a white shirt with pale grey embroidery. Two more skirts and several tops meant Marjorie was very grateful she had brought such a large suitcase.

A further visit to the lingerie department ended up with Marjorie threatening to leave the store as Claude mischievously produced some very tiny pairs of knickers which she suggested that Marjorie buy. 'I would be too embarrassed to even hang them on the washing-line, let alone wear them,' she retorted. 'I don't mind my skirts going up an inch, but that is a step too far. Totally unsuitable for a woman of my age. Underwear must be comfortable for me. Thank God for Marks and Spencer and John Lewis,' she added.

Claude had to drop her serious face and admit she had suggested them only for Marjorie to laugh. Looking back on it over lunch, she did see the funny side of it.

When it was time for Marjorie to return to England and home, Pierre insisted on driving her to the airport. She was delighted to see that Pierre's elderly Mercedes had ample room for her luggage and four adults in the car. She insisted they only go as far as the entrance and was grateful when Pierre found her a trolley and loaded it with her cases.

Marie's eyes were glassy with tears when she hugged Marjorie. 'We have so loved having you,' she said tearfully. Pierre kissed Marjorie goodbye on both cheeks and insisted his wife get back in the car. Saying goodbye to Claude was not too painful as she knew they would see each other in Portbradden in July. With one final wave before the automatic doors closed, Marjorie pushed her trolley to the nearest check in.

The flight was not particularly full and she had a row to herself. She had bought her father his favourite bottle of brandy at the duty-free, and in her suitcase was a beautifully wrapped mohair scarf for her mother which she could wrap around her shoulders when she complained of feeling cold.

Marjorie thought back to her goodbyes with Claude's parents. Marie's tears because Marjorie was leaving them and her assurance of how much she had enjoyed seeing her had really affected her emotions. On all the occasions she had said goodbye to her mother leaving India for boarding-school or leaving to go to university, she never saw her mother shed a tear, she had never been told she would be missed. Seeing how Claude's entire family showed love for one another had made Marjorie realise she had never had that commitment from her parents or her sister.

In fairness she realised that her father had regretted not seeing his children more and she was grateful for the fact he was trying to make up for it now. 'You must make allowances for your mother, Marjorie dear,' he had told her. 'She comes from a very different time and from a different kind of family. She lost two of her brothers in the First World War and her mother had grieved ever since. It's a different world now, Marjorie, and a better one, I think.

'There was never any question that I would not have to work for a living. I had a good schooling and my father paid for me to study Medicine but after that I was on my own. Your mother was simply expected to find a husband who could take care of her. I do believe I've been a great disappointment to her,' he smiled ruefully. 'But you, dear, are you happy?' he asked.

'I'm fine, Father, I really am, I just wasn't interested in finding a husband and Daphne had no time for one.' They both laughed.

Thinking back, Marjorie gave a long sigh as she thought about going home after experiencing what she thought of as a proper family. Now it felt as though she had a family of her own in France.

As promised, her father had sent his driver to pick Marjorie up at the airport. Although it had been a short enough flight, Marjorie was tired and grateful she had only to sit in the back of the car and admire the scenery. Although the countryside was well known to her she felt strangely unfamiliar with it. She supposed it must be because she had found herself so immersed in life in and around Rouen.

Sam, the driver, assured her all was well at home and he had taken the colonel and Mrs Kirkpatrick out several times over the last couple of weeks. 'They seemed to enjoy The Fox and Hounds all right, they went twice and Mrs Kirkpatrick went to her bridge club every Tuesday. Nothing for you to worry about, miss.'

Her father came to the door the second he heard the car wheels on the gravel. Sam drove round to the back of the house and carried her cases to where her father was standing. 'Marjorie, my dear, lovely to have you back, did you have a good flight?' her father asked.

'Excellent, Father, and so good not to have to find my car in the car park. How are you?'

'Well, I'll not deny it's good to see you back, but we managed perfectly well and Maeve has looked after us royally.'

Maeve, hearing Marjorie's voice appeared as if by magic. 'Here, miss, let me have those suitcases and I'll take them up to your room. Nice to have you back, miss.'

While her father went out to settle up with Sam, Marjorie looked to see where her mother was and found her reading the paper in the morning room. 'Marjorie, is that you?' she asked, looking over the top of her spectacles, 'Your father has been waiting for you all morning. Did you have a pleasant sojourn? The weather has been perfectly lovely here, I expect it was even better in France.'

Unused to her mother taking any kind of interest in anything she was doing, Marjorie replied that it had been a lovely couple of weeks and the weather had been marvellous, thank you.

'I hope you're not getting ideas about going over to teach in France,' her mother asked, much to Marjorie's complete surprise.

'Why of course not, Mother, what on earth gave you that idea?

'Well, it's your father, dear, he seemed quite unsettled when you were away and I thought perhaps he was worried you mightn't come back.'

'What was that, Sybil? I thought no such thing,' her father replied indignantly. 'I knew she was with Claude's family.

Never doubted it.'

As Marjorie sorted out her suitcase she thought how extraordinary her homecoming was. She hadn't thought her mother had taken any interest in where she was, but noticing how frail her parents were after such a short absence, she imagined they might be feeling a little more vulnerable when she wasn't around. She wondered how they would react to her going away for the summer. Finding the bottle of brandy for her father and having retrieved the scarf for her mother, she went down to dinner wondering what else she might hear.

Maeve had made her favourite dinner in honour of her coming home. She even volunteered to do the clearing up before she went home. Marjorie thought again what a treasure she was. 'Steak and kidney pie, miss, creamed potatoes, carrots and green beans. I've a nice apple crumble for afters,' Maeve said, setting down the plates from the side table. 'Now just you take the weight off your feet. Travelling takes a lot out of you, I've heard.'

Marjorie noticed that her father was particularly jolly throughout dinner and her mother slightly more communicative. 'He missed you something rotten, the colonel did,' Maeve told her. 'I reckon he missed having someone to talk to proper like. Your mother isn't that talkative mainly, is she?'

'I suppose not,' Marjorie replied, 'I do know he misses the hospital a lot and not having to prepare lectures for the young doctors, but maybe some night we could invite a couple of his old friends to dinner.'

'I reckon he'd like that and I'd be perfectly happy to stay and serve it up for them,' Maeve replied, 'you just let me know. And I'll be getting off home now, if you're all right. Can't wait to share those French chocolates you brung me, but maybe I'll keep them for the weekend, special like. Thanks ever so much, miss.'

Marjorie gave her mother her present and watched as she opened the box and took out the scarf from its tissue paper. Marjorie had chosen lavender as it would flatter her mother's silver hair.

'Well, this is just perfect, so nice of you, dear, you really shouldn't have bothered,' she told Marjorie as she pulled it over her shoulders. 'Well, this is just what I needed. I swear there's always a draught from that window. Very thoughtful of you, dear.'

Marjorie couldn't stop smiling for whilst her mother was always polite when she received presents, she was not usually this enthusiastic.

They all had a glass of her father's brandy in front of the fire while her father switched on one of his favourite records on the radiogram. As they listened to 'A Nightingale Sang in Berkeley Square', Marjorie realised that it hadn't been the homecoming she had dreaded, but quite a welcoming one. She would have to think long and hard about the summer holidays, but for now she would just enjoy it as it was.

65

After her holiday Marjorie noticed an almost daily deterioration of her father. Although he remained in cheerful form he seemed to find the simplest things more difficult. He could no longer walk around the garden but instead sat on the garden seat, leaning on his stick and taking in the new growth and admiring the flowers. At weekends, when the weather allowed her, Marjorie would sit with him, trowel in hand, to take his instructions on whichever flower or bush he believed needed tending.

As the summer weather approached, she knew she couldn't leave him and had the hard task of telling Claude she could not make the visit to Portbradden they had planned. Claude understood totally, knowing how she had felt when her father had his stroke. Marie and Pierre wrote to Marjorie and wished her father well. Madeleine sent a photo of her taken in the garden by Philippe, showing her blossoming pregnancy. Marjorie's heart was heavy, but she took each day as it came, helping her father as much as she could and even warming to her mother knowing that she too could see Henry's abilities lessening.

In August Claude flew to London, where Marjorie picked her up from the airport. It had been quite a surprise for Marjorie, but a welcome one. She had bought new bedding for the guest room and picked bunches of sweet peas for the dressing table.

Maeve was excited too and made sure the rooms were sparkling for their visitor. 'What about a nice rack of lamb for dinner when your friend arrives? I'll get Alfie the butcher to cut me some and I'll do a nice apple pie for afters.'

'That sounds perfect, Maeve, I'm sure Claude will love it.' Marjorie replied. 'Mother and Father will too.'

'Yes, miss, I think they're quite excited to have visitors. Do them good too.'

Marjorie had noticed that her father's mood had lifted quite considerably since he heard Claude was arriving. 'I'll book the Bull and Crown for Sunday lunch, shall I? And Sam can take us there and back. I'm sure Claude will enjoy a real English pub."

'That's a wonderful idea, Father, I'll tell Maeve to take Sunday off.'

Maeve, however, insisted on coming round to make breakfast on Sunday morning and she would leave some cold meats for Sunday tea.

Claude was, as always, dressed in a way that was unmistakably French. Little black dress with a string of long pearls, fine black stockings and black patent heels. Draped around her shoulders was an off-white trench coat and her hair was in a smooth, French pleat. 'Darling, it's so good to see you and you look wonderful!' she exclaimed the second she set eyes on Marjorie. 'I am so happy to talk again in person. Maman and Papa send all their love and Maman said to give you this.' With that she embraced Marjorie warmly.

On the drive home Claude seemed delighted to be in the

middle of English countryside. 'It's quite different from Ireland, but very beautiful.'

Marjorie couldn't help comparing Claude's reaction to the week she spent driving round a France with Claude. 'I think perhaps we take our own scenery for granted,' she observed. 'Father is so excited about having you to stay. He has even booked an English pub lunch for us on Sunday.'

'That is very sweet of him and I am quite excited to see him also. And your mother of course,' she added.

'Actually, Mother is quite excited at the prospect of seeing you also. She insisted on wearing her lilac blouse this morning, in your honour.'

Maeve was waiting by the front door to take Claude's case for her. Marjorie introduced her and Maeve gave Claude a broad, welcoming smile. 'Lovely to meet you, miss, Miss Marjorie has told us so much about you. Give me your coat and I'll hang it up for you. The colonel and Mrs is waiting for you in the morning room.'

Marjorie's father stood up immediately to welcome Claude, leaning heavily on his cane. 'Delighted to meet you at last, Claude, if I may call you that.'

'But of course you must and it is my pleasure to meet you,' Claude replied. 'Now please, you must sit down while I say good morning to your wife.'

'I'll not stand up if you don't mind,' said Marjorie's mother, 'but I'm very pleased to meet you, and as you are staying with us you must call me Sybil.'

Marjorie could barely suppress a smile as her mother was normally so formal.

'Would you like to come in for lunch now?' Maeve asked,

'I've everything ready in the dining-room.'

Marjorie helped her father get up from his chair while Claude offered her arm to her mother who accepted it surprisingly well.

'It's all ready, Miss Marjorie, you just sit yourself down,' Maeve said. 'The colonel has a bottle of wine chilling for you, shall I bring it in?'

'Please do, Maeve, and I'll pour,' Marjorie replied.

'It's a rather nice Chablis, I hope you'll enjoy it,' her father addressed Claude.

Claude assured him she would and began to chat to Marjorie's mother, who was really quite elated and not her usual self at all. Her father had picked up considerably and Marjorie noted that his appetite appeared to have improved. It was a simple ham salad with some French bread Maeve had fetched from the local bakery. They had some late fresh raspberries from the garden served in a meringue basket with clotted cream on top.

'This is delicious, is it not?' Claude once again addressed Marjorie's mother. 'I have to admit I have - how do you say? - a very sweet tooth! And you, Sybil, are you like me?'

'Indeed I am, but not a word to Henry, he doesn't approve,' Sybil replied. And as Henry heard every word they laughed.

After lunch, while her parents went to sit in the conservatory, Marjorie took Claude for a walk around the garden.

'Your parents are delightful,' Claude told her. 'Your father is every bit the English gentleman and your mother is just how I expected.'

'To be honest, I don't remember my mother ever being

quite so sociable, your visit appears to have lifted her out of her old self completely,' Marjorie explained, 'and my father is quite over the moon at your staying here.'

'And Maeve is so lovely, Marjorie, I can see how much she likes you.'

'The feeling's mutual, I can assure you. I have no idea how I would manage at all without her. But seriously, Claude, can you see how difficult it would be for me to leave them alone all summer? Getting Father up the stairs safely is difficult enough and I can't expect anyone else to do it.'

'No, *mon amie*, I can see just what you mean. My parents are younger and of course I have my sister and my brother also, but for you it is more difficult.'

'There will be other times, I know that, but I miss Portbradden so much in summer.'

'Oh me too, and I miss Connell's lovely drink times and the evenings in front of the fire. But I am happy just to see you again and I can give you all my family news when there is time.'

After the rack of lamb that evening, which was declared a great success by everyone, Maeve blushed when complimented by Claude. Marjorie's parents retired early, the excitement of the day having taken it out of them. After helping them both upstairs, Marjorie bade them goodnight.

'Charming girl, Claude,' her father announced, 'as beautiful inside as out. She must come here more often.'

'Thank you, Father, I will tell her. Now, Mother, can I get you anything else?'

'No, dear, run along and join your friend. Such a lovely girl, very good manners.'

Marjorie smiled all the way downstairs. She hadn't seen her mother so animated since before Aunt Margaret died. She had been as close to affectionate as it was possible for her to be.

Finishing off the red wine her father had chosen for dinner, Marjorie and Claude were able to totally relax at last.

'You know, *mon amie*, I can see for myself how difficult it has been for you,' Claude remarked. 'Once again I wish I could help you, but we are so far away from each other.'

'Perhaps if we were both English or both French it would be easier, but I think the fact that we live different lives makes it all a little more interesting,' Marjorie replied. 'Meeting your family has certainly broadened my outlook and I'm grateful for that. But now, tell me more about Philippe and Madeleine. I did receive a photo from Madeleine and she looks so content and happy.'

Claude's face lit up. 'She is. Pregnancy suits her and already she has prepared the room for the baby. They are hoping to visit us all in September, but it is a long drive, I think. Philippe hopes one day to live in Paris as he can work there and it is more central for flying to other countries, but Madeleine hopes it will not be for quite a while. You know how much she loves their cottage. I am being selfish thinking that Paris will be closer for me, but maybe one day.' She laughed.

They stayed up very late, reminiscing and thinking about the new baby's arrival. Apparently Philippe had become more excited as the time came closer and was planning to take his holidays once the baby was born.

'Madeleine says the doctors now believe the baby will arrive in October so I hope it is during half term, then maybe I could visit, but I have to remember that it is Brigitte's time to enjoy being a grandmother.'

Marjorie had decided to leave buying clothes for the baby until they knew if it was a boy or girl. She and Claude would go to John Lewis on Monday and perhaps they would find something suitable for an English aunt to send her French great-niece or nephew.

They were still smiling at the thought as they tried to climb the stairs quietly.

66

Monday morning at John Lewis was the most fun Marjorie had experienced since she was in Rouen. The naughty side of Claude was very apparent as they walked through the lingerie department. Lifting a matching set of black bra and knickers, she giggled, 'What would Sybil say if she saw these on the washing-line?'

Despite her indignation Marjorie had to laugh at the thought. 'Nothing wrong with my whites I can assure you,' was her reply.

After purchasing some back-to-school shoes and jumpers they headed to the children's department to look at the baby wear. There was a bewildering array of colours from white through to navy, and Marjorie, although tempted, was a little superstitious about buying before the baby was born. Claude, however, couldn't resist buying a white knitted coat with a fur-lined hood as the baby would be born just as winter arrived.

Afterwards they had lunch in one of the English pubs Claude chose, where they had fish and chips with mushy peas.

Claude had so enjoyed the lunch they had with Marjorie's parents at their local pub and Marjorie didn't think she had seen her parents so animated in a very long time. Daphne had joined them, much to everyone's surprise. Claude made herself popular with Daphne, having asked all the right questions about horses, but Daphne declined to join them back at the house again as she had several children from the pony club to instruct later that afternoon. Claude gave Marjorie a knowing wink, letting her know that Daphne was just as Marjorie had described her.

Henry had insisted on Claude having a glass of the local ale and was delighted when she pronounced it as 'fantastique!' Even Sybil smiled more before making Marjorie realise that Claude simply brought out the best in everyone.

Even the waiter in the pub where they had lunch after shopping appeared to be under her spell. He served everything with a flourish and beamed with delight when she thanked him in her exaggerated French accent.

On the way back they stopped at the shop where Marjorie had bought her blue dress with the pleated skirt that everyone admired. In the window a dress was displayed in a floral print of white and several shades of green. 'Not only is it beautiful, Marjorie, it is perfect for you and oh, *mon dieu*, it is in the sale!' Claude exclaimed. You must try it on.'

Knowing she had no other choice but to obey, Marjorie opened the door and stepped inside. The same assistant who had sold her the blue dress was standing behind the counter. 'My friend would like to see the dress in the window please, if you don't mind,' Claude asked, smiling warmly at the girl.

Having ascertained she had Marjorie's size on the rail beside her, the girl led her into the dressing-room. Five minutes later Marjorie emerged, barefooted, in the dress for Claude's approval.

'*Non, non*, you must wear the collar this way, see?' Claude explained as she adjusted Marjorie's collar. 'Bring it up at the back and down at the sides.' Then she adjusted the narrow, white leather belt and asked the assistant for some high heels so Marjorie could see how it looked.

Feeling incredibly awkward getting into the strappy shoes the girl handed her, Marjorie surveyed herself in the mirror Claude directed her towards.

'And with your hair like this,' Claude said, pulling Marjorie's hair back, 'you see?'

Marjorie hardly recognised her own reflection as Claude instructed her to put her hands in the hidden pockets of the full skirt. Even she could see the colours suited her and also that the dress showed her figure off to perfection. The sales assistant declared that she had not seen it look so good on anyone else.

'But when will I wear it?' Marjorie asked as she walked along carrying the bag containing the dress.

'That is simple,' Claude replied, 'you can wear it tonight when we go to dinner. It's a perfect day to wear a dress like that.'

Marjorie had chosen a little restaurant she had been to occasionally with two of the other teachers from school. It was small, but had an area outside for sitting in when the weather was good. Her father had arranged for Sam to drive them there that evening so she thought she might be able to tolerate high heels as she would not have to walk far.

'But what colour should I wear with the dress?' she asked, 'I really only have black patent heels that are smart enough.'

'Do you have a black belt?'

453

'Well yes, but how...'

'It's simple, there is a little bit of black in the pattern of the dress, so you change the belt, wear black shoes and I know you have a small black bag.'

'Well yes, but...'

'No more buts, Marjorie, it is settled,' Claude replied with a mischievous grin.

When they were ready to go to the restaurant, Marjorie and Claude went to say goodnight to Marjorie's parents as they sat in the drawing-room.

Her father, who was reading the evening newspaper, looked up and raised his eyebrows. 'I say, my dear,' he said in a surprised tone, 'you look exceptionally well,' and then looking at Claude, 'and you look wonderful, just wonderful.' Turning to his wife he asked, 'Don't they both look wonderful, dear?'

Then, to Marjorie's total surprise, her mother answered, 'You look splendid, both of you.'

Marjorie couldn't for the life of her remember her mother ever telling her she looked well before. 'Smart' maybe in her school uniform, 'comfortable' in a new coat and 'suitable' in a new outfit for work, but 'splendid'? Never!

Claude, looking marvellous as ever in a blue and white polka dot dress under a short white jacket, kissed both Sybil and Henry before bidding them goodnight.

Marjorie told them not to wait up and not to worry, she had her key.

The restaurant looked out over a river and members of the local rowing club were out practising in the perfect weather conditions. Whilst they watched them from a table outside, they enjoyed martinis made specially for them by the barman at Claude's request.

'I think your father approved of your new dress, don't you?' Claude asked.

'I know,' Marjorie replied, shaking her head, 'I can hardly believe it, but when my mother said I looked splendid, I wondered if I'd ever recover. My mother took no interest in my clothes when I was growing up other than to have her dressmaker adjust my uniforms. When we went shopping it was always for her. I so wish I'd had someone who would have taken an interest in me but I think I was always regarded as too plain. Aunt Margaret tried but as she herself was plain I don't think she would have known how. But you, Claude, you were born with style.'

'My dear Marjorie, you are far from plain, you must believe me,' Claude replied. 'For me it was easier as my mother was a dressmaker and used to copy clothes from magazines she bought. We didn't have a lot of money, but she knew where to buy material for a good price. Then I would go up to bed and in the morning my new dress would be ready. She stayed up late until she had finished. Then the next day she would be making clothes for other people.'

'What a wonderful woman your mother is. I'm looking forward to meeting her again soon. Now we'd better go inside as the waiter is waving to us.'

They had the table Marjorie had particularly requested, by the window where they could see the river, both up and down as the boats sailed by. Marjorie had melon served with ginger for her starter while Claude had the lemon sorbet and fresh mint. Marjorie had Dover sole off the bone while Claude had the sea bass, served with asparagus and new potatoes. The flavours of the fish were delightful, complemented by herb sauces beautifully presented.

'They have an Italian chef and I can thoroughly recommend the home-made ice cream,' Marjorie explained as they searched the dessert menu. The waiter poured them another glass of the Chablis they had ordered and Marjorie had just taken her first sip when she heard someone call her name. She turned round to see two familiar faces looking down at her.

'Marjorie, is that really you?' one of them asked.

Marjorie looked up at them both and recognised the science mistress and the art mistress from St Augusta's, the school where she taught.

'Oh hello,' she answered rather awkwardly, 'How nice to see you both. Oh I'm so sorry, this is my friend Claude who is staying with me for a few days. Claude, this is Barbara and Jennifer from my school. Claude teaches English in France,' she explained. Once Barbara and Jennifer had introduced themselves to Claude and shaken her hand, the attention turned to Marjorie again.

'You look amazing, you really do,' Barbara said, examining Marjorie from head to toe. 'What wonderful colours, and your hair is quite different.'

'I have Claude to thank for that,' Marjorie replied a little nervously. 'She's awfully good with hair.'

'Well I must say, it's quite a transformation,' Jennifer remarked. 'We had to look for quite a while before we were sure it was you. I hope you didn't think we were rude staring.'

'Not at all,' Marjorie replied, 'we were too busy talking away, but it's lovely to see you and of course we will see each other in a couple of weeks.'

'Absolutely, old thing,' Jennifer replied, 'back to the little fiends.'

Bidding goodbye to Claude and Marjorie in a rather theatrical way, Barbara and Jennifer went on their way.

Marjorie took a couple of minutes to recover whilst Claude found it all rather amusing. 'Honestly, their faces, you should have seen them, Marjorie, they couldn't believe their eyes. Amazing what two little combs in your hair and some very pretty lipstick can do. And the dress of course. No more boring grey suits from now on.'

While she enjoyed her ice cream, Marjorie began to see the funny side of it. For her two colleagues, it must have been quite a shock to see someone they knew and were used to seeing in grey suits and lace up shoes, suddenly in a restaurant wearing a glamorous dress, high heels, hair back combed and wearing pink lipstick. If the truth was told, she barely recognised herself but she imagined that, with time, she might just get used to it.

Lifting her glass up, she tapped Claude's glass with hers. 'Here's to lots more happy days, my friend. You really have made a huge difference to me and my family.'

'And you to mine, *mon amie*, my family believe you're adorable and so do I.'

Linking arms and laughing, they climbed into the back of Sam's waiting car.

67

Seeing Claude off to the airport was particularly poignant this time as they really didn't know when they would next see each other. Marjorie drove home in silence not bothering to turn the radio on. They had had such a great time together but it had passed by too quickly.

Claude needed to prepare some papers for her students and Marjorie had pupils applying to Oxford in September so she needed to prepare for that. There was a vague chance they might see each other at half term in October but it would depend on how well Marjorie's father was. Her mother was also becoming more and more forgetful but for some reason she was much more agreeable.

Marjorie drove through the village and up the narrow road to home. The house felt terribly empty when she returned home. Her father was in the morning room reading *The Times* whilst her mother was sitting looking out the window watching the gardener.

'Did Claude get off all right? Plane on time?' her father asked, lowering his newspaper and peering over the top of his glasses.

'Yes, I imagine she'll be in the air by now. The traffic was heavy on the motorway coming from the airport. Can I get you anything, Father?'

'No, my dear, Maeve will bring us some tea in the conservatory at three. I imagine you'll be glad of a cup after the drive.'

'Yes I really would, I'll go and see if I can help Maeve. Can I get anything for you, Mother?' Marjorie asked, walking towards the window. 'Are you warm enough? It's cooler today.'

'Oh no thank you, dear,' her mother replied, 'lunch will be ready soon.'

Her father put his paper down again. 'Sybil dear, we've had lunch, it's almost time for afternoon tea.'

'Is it really? I must have fallen asleep and forgotten. Will Claude be joining us?'

'No, Mother,' Marjorie said, 'Claude has gone back to France. She said goodbye to you this morning.'

'Well, there you are, I must have fallen asleep to have forgotten that. I shall miss Claude. Terribly nice gal.'

'She enjoyed meeting you both very much,' Marjorie told her mother. 'I shall go and see Maeve and help her bring the tea in.' She noticed her father looking quite concerned.

Marjorie told Maeve her mother had forgotten she had lunch.

'Oh she was the same yesterday, miss,' Maeve answered, 'wondering where you were all day. It's getting a bit worse I have to say, but at least she's not gone wandering yet like my old mother-in-law did. Nearly drove us crazy chasing after her when she set off on her own. In her slippers, mind. Pass me the teapot will you? Yes, she was always looking for her husband and the old boy had been dead near ten years. Fancy a piece of fruit loaf?'

'Yes, I'd like that, I'll slice it shall I? I'm feeling quite peckish having missed lunch.'

'You're going to miss your friend an' all, miss, lovely woman she is. Lovely manners thanking me for everything. I think she was good for the colonel too. Don't you?'

'Yes he did perk up quite a bit and Mother quite surprised me. She seemed to really enjoy having Claude around,' Marjorie replied. 'I'll carry the tray in for you. You take your time.'

Her mother seemed quite normal when Marjorie served the tea. She wondered what her father thought about it but decided not to ask him and wait instead until he broached the subject, which he did that very night when her mother went to bed.

'I'm afraid your mother is becoming very forgetful. Not unexpected given her age but worrying all the same. I'll have to ask old Forsyth to give her the once over. We can tell her it's just a blood pressure check. She's had those before. Hardening of the arteries I'm afraid but with a bit of luck it won't get any worse.'

'I had noticed it before, but it seemed like just a little forgetfulness about her book or her glasses,' Marjorie replied. 'I wonder if Claude being here made it any worse?'

'Oh I shouldn't have thought so. She seemed to quite enjoy having her here, we both did. I hope she will come more often,' he replied, smiling.

Marjorie returned the smile and assured him Claude would be back when she could.

Two days later Marjorie drove her parents to see Dr Forsyth who had known them both for years. She sat in the waiting-

460

room waiting for them both to come back. They were the only patients that afternoon and the doctor accompanied his parents back into where Marjorie was reading a copy of *The Lady*.

'Marjorie my dear, how lovely to see you,' Dr Forsyth said. 'You must be fit and well or I would have seen you before now. Well, your mother will need a few pills from the pharmacy. Nothing too serious, just to keep the blood flowing. Your dear papa here could also do with popping a few himself. Make sure they take them, I know what we doctors are like.' He tilted his head towards her father. 'But in this instance I think he knows I'm right. Good to see you all,' he said heading towards the door. 'I might just manage a few holes if I head off now, shame you never played golf, Henry.'

And with that he disappeared.

'A lot of fuss about nothing,' her mother told her, 'I'm perfectly all right.'

'Of course you are, Mother,' Marjorie replied, 'but it's sensible to see the doctor now and again. Now let's go and pick up your prescriptions and we'll have a nice cup of tea in your favourite tea shop before we go home.'

By the time September came and Marjorie had started the new school term, her mother was even more forgetful despite the fact that either Marjorie, her father or Maeve made sure she took her pills. Her father was also struggling to climb the stairs at night, making Marjorie feel quite guilty leaving them. She was too busy to think much about it during school time but driving home she was never sure what she was going

461

to find. Maeve's niece had started coming in the mornings to do the cleaning so that Maeve could keep a closer eye on things and do the cooking.

Marjorie's new clothes did not go unnoticed by other members of staff. They looked up each time she went to the staff room to see what she was wearing each day. Having learnt from Claude how a change of blouse or a smart shirt could give her suits a new lease of life, she had also learnt how to back comb her hair and how to tie a scarf over her shoulders. Barbara and Jennifer had obviously told other members of staff about seeing her in the Riverside Restaurant and they had worked out there was perhaps a man in her life.

She had to laugh at that idea. She was simply grateful that she felt younger, better and more confident by making the changes she had to her wardrobe. A man was the last thing she wanted.

'So, have you been to any new restaurants lately?' Jennifer asked sweetly.

'Sadly no,' she replied, 'unless you count The Village Tea Shoppe with my parents. And what about you, Barbara, have you been anywhere nice?'

'Well actually, my husband and I joined the golf club. They do a really good steak,' was Barbara's reply, her and Jennifer's disappointment quite obvious.

The younger members of staff almost all complimented Marjorie on her appearance, and even the head was spotted looking over the top of her spectacles when she met Marjorie in the corridor. 'Well, my dear, it's obvious your summer holiday has done you the world of good,' Mrs Hardcastle observed. 'I take it you were further than Ireland this time.'

'Sadly no,' Marjorie replied, 'I didn't feel it responsible to leave my parents as they are both quite frail and both in their nineties.'

'You have all my sympathy, believe me,' the head replied. 'I'm an only child myself so I know just what you're going through. Don't be afraid to ask for time off if you need it,' she added before strutting off, her robes flying majestically behind her.

And so time passed by and it was almost half term. Marjorie hadn't dared mentioning a trip to Paris with the way things were at home. When her autumn break began, she promised herself time to catch up with her reading and she booked a hairdressing appointment to have a trim and a colour rinse for the first time that morning.

She hadn't driven as far as the gates when Maeve came racing down the drive after her. 'It's the colonel, he's fallen down the stairs and I can't lift him,' she cried.

Marjorie reversed the car to the black door and raced inside as soon as she could.

Her father was lying between the third tread of the stairs and the hall floor. The colour had drained from his face and he was in pain but still conscious. 'It's okay, nothing broken, I can move my arms and legs. Just phone Forsyth and ask him to call.'

Not wishing to upset him, Marjorie rang the surgery and asked for an urgent home visit. Meanwhile, between Maeve and herself with Maeve's niece reassuring Sybil, they managed to get him firstly into a sitting position and secondly on to a chair. After allowing him to catch his breath they helped him on to the sofa in the morning room and lifted up his feet.

'He's had a bit of a stroke, I'm afraid, Marjorie,' Dr Forsyth explained. 'Not too severe but it could be the first of many if he hasn't already had one. You need to get him upstairs and let him rest. I've promised I'll not send him to hospital this time, but he'll need to take these.' He shook a little brown bottle with pills rattling inside. 'We need to keep his blood thinned and it might be an idea to have a nurse call in each day. Don't worry, I'll sort that out for you. Sorry, m'dear, not easy for you, but you'll have to get yourself some help. One good thing, I'm not sure your mother really understands what's going on. I've told her Henry's had a nasty fall.'

'Thank you so much, doctor, I'll make sure he gets those pills,' Marjorie replied gratefully.

And so it began. Everything revolved round her father who was confined to his room with only small walks along the corridor allowed. Her mother couldn't understand why Henry lay in bed so long, but she was quite content to sit in the morning room, doing her embroidery and watching the birds in the garden. She slept for most of the day and only ate a little, but miraculously she didn't complain.

On the twenty-third of October, Marjorie unexpectedly lost her father, peacefully in his sleep. Marjorie had tucked him in at bedtime, assured him she was only next door and to ring the bell if he needed her. He had told her he felt well and was looking forward to a good night's sleep.

Her mother wept and asked to go to bed, and Marjorie turned off her light and kissed her on the head, not something she had ever done before. The following morning, her mother was found looking like she was sleeping peacefully, but she had gone to join Henry.

On the thirty-first of October, Madeleine gave birth to a daughter. She and Philippe named her Amelie Brigitte Claude.

68

After the funeral, Marjorie poured herself a gin and tonic before kicking off her shoes and lifting her legs up beneath her on the sofa in the drawing-room. Sadness enveloped her, the signs everywhere that her mother and father had been here just days ago. She longed to hear her father's voice again, or even her mother complaining, but all she heard was silence.

She had insisted Maeve go home, as the latter hadn't stopped working since she heard the news about Henry and Sibyl, and she had made the most wonderful buffet lunch for the family and friends who came back after the service. Marjorie hadn't expected so many people to turn up, as so many of her father's generation had died before him, but such was the respect for him that almost all of the younger doctors he had taught turned up for the service. The church had been filled to capacity and she was so happy that the hymns which her father had requested were sung in full voice.

It had been difficult not to be overawed by it all, but she felt immensely proud of the man she had got to know so much better after their last few years together. Her mother was referred to as gentle and dignified, always happy to stand by her husband. She listened to stories of their time in India and the amazing number of people whose sight her father had restored.

After the service she seemed to shake hands with hundreds of people all of whom had wanted to share their respects. Thankfully only a few had returned to the house for lunch. Seeing cousins she hadn't seen for years was very pleasant, and seeing Louisa, her friend from boarding-school and later Oxford University, and her parents really touched Marjorie. Louisa was doing so well, following her father's footsteps just as she had wanted to.

Marjorie was reminded, although she had never forgotten, what a wonderfully close family Louisa had. She had loved staying with them at half term and wished so hard that she could be one of them, but that was before Aunt Margaret took her under her wing. She wished Aunt Margaret was still here, but all those days were behind her now and her future lay ahead of her.

Marjorie had discussed with Claude the possibility of taking early retirement after the present school year ended. She had been left very comfortably off; the house was to be sold with two thirds of the assets to be hers. Daphne was keen to sell as the cost of looking after horses seemed to rise at an alarming rate. The money from their father's estate was to be divided equally between Marjorie and Daphne. Marjorie was to have her choice of anything she wanted for herself but apart from one or two items she held particularly dear to her, she was happy for Daphne to take what she wanted. Daphne's house was very large and sparsely furnished so she would benefit a great deal more.

Marjorie decided to go back to school as soon as she could. She felt she owed that to her pupils and at weekends she would try and make arrangements to sell the house the following summer. She intended to spend most of the summer in Portbradden as she had never accepted Hampshire as her home. It was what she had always wanted to do and now there was nothing to stop her.

If she stopped work she would have time to visit Claude and her parents and even, if she chose, to go back to Marseilles. She had always held a hope that Claude might be able to stay in Portbradden for long periods, but she had accepted that could not happen as Claude would have to teach for at least another ten years. Now that Claude had Philippe and Madeleine in her life, and of course her new grandchild Amelie, Marjorie imagined Claude would not have much time left to travel to Ireland. She had, however, already decided to pay for Claude's trips as she knew it was not always easy for her.

Marjorie's mind turned to Maeve and how much gratitude she owed her. She already knew her father had made an allowance for Maeve in his will, but she wanted to do something for her also. She would certainly be keeping her on until the day the house sold, if she agreed of course. Marjorie would have loved to have both Maeve and her husband to stay in Portbradden, but she knew it wouldn't be the best idea as there were no pubs or bingo halls within a ten-mile radius. Instead she would pay for them to have a great holiday wherever they wanted to go.

So many decisions to be made, but plenty of time to do it.

Unfolding her legs, Marjorie went into the hall to pick up the mail which was delivered earlier. More letters and cards of sympathy, each one special and each one needing to be thanked for. Seeing an airmail envelope she opened it first. It was from Madeleine. She slumped into her father's armchair and began to read.

My dearest Marjorie,

Philippe and I would just like you to know how sad we were to hear about the death of both your parents. It must have been so difficult to accept, but we know you will do so with grace and dignity.

It is important for us to let you know that you will always be welcome in our home. We loved having you with us and you are one of the kindest people we know. I do not see my parents very often as they moved further south in Provence and they have very busy lives. Now they have a very large garden and if you remember, I told you that was what I wanted when I was little. It is a little ironic to me.

Philippe has been thinking that sometime we will have to live in Paris as otherwise he will not see us very much. I could not bear for my children to live in an apartment without a garden, so he says we can keep this house which I love and he will also try and find a house with a little garden in Paris. Then you can come and stay in Paris with us, but I know you will prefer our home here.

We cannot wait for you to meet Amelie. We will send you lots of photographs until you get the chance to

*meet in person. We are hoping Claude will be able to
come perhaps near Christmas time when she is not
teaching.*

*I wish I was closer to you so I could give you a very
big hug. We are both thinking of you at this very sad
time.*

*With much love from
Madeleine and Philippe*

It was signed by both of them and Marjorie felt a tear fall
down her cheek and land on the ink from their names. It was
almost like receiving a letter from a niece and nephew. Well,
she would just have to be the best Great English aunt she
could be!

69

The news of Amelie's arrival had helped to dispel some of the grief Marjorie felt about losing her parents. She smiled as she thought about it on her journey to school. Claude sounded so excited not only with the fact that the baby would have her name but just by the fact that it was indeed a girl. Marjorie was so happy for the whole family and delighted by the fact that she could now go out and buy a suitable gift. She would go to John Lewis on Saturday; it would cheer her up being able to get away from the never-ending drawers and cupboards which she had to sort through.

Then there was the thought of Christmas arriving and she really couldn't bear the thought of Christmas on her own in a house where already she felt alone. She hadn't mentioned anything to Daphne but she couldn't imagine her wanting to join her for Christmas lunch now that her parents were no longer there.

She drove through the school gates and found a parking space close to the school door. The staff room was already half full but she found an empty armchair and proceeded to check her briefcase to make sure she had the papers ready for her A level class later in the morning.

She had just found them when she saw Barbara coming towards her. 'Morning, Marjorie, just wanted to know how you're coping with things at home,' she asked kindly. She sat on the armchair nearest to Marjorie's and looked enquiringly at her.

'Well, you know how it is, I'm sure. Mountains of paperwork but I'm getting through it slowly but surely,' Marjorie replied.

'I do know, my father passed away five years ago and my mother simply wasn't well enough to cope with it so it all landed on me. You do have a sister, don't you?'

'I do, but she's always busy with her horses and ponies, so I don't ask, I'm afraid.'

'Oh poor you. What about the lovely friend we saw you with before term began?'

Marjorie knew she wasn't going to get away from Barbara so she tried to change the subject. 'It's funny you should ask. Claude became a grandmother just last night, so I'm really looking forward to shopping for the little girl this weekend. I'm also looking forward to seeing the photos they've promised to send. I'll let you see them when they arrive.'

'I'd love that,' Barbara replied. 'I can't wait to be a grandmother myself. I just can't imagine your friend as a grandmother though, she looks so young.'

'Older than you might think,' Marjorie replied. 'Now you must excuse me, I have third form first period and it will take them half the morning finding their books.'

As Marjorie gathered up her things, Barbara said she would look forward to seeing the photos. 'Oh, I didn't ask, has she a name yet?'

'Amelie,' Marjorie called back to her as she grabbed her gown and placed it round her shoulders, 'seven pounds, eight ounces.'

Marjorie had to laugh at herself as she headed towards assembly. In all her years of teaching, she couldn't remember sharing baby news with anyone before. Even more strange was the fact that she rather enjoyed it.

Third form were as noisy and disorganised as usual. They hadn't yet realised that they had only two years before they took their GCE's. She reminded them of the fact and told them that from this day on until Christmas, there would be punishment issued if their homework wasn't ready in time.

There, she had said the word again, and reminded herself of the fact that it wasn't going to go away. Before she knew it the Christmas tree would be going up in assembly. Thankfully there was no mention of it with the sixth-form pupils. They had produced some excellent written work and she rewarded them by not giving homework for the weekend.

As usual Maeve had left Marjorie's dinner prepared and she had just to pop it in the oven. While she waited, she opened a few more of the condolence cards and made a note of who they were from. The final one she opened was quite large and had several signatures. Narrowing her eyes to read the handwriting, she discovered it was from the three pupils she had introduced to her father, as they were considering studying Medicine. She remembered now how gentle her father was with them and how much he had enjoyed meeting them.

She read the few lines written by one of them.

Dear Miss Kirkpatrick,

We just wanted to say how sorry we were to hear about the death of your parents. We will never forget

*the kindness shown to us by your father and as a
result of talking with him, two of us decided to study
Medicine at Oxford. You must miss him terribly as he
was such a lovely man. It was so kind of you to
introduce him to us.*

With deepest sympathy, we remain,

Yours sincerely,

*Catherine Whitehall
Marianne Burgess
Valerie Jones*

Once again Marjorie's tears dropped on top of the
signatures and she used her handkerchief to dry them. How
lovely of them to remember and she knew how much her
father had enjoyed meeting them. She sat thinking about him
and her mother and how lonely mealtimes had become.

She was marking papers later that evening when the
telephone rang. It was Claude again, much to her surprise.

'I hope I am not disturbing you but there was something I
forgot to say to you this morning,' Claude told her, 'I meant to
tell you, you had better book your tickets before it's too late.'

'Book my tickets for what?' she asked in a very surprised
voice.

'Your flight tickets for Christmas of course,' was the reply.

'Now you really have lost me I'm afraid, I'm not going
anywhere for Christmas.'

'Of course you are, Marjorie. You're coming here to France to stay with me. Where else would you go? You have no entertaining to do so you have no excuse not to come. We are all looking forward to having you. Maman is cooking goose this year and she said to tell you it is in your honour as you have never had it for Christmas dinner. You have no excuses, you must come. I can't wait to see you.'

Once again Marjorie was crying. 'But I didn't expect, I mean, I hadn't thought about it, but it would be so wonderful. Of course I will come. Please thank Marie for thinking of me,' she stammered between her tears. All of a sudden, the time she had dreaded arriving was now something enormous to look forward to.

Claude continued, 'Philippe rang me earlier and I told him you were coming and he was so pleased to hear that. And guess what? They are going to Paris just after Christmas to stay in a hotel. They are going to look at an apartment which might be coming on the market and it has a garden for Madeleine. It looks like we are going to meet my granddaughter and your great-niece.'

This time Marjorie was lost for words. More tears arrived, but they were tears of joy.

Finishing her marking she gathered up her books and placed them back in her briefcase. She had probably been a little too generous with her marking, but why not? She wasn't often lenient although she was always fair. She was just so happy that Christmas was now a time to look forward to. Smiling to herself she realised that she would need to start Christmas shopping, so many presents to buy. Now there was an extra one, a special one for the baby.

She had better tell Daphne but she knew it would come as a great relief to her. Maeve would also enjoy having time at Christmas with her own family for a change. She knew there were going to be tears for the first Christmas without her parents, but she knew her father would be pleased for her. And who knew? Maybe her mother would be, too.

While it was the end of a long chapter in her life, a new one was just beginning.

70

Marjorie settled into her seat on the aircraft and breathed a huge sigh of relief. The last couple of weeks had been manic for her, marking exams, writing reports, giving extra classes for her Oxford girls and all the while trying to pack away her parents' belongings. She did enjoy her day Christmas shopping and she felt she had done quite well with her choices. She had brought an extra suitcase filled with presents for almost all of Claude's family. The rest she would do with Claude the day after her arrival.

She had never been away at Christmas before and the atmosphere at the airport had given her a taste of what it was like. Huge Christmas trees, all lit up, carol singers and excited children really added to the buzz and Marjorie felt her mood lift enormously. She had visited the duty-free and had bought some perfume she knew Claude particularly loved. The sales girl had been very helpful and gift wrapped it for her and asked her if there was anything else she would like.

'Going home for the holidays, are you?' she asked.

'Well no, I'm going away actually to spend Christmas with family,' Marjorie replied, thinking to herself, well it was not a lie, I am, and she smiled at the thought.

'Nothing like family at Christmastime, is there? There's going to be nearly twenty at our house, two grans, uncles, aunts, all squeezed into a three up, two down, but my mum wouldn't have it any other way. Now, what colour are you wearing on Christmas Day?'

Marjorie looked a bit startled and then replied, 'A very pretty shade of mauve, I think.'

'Lovely, that'll be really nice with your colouring. Come over here and look at the lipsticks.'

Twenty minutes later, Marjorie had new lipstick, eye shadow, rouge and mascara. Then there was a bottle of Dior perfume as well. 'You have yourself a really lovely Christmas and come and see me next time. Lucky you! I've never been to France, or Spain or Italy for that matter. Isle of Wight's the furthest I've been. One day maybe.'

Now she was ready to take off and if she had forgotten anything, it really didn't matter.

Claude was waving frantically for Marjorie when she stepped into the arrivals lounge. Claude was wearing a red coat trimmed with black fur and black boots. She looked so welcoming and Christmassy that Marjorie felt happy just looking at her. They hugged each other tightly and all the stress and sadness of the last few months began to fade away.

Claude told Marjorie how fabulous she looked in her new fur lined coat. 'You're going to need it here, it's really very cold. Here, give me that trolley and I'll push it. I'm not parked too far away. Anyway, Christmas starts now,' she laughed.

'Actually it started for me the moment I sat down on the aircraft,' Marjorie told her. 'I am so happy to be here'

'And we are all so excited to have you. Papa is sorting out

the wines as we speak,' Claude laughed.

Twenty minutes later they were leaving Paris behind them and heading for Rouen. Although the roads were busy, neither of them felt that the journey was long. Marjorie told Claude all about the funeral, the solicitor, the packing up of her parents' things and Maeve being even more wonderful than ever. She told her about her friend Louisa coming with her parents to the funeral. 'I hadn't seen her mother and father for so many years I hardly recognised them, but Louisa was just the same. It brought back so many memories.'

Marjorie added that Daphne had been very kind and helpful at the time leading up to the funeral but was now once again back to her busy life. 'And the teachers were also really kind helping out with my classes, so it hasn't all been bad. What I would do without Maeve, I dread to think.'

Marjorie went on to tell Claude about taking the photos of Amelie to the staff room and how everyone thought she was a very beautiful baby. 'And she is of course,' Marjorie smiled.

Claude told her how well the baby was doing, how Madeleine sent photos all the time and kept her up to date with all the progress. 'She still doesn't want to leave the cottage and I can't blame her, but at the same time she and Amelie will see much more of Philippe if they have somewhere in Paris.'

'How wonderful it is to be young and able to adapt to things so much more quickly, but I know they will sort it out between the two of them as I could see how good they were together,' Marjorie agreed.

Before they knew it they were pulling up in front of Claude's apartment. Claude lifted the suitcases out of the back of the car and pulled them over to the doors of the lift. Marjorie followed with what felt like endless bags full of parcels.

Stepping in the doorway Marjorie saw that the apartment had been transformed. There was a beautiful tree decorated as only Claude could do. There were candles everywhere and fairy lights hung everywhere. Marjorie stood back to take it all in. There was a nativity set made of carved wood with a candle illuminating the manger, sitting on a side table and lights hung over the window. It was quite a winter view over the lake and she could imagine what it would look like if there was snow.

'Claude, you have worked so hard doing all this but I love every bit of it,' Marjorie exclaimed.

'Wait until you see Maman's house. The children all help to decorate it and then when it's done, Papa switches on the lights of the tree. Maman makes punch for the children and then they have toasted sandwiches and hot chocolate. It's one of my favourite parts of Christmas.'

'It sounds wonderful, I can't wait to see them all. Tomorrow I need to get gifts for the younger ones. I have no experience of children that age I'm afraid.'

'Yes, we can do that, but only little gifts please. Now, go and empty your suitcases and I will heat up some soup and some warm bread. You must be so hungry. And look, I will light the fire for us.'

In her bedroom unpacking her clothes, Marjorie thought of how different this year was going to be compared to last year. She was so glad her parents had enjoyed their last Christmas so much. All the hard work had been worth it and she remembered them sitting in front of the drawing-room fire opening their presents. A lump caught in her throat again, but she didn't allow any tears. This was a whole new experience for her, a Christmas with her dearest friend and her family. Children around them on Christmas Day. She had never expected anything like it, but she knew it would be wonderful.

After she hung up her clothes she joined Claude in the kitchen. The smell of soup and hot bread made her really hungry, but first they had a glass of champagne before they sat down. Claude lifted her glass and proposed a toast to Marjorie, how joyful it was to have her and how grateful she was to have a friend so dear.

Once again Marjorie felt the tears rising, but she lifted her glass and quietly said, 'This is to you, Claude, thank you for saving me from myself.'

The toasts over, they sat down and enjoyed Claude's French onion soup, hot bread and cheese. Claude said, 'I thought tonight we would stay in so we can both rest before shopping tomorrow. Maman and Papa like to follow the old tradition of eating on Christmas Eve, *Le Réveillon de Noel*, but on Christmas Day we have roast goose and all the trimmings. We are allowed to open one gift on Christmas Eve but on Christmas Day the children are allowed to open the rest. All of us help Maman and then on Boxing Day we rest. With more food, of course!' she laughed.

'It all sounds wonderful. I think I need to pinch myself in case I'm dreaming. I wasn't looking forward to Christmas with Daphne,' she smiled, 'but she has so many invitations, I don't need to worry about her. This is so much better.'

'And don't forget,' Claude reminded her, 'it's my first Christmas ever as a grandmother, isn't that wonderful? I never imagined for one minute it would happen, but here we are. Happy Christmas, Marjorie.'

'Happy Christmas, Claude.'

They clinked their glasses and sipped their wine as the logs crackled in the fire. It had begun and they were ready.

71

Much as Claude and Marjorie loved being with the family, they decided to spend St Stephen's Day at home. Neither had had much of a chance to relax after term broke up as they had been so busy with the lead up to Christmas. They had accepted an invitation to visit Claire the following day and Josephine's the day after that. So they now had time to do as they liked and also to pack ready for Paris.

Claude was so excited to see the new baby but also grateful to have a few days' rest before then. They read books, flicked through magazines, drank lots of coffee and tea and did what friends do best: they talked.

Claude explained how difficult it was to remember what Philippe was like as a baby as she had such a short time with him. She had forced herself not to bond with him and of course her mother was there for them both. Brigitte had sent photos of him as a baby to Marie but she had decided not to let Claude see them as she was at school and preparing for exams. Instead Marie had kept them in a special album ready for the day when Claude would ask.

Now Claude showed those photos to Marjorie so they could compare Philippe with Amelie.

'I rather imagine she will look more like her mother,' Marjorie pondered over a photograph of Philippe at the same age beside the new photos of Amelie. 'Perhaps with his father's features. I've not had any experience with babies, I'm afraid.'

'Well, of course I have had my nieces and nephews since they were born and I have babysat a lot of course,' Claude replied, 'but this is quite different for me.'

'Of course it is and it will be a wonderful experience for you, and a delightful one for me.'

Three days later, they stood at the station waiting for the train to Paris. It had become quite cold and Marjorie was grateful once again for her fur-lined coat. However, the temperature inside the train when they eventually boarded was extremely comfortable. The journey was quite short, less than two hours, and they both relaxed at the table they had to themselves.

It was not first class - Claude refused to allow Marjorie to do that again - but the seats were comfortable and they enjoyed the scenery as they passed through, with Claude pointing out places where she had relatives or places of interest. Marjorie fell asleep with the rhythm of the engine and was quite startled when Claude woke her to tell her they had just ten more minutes before they arrived in Paris.

They managed to grab a taxi from the rank outside Gare Saint-Lazare and as it was a reasonably early hour, the journey to their hotel was just over half an hour. They had booked a small hotel near to where Philippe and Madeleine would be staying. They arrived just in time to unpack their clothes before going out for lunch.

Marjorie and Claude walked along the avenues, gazing in windows and looking at menus. They found a restaurant which looked comfortable although small. The waiter who met them was friendly and welcoming and he suggested they take a table close to a radiator. They did and warmed their hands before choosing from the menu. They both decided on soup followed by pâté and bread of the house.

'Shall I bring you a carafe of house wine?' the waiter asked.

They decided a half carafe would be plenty. It was a good choice and the soup was delicious and warming. The pâté was excellent and the wine quite sufficient. Over their coffees they discussed what they might do in the afternoon. They agreed the museums were better visited in the morning so this afternoon would consist of some leisurely shopping.

They finished the day having dinner in the same restaurant as it was close to the hotel and they knew how good the food was. Marjorie had bought a warm outfit for Amelie, and Claude had bought her a tiny gold bracelet. It was being engraved with her full name and date of birth and would be ready the following morning. They would meet up with Madeleine and Philippe on the morning of New Year's Eve.

Marjorie smiled as she recognised how excited Claude had become since they reached Paris. 'Only one more night to go until you first get to hold your grandchild,' she said, tapping her wine glass against Claude's. 'It must seem like forever to you.'

'Oh no, Marjorie, I am enjoying my time with you so much. I like that we don't always have to say things to each other, we just know. Like now when I was thinking of the bracelet, how tiny it was. Andre is my youngest nephew but he is three now and I can't really remember how small he was.'

'And now Amelie is almost two months old so she must be changing all the time.'

'She is, but Madeleine has been so kind sending me a photograph almost every week. Philippe is so lucky to have such a lovely wife. I hope he knows that.'

'I'm quite sure he does,' Marjorie replied. 'When he looks at her I think that is obvious.'

Back at the hotel they were grateful to climb into what were very comfortable beds. They had sat in the hotel lounge for a while, sipping Pernod and watching the tourists who were arriving in time for New Year's Eve.

While Claude slept, Marjorie thought about the life changes she had experienced over the last few years. Buying the house in Portbradden was the first one, her parents dying was the second. Selling the family home would have to be done before summer of the new year. Meeting Philippe and Madeleine and the arrival of their baby had been a very welcome change, but it made Marjorie wonder how life would change for Claude. It was obvious the immediate bond Claude and Philippe had felt. She couldn't just walk back out of his life. And then there was the baby, an opportunity to be involved in her life.

Marjorie couldn't see how Claude would manage to come to Portbradden as often now that she had other people to consider. She was going to miss Claude, that was for sure, although when she gave up teaching she would be able to travel to France. She was always amazed that Claude did not have a man in her life, yet when she broached the subject Claude always had the one reply: 'One marriage was enough for me, never again.'

Claude rarely talked about her ex-husband Antonio but Marjorie knew how deep that hurt must have been. Claude's marriage had been violent and degrading; it had been a terrible time for her. She made light of the experience but she must bear scars. Philippe was helping to heal those scars and Brigitte and Madeleine were happy to stand back and let her have this time with him.

Although Marjorie knew how much Madeleine loved her cottage near Marseilles, she couldn't help hoping Madeleine and Philippe would also live in Paris so it would be easier for Claude to keep contact with the little family she loved so much. Marjorie was sure they would work it all out but she knew, whatever happened, she would always be there for Claude.

Then she allowed the restful feeling of approaching sleep envelop her.

72

B y New Year's Eve, Marjorie and Claude were exhausted with shopping, walking round art galleries and museums and generally sightseeing. There was such a buzz around Paris, more and more people arriving in the city to celebrate seeing the old year out and the new year in.

But today, Claude had much more important meetings to look forward to and Marjorie found herself caught up in the excitement of it all. They had been invited to the apartment where Philippe was staying at four o'clock. Philippe had booked a table at the restaurant in the street close to the hotel Claude and Marjorie was staying in so it was just minutes away from where they were all staying.

Marjorie and Claude agreed amongst themselves to stay at the apartment for two hours only to allow Madeleine to rest before they met up again. This morning they would take a leisurely stroll around the shops, taking their time and stopping for coffee whenever they felt like it. The two were so easy in each other's company, they didn't need to make excuses when they needed to sit down.

At ten o'clock they stood outside the jewellers where Claude had bought the bracelet for Amelie. She was always thoughtful about Brigitte and didn't want to do anything that could in any way upset her. She had seen a very sweet little necklace and thought she would like to look again. Marjorie asked if Claude would mind if she looked in the bookshop across the road and of course Claude told her to take her time and they could meet up again around eleven at 'their' coffee shop.

Walking past the bookshop, Marjorie noticed an estate agency just next door and stopped to look in the window. All the apartments for sale were from the immediate area where they were staying. She was amazed to find that properties in Paris were actually less expensive than similar properties in London. One which drew her eye was just two streets away from where she stood. It looked wonderful and to her amazement the furniture was included in the price.

Looking round to see if Claude was still in the jewellers and seeing that she was, she walked inside the estate agency.

'Good morning, madame, how can I help you?' The gentleman addressing her was immaculately dressed in a dark grey suit, sparkling white shirt and red silk tie. His cuffs were held together with gold cuff links set with rubies and diamonds. He had silver grey hair which was immaculately styled. She imagined him to be in his early fifties and she felt slightly overawed by him.

'Good morning,' she replied, 'I'm curious about an apartment you have in the window, the one with the Juliet balcony.'

'Ah, we have several like that, let me show you over here.'

He brought her to a wall at the back where photographs of apartments, including their interior, were displayed. She immediately saw the one which interested her.

'Ah, this is it, this one here,' she said pointing to the top row.

'Ah, that is an interesting property. It has been used only a few times a year. The owner is a musician and is moving to New York. He has two properties in France to sell and wants to sell the apartment quickly. But madame, although your accent is impeccable I detect you are not from Paris. Am I right?'

His manner was slightly condescending and although his smile was bright, she rather imagined he was amused by her.

'You're absolutely correct, I'm English, but I have an interest in having somewhere in Paris where I could stay from time to time. Now is the asking price negotiable? You mentioned the owner is anxious for a quick sale.'

'Well, yes, madame, it is not generally our policy, but I'm sure we can come to some arrangement.'

'I imagine we could, but first I need to see it. My time is limited. May I arrange a viewing for two o'clock this afternoon?'

'Well, that is rather soon, but I'm sure one of my staff could meet you there. May I have your name?'

'Of course, here is my card, it's my father's actually but it is my address. I'm staying at the Hotel Normandy and I will see you at two o'clock precisely.'

'Thank you, madame, I may even be free to show you around myself,' he added.

Claude was walking on the other side of the road when Marjorie stepped out on to the street again. Catching up with her, Claude noticed that she wasn't carrying any parcels.

'Good heavens, I quite forgot,' Marjorie replied. 'I rather think we may have to have an early lunch. I have an appointment, just here.' She pointed to the street to the right of them. 'Number twenty-four E.'

Claude stood still and looked at her friend, surprise written all over her face. 'Marjorie, what are you talking about? You only crossed the road to buy a book!'

'Yes I know, Claude, but you see it just struck me, we should have a place to stay in Paris.'

'Now, Marjorie, I am beginning to think you've gone a little bit mad. I could not possibly afford to have property in Paris.'

'Yes I know, dear, but the thing is, I can!' As she said it, she realised it was true. 'I've been thinking how difficult it is going to be for you, with your new little family to visit, and as you will still be teaching it won't be easy for you to find time for Portbradden. I shall be selling Father's house and there really is no need for me to have any property in England any more, not if I retire next year. What do you think, Claude? Doesn't it make perfect sense?'

'What I think, Marjorie, is that I need a glass of something strong and very quickly.'

They reached the restaurant they loved and the waiter waved, happy to see them again. 'And for New Year's Eve, we have a different menu, I can highly recommend the sole, it's magnificent.'

'Then that is what we will have, no starter and a large carafe of wine, please.'

'For both of you?' he asked. 'You will both have the fish? It is sole Veronique,' he added.

'Delicious, that's good for you, Claude?' Without waiting for an answer she told the waiter to bring two glasses of brandy before the entrée.

'Marjorie, have you completely lost your mind?' Claude asked, 'This is so unlike you. It has been difficult to persuade you to come to France until now,'

'Of course it was. I had my parents to look after and my time wasn't my own. But now I have the freedom to do as I please,' she replied with a very satisfied expression on her face. 'I miss my parents, I really do, but since the war I have been limited in what I can do. Now I think I should be doing things for myself.'

'Of course you should, but *mon amie*, this is all so sudden. In all the conversations we have had over Christmas, you have never mentioned living in France. I'm just very, very surprised.'

'I'm surprised myself,' Marjorie said with a smile. 'I've been thinking about it when I couldn't sleep. Then I looked in the window and saw this dear little apartment which looked as though you or Madeleine had furnished it. It's the answer to my prayers. I shall live in Portbradden and at holiday time I shall come to France. Meanwhile, you can come to Paris to see Amelie whenever they are in town and in between so can Marie and Pierre and any of your family who would want to can stay in it. Isn't it a wonderful idea?'

'Well yes, but it wouldn't be fair, we would be using it much more than you.'

'Good, then it will be lived in and that is what I want. What else should I do with my money? Portbradden has enough furniture and I intend to put heating into it, but I need little else. Oh look, here comes lunch. Finish your brandy and I'll pour us some wine.'

At two o'clock precisely, the estate agent Monsieur Mercier met Claude and Marjorie outside the door of number 24E. 'Delighted to meet you,' he said, shaking hands with Claude. 'Your friend has very good taste. I think you will find this apartment very charming.'

And it was. The salon was a comfortable size and the two bedrooms both had double beds and excellent wardrobe space. The kitchen, which was painted yellow and blue, made Claude smile. Saucepans and frying pans hung from the walls and the cupboards were full of cups, saucers and plates, all in a very pretty yellow and blue floral design. The Juliet balcony was approached by French windows from the salon and was furnished with a circular table and four wicker chairs. The window boxes, Marjorie imagined, could be ablaze with colour in springtime.

Claude walked from room to room with a look of disbelief on her face.

'Well, do you like it?' Marjorie eventually asked. 'Is it not exactly the style we both love?'

'Well, yes, of course it is and I love it, but -'

'No buts, Claude, for once in my life I'm doing something that I want to do. Now I just need to talk to this gentleman and we'll see how quickly it can be done.'

Monsieur Mercier looked delighted. Must never judge a book by its cover, he thought to himself. 'I managed to speak to the owner in New York. He has agreed to drop the price a little for a cash deal. But first, madame, you must find a lawyer.'

'That's not a problem,' Claude intervened, 'my son is an *avocat* and we will see him in Paris this evening.'

'Excellent. Then if you can give him power of attorney, I can conduct the sale with him. Thank you so much, madame. I think you have made a wonderful decision. I will see you before you leave on January the second. It has been a pleasure and may I wish you both a Very Happy New Year.'

Back in the hotel, Marjorie and Claude went up to their room and flopped down on the bed laughing.

'I know it is all slightly ridiculous but I have no regrets at all,' Marjorie confessed. 'We can come here together during the winter, perhaps at half term, and in summer we can divide our time between Ireland and France. I have no particular desire to be in England. I have no family there that counts but I have my wonderful French family here.'

'Oh my dear Marjorie, you are the most generous person I know. It would be so wonderful for Maman and Papa to stay when their great granddaughter is here. Marseilles is so far away from them. For me, I can see Philippe and Madeleine far more often and you and I will have so much fun together. I can hardly believe it.'

'Neither can I,' Marjorie replied, 'but the money is in the bank and all we need now are papers to sign. It really was made for us.'

'Good heavens, look at the time,' Claude exclaimed, 'we need to leave in half an hour. Now we get to meet Amelie. Could a day be any more perfect?'

Marjorie had to agree, it couldn't have been any better. Silently she thanked her father for all the careful work he had carried out to ensure there would be plenty of money available for Marjorie. She remembered the letter he had left with his solicitor. In it he said that Marjorie was a daughter he didn't deserve for her kindness and her unselfish nature:

I hope you know how much your mother and I appreciated all you did for us. I hope the money will enable you to live the life you richly deserve. Spend it as you please, whatever you do will have my approval. Your sacrifice gave us a very secure retirement. Look after your friend Claude, she is a delightful woman and I wish we had known her longer. Look after each other.

She would show it to Claude the following day. Today was Claude's day. At last she would meet Amelie and hopefully the apartment in Paris would enable her to see Amelie more often. She was excited herself to meet this precious baby and to see her parents again.

'You are right, Father, we have to look after each other. And thank you,' she whispered to herself.

Half an hour later they stood outside the apartment where Madeleine and Philippe were staying. They rang the bell and waited.

73

The door opened and Madeleine was standing in the doorway. She hugged them and welcomed them inside. She was casually dressed in a grey sweatshirt and matching pants. Her hair was caught up in a ponytail and Claude immediately noticed dark circles under her eyes.

'Claude, Marjorie, you look amazing,' Madeleine said. 'I look like such a mess but the journey was so long and then I had to change Amelie and bath her in the sink. Oh dear, I must sound pathetic, forgive me. Come inside, Philippe was on the phone but he's finished now, but first, you must be dying to see the baby. Come on, she's asleep in the bedroom. Don't worry, you won't disturb her.'

She gently opened the door to the left. Although the room was in darkness, the light from the hall lit up the crib where Amelie was lying. She was dressed in pink, her arm outside her blankets. Her hair was dark and quite curly, the tiny curls jutting over the collar of her sleep suit. Her other little hand was under her cheek which was flushed with sleep. Even from the doorway Claude could see the long, dark eyelashes lying on her cheeks. Beside her lay a pink and white bunny rabbit which was the same size as she was.

'Oh my, she's so pretty, so tiny and perfect,' was all Claude could say. She was quite overcome by emotion, the reality of her seeing her granddaughter, being able to touch her little hand, was all of a sudden too much. Taking a hanky from her pocket, she dabbed at her eyes. 'Marjorie, you must look closer. Isn't she perfect?'

'Indeed she is,' Marjorie whispered, 'like a little doll sleeping.'

'Come, she will be awake in an hour and you will see her properly then,' Madeleine said. 'Let's catch up while we can.'

Philippe was standing behind them in the hall waiting to greet them. Madeleine pulled the bedroom door to and joined them in the hall. Philippe led Marjorie and Claude into the salon, an arm round each of them. He hugged Claude warmly, leaning back to look at her. 'Well, you obviously have not been missing your sleep like we are, you look so well. And you, Marjorie, you are looking fantastic, how lovely to see you both at last.' He ushered them into chairs while Madeleine sat on the sofa with her legs tucked under her.

'So Amelie has been keeping you up, no?' Claude asked.

'Only for the last couple of nights,' Madeleine replied, 'I think she is not getting enough milk, so tonight we are going to give her a bottle as well.'

Marjorie, unused to such conversation, felt mildly uncomfortable, but then Philippe joined in, making her feel better. 'I think it is better, for I can give her a feed at night before I go to bed so that Madeleine can get some proper sleep. You can see she already she has her Papa round her little finger.' He smiled, taking Madeleine's hand and squeezing it. 'She is perfect during the day, but late at night I think she wants to have a party.'

'And you are very busy, are you not?' Claude asked him. 'Madeleine tells me you have a lot of work at the moment. I hope you can rest for a few days now.'

'It's very difficult for me to turn down work. I have to take the work I'm given as I'm not senior enough to turn work down. But it's ok, just a bit difficult as I have had to be in Paris quite a lot on a case I'm working on. If I win, it will be very good for me.'

'That all sounds exciting,' Marjorie told him. 'I'm sure you will win after putting so much effort in.'

'I hope so, Marjorie,' he replied, 'but how are you enjoying Paris? Very different from Rouen, no?'

'I love it. The museums and galleries are just wonderful and I never tire of them. We have had a very busy few days, haven't we, Claude?'

'You could say that,' Claude replied, 'but we will keep it all for dinner time. Are you very tired, Madeleine?'

'Not so bad, but travelling is always tiring, no matter what way you go. Philippe! You are very remiss. Please offer Marjorie and Claude a drink.'

'Oh no thank you, you're very kind,' Marjorie said, 'but I think it's better to wait until dinner time, don't you?'

'Absolutely,' Philippe agreed, 'we shall have good wine with dinner, then we have champagne in the fridge to see in the new year. It is easier for us to be here in the apartment if you don't mind. It means we can have Amelie settled for the night.'

Amelie woke, just as her mother had forecast. Madeleine went to the bedroom and carried her back with a blanket round her. 'Here you are, my little one, you need to meet two very special ladies,' and she handed her to Claude.

Amelie was indeed awake and her eyes were bright as she studied the face looking down at her. She squirmed a little and then, as Claude cooed at her, she smiled.

'You see? Right away she knows who you are,' Philippe said. 'We have decided that you will be Mamie Claude and Brigitte will be Mamie Brigitte. We don't see very much of my mother so Amelie won't be too confused. When she's older we will explain how lucky she is to have three Mamies.'

Claude was simply mesmerised gazing at the baby in her arms. As she talked to Amelie, her tiny mouth began to form shapes. 'Look, already she is trying to talk,' Claude smiled.

'Obviously highly intelligent like her father and talkative like her grandmother,' Marjorie laughed. 'She is quite delightful. I don't think I've ever seen such a young baby before. I did go to the christenings of Louisa's children, but they seemed so much bigger, practically walking I imagine.'

'Here, Marjorie, you must hold her,' Claude insisted. 'You are her honorary great-aunt after all.'

Marjorie sat back, quite shocked at the prospect of holding such a tiny human being. 'Oh no, please, I'm quite unused. Perhaps when I get to know her better,' she protested and they all laughed in the kindest way.

'Perhaps tomorrow,' Madeleine suggested, 'but now she's ready for her feed.' She looked at Marjorie. 'Do you mind if I feed her here? I can take her to the bedroom so don't worry.'

'Oh no, please don't change anything because of me. I'm very happy just being here.'

Madeleine lifted the baby carefully from Claude and, draping a towel over her shoulder, she covered herself up before beginning the feed. Any embarrassment Marjorie felt was overcome by the sniffling sounds from under the towel.

'Amelie loves her feeding times, there have been no problems about that from the day she was born. She's just very greedy I'm afraid,' Philippe explained and Claude thought what a good father he was.

'Such a pity Philippe has to work so hard,' Claude thought out loud to Marjorie as they arrived back in their hotel bedroom to change before dinner.

'I know, but we must remember he's still very young and making his way. When I first started teaching in Jersey, I took it all very seriously and sat up late writing helpful remarks on every girl's homework. He's young and ambitious and Madeleine doesn't have to work, which is a great blessing,'

'You're right of course,' Claude agreed, 'I still look at this man and wonder how on earth he can be my son. I held Amelie tonight and kept asking myself, are you really mine? But then there was just a tiny movement in her face and suddenly I saw Maman. It was amazing really because now I know she is part of me.'

Claude looked so happy and Marjorie instinctively hugged her. 'She is very much a part of you, Claude. Even I who know nothing about babies could see the likeness.'

'Oh thank you, my lovely friend, you always see the happy side of things,' Claude whispered.

'Not always,' Marjorie replied, 'but that was very obvious. Now, I shall use the bathroom while you choose what you are wearing. I'm wearing the blue blouse again as I feel so good in it.'

'You look great in it,' Claude told her as she opened the

door of the wardrobe. She decided to wear the little black dress with the new scarf Marjorie had bought for her. Charles and Charlotte had given her a joint present of black beaded earrings and she decided they would go nicely with the dress.

When Claude and Marjorie were both ready to go, the room smelt of a heavenly scent, hair spray and body cream. Donning their coats and wrapping scarves around them they headed for the lift.

'I do hope Madeleine is feeling better,' Claude remarked. 'She looked so tired when we arrived. She had dark circles under her eyes.'

'I'm sure it was simply the journey,' Marjorie assured her. 'I'm always exhausted after a car journey, whether I'm driving or not.'

There was no sign of dark circles or tiredness in Madeleine when they arrived at the restaurant. She was looking like a picture in a taffeta dress in a beautiful shade of sapphire blue. Her hair was brushed away from her face displaying beautiful sapphire earrings.

'My Christmas present,' she explained when she saw Claude looking at them. 'A kind of thank you from my husband for giving him a daughter.' She smiled over at Philippe. 'And you two look gorgeous. Marjorie, that colour is stunning on you and Claude, you are like Audrey Hepburn. Now have a quick look at your granddaughter before we cover her up.'

Amelie was lying in her carrycot with the hood up to shield her face from the light. She was wearing a blue velvet dress, similar to the colour of her mother's, with a white lace collar and white lacy tights. She was fast asleep, her little hand behind her face again. Philippe threw a navy blanket over the hood and placed the carrycot on two chairs the waiter had left for him. 'She won't wake up until we get back, so let's enjoy dinner while we can.'

A large bottle of champagne sat beside the table and Philippe skilfully poured it into the four glasses on the table. Marjorie thought how handsome he looked in his navy suit and blue shirt. It brought out the colour of his eyes which were so like Claude's. Claude was also thinking how handsome he looked, how wonderful the night was, with her son and his wife, her granddaughter and the best friend anyone could wish for.

'What shall we drink to?' Philippe asked, holding up his glass.

'So many things to drink to,' Marjorie said, 'but tonight it has to be to Amelie and her lovely parents,' and she clinked her glass against Philippe's then Madeleine's. 'And lastly her grandmother, who will always be there for her,' and they clinked their glasses with Claude's.

'Then I must make a toast,' Philippe replied, 'to Amelie's English great-aunt who has come into our lives and made them better.'

Overcome by his kindness, Marjorie wiped a tear from her eye. Overcome by her emotions, Claude felt a tear run down her cheek. With her hormones all over the place, and feeling overcome by the love there was for their little family, Madeleine also shed a tear.

Philippe looked on in horror, not knowing who to give his handkerchief to first. 'Ladies, please, this has to be a happy night for us all. Why are you crying?'

'Because we're happy,' Madeleine tried to explain, pulling the handkerchief out of his hand. 'It's what people do when they're happy.'

'Then I sincerely hope I'm not around when you're all bloody sad,' he said in an exasperated voice.

Seeing the funny side of it, Marjorie began to laugh. Claude started to join in and then, because it was infectious, Madeleine laughed too.

'The next one must be a boy,' Philippe told Madeleine, 'as I am totally outnumbered.'

When the waiter came to give them their menus and to explain some of the less familiar dishes, Marjorie took her first proper look around the room. It was beautifully decorated with glass lanterns hanging from the ceiling. The shadows cast by the candles echoed around the walls. From every window hung smaller lanterns lit by tea lights. The tables were dressed in green and red with Christmas roses in the centre.

It really was glorious, as was the food. At the end of the main course, they could feel the atmosphere in the room as diners looked forward to seeing the old year out and the new year in. Claude decided that it was time they told Philippe and Madeleine what they had done that day.

'Don't tell me,' Philippe laughed, 'you bought more new clothes, it is Paris after all.'

'Oh no, we've done enough of that,' Marjorie replied in a very serious tone.

'Actually I bought an apartment, just round the corner from here. I rather need your help with it, I'm afraid.'

All eyes were on her as she tried to explain that she thought it was a jolly good buy. 'I shall use it to come and visit you all, and Claude and her family can use it whenever they like. You may too if it's any help.'

'So you go out to buy a handbag and come back with an apartment instead,' Madeleine laughed. 'I absolutely love it.'

'Not quite,' Marjorie replied. 'As you know, I lost both my parents just days before Amelie was born. I'm selling my family home as it would be ridiculous to stay on there and also some of it belongs to my sister. I've already bought my house in Portbradden where I hope you'll come again very soon, so it seemed like a really wise decision to use some of the money to buy somewhere here. I've no particular need for anything and I don't really have any family apart from my sister, whose family consists of horses and ponies, but Claude's family have treated me like one of theirs, so now I have something to give back. It all makes perfect sense to me,' she added, realising she had spoken longer than she intended.

Madeleine put down her napkin before standing up and hugging Marjorie. Philippe did the same and then Claude threw her arms around her. 'Oh Marjorie, sometimes you are just amazing and then at other times you are magical,' Claude exclaimed. Addressing Madeleine and Philippe, she explained, 'Her idea was that if you two do buy anywhere in Paris, I would have somewhere to stay and maybe babysit for both of you.'

'Well, on the second of January, we are going to look at a garden apartment not too far from here. It only has two bedrooms but that's enough as we will always have the cottage,' Philippe told them. 'And Marjorie, I should be delighted to look after the legal side for you. I cannot do it personally but I have a lot of friends who specialise in conveyance. This is wonderful news.'

They saw the new year in at the apartment. Amelie was wide awake and when Marjorie felt confident enough to hold her, Madeleine placed a cushion behind her left arm before gently placing her in Marjorie's arms. The little one looked straight into Marjorie's eyes with an expression that seemed like she knew this was a very special aunt.

As Marjorie held Amelie's little hand and felt her fingers clutching her own, she gazed at the reflection in the overmantel mirror. There she was with a baby in her arms, holding her hand and staring at her while Philippe, Madeleine and Claude looked on. She wished that time would stand still, that she could be this happy forever, but as Amelie looked at her maman, Marjorie realised it was time she was fed.

It was a magic moment, one she could never forget, but it was also the beginning of a new life for all of them. The long, often lonely years were behind her. She had a family now and everything she achieved from now on would be shared with them, just as she knew they would with her.

The bells of Paris rang out as they stood together in a circle, Amelie in her mother's arms. 'Happy New Year,' they shouted in unison and Amelie joined in, determined to be heard. It was, both Claude and Marjorie knew, the happiest new year they had ever experienced. It was full of love, hope and caring. And the greatest of those was love.

THE END